books by Kim Chernin

The Obsession

The Hunger Song (poems)

In My Mother's House

The Hungry Self

The Flame Bearers

The Flame Bearers

The Flame Bearers

a   n o v e l   b y

Kim Chernin

R a n d o m   H o u s e   N e w   Y o r k

Library of Congress Cataloging-in-Publication Data

Chernin, Kim.

The flame bearers.

I. Title.

PS3553.H3558F5   1986   813'.54   85-29042

ISBN 0-394-55649-6

Manufactured in the United States of America

Book design by Iris Weinstein

9 8 7 6 5 4 3 2

First Edition

For Renate Stendhal, F. T.

part one

The Homecoming

The Present: 1974

1

Wh *a t* do you say, after ten years of absence, to someone you have loved and failed? Rae, who had prepared any number of greetings, couldn't produce a single word. She stood silently as the door to Maya's house slammed shut behind them and she remained silent as the two of them, their arms linked in brave imitation of their old camaraderie, walked quickly down the hall into the kitchen. And then, because she was profoundly ill at ease, Rae told herself it was a good sign, this silence between them, and she found time to wonder which one of them would speak first.

It was the first day in the festival of unleavened bread and Rae had finally managed to get herself back to San Francisco. She had wanted to make up her mind about their grandmother (if that was possible); and about the "legacy" that was intended for them, the three cousins of this first generation born in America. But she hadn't expected the arrival itself to restore her, not quite that fast, to the person she'd been ten years earlier. Within the half-hour it had taken her to gather up her luggage, hail a cab, and set out for Maya's house, she had ceased to believe in the urbane, somewhat world-weary, sophisticated woman she had stitched together so carefully over the years. It seemed to happen in an instant, but she knew perfectly well the fraying of thread had been under way for months.

She stood there, fumbling about in her coat pocket for a cigarette, wishing Maya would say something. Then she caught herself wondering what Maya was thinking about her, the "renegade daughter" who had broken away. But it all kept happening in silence. Maya, her face averted, took Rae's bag and carried it over to the table near the window.

That was it then, the homecoming she had in some sense known was inevitable from the moment she'd left home? Maya, her back practically turned to her, was bent over the old traveling bag with its brass clasps and deep, oiled leather wrinkles. The name Sarah Rachel Shadmi, their grandmother's name, was hand-tooled into the surface. Beneath the handle, cut into the leather in an intricate, archaic script, were the initials of the sect whose leadership Rae was expected to take on.

F.T. *Flam-Trogers. The Flame Bearers.*

Rae felt dizzy. The tiled floor of the kitchen, the dark beams in the ceiling, Maya's dark head bent over the traveling bag, her own hands pressed against her thighs—all rushed together in a sickening whirl that did not manage to keep out a disturbing impression of her grandmother's face looking down at her reproachfully from the upper story of their house on Scott Street.

And yet, there had been a time when she had loved the stern face with its piercing gaze. And she had loved the endless stories the old woman told. When Rae and Maya and Naamah were children, growing up together in their grandmother's house, the old woman had taught them the customs and practices of their sect, which had existed within the framework of traditional Judaism for thousands of years, the teachings passed down from mother to daughter in every generation. The old traveling bag, which had seemed to them the most mysterious of their "treasures," by now was so familiar Rae would not have been able to see it any longer if Maya hadn't been making such a fuss, turning it this way and that, breathing on the surface and rubbing it with her sleeve. It had caused trouble between them from the day, some twenty years earlier, when the old lady had first given it to Rae.

"Idiot," Rae muttered to herself. It was a habit she'd acquired as a child, imitating the old lady, "Couldn't you have left the damn thing in New York?" But the truth was, dragging the bag down from the top shelf in her closet to throw some clothes into it once she had finally made up her mind to come home, she hadn't given the bag or its meaning a moment's thought.

Rae had spent the last ten years of her life running away from the old woman and the family. She had, it was true, written a strange, somewhat scholarly, and then unexpectedly popular book on the oral legends of Eastern Europe. But the book, too, during the last half-hour had wafted away into an eerie insignificance. It was so small a tribute it would count for nothing when set against the expectations the old woman had of her. She had gone back to the university for an advanced degree and been invited, these last two years, as a visiting writer to a much-respected Eastern college. "A pack of nonsense," she said, in unexpected agreement with the old lady, as Maya set the bag down carefully near the window, "you actually thought these things mattered?"

She had remained standing awkwardly at the kitchen door but now she walked into the room with a determined stride as if she had made up her mind at last to confront some difficult question. Then she was aware that Maya had spoken and that the words were disturbing. "I expected you sooner," Maya had said. But she still did not turn to look at her cousin.

There was silence again and in it Rae was asking herself how she should respond. Maya's son had died four years ago. And Rae, who loved him, had not come home to attend the services. She could of course burst right out with explanations and apologies about the funeral. But she, who had practiced the art of evasion for far too many years, heard herself taking the easy way out, and then it was too late to do it over.

"I stopped at the house on Scott Street," she said. "I had to see it again after all this time." She hesitated then, because she could not tell if Maya was listening. She was standing at the window, her arms crossed over her chest, holding her shoulders with her hands. It was a characteristic posture, but one that Rae had forgotten. "It's altogether changed," Rae went on, afraid that she was going to start chattering and would not be able to stop. "I didn't know what to expect. After we sold it, I mean. But not certainly that kind of renovation."

"A lot changes in ten years." It was the same ambiguity.

"Are you talking about me?" Rae had decided to laugh. There she was, walking over to her cousin with an exaggerated strut to show off the new clothes she was wearing. And meanwhile, she was telling herself to cut it out, the contrast between them wasn't the least bit funny.

"Oh sure," Maya answered with a catch in her breath. "What else would I have to talk about?"

That shut Rae up and this time she kept herself silent. Maya had gone over to the stove and was fussing about with coffee beans, the roar of the grinder making further conversation, for the moment at least, impossible. That was good, because Rae by now had figured out what had been happening since the door opened and she had looked, without wanting to know what she had seen, at Maya's face.

The moment before, when she had been running up the steps excited for the first time really by her arrival and longing suddenly for the sight of Maya after all those years, her cousin's face, wrinkled up against the sun, had come rising directly out of their childhood. And it had been there still as Rae pressed the bell, Maya with her dark hair loose around her shoulders, her fine, curved lips parted in laughter, the black eyes flashing with mockery, her dark beauty even richer and more breathtaking than Rae, who had always been susceptible to it, had realized at the time.

Maya was glancing at her over her shoulder. Was it possible? That beauty, which had deepened and become even more evocative as Maya matured, rubbed out so completely it had been hard to recognize her cousin in that first, anguished glimpse from which Rae, during these moments of silence, had been turning away? And how, in the tension of all that remained unspoken between them, Rae blurted out awkwardly: "I can't get my eyes off you. I keep trying to find . . . what I remember."

And then, for the next moment or two, neither of them said anything as Maya poured the steaming water into the paper cone, adjusting the flame so that the coffee, dripping slowly down into the ceramic pot, would not begin boiling. Finally, Maya was done and she turned, very deliberately this time, to look at her cousin. She had put her hands into her pockets. "I know I look ghastly," she said, "you don't have to tell me."

Maya was dressed in a loose pair of corduroy trousers, a baggy T-shirt, and a heavy green cardigan with some flecks of white paint on the sleeve. The pants and sweater were several sizes too large for her. All this was, in itself, surprising. Ten years earlier, it was Maya who used to beg Rae to buy new clothes and do something about her hair. And now it was an uncomfortably elegant Rae Shadmi, conscious of her white woolen slacks and cashmere turtleneck, who leaned against the oak hutch in Maya's kitchen, aghast at the way Maya looked.

She had cut her hair short and wore it in no particular style, flattened back on her head. She was very thin. Her eyes were larger than ever but they looked strained and frightened in her thin face. Was it grief that had changed her like this, Rae asked herself, knowing perfectly well that it was more than grief. She looked old, with her yellowing teeth and brittle, lifeless hair. And yet, at the same time, there was something strangely and disturbingly youthful about her.

So this is what happens if you don't get away, Rae found herself thinking, and then she was aware that this thought had been trying to intrude from the moment Maya opened the door, grimacing at her in an attempt to smile.

Rae forced herself to watch the way Maya was preparing the coffee. She was worried about her own tendency to say more than she intended at one moment and less than would have been appropriate at the next. She took a few steps toward her cousin, as if there were still some possibility they could carry off this reunion like two perfectly ordinary people meeting after a long and difficult separation. "You look older," she said, holding out her hand to her cousin, who looked at it with a dull stare, as if she were puzzling out the meaning of the gesture. "Much older, okay? But that's not really what I meant."

Maya was looking hard at her, her face pinched and watchful. But then she said, in a bitter voice, "How could you," with one of those sharp moves that had always marked her conversation. And Rae knew that they were at it now. "How could you stay away when Hillel died?"

It was then, with the steam still rising from the pot of coffee and the light fading perceptibly in the room as the curtains on the window billowed, that Rae realized something. It came to her abruptly and surely. It was, she kept insisting to herself, a shock, a surprise. But she knew it was a confirmation. Years before, she had felt instinctively that Maya would fall apart after Hillel's death. Years before he had died, so tragically, so unexpectedly at the age of thirteen, she had known that death was going to happen. And now, with the same sense of certainty and with the same desire to turn away from it, she realized that Maya was wearing her son's clothes.

Her cousin was talking in a loud voice. "So you knew, you knew he would die. Was that a reason not to come? Even more reason to come home, I tell you."

Rae shoved her hands into her pockets and balled them up into a fist. But the fact remained, Rae had failed her cousin. And she knew, too, that it would not have been so terrible after Hillel's death if it hadn't happened once before. That time it hadn't been her fault and they both knew it. But Maya, in grief, collapsing the two events together, blamed her because both times she hadn't been there. Not when Hillel died. And not five years earlier either, when his father was killed in the Golan Heights, on the fourth day of the Six Day War. The telegram about Lev had arrived in New York after Rae had left on a trip to Algeria. But this mischance of timing, for which she was in no way responsible, only seemed to make it all worse. The trivial glamour of her own life, weighed against Maya's tragedy; and both women, in some ultimate scheme of things they shared, weighed together. Whatever else was between them now, this, too, was there, uneasily.

Maya had turned away from Rae. She was keeping herself busy with a gilt Florentine tray she probably no longer remembered Rae had sent her. But Rae had decided by then that if she had to be out of control she might as well use it to some purpose and she heard herself say in a voice that was far too shrill: "I failed you. I admit it. I should have come home when Hillel died. And yes, in spite of the impossibility, I should have been here when Lev was killed. What is it you want from me, Maya?" she asked suddenly, her voice rising. "Is that what you want me to say? I should have known Lev was dead even without the telegram? But, Maya," she rushed on, unable to face the look in her cousin's eyes, "you know how sorry I am."

Maya said nothing. She expected Rae to chatter on and on in her rather pompous way before she came to the point. She waited, smiling grimly to herself, knowing full well that her silence was unnerving to her cousin.

"You can of course sum up a whole relationship, an entire life by a single act," Rae said, fulfilling Maya's prediction. "No one will argue with you. But there are other ways to look at these things. It's a question of competing urgencies, a moment in two lives when neither person can be available to the needs of the other. Even if they wish to . . ."

She had added the last comment after a moment's pause, but the brief silence was sufficient. She had managed to change her tone. "I wanted to come back, but what was the point? I just couldn't make myself do it. I couldn't. Not yet . . . Don't you know how much I loved him? I never planned to have children. Hillel was . . . to me . . .

more than my own child would have been." Her voice had taken on a warm, confessional tone that always won her the confidence of another person. But Maya knew her too well to be taken in by it.

"Never mind that stuff," she said. "You think I care how you feel about Hillel? Get to the point, can't you?"

It had always been like that; if Rae rambled and tried to evade, Maya pounced. If Maya became too emotional, waving her arms and walking about in furious little circles, Rae quieted her down. But this time something else was needed; Maya was asking for truth and Rae, who recognized her right to it, didn't know if she had it to give.

"Do you remember? That day you took me to the airport? Do you remember what we said then? That I'd stay away until I figured out how to come back here as my own person?"

"It took ten years?"

"It would have taken more than ten. If I'd been able to accomplish it."

"You're not 'your own person' yet? You could have fooled me." Maya, her arms circling in front of her, had made a disparaging gesture that seemed to take in Rae's new clothes and stylish haircut and that cultivated air she had been trying, without success, to subdue from the moment she walked into the house. "Just look at you. Every inch the woman of the world. You're so proud of your book and your thesis and those little lectures you give about our grandmother's stories? 'The Oral Tradition of Eastern Europe,'" she said, stressing each word with heavy emphasis, "as if you knew more about it than I do. I listened to the old woman's stories even better than you. But you're the one who goes off and makes a fancy career out of it. Why you? And meanwhile . . . meanwhile you leave me. You leave me here buried in the family. You never even asked me to come for a visit. And my life? Did you care about that? Did you ever think what it was like trying to take care of the old woman? You thought Naamah was doing it all. But it was me. I was the one who had to assure her you'd come back again. She was always asking, whenever I came to visit. 'Where is she, where's the little wrestler? You are keeping an eye on her, Mayechka?' Three thousand miles away and I should keep an eye on you! Do you know what happened when Hillel died? How would you know! She had Naamah call me up on the telephone late one night. 'She's at the airport.' That's what she kept saying to Naamah. 'Tell Maya. She's coming now, I see her already, she's coming.' I believed her, Rae. I believed her. Who could think you wouldn't come back, even for that?"

"I went to the airport the minute I heard." Rae answered fast, but she was not surprised that their grandmother had "seen" her. The old woman was like that. "Yes, Maya, I did. I actually got on the plane. But I couldn't do it. I was that scared. It must have looked as if I were having a heart attack. You don't believe me? I went back to the airport the next day, too. They put me on the waiting list but somehow I managed to talk my way on to the flight. And then it happened again. I couldn't go through with it. I had to get off that plane."

"Scared? You, scared?" Maya had started to laugh. "You got yourself made into the successor, didn't you? Then sure, you could go away. Ten, fifteen, twenty years you could stay away and what would it matter? No one would ever take your place, after that."

"You think I wanted to be the successor?" There was something in her voice; it made Maya stop to listen to her for the first time really, as if this time she were going to hear the truth. "Don't you know what our childhood was like for me?" Rae heard it too; that clear steadiness without false emphasis or exaggeration. It didn't last for long but it was enough. By the time she'd lost it again they were both listening about as hard as ever they'd listened to anything. "Until I went away from here I never existed. Never in my own right and not for my own purposes. My whole life was for the old woman—to meet her needs, to fulfill her vision, to live so that she could live through me—so that I could, in every way possible, from the largest to the smallest choices, carry out her view of the world. Don't you see? Never to exist for oneself? Never to find life sufficient for its own sake? Always to be spread out and made available for another's use? And how could I protest against it? Only by disappearing, by getting out of here, by going away. You knew that, Maya," she went on, as if recalling the fact for the first time herself. "What do you think we were talking about for months before I left? Of course I was scared. I was scared ever since I was a small child, the fear was always there, always just about as large as the love for her. We never knew exactly what was ritual and what was abomination. We were always afraid to make a mistake. And I, I was terrified I'd do something to lose her love, afraid to offend her centuries of tradition, afraid to fail her, afraid she'd love you better or pay more attention to Naamah. I wanted my own life, Maya, is that such a crime? I wanted to . . . I don't know," she said, waving her arms in a way that was not at all like her. "I wanted to . . . create myself! Yes, laugh. I know perfectly well how pompous I seem to you. When Hillel died I was terrified that if I came back here, whether I wanted it or not, she'd gobble me up. Yes, that's the truth. I was afraid she'd eat me alive and spew me out again, her successor."

Maya, who had been listening with her hands pressed flat against her cheeks, answered as if she were after all considering the possibility. "Now you're not afraid any longer?" And then for a moment she was smiling. It was the old smile, with its infectious delight; it seemed to say that no disorder or even tragedy would ever be too much for her. Rae wanted to go over to Maya and put her arms around her and rock her in that little dance step with which, from the time they were children, they had always greeted each other. She didn't expect Maya to forgive her. There were things you did, she had known this even at the time, for which you would not be forgiven.

Silence came again; the silence of not knowing what to say after ten years of absence to someone you have loved and failed. "I avoid things," Rae said after a while. "I've learned how to shut out everything you've been living with. I made a life for myself, with my own little tasks and purposes. It meant something to me because it was my own, even if it was so much smaller than what she had in mind for me. When I was living in New York," she said, as if referring to an era that had ended ages before, "I used to feel that I was fighting my way against an overpowering undertow that would topple me over and suck me back here if I didn't use all my power to resist it. And now," she added, "the undertow is winning out. Maya, you do understand. You don't want my apology. It won't do, will it? From the minute I got off that plane I knew I'd made a mistake and could never undo it and I'm so sorry I don't know how to find words to utter it. My whole life tastes like ash. It's crumbling apart in my hands. I've lost you. I've lost you for my friend. Are you listening to me? I gave you up because even my love for you couldn't hold out against my dread of being taken over by the old woman. You think I'm asking you to forgive me? I'm not. Believe me I'm not. I'm just telling you, I want you back again."

Maya was pacing about in the kitchen, her hands behind her back. Rae had seen her do it before, with a deep frown and an odd tilt to her head, as if she were trying to hear beyond the spoken words. She looked small suddenly and quite infinitely forlorn and she reminded Rae of their grandmother during those years, after the fire, when she had withdrawn from the family and kept herself apart in the upstairs room. And then Rae felt the full measure of what she had lost in closeness to this woman. There would be no reconciliation. Never, it would not occur. No matter what sort of superficial accord they might someday achieve, the hurt had gone too deep.

"I had a life back there too, you know," Maya said with an air of not quite believing it, so wistfully Rae wondered if she was going to cry. "Once upon a time, I, too, had got away."

The two women stood there in the large kitchen. They stood in that silence which once, so many years ago, had measured their companionship, the two of them capable then of creating solitude for one another. But now, finally, Rae had an inspiration. She managed to deliver it in a quick true voice, which reminded Maya of the old Rae, her childhood companion. "You're wrong if you think I'm proud of myself for these ten years. The truth is, I'm not."

Maya glanced at her; it was the kind of look that sifts out the pure from the base; it was also a sharp glance, like a knife that had been honed and set aside for an essential thrust. Rae returned it, finding it not at all easy to hold Maya's gaze. But she managed it, with the odd sense that she was opening the book of her life for Maya's scrutiny.

Then, Rae went even further. "Why don't you forgive me and be done with it?" She had just remembered the way they had agreed, years before, to end arguments. "You know you're going to do it sooner or later anyway."

It was the right tone and the smile was right and the way Rae was standing there, her hands in her pockets, looking, Maya thought, like an awkward, well-intentioned adolescent, her red hair escaping from its smooth cut, curling over her ears the way it used to; her wide mouth puckered, that fierce light softening in her upturned, slanting eyes. Maya, unable to go on hating her cousin, walked over toward her, dazed by this sudden beauty that would come over Rae, in spite of all the incongruity of her features. Maya lifted a finger and shook it at her cousin. "Dybbuk," she whispered, knowing there was no force in the world great enough to keep her from falling for Rae's charm. "You do, you really do. You look just like an overgrown imp of some sort." And then, when Rae stepped forward to put her arms around her, she lowered her head onto Rae's shoulder and stood there, dark and tiny and tragic.

Rae held her, painfully aware of the sharp, unprotected ribs, the jutting bones in Maya's hips, the sheer minuteness of her cousin. Ten years, she was saying to herself; ten years, and until this moment I've felt nothing.

"Mayechka," she murmured, wanting to press the other woman so close there would be no smallest space of separation between them. "Mayechka," she repeated, knowing that one word would have to carry the rest of it. Her voice, in its unaccustomed vibrancy, so much like the old woman's it frightened her with the sense that she was losing control.

Maya stood up on tiptoe to press her forehead against her cousin's.

"They've been trying to get me," Maya whispered, her hands rising to grip Rae by the shoulders. "Ever since you went away. They've been trying to get me."

"Maya? Tell me. What do you mean?" It seemed to Rae they had just made a dangerous move and would undoubtedly regret it. She was doing a good job keeping her voice low but she didn't know how long she could manage it if this is what trust between them was bringing out. She wanted to clap her hand over Maya's mouth to keep her from saying another word. And meanwhile, she longed to lean down and wrap herself around Maya to protect her from whatever she believed was out to get her.

"I'm telling you. They've been trying to get me."

"But who? Who has been trying . . ." Something told her to pick Maya up as if she were a child and stride all over the room, rocking her in her arms. There was something wrong here. She had seen it from the first moment she glanced at Maya. It was more than the shorn hair, the pinched face, that premature aging.

Maya drew back; she tipped her head and cast a long look at Rae, who fairly winced from it. There was suspicion in that gaze, an infinitely careful "reading" of her cousin: Hope was there, too, but fading almost in the same instant it had let itself be seen. And a raw yearning, to which Rae responded with what was best in her. "Try," she urged, and her voice had a really remarkable tenderness in it. "Tell me, won't you? Who has been trying to get you?"

"You won't tell?" Maya, bending forward again and reaching up on tiptoe to whisper in Rae's ear said, very distinctly: "It's the voices . . ."

Rae knew all about fear. The last year had given her a good hard shake. Dreams that woke her at midnight, out of a sleep that had begun to seem more trance state than slumber. Voices that seemed to be chattering, far back in her mind, just at the edge of audibility. Sometimes she could hear the old woman speaking to her, the familiar voice as distinct and commanding as it might have been over the telephone, which her grandmother had never used. "So, Rae, you are listening?" the voice would say and she would actually have to sit up in bed and stare around her, each time unable to resist the impression that her grandmother had just walked into the room. But those words of Maya's brought Rae to one of her worst moments. "The voices," Maya had said, and her cousin had immediately caught the note of an inconsolable despair in it. Then she said to herself, This woman is going mad. But what she meant was: Why Maya? Why not me?

Because she knew, in spite of everything: what was happening to her, even at its worst, that was not madness. At first, that "worst" had occurred on nights when she stayed up late. Later, it began to happen in broad daylight. Only toward the end of that year did it happen when she was with other people. Suddenly, she would be somewhere else. How else could she describe it? Somewhere else . . . and aware of having been rapidly lifted and carried off and set down, while at the same time she was dimly aware of the world of her ordinary life. She knew people were walking along next to her and she knew too that she had retreated so far from them it was as if she had moved forward or backward in time. She was standing, for instance, at the edge of a forest. She could smell the pine. It was all bright and vivid, with the luminous presence of a nostalgic childhood scene. And then once again she would hear voices, calling out joyfully, in Russian and Yiddish and Ugaritic. She would have the sense of someone, or perhaps a band of people, coming to meet her. They were there, within earshot. They were coming closer. They were just about to burst into the clearing. Something momentous was about to happen. And the terror she felt, the sense of urgent dislocation, the sharp, returning awareness that she was being dragged back into the old woman's childhood stories, would waken her out of the trance. She would be walking along on the tree-lined cement street, her companion gazing at her with a worried frown, taking her arm, asking solicitously, was everything all right?

It was not all right. These "visions" or "transportations" or whatever they were left her with a sense of unbearable urgency. It was the same feeling she got from her grandmother's ghostly voice, insisting she come home before it was too late. A sense that something was making a terrific assault on the identity she managed to piece together over the years, tearing her out of this worldly life of her own choosing and forcing her back into her childhood. But all this nevertheless was, she knew, far different from what was happening to Maya.

As a child Rae would have thought she had reached the Time of the Calling—that great event for which, according to their grandmother, every Shadmi girl over countless generations had been taught to wait. Grown up now, bitterly estranged from the old woman, she did not like to admit that she was being drawn back into the sect, against her will, as the old woman's successor.

"Don't be afraid," she said, pressing both her hands firmly on her cousin's shoulders. Maya snuggled up against her. "I'm here, Maya," she whispered. And then, because she thought there really was good ground for Maya's fear she burst out, absurdly: "You can trust me."

"Trust you?" Maya was no longer in Rae's arms. For a moment she stood there a few inches from her. Then, moving abruptly, "It's too easy," she cried out, "it's too easy. I tell you, it's too easy." She lifted a tray from the counter next to the stove. She carried it over to the round table near the window. "We've become enemies," she shouted. "I've hated you, Rae Shadmi. You, the successor . . . " she concluded with unmistakable contempt. "I've hated you for years."

Maya had been arranging the table as she spoke, her eyes fixed stonily on her hands. Her voice had all the contradictory vehemence Rae remembered, an uncompromising harshness, a hidden longing for reconciliation. But this time Maya did not go off into one of her truth-telling bursts. She seemed suddenly to have drawn a curtain of snow around herself. Maya the Irrepressible, as Rae and Naamah had always called her—what could have driven this woman with her rare vitality and love of life to wrap herself in ice?

She was helping Maya set the table, moving with deliberate care to give herself the sense that she was in control. She arranged the cups and glasses from the tray, watching Maya from the corner of her eye. Maya set out a cylinder of white Sonoma goat's cheese. She placed next to it a small basket, filled with figs and almonds. There was a plate of black Greek olives, a wooden board with a loaf of un-sliced black bread, a small dish of pale, unsalted butter. They were

Rae's favorite foods. And Maya, managing it somehow, in spite of the season, had found poppyseed cake for Rae. Probably, Rae thought, she'd had a neighbor bake it.

The light, falling upon the white, wrought-iron birdcage that stood near the window, caught Rae's eye. A small, yellow bird swayed back and forth on its little wooden swing. Rae glanced at it with surprise. Maya had never liked to keep pets. Once, for an entire week, she had not talked to Rae when a little dog had followed them home from the park and Rae, having fallen in love with it, refused to give it up in spite of Maya's insistence that they take it back to the park and set it free again.

Maya broke off a piece of cake and slipped it between the bars of the cage. "Why not?" she asked in a light voice. "We're all caged now, aren't we?" And then she threw back her head and laughed with that old exuberance Rae had imagined lost forever.

They had settled themselves in a bright corner of the kitchen. They sat easily, because they had sat there together so many times before, these two cousins who loved each other against all odds—having been set by birth into so terrible a rivalry. And Rae, stirring the ribbon of cream into her coffee, gradually realized in their silence and familiarity that everything on the table had been chosen with care. The single damask rose in the pewter vase she had sent to Maya when Hillel was born. The tiny, gold-rimmed demitasse they bought together from the little Italian import shop near the church in North Beach. The beautiful silver spoons with Ugaritic letters, given to each of the cousins by their grandmother when they had begun to menstruate—spoons each would give in turn to her first girl child.

And then, because Rae still said nothing and Maya thought she was angry, she reached out to touch Rae's arm. But that, too, was familiar. Always it had been Maya who yielded, moving against Rae's silences, her stubborn insistence upon being reasonable, until everything broke and Rae sat there, still struggling to keep her face rigid, with no idea apparently that her eyes had softened.

"Talk to me, Rae," Maya said and this, too, was from the past, part of their private code, a concession.

"I have been called home," Rae said at last. "Maya, are you listening to me? We have to talk, you and Naamah and I. Only one of us is going to be chosen."

Maya had not heard a word her cousin said. From the moment

Rae had started speaking she had been humming to herself, swinging her feet against the heavy chair and gazing upward at the ceiling. And now, in an unfamiliar, wheedling voice, she suddenly asked:

"Will you make the Havdalah with me?"

"The Havdalah?" Rae glanced sharply at her. "Now, at the beginning of Shabbas?"

"Don't be angry, Rae," Maya said again, in a whining, childish voice she had not used even as a child: "You know what I mean."

She had picked up the silver spice box from the window sill. Rae noticed the goblet of dark wine, the braided candle. It was one of the few customs they shared with the Jewish patriarchal tradition. Somehow, in spite of the vigilance of the scribes in weeding out all trace of Canaanite worship, Jewish orthodoxy had retained their own beautiful ceremony of parting at the end of the Sabbath with the Queen of Heaven—she who, as the Sabbath Bride, had come to dwell with her children in exile. But why would Maya begin the ceremony now?

Maya had opened the spice box and was sniffing the aromatic herbs. She was looking over at Rae with a coy, knowing look, pushing the candle toward her, as if she expected her to light it. Without thinking, automatically, Rae reached into her pocket for a match. But then, hesitating, she understood. She saw the crazed smirk of triumph on Maya's face. And now, with a sense of growing alarm, she watched Maya reach out, her hand trembling slightly, the palm cupped, as she held her hand over the candle to light it, the way their grandmother used to, without a match.

2

Up s t a i r s, Maya was running water into the tub. Rae listened to the steady stream of it, settling her thoughts in that way the old woman had taught them when they were children, showing them how to focus their attention upon water running, the barking of a dog in the distance, the scraping of a branch against the side of the house, until they had entered completely into the sound and had calmed whatever uneasiness or restlessness they might have been feeling. But Rae was out of practice; she couldn't hold her mind steady, it lurched and stumbled with that same dizzy sense of dislocation she had felt from the moment she had stepped from the plane. And anyway, Maya had always been better at those games of concentration, had tried harder, had been more eager to please.

She wanted to believe that her sorrow was for Maya, for all that extravagant beauty effaced. And because of their lost childhood. And for those months after Maya returned from the East Coast and they were again for that brief time together in those late afternoons when they had taken Hillel and Ruthie to the playground in the park. They had found their own childhood there with the sweat and dust marks on bare knees and elbows. Maya in braids, shrieking on the painted horses of the merry-go-round as Ruthie waved at them, straining against her belt and then she managed to pull the gold ring from the holder and put back her head and bellowed with joy and triumph as if she were Maya. But it was not for that, not really.

A few hours earlier, when Rae had stopped the cab in front of the old woman's house on Scott Street, she imagined that she had forgotten almost everything about her childhood. But then she had walked out onto the familiar street and she had kept on walking to the side of the house. From there she could see a corner of the garden where the old woman had grown her herbs and tended her little altar under the fig tree. "Good," she had muttered savagely to herself, seeing that the beautiful garden had been bricked over and filled with pots of carefully tended bonsais. And the fig tree? And the altar? She walked on down the drive and pushed at the iron gate. It was one of those gates with heavy scrolls and sharp, pointed prongs. She tried the handle and then, finding that it was solidly locked, stretched out her arms to grasp the bars and began hoisting herself up.

Perched at the top, she could see down over the garden. The fig tree was still there. But it looked now like any other flowering tree and no longer like a sacred presence. The altar had been removed, and the dovecote and the carved wooden figure that was set into the ground each year at the festival of unleavened bread on the raised mound under the fig tree. "Good," she repeated, looking around for the little fountain, where the wrens and robins and sometimes even a jay had splashed and bathed, with that nonchalant innocence she had always attributed to the old woman's presence and had never really observed again since she had left home, "all trace of it effaced." But she did not mean it. Her bitterness, so carefully guarded over the years as a protection against the old woman's power to draw her back into the sect, could not hide the sorrow she felt as she jumped down into the garden, bending her knees and wrapping her arms expertly around her legs to keep her balance. She straightened up and put her hands in her pockets. She was home again. She remembered.

During their childhood, in the years before the old woman had withdrawn from active leadership of the sect, she would stand with them in the garden at dusk during the twelve days of the spring festival, remote and wrapped away from them, as she lifted one of the cakes left in offering, blessed it, and divided it among them. Then she would go through the house lighting the lamps and candles without a match, her palms cupped over the wick as she recited the blessing to call fire. After that they were not permitted to eat until she roused them at dawn and took them into the kitchen to break their fast.

But Rae, when she was maybe four years old, had crept out of bed and gone down into the garden. She had walked boldly toward the altar, with an exaggerated swagger, knowing that Maya was watching her from the upstairs room. And then, snatching at the little mound-shaped cookies, she slipped them into her bathrobe pocket and held her breath.

Nothing happened. She looked around, without moving her head, letting her eyes slide over to the left and back again. She made another snatch, grabbed several cookies this time and stuffed them into her pocket. Bolder now, moving more slowly, she reached out, she touched the altar, she waited. But this time she noticed the wooden image with its painted eyes and heavy, pendulous breasts. It was an instant only. But in it the wind had come up in the little fig tree, giving her the sense that the tree was alive. The carved face had moved, the painted eyes shifting and opening as the spray from the fountain, beating down on her, touched her face. She stood there in astonishment, paralyzed with joy. The statue had spoken. And then she was laughing out loud, waving both hands at Maya and prancing around on the wet grass, leaping and jumping. The statue had spoken.

But when she had gone back upstairs, moving cautiously to keep the boards from creaking, she became aware that this act of daring she and Maya had insisted was a game, had become in fact something far different. She was scared; it was not the first time she had felt like that and she stood there, outside their grandmother's room, the sacramental cookies in her fist, holding her breath, leaning forward, listening.

The old woman had opened the door, the prayer shawl gathered over her head. Her eyes had been bright and demanding, with that odd, fixed stare that used to awe them into obedience. She was holding in her hand one of the large leather volumes from which she would one day teach Rae Ugaritic, the ancient, holy tongue that had come down from prebiblical, Canaanite times. And Rae, who still in those days loved her beyond awe and even terror, had reached out cautiously to touch the old woman on the shoulder. It was the traditional greeting.

The old woman's room smelled of mustard. She had every kind of herb hanging on little hooks around the walls, cloves and garlic and wreaths of bay leaves gathered from the trees in the park. The other old women looked at Rae with startled faces and one of them, without seeming to hurry, reached out, gathered some papers, and put them in her grandmother's old chest. Then, the door closing behind her, Rae had walked boldly into the room, forcing herself to overcome the trembling in her legs. She was too young to be walking in there like that, where the old ladies were at work. It was too soon, she had not yet passed through the initiation. Their whole childhood was like that, they never knew when they would stumble against something they were not supposed to do or when they might have neglected some rite or observance they must have been taught. It occurred to her she could still bolt for the door before it was too late. Too late for what? She never knew. She had made herself keep walking with her little forbidden hoard of sesame cakes. And then, while she was still think ing about running away (from the danger, was it, of transgressing against things that remained always nameless?) she had stopped before the smallest and most frail of the old ladies, bowing her head and bending her knee, to present the offering.

There had been, really, nothing more to tell and no reason to remember. Rae never knew if she had done something wrong and pun ishable, for which she had been instantaneously forgiven, or whether instead in breaking the apparent rule she had chanced upon yet an other hidden and mysterious custom and had found favor in their eyes. From her grandmother she could not tell. The old woman's eyes were fixed upon her granddaughter as she made her way, head bowed, from one old woman to the next. But when her own turn came and Rae knelt down before her the old woman had placed her hand on her granddaughter's head. Nothing more. And muttered something to which the other women, with a collective sigh, murmured assent. Rae, feeling a sudden devotion for her grandmother, had grabbed the gnarled, blue-veined hand and pressed it to her lips. That's the way it was with her; she never knew if she would shake with fear or be bowed suddenly with inexplicable love.

And yet, during all those years that came later, when Rae began to be late for Shabbas, and frequently stayed away even from the hol iday of the unleavened bread, she recalled that night when she'd been with her grandmother's students in the large attic room. Vaguely, it had given her the impression that her role as successor had been confirmed that night. But why? Because she had dared to break with custom and steal down into the garden? Because the statue, to place the seal of approval upon her deed, had spoken?

Trying to tell Maya about it she found that she could not talk; her tongue actually stuck to the roof of her mouth, she could no longer remember what the statue had said or why she had been so terrified walking into the old woman's room. There was a choking sensation in her throat and she felt, suddenly, as if a firm hand had pressed itself down upon her forehead, leaving behind a fiercely burn-ing sensation. The smell of musk and myrrh and cloves and mustard, the burbling in the samovar, that firm, erect manner in which the old woman stood watching her beside the door, had all impressed Rae, who was above all an impressionable child, with an air of mystery and consecration. Yet, somehow, it was forbidden to speak of it, even to Maya. It had been the first great loneliness of her life.

And that, thought Rae, standing once again after all those years in the kitchen of Maya's house, forgetting herself in a revery that was not really any longer characteristic of her, except recently—that was probably why they had all still come for Shabbas even in the years of the old woman's decline. There was, in spite of everything, some qual-ity of authority in the old woman, never entirely effaced. They all came. Naamah, with her son Michael. A few teachers from their grandmother's school. And of course the old women who were still alive and who had continued to live in their teacher's neighborhood. Even Maya had come, after she returned to the City with her new young husband from the East Coast.

They were always there, in spite of frequent resolutions to the contrary taken by Rae and Maya, on those nights when the old woman, dressing herself in her white lace, with her tattered prayer shawl, came down the staircase without support. And even then, Rae had known they came because of some quality in their grandmother which seemed both to wring the heart and conquer the will. It was not that her hands shook. Indeed, they shook. But it was not age that made them reverent and brought down their heads. Tragedy perhaps, the old woman's loneliness, the failing grandeur with which she brought herself down the stairs, trailing centuries of custom behind her in the way she held out her arm to bless them. She was the first of the Flame Bearers to have reached the New World, the last as she believed in the long line of the Old World descent—in which the successors had been selected practically from birth by signs and por-tents. She was, as she so often told them, the last of her line alive on this earth. To her had descended the terrible responsibility of selecting the successor.

Rae listened to Maya singing away upstairs in a shrill voice. But was it really Maya? This woman with the pinched face and anguished eyes? Rae got up from the table and paced over to the birdcage. The little bird, agitated by the sudden movement, hopped up on its perch and then, clutching the bars with its sharp claws, scurried up the cage. "Never mind, little one," Rae murmured to it. "I'm home now. No one will hurt you."

She began to wander about the room, her arms folded behind her back. Turning abruptly, she went over to the window and stared out into the street. I never forgave her, did I? she said to herself, her forehead pressed against the window, for making our childhood so impossible. She walked over to the telephone and stood there impatiently, waiting for it to ring. That's it, then? More even than fear? That was the reason I stayed away?

Rae's forehead beaded with sweat. "Don't let her be dead," she heard herself say and then indeed the telephone rang and she leaped back as if it had burned her.

"Naamah, is that you? I can hardly hear you . . ." But then with an abrupt movement she drew herself up to her full height; she nodded once or twice, her mouth open slightly, glanced up uneasily and, hesitating, nodded her head vigorously.

"Rae," the old woman said in her high, rasping voice. "Rae, you are coming to get me?" But she had never called her by her American name before. "Slevka," she had always said in her peculiar way. "Little wrestler." And never before had she used the telephone.

So that was it; the homecoming as the old woman wanted it. She had sent Naamah back without her. She would wait there, at the Home for the Jewish Aged, for Rae to come get her.

Rae lifted her left arm and held it out at shoulder height with the palm turned toward the ceiling—a gesture that would have surprised her if she had noticed it. Nu, it seemed to say with an unmistakable, Old World inflection, what else would you expect?

But she heard, from around her heart, the sudden terrifying crack of ice melting. It was the first time in a decade she had heard the old woman's voice.

After that, not more really than a few moments later, there was the flurry of beeps and calls with which her older cousin was trying, Rae knew, to welcome her home with a fanfare. She stood up and leaned forward through the window, waving and calling out greetings in an awkward Yiddish that seemed reluctant to leave her mouth. And meanwhile, she was saying to herself: I don't want to love them.

She stood at the window, watching the careful way Naamah

pulled up the street. The car door on the passenger side swung open, the legs of a little girl appeared suddenly and vanished quickly, leaving behind an impression of red sandals and white socks, as the door slammed shut. "Brucha," she murmured.

Rae wanted to race down the hall and grab the little girl in her arms as she came through the front door. Ten years ago, she would have done it, whooping and hollering and spinning the child around over her head. This time she waited, her hands in her pockets. Don't be absurd, she was telling herself. Cut it out now. She listened to the quick patter of feet down the hall. And then she, too, was running, across Alamo Square, down the ornate staircase, past the jacaranda tree, waving to the old woman looking down at her from the window of the house on Scott Street.

Brucha stood at the kitchen door. She was "taking a reading," as their grandmother would say. Her little mouth was open slightly, her eyes darted rapidly, and she stared over at her aunt, curious and demanding.

She was waiting to see whether Rae would return this look, which acknowledged the special bonding of the sect and allowed the "reader" to determine a great deal about the character of a new acquaintance. But Rae, delighted by this sturdy child with her sharp eyes, winked at her instead and opened her arms. She had never seen the little girl before.

Brucha came toward her slowly, her bottom lip caught between her teeth. But now, catching sight of the food spread out on the table, she grabbed for a cookie and looked up at Rae. "What's your name?" she demanded between bites, as she reached out to grab another cookie, hurrying to stuff herself before Naamah entered the room.

"I'm your Aunt Rae," the tall woman answered, bending forward to offer the child her hand. "As if you didn't know."

But the little girl once again hesitated, wrinkling her forehead and biting down on her lip. And then, with a great boom of laughter that sounded like Jacob, her father, she reached out her tiny paw, in which the soft cookie had already been squeezed to a pulp.

Are you one of us? she wanted to ask, putting into words what she knew must never be spoken directly until you were absolutely sure. And then, as her mother had said to her, what need to ask? She had the haughty, overbearing, rather comical manner that sometimes appears in a child introduced early to the teachings of the sect. Rae smelled, she thought, like the Havdalah spices for the end of Sabbath. She wasn't sure yet if it was a smell for the nose or for the larger knowing her mother had begun to teach her. She was confused by this woman, who had not met her eyes or acknowledged her "reading." She knew she was good at it. Much better than Ruth, who was years older. And she knew that Rae was not a hopeless case, a "fallen spark" like her Aunt Maya. She liked the bright light in Rae's red curls. She liked the fierce look in her yellow eyes. It did not frighten her, although she thought maybe it was supposed to. But something told her not to cross too fast into her aunt. Not even with love. Was she like Maya then, someone you had to treat with caution? The little girl narrowed her eyes and pressed her elbows into her hips. Rae was not like Maya. And suddenly, unable to restrain herself, because she was still so new at the practice and was constantly lapsing into being only a little girl, she reached up and tugged at Rae's arm, pulling her down so that she could throw her arms around her neck.

"Meydele, meydele," Brucha crooned, in the old woman's voice, "dayn harts is asey greys me ken arein leygen di gantse velts tsoris?" Rae felt the child's breath against her ear. "My child," she was saying in Yiddish, "your heart is so big we can put in the whole world's troubles?"

Rae took the girl by the waist and held her at arm's length. It was not too late. She did not have to love this little elf. She did not have to be drawn back into the family. She still had a life on the East Coast. She did not have to do what the old woman wanted. She looked at the child, her auburn hair coiled up on her head, the dark, searching, intelligent face. She drew her closer and the little girl, rubbing their noses together, wrinkled up her eyes and pursed her lips.

Yes, it was there. The suggestion, at this early age, of a complex inner life, the quick flashing of intuitive gifts—these signs of the familial tendency to produce personalities for whom daily life would never be easy. The aloof, rather impersonal tone to it all, as if the child knew she had been set apart from others. And then, in full contradiction to all the rest of it, the breaking through of an undeniable warmth, a yearning for, even a highly developed capacity for human closeness. It was all there, the unmistakable Shadmi cast.

"So little and so wise," Rae said to her in a mocking voice, using words she had not once recalled in all those years since they had been spoken, quite seriously, of herself. She did not want to show that she was moved.

"But not so wise as I'm going to be," the child answered smartly.

"Oh, yeah? Who says so?"

"Mama says so," the child responded at once, with a toss of her head. "And you know what, Aunt Rae?" she asked with a little giggle, winding herself up to boom and laugh and choke and cough again: "You know what else she says?"

Rae glanced down at the little girl. She had just remembered what it was like to grow up a Shadmi, knowing that she had an important place in the family, which had played for hundreds of years so meaningful a role in the sect. Briefly, she felt again the force of that great tradition of female worship they tended and guarded, with its cherished mysteries, its awesome powers, and those old tales that had survived for so many thousands of years.

"So, tell me, what does Mama say?"

"She says you're not as wise as you're going to be, either. And you know what?" the child added with a little scowl: "You're not."

Brucha had stamped her foot for emphasis, half in play, half in earnest. But now, turning her head sharply, she saw that Naamah had entered the room and she threw her hands up over her head, kicked her feet, and cried out in genuine consternation: "You fooled me. You did. I couldn't read your coming."

Naamah walked rapidly across the room. She opened her arms to Rae, she embraced her quickly. Then, her head tipped to the side, she stepped back, her hands on her hips, silent, staring at the floor. Naamah, who had not seen or talked to Rae, not once in all those years.

And Rae, aware of a longing she would not have expected Naamah to inspire, stood there like a great fool (she, Rae Shadmi!), staring mutely at the tips of her highly polished red boots.

3

A *d o o r* opened. It led to a room on the second floor of the
house on Scott Street. This room, filled with stocking dolls and the
Swiss clock Rae's father had repaired and the little handwritten texts
their grandmother gave them, had been Rae's ever since she could
remember. It was set aside for her on the Sabbath and for the holidays.
She had managed to seal it off more completely even than her childhood's fear and its heartbreak because it held another story. It was
made up of little snatches of memory, odd tattered fragments that had
survived her efforts to wall up the entire thing. Smells and tastes and
the recollection of touch. The fine order of daily life the old woman
had given them, with her rich, ceremonial sense of things.

The way, for instance, she had taught them to polish the silver
with a pattern of interlocking circles as they chanted together preparing for the Sabbath meal. She had filled their laps with almonds late
on Friday afternoons when they got home from school, sat them down
at the long table in the kitchen to tell them stories about the Sabbath
Bride. It all came back to her in that brief moment when she grabbed
hold of Naamah's hands and pressed them against her cheeks, she who
had learned to keep such careful watch over what she was feeling. "So,
Rae, home again after all these years . . ." Naamah had said, finally.
And there was no reproach in it. None. Her low, rather husky voice
had faltered, leaving behind an echo in which Rae heard how much
her cousin, in all those years, had longed for her. The egg smell of
challah baking, the smell of the tallow melting, the feel of the warm
wax in her hands as the old woman, lifting her head and looking down
at them from the corner of her eye, told them how to braid the strands

for the Havdalah candles. Naamah's face with those gray eyes of hers; they had, all of a sudden, looked like homecoming.

And earlier, before her parents had been killed in the fire, walking down the long afternoon streets, it was autumn and there was Maya, who had come with her mother from the other side of the park. She would wait for them at the corner, tearing free from her mother's hand and racing to greet them. Maya, the Irrepressible, as Rae's father also called her, lifting her up in the air, her legs kicking and dangling as she shouted and tugged at his hair. The old women, their grandmother's cronies, had come out onto the porch to watch this Shadmi procession to the home of the Matriarch. She had loved those old ladies, who would stop in during the years of her grandmother's decline to bring her a loaf of bread or a pot of soup. And of course, because Sarah Rachel Shadmi had been their teacher and mentor, they stayed and did some little service for her—dusting the books in their worn leather bindings, weeding out the little pots of herbs that grew in the kitchen, polishing the ceremonial silver, preparing the Shabbas libation of honey and myrrh. And so grandmother's house had kept itself up, even while the old woman herself had become unkempt and disheveled, gnawed it was clear by some secret sorrow or doubt she could never bring herself to confide in anyone.

Rae had always been grateful to these old ladies, her grandmother's students and coreligionists. When she had first come to live at her grandmother's house, after her parents had been killed in the fire, the old women (already old when she was a child) would come to sit by her bed at night, crooning and chanting in their strange language. Or sometimes, she would awaken to the touch of a cool hand upon her forehead, naked in bed, feverish with the unwept anguish of the loss she never thought about during the day. She would feel the skilled fingers kneading her limbs and searching over her body (as she later understood) for the sign of the flame, the mark that came sometimes at birth and sometimes later, to designate the successor. And she loved them, soothed and comforted by their attentions, by the way they seemed to know what she needed before she knew it herself, by their chanting and their sacred silence and by the sense they gave her of her own importance.

And there was: the taste of cumin in the ceremonial meal of spiced baby goat; the dry, flat bread with its thick crust; the embroidered tablecloths that were hundreds of years old. The old woman sat with them in the long wet nights of the rainy season in front of the kitchen fire, bent over to show them how to hold their fingers around the yarn, playing the thread game of the lion's cradle.

One day, when Rae was eight years old, she had shown her how to pluck out the piece of dough she had thrown into the fire when she was making the challah. "This we do because also we have to feed the Bride of the Sabbath. And how else will we feed it to her, this bit of the dough? Only by the fire. By the fire. But now you ask, why do I teach you to pluck out the dough? That is because with you, with you, Little Wrestler, the Sabbath Bride is willing, you understand? to share the offering."

Why, Bubbe? Why me? That is what Rae had wanted to ask. But she had said nothing. And then she had felt the coals hot against her hands as she dug around in them for the little piece of dough that was rapidly turning black. "So," the old woman had said, coming to stand next to her, "you have found it?" Why, Bubbe, she had wanted to ask, why aren't my hands burning? But she had said nothing. And then the years had grown up over her and she had wanted to forget it, along with other things half understood and the things that frightened her because they were all, taken together, too heavy a claim on her. And now here was Naamah, with her high forehead and her patient, pale gray eyes bringing it all back and her wonderfully expressive mouth, and that way of holding herself absolutely straight walking next to her as they went out to carry the pots and dishes in from her car.

Brucha ran ahead of them down the street, twirling and hopping and keeping a careful eye on them to make sure they followed her over to the car. "Time to bring the pots in, time to bring in the pots," she was singing to herself and Rae remembered something else she hadn't thought of for years.

She turned to Naamah and took her by the elbow, shaking her arm lightly. "That time, you remember? Maya ran out of the house in her red raincoat and hung it up from a branch and danced naked under the tree in the rain?"

"You are worried about Maya."

"Worried? Aren't you? Or has this . . . strangeness come on so slowly you have taken it in bit by bit until at last you don't see it?"

"I see it, Rae. Believe me, I see it."

"And you do nothing? You stand there and look on as if it were her fixed, unalterable destiny?"

"Fixed and unalterable it is not, I agree. But does this mean you and I know how to change it?"

"I don't want to argue with you, Naamah," Rae said. Her hazel eyes had turned yellow. "I want you to help Maya. That's all I want from you . . ."

Naamah liked her fierceness, the quick outrage on Maya's behalf.

"Don't you remember?" Rae had kept her hand on Naamah's elbow. "That wildness of Maya's, the unpredictability? I was sitting in the window seat in the living room. That day she danced in the rain. Bubbe was with me, I saw something in her face then. She was watching Maya twirl around with her arms straight up over her head. I thought, maybe she's sorry she chose me instead?"

Rae folded her arms over her chest and hunched forward, her eyes on the ground. Naamah remembered the posture, the intensity of it, turning inward.

"This she never regretted."

"You are so sure of these things, Naamah?"

"Of this I am sure."

Brucha had been leaning against the car, listening to them with an impatient expression. "Hurry up, you two," she shouted out. "You'll talk all day and what will we eat for dinner?" And then, before either of them could say a word, she began pounding on the trunk of the car, pressing the button and slapping it with her hands. Naamah came over to open it for her, going through the same pounding routine but with considerably more result. The trunk, giving an odd little groan of protest, finally sprang open and Naamah looked over at Rae with a rueful smile—years ago Jacob had been planning to fix it. The child stood up on tiptoe and peered into the trunk, where the pots and dishes for the feast had been neatly arranged. "Mine, give me, Mama," she said in the wheedling tone of a little girl who has forgotten all about her mysterious powers. She was pointing insistently at a plate wrapped in tin foil. And this time Rae burst out laughing.

"A safe plate?" she asked. And now she saw that Naamah had prepared several such plates for Brucha to carry so that she would not make a fuss when they were at work transporting the pots and dishes across the street. Naamah picked up the plate and placed it grandly in Brucha's outstretched arms. The child was holding her elbows together, wiggling her fingers impatiently, but the plate rode there with

great equanimity as she arched her back and began to stride impor-
tantly across the street, Rae walking behind her with the same proud
strut, Naamah bringing up the rear of the little procession.

But when they were inside again Brucha began to caper around
the table, grabbing bites of food, stuffing them in her mouth, making
strange faces and little gobbling noises.

"You know why she does this?" Naamah had leaned forward to
whisper to Rae. "She knows how shy I am. This is her way . . . just
look at her . . . to set up the rescue operation. But why should I
whisper?" she interrupted herself, still whispering. "She hears every
word I say anyway."

"Come here, you elf," Rae called to the little girl. "And stop your
racket. We'll manage it, somehow, just the two of us."

Brucha, who had just cast the most extraordinary look at her
aunt, went on eating anyway. But it was clear that Rae had taken her
by surprise. She was one of those children who easily guess the meaning of whispered conversations, and who acquire therefore from an
early age a great contempt for grownups. But Rae had shattered
through the absurd pretense and the effect on Brucha was immediately
apparent. She sat down at the table, leaned her head against her elbow and listened to them with open fascination, her mouth full of
food she had forgotten to chew.

"The old woman says Brucha's a throwback," Naamah went on,
"born with the knowledge. You have seen her eyes? Such a strange joy
in them . . ." But she was no good at this kind of thing. Their grandmother had prepared her to receive the successor. She had not taught
her how to make conversation.

"Joy? Is that joy you see?" Rae had glanced at the child, who was
kicking her feet against the oak chair, listening to every word with an
anxious expression. "I see precocity. And maybe also the strain of
bearing too much expectation."

Naamah blushed with joy because Rae had taken her by the wrist.
Her face brightened; she caught her breath as if she were now, finally,
after all these years about to tell Rae how much she loved her. But the
moment passed. Naamah coughed once or twice and looked down
with embarrassment at the silver thread in her embroidered shoes.
Patting her cousin's hand, she murmured: "The strain we all of us felt
growing up in the old woman's house? Is this what you mean?"

Brucha came tearing back from the table and began to run in circles around them. "Bruchelle, little wild one," Rae called to her, "let me see those eyes of yours. You know what we're talking about?"

"Hoich," snorted Brucha as she came to rest on Rae's toes. "That's easy. Mama just asked you if you loved me. And you said you do. You do. You do."

She capered off, lifting her little legs and holding out her hands to tug at a pair of invisible reins, clucking and clicking and tossing her head.

"A joy child," Rae murmured in assent. "She must be a throwback. Where else, in this family, would joy come from?"

"For shame, Rae Shadmi," Naamah answered. "You should see Michael." She had been arranging the pots and dishes on the stove while they talked, stirring and tasting, wiping her hands on the apron she had brought with her, folded carefully on one of the pots. "But of course," she added, wondering how she was doing with the "art of conversation": "you will see him. He and all the others from the band. You know what they call themselves? The Matzoh Balls. But believe me," she said, talking quickly and feeling altogether like a fool, "they are very serious about the music."

"Another joy child?" She remembered an awkward, gangly boy, shy and reserved, given to long silences and sudden, uncomfortable bursts of speech. It was hard enough to imagine Michael a grown man. But a grown joyous man it was impossible to imagine.

"So, joy maybe is too big a word. But you'll see, believe me, you'll see. His face, when the music is playing, that, too, is a throwback. Jacob says . . ."

"Jacob says. Jacob says. I can just imagine what Jacob says." Rae put her hand to her forehead, imitating Jacob and managing somehow to make her eyes look myopic. "'Such a gift, such a feeling for melody, such deep understanding of tone. A boy like this you don't see in the world every day.'" But then she said in an altogether different voice: "To think I still feel so much love for that man." And Naamah, looking up to glance at her face, thought that it might as well have been streaming with tears. "You see what you did to me, Naamah? You snatch him up and leave me to . . . to the rest of them . . ."

Naamah laughed. "You and Jacob?" She put down the wooden spoon she had been holding out to Brucha, her left hand cupped underneath to catch the drippings as the child leaned over to take a taste. "Oy, mother," she said, "I already see it. This is a match. This wild one, this wanderer no less, married to the stay-at-home dreamer."

Rae reached out to take Naamah by the shoulders. "But why are we laughing?" she asked herself. Was it so funny, really, that she had loved Jacob all those years? "You didn't know? Great reader that you are? You didn't guess? You are perceptive only for the sect, is that it? You see only for those 'larger purposes'? Cousin, I fell in love with him too. No, I'm perfectly serious. Why should we laugh? Jacob, I assure you, is the one man in all the world I might happily have taken."

Brucha, who had galloped off and come to rest next to the oak hutch, was watching her mother's laughter. "Stop," she said, her hands on her hips, "she'll pee in her pants."

"Fresh one," Naamah said. "Is that a way to talk to the mama?"

"You're not," the little girl snapped back. "I don't want you anymore. I want Rae instead."

Naamah looked at her. "Yes?" she said, taking the words very seriously. "Already you have decided?" Brucha began to tap her foot impatiently against the leg of the chair, upsetting the small, yellow bird so that it began hopping around on the floor of its cage, scattering birdseed.

Rae said: "She's too young, Naamah. Leave her alone. How can she know yet who she wants to follow?"

"Nu, kum a her, meydele," Naamah said, opening her palm to the child, "we'll ask again another day. When you are older." But Brucha, with a characteristic toss of her head, went to stand next to Rae.

Naamah, looking at them as Rae stooped down to gather the little girl in her arms, smiled to herself. She had recognized the quick stab of jealousy that always rose in her when she was with Rae, who had that effortless capacity to open a heart, and used it; oh yes, Naamah thought, she used it, with merciless precision. The demanding little girl, who had seemed for all of her life merely to tolerate rather than actively to need or love her mother, was already smitten. She was perched there in Rae's arms holding herself very straight and proud, looking at her mother with a severe little frown, forbidding her to upset this beloved stranger who had been sent back to them.

Ridiculous, ridiculous, Naamah was telling herself, this childishness still in me. This envy of Rae's charm.

She was a difficult woman to understand; more difficult still to resist loving. She had a streak of charismatic wildness that came, Naamah had always suspected, from her lifelong struggle to subdue a passionate nature. That struggle gave to Rae a restless, contradictory intensity, as if she were constantly racing to put out a fire she herself had kindled. When they were girls, at a party in the neighborhood, Rae would stand by herself in a corner, her arms folded over her chest, so consistently refusing the boys who came up to her that soon none of them dared. Then, changing her mind, she'd stride across the room with her head back, pick the first boy she saw, and dance for the rest of the night with an abandon even Maya had to envy.

There was something about Rae, with her high cheekbones and slanting, yellow eyes. Watching them, as they romped around the room, Brucha squealing and shrieking from Rae's shoulder, caught up in one of those exuberant bursts through which her aunt hid so much inner turmoil, Naamah felt it again. Something that made you think that if you went over and put your arms around her she'd probably burn you.

Naamah sighed. Stop it, she said to herself, you can't afford to be tired. But she wondered if it was all too late. The old woman's powers were failing, there were secrets she would tell only to her successor. But would Rae be able to receive them?

Naamah wanted to sit down in the chair next to the window and close her eyes. She wanted to gather the child into her lap and place all her hopes on the next generation. She was worn out by the last months, during which she and the old woman had spent so much time together, preparing. But she knew that Brucha was watching them and she wanted the little girl to be part of this homecoming that might play such a momentous role in her life, too. And anyway, Naamah had loved Rae from the moment she was born. She remembered that, vividly.

"A *meydele, a meydele,*" the midwife had said. "*Freylakh zulzayn.* Great joy is upon us today. It is a girl." She set the infant down in the tepid bath. Naamah, pushing her way forward, had looked for the birthmark, the sign of the flame, even before the older women began the search. The infant's flesh was unmarked. But Naamah knew. No one was disappointed. She could feel it in the way they wiped Aunt Esther's forehead and chanted their congratulations for having birthed a girl. She could sense it in the way the candles were lighted and the thanksgiving was sung as the moon rose over the fig tree in the garden. She was too young still to have understood that this child (unlike

Maya, from whom no one expected very much?) would become their grandmother's favorite. She knew only that the women were fulfilled in some long-awaited, silent expectation of which she, too, was a part. She walked forward, holding little Maya by the hand, to receive the blessing from the new mother. Then she had bowed her head and she had felt her aunt's strong grip upon her shoulder, the lingering pressure of her palm against her belly (wishing her a bountiful harvest of girl children), the touch of her fingers on her breast (wishing her a plentiful nurturance), and she received the shock of power rushing into her.

Standing there, looking down at the infant Isarael, she whispered to Maya: "You know what it means? You understand the name Isarael? It means she who wrestles with God and prevails." Then she understood the grim and ironic meaning of this name that had already been shortened protectively to Rae. Child still herself, she recognized the sect's expectation for this girl, last of their generation and carrying (but how, how was this already known?) the particular hope she and Maya would not be able to fulfill.

"My little wrestler," Grandmother Shadmi had called the tiny girl, coming forward without her cane to take the infant in her arms and place her against her withered breast. It was she as the eldest who would give first suck.

Naamah remembered the way they had all leaned forward to watch the infant open her mouth sucking air as she balled up her fists and twisted blindly, seeking the breast. They were waiting to see what the old woman would say. But then, as she closed her eyes and sighed, patting the child's bottom and grimacing in mock pain to indicate the force of the sucking, they had sighed responsively and taken each other by the arms and bent over to kiss Esther and they had passed the sweet wine and almond cakes, as they chatted and joked about the power of the little wrestler who was receiving the milk of wisdom through Sarah Rachel Shadmi, descendant of those days, thousands and thousands of years before, when this ceremony of welcome had been performed in just this way, before the Ibiru and their hoards had come up out of Egypt into Canaan.

But Isarael (whom everyone but the old woman called Rae, even within the most intimate family gatherings) had never taken to Naamah. From the time she could first toddle about by herself it was Maya she had reached for, and then their grandmother and then her father and only after that her mother and then it was Naamah's mother and last of all, toddling around the circle from one to another, showing them how she could stand on her own two feet, grabbing from them the little candies wrapped in colored paper, only then had she reached for Naamah's hand and accepted the sweet.

Did it make sense to say that she had on that occasion broken Naamah's heart? Of course, it made no sense. And yet, Naamah never forgot the way she felt that day, the hot tears rushing into her eyes, as Maya, who was scarcely three years old herself, put her arms around the smaller girl and toddled about with her inside the circle, taking funny little bites at her red hair and tickling her under the arms. The old woman had come to stand next to Naamah, pressing her hand to bring her comfort. "Shah," she said in a whisper, "it is so because already she knows. You are hers. You she does not have to win over. Wait only, the time comes soon enough when it is you and Rae. You and Rae together . . ."

"Isarael Shadmi," Naamah said, using her cousin's birth name for the first time. It had just come to her, standing in the kitchen with Brucha and Rae that even then, as they were romping and dancing, the old woman might be dying.

Rae set the little girl down on her feet and walked over to Naamah. And then Rae was in Naamah's arms, she was caught up against the hammering of her heart, losing herself in the strong scent of musk their grandmother also wore. Naamah took the younger woman by the chin. She had tipped her head back. Their eyes met, this time it happened.

"You remind me of things I haven't thought about for years," Rae said. "I stand with you, here on a spring day in 1974. But it seems only a day or two has passed since you and Maya and I . . . I actually can see my bedroom and that absurd old blue rug I wouldn't let Bubbe throw out and the patchwork quilt, you remember? Was it you? Did you make it for me?" she asked, interrupting herself on a sudden wild inspiration.

"The quilt?" Naamah shook her head. "That quilt I think was made by Hannah Leah. Yes, yes, when she was a child," she went on in her slow, deliberate way, working it out for them. "Old it certainly is; much older, I assure you, little cousin, than you remember. And the pattern, this, too, is very old. An intertwining of pine branches with little stars of flame? This is from the Flame Bearers, handed down each generation to the successor."

"Naamah! You say it, just like that? No bitterness? No resentment against me for gobbling up our grandmother's love?"

"Oh, bitter," Naamah said, shaking her head. "This I have been, surely. But I have waited for you to come home for such a long time now. Who knows? The longing to see you, it maybe ate up the bitterness?"

"What does she want from me, Naamah?" Rae blurted out.

Naamah stepped back, involuntarily. She drew up her shoulders and lifted her chin. "Tell me the truth, Rae. Please. You read my letters? You read what I wrote you this last year?"

Brucha, sensing the quick rise of tension in the room, had been inching closer and closer to Rae. She stepped up to her now, leaned against her and then reached into her aunt's pocket to tug at her hand so that she could hold it in her own, protectively.

"I didn't," Rae said after a momentary hesitation. She had expected this question, been prepared to lie, and found herself speaking the truth instead. "I didn't read them."

And then Rae said something she had wanted to say for almost thirty years. "Naamah," she said, and her voice betrayed her, "why is it I have to keep justifying myself? Why? When I never wanted to be the successor?"

Naamah wanted to put her arms around Rae, to draw her close, comfort her. But she had restrained the impulse too many times when Rae was a small girl, turning to Maya.

"I'm not judging you, Rae." That is what Naamah said finally, with a tone of authority she had acquired, without realizing it, from the years of labor at the old woman's side. "But for you, if only you'd read my letters, there would have been comfort. Rae," she said, taking her cousin by the hand, "we know much more now, the old woman and I. Listen, please. We understand the mission."

Rae's face had gone pale, with that sudden, greenish pallor that accompanies nausea. Tricked me, yes, they have, she thought. For half an hour I let myself be glad I came home. And now, they've got me. She was shaking her head, mournfully and with violence, as if she were trying with this inadequate gesture to throw off the weight of Naamah's words. "Comfort?" she barked out, "you speak to me of comfort? Do you know what the last year has been like?" And then, feeling that in spite of all her efforts she was at last completely out of control: "You expect me to tear my whole life apart? I tell you cousin, I wouldn't put it past you. You stand there and you actually expect me to go out on some insane mission the old woman has cooked up?"

4

"**T**a k e me back to the airport," she said in a muffled voice as she leaned forward, fiddling with the lever under the seat. "Damn thing's broken," she muttered, without looking at Jacob, "what am I going to do with these legs?"

He reached over and shook the seat a few times, frowning. His glasses slipped down on his nose. "I didn't notice," he said, looking worried when the seat refused to budge. "You are uncomfortable? You want me to pull over and try?"

"Family of midgets," Rae answered, giving the seat a furious push, so that it lurched back finally, giving her room to stretch her legs. And then, when he glanced at her, she reached out and took his hand. "Take me to the airport. Send my bags after me. Tell them I suddenly remembered an urgent appointment. Tell them I ran into an old friend and jumped out of the car and ran off to Europe with him. Or better yet," she went on, "just tell them you took me for a walk on the beach and I ran into the water and disappeared."

Jacob was a terrible driver. He always waited too long when a light turned green, to make sure, he said, that no one was going to run the red. And then, if he got into a conversation, he frequently forgot to go on at all until a car came up fast behind him, blowing its horn. Usually, she kept an eye on him, on those rare occasions when she let herself become the passenger. But tonight, because they were driving through the park on their way to the Home for the Jewish Aged, Rae let him go along in his own desultory way, laughing when he drew up at the stop sign at Ninth Avenue and remained there, his face turned toward her, his arms wrapped around the wheel.

She sat back and closed her eyes, feeling a quick rush of relief to be out of the house, alone here with Jacob in the gathering dark. The sense of urgency that had been with her for the last few days had vanished completely. She knew, all at once and undeniably, that she had come home for this. For Jacob, for the way they were together. In silence and in conversation. And now suddenly she was talking as if she'd reached some point of no return and was going to say it all and have it done with, whatever he might think. "Jacob, it's no good. I'm not what they want or need. I've forgotten the teachings. I don't know what to make of these mysteries and powers. They're not for our time. The old woman had them, I know. But something happened to all that business when it left the Old World. It can't be transplanted. Here, it's a grotesque. It's driving Maya insane. If Brucha were my daughter I wouldn't encourage more of that stuff. Jacob," she cried out, sitting forward and turning to look at him. "How is it we never really talked about all this? I haven't the least idea what you think of it or why you hang around here or why you married into this family in the first place . . ."

A car came up behind them blowing its horn belligerently when they did not move on. They had remained standing at the stop sign and Jacob, rolling down the window, made a vague gesture with his arm, waving them on.

"Whatsamatta hey? You love birds? You can't find nothing better . . . ?" The car swerved around them, horn blowing, hands waving, middle fingers gesturing, heads turning.

Jacob seemed unaware of it all. He stayed where he was, his arm still extended, with no apparent intention to move on. But that was like him, Rae thought, admiring him all over again for this ability to attend to one thing at a time, regardless of consequence, giving himself so fully to the moment you felt, when he was listening to you, that nothing in all the world mattered more than what you were about to say. "Such a deep look," he said to Rae, whom he still regarded, after all these years of absence, as his closest friend. "Maybe you see something I should know about?"

"I see a happy man, Jacob Isaac Paltiel," she answered lightly, charmed out of her somber mood by the love and devotion she saw in his eyes.

For some reason, and particularly when she felt the most affection for him, Rae had always called him by his whole name. And he, with his eyebrows raised, answered gravely: "A happy man is such a miracle?"

"Rare anyway," Rae said, her voice serious again. "Very, very, very rare . . ."

Jacob crossed the boulevard, swerved to avoid a car, and moved too fast over toward the lake, where he drew up too quickly on the grass and stopped the motor. He took off his glasses and put them in his pocket, "to listen better," as he always said. It was an habitual gesture and he made it now although he'd recently stopped wearing suits and today he had on a thick white turtleneck sweater, a gift from Naamah's son, Michael. The glasses dropped to his lap. He reached for them, gesturing toward Rae, who took them from him and set them down carefully on the dashboard for safekeeping.

Jacob brushed at his sweater. "A man of fashion you have here, Rae. So, what do you think? Do you like the new man Michael has created?"

She knew perfectly well that he was stalling and she was glad of it. The old woman was waiting for them. And nevertheless, as he seemed to be saying, there was time. Time for Rae and for the two of them and for this effort at light-hearted banter, through which, in time, they would find their old, lost intimacy again. "Michael's done a good job on you, my dear Reb Jacob," she said. "A few snips of the scissor and a Lubavitcher is made over into the near semblance of an American professional man."

"Shah, Rae, be careful what you say here. You don't want to let Michael hear this 'near semblance,' do you? He tries so hard. And believe me, it's a work of love. He got me jogging with him in the mornings. He got me even to lift up weights. Every birthday, every holiday, there's a new garment. He found me also a new barber, who will make me look a bit more like I should look. Michael, as you know, is a good boy. He's not ashamed to be a Jew. But why, he says, does a Jew have to be ashamed to live in the twentieth century?"

"You say that to me, Jacob?"

"And why not? You think it is not also a problem for you? How to be what you were born to be and still also this . . . glamorous woman of the twentieth century that has come home to us?"

She bent over and rested her head against Jacob's arm. "What I was born to be? Look at me. Look. Does this," she insisted, lifting her head to point at herself, "look to you like a 'successor'?"

"I, too, have gone off a long way from my family," he said, trying hard to strike the right note. She was never easy to be with in this mood, jumping from one thing to another, suddenly open, in the next minute evasive and closed. "For them, as you can imagine," he went on cautiously, "I have dropped out of the world. From their point of view I had a mission. I was sent here by our own rebbe to organize a Lubavitcher center. And what do I do instead? I become a teacher in a secular school, with a founder who is, to say the least, not the kind of woman our rebbe would admire. Well, you say, so maybe it's not so terrible for a man to do this? But for them, believe me, it's terrible. Because of this they lose their only son. Epicorus. Apostate. That's how they see me. I gave myself grief over it, I assure you, Rae. But such a grief a human survives. If you must break finally with the old woman, then you must do it. If this is what you decide I will stand by you, believe me."

Jacob had pointed a finger at himself and now he was tapping nervously on his chest. He reached into the pocket that was not there to find the glasses that were on the dashboard. And then, shaking his head in mock despair at himself, he pushed the heel of his hand against his forehead and picked up his glasses.

"Rae," he said, "do me a favor. If I talk about myself it is, as you know, only an invitation. Don't misunderstand me. Take a minute, tell me what you need to say."

"Yes, Jacob. Yes. Yes. But not yet, give me time," she answered quickly, taking his glasses away from him again and putting them on herself.

He bent over closer to look at her and she, staring back at him with his own veiled expression, guarded herself from him. She loved the way his long hair, combed straight back from his forehead, fell into his face when he was moved or excited, parting itself perfectly down the center. She loved the deception in that gentle expression of his, which did not quite manage to hide the sharp edge of his brooding intelligence. His black eyes, with their myopic innocence, so strangely at odds with the lean scholar's face, the too full, sensual mouth— these features that made no sense together and charmed her therefore with their contradiction. He was self-absorbed and light-hearted and unpredictable and tender and it was true, as she had told Naamah, she'd always been in love with him.

"I have begun to have strange thoughts, Rae," he said, driven back to himself by her need for self-protection. He was speaking in that manner that always provoked Maya to so much contempt. It was the Jacob Rae loved best, the yeshiva boy whose family had joined the Lubavitcher movement when he was six years old. He had lived his whole life in the Hasidic movement and was, as he used to say, in the early days of talking to Naamah and Rae, a bit of the eighteenth century wandering still in the world. And now he said: "Sometimes when I have been walking about in the school garden, showing the younger pupils how to name the flowers in Yiddish, it seems to me that maybe the distinctions we make are not good. You take a vegetarian. He's convinced he's a more moral person if he doesn't eat meat. And yet, is there something less worthy about a carrot than a cow? It sounds foolish, I know. Yet, I ask you. Whose division is this? Is it from man or from God? If God exists, surely he cares as much for the carrot as for the cow?"

"Or, equally possible, he cares as little for either?"

She broke off, unable to speak in this bitter irony that did so little justice to her feeling. Jacob Isaac Paltiel, for all his apparent gentleness, held her in a strange suspension of will that had always fascinated her. She could count on him to take her by surprise. His thought never ran along any predictable path. To Maya he seemed an embarrassing man, to be endured at best because he was married to Naamah. But Rae knew better. And now, taking his hand and holding it against her cheek, she said: "Don't listen to me, Jacob. Talk instead. Talk on and on as if we were not in a hurry. As if the old woman were not waiting. As if I were not terrified of her and what I have to face when I confront her. Talk, Jacob, do me a favor. Talk."

"So, what am I trying to tell you?" he went on, looking as if he did not remember why he was talking like this when silence would have been much better. "So," he repeated, "what am I trying to say? That maybe we look at the world, not the way God does, but from our own very limited human point of view?"

But now she interrupted him, growing impatient and not even trying to keep the edge out of her voice. "Do you really believe in God? Or is it just a way of talking? Nothing but a figure of speech perhaps? A habit you have, a verbal tic you've acquired?"

"You think I don't ask myself the same question? As for belief, I definitely believe. But what I believe in, who knows? Every epoch of my life what I believe in changes."

"That's too easy," she snapped, her voice harsh. He glanced at her, his eyes suddenly sharp. "For a solid year," she said, "every night when I'm falling asleep I've heard my grandmother's voice. For months now, waking and sleeping, something's been happening to me that would, in our enlightened times, be called a breakdown. But I think it's worse than that, if you want to know the truth. I think my grandmother is making claim to me, against my will. I think she's capable of it and I'm not sure that I'm capable of resisting. She wants a successor? She wants me? She knows perfectly well how to make me do it. And what of me then, Jacob? What of what I want? You understand what I'm saying? You know what it feels like to be drawn back against your will? To be compelled? To be . . . ordered?"

"Naamah had heard these voices too, Rae. Not that she would speak of them to me directly. And you, too," he added, looking at her carefully again, "perhaps should not speak. You have considered that?"

"Spare me," she muttered, shaking her head at him. "I hate piety, Jacob. Even in you. If these women felt they had to keep their deepest secrets from the men for thousands of years, well and good. I don't argue with them. They were right to protect a knowledge that would have been feared and despised and for which, undoubtedly, they would have been punished. But to keep all these powers mysterious in this day and age? What for? To make them seem more than they are? My grandmother can read thoughts? Well and good. My grandmother knows how to heal with herbs? It's a gift, would I deny it? She's an old woman from a dying culture that she cannot leave to die. I'm not saying we have anything to take its place. You think I don't know that? And I know also that psychic phenomena exist . . ."

And now, finally, she had provoked him. He reached over and was holding her in a firm grip, his fingers pressed tight against her arms. "So listen," he said, and she could tell that he was angry: "Listen well. You are confused? I understand this. You are frightened? How else could it be. But you may not make yourself less than you are, Rae. With me, you may not do this. It is not easy, all this the old woman expects of you. But it is larger than you are. Larger even than the old woman herself. If I know this, I who have always been kept at a distance, how much more it must be known to you, even if you deny it. You think you have solved the mystery by calling the mystery 'psychic phenomena'? This is not worthy of you, Rae. It is not, I tell you. You think you can cast it off like that and run away and leave it behind? You cannot. Whatever you decide finally, you must do it by suffering in the ambiguity. How do you know yet what it means to be the successor? Tell me, I demand it from you, how do you know?"

5

"**L**eave me alone, Jacob," she said, pulling herself away from him and turning her back. She rolled down the window and put her arms on the window frame, leaning out of the car. "It's easy for you to talk. Nothing is wanted of you. They make use of the men. But they do not call you. Such words," she added contemptuously, "The Time of the Calling, the Coming of the Summons." She reached into her pocket and brought out the little tin of Dutch cigars. Lighting one for her with the matches he took from her hand, Jacob stayed close to her, pressing his shoulder against hers. "She told us when we were children. I'll give her that. She prepared us for the time when we would be called. Only, she forgot to say it would disrupt whatever life we were living at the time it came. She didn't bother to tell us we would hate it and resist it and run from it and be pulled back. She didn't say it was nightmares and transportations and terror. She neglected to let us know we might want to belong to the world instead and not forever and inexorably to her damnable sect. And for what Jacob? For what? What does she have in mind for me? What is this incredible mission? I'm supposed to go out wandering all over the place in search of women who also have forgotten the teachings of the sect? Recognizing them, how? By the use of my own latent powers? Is this serious, Jacob? In our time? You know what she used to tell us? 'In a time of trouble,'" and here Rae launched into a savage imitation of the old woman's voice: "'When the world trembles and shakes, knowing it stands at the edge to lose itself into the voids, the Flame Bearers gather. From the four corners they are called back to the place where the four corners meet . . . '" But she could not go on like that. It was no longer funny, nothing from which she could continue to make derisive stories. "'When the world trembles and shakes . . .'" she repeated, turning back to face him again. "Look at me, my friend," she whispered to him. "You really believe I can set out to find . . ." But she could not bring herself to speak the name Kiryat Sefer. "You think," she rushed on, startled by this sense that she was keeping the secret of the ancient city, even from Jacob, unable to tell him the greatest mystery. "You think, even if I found . . . you think it could matter at all to this twentieth century?"

"I do not want to know these things. They are not mine, not part of me. My work is with the school and with the children. My love is for Naamah and Brucha and Michael. And for you, too," he added, noticing the expression on her face but not understanding all that it implied. "Who am I to say what is a dream and what is real? The world is larger, it is far larger than the rational order we impose on it. Rae, what is it? I have hurt you somehow?"

"I don't want to cry," she said and he drew away from her, having taken the words to mean their closeness was part of that temptation. "Hold me," she wanted to say. "Love me more than you love Naamah." He had wrapped his arms around the steering wheel again and was watching her closely. "I can't take in a word you say, Jacob. What do I care about the rational order of the world?"

Something told him not to reach out for her. In her own time, he kept reminding himself—you do not tamper with a nature like this. And then, because she had withdrawn again into that locked silence of hers, he began to say anything at all.

"The first time I came to visit the school . . . did I tell you this already? I didn't introduce myself. I decided to make a visit, to announce myself a representative of the Lubavitcher rebbe. This was my plan for every school in the area. But when I walked in I heard girls' voices chattering in Yiddish and Hebrew. They were laughing, Rae, I heard them yelling out and suddenly I thought, in all my life I didn't hear Hebrew spoken like this. So I stood there and I heard these little voices shouting and complaining and gossiping in Hebrew. I had to go over to have a look. I peeked in the class and what did I see? A dozen bright little faces, learning their Hebrew as they marched about the room. And the teacher, with the face of an angel, also laughing and marching along with them. And that, of course," he added, interrupting himself to glance at her with an expression for which she would, perhaps, never be able to forgive him: "that was Naamah."

But now he could not go on. Rae's face, which had been still and attentive, seemed all at once to be covered in shadow.

He loves her, he really does, he loves her, she was saying to herself, discovering a pain she had avoided all those years by believing that his real passion had been for the younger cousin whom he had not chosen only because (as she had always told herself) Naamah seemed so much more suited to be his wife. To cry alone in Maya's kitchen. That was one thing. To cry in the arms of this man who did not, after all, love her. That was something she would never do.

"Go on," she said to him and turned toward the lake. She could not tell if she was watching the final moments of a long and exhausting day or the gradual extinction of the universe. "Jacob? You were saying?" she prompted him, afraid of this yearning that had taken hold of her, this desire to escape from her body, to move out into nature the way she could as a child, holding her grandmother's hand as they walked along this very lake at sunset, while the old woman, closing her eyes and opening her arms at shoulder height, taught her how to enter the flight of a bird. "You were saying?" she repeated, urgently now.

"I was saying . . . ?"

It cost her to keep her voice steady. "The girls, marching around the room there . . ."

". . . Something happened to me then. Rae, what is it? Why have you . . ."

"I'm listening, I tell you."

"In that moment I . . . understood. We Lubavitchers had lost the simple spirit of the original Hasidic movement. We had lost its simple joy. We had severed our connection to the Baal Shem Tov, our founder. And now here in Naamah's classroom I saw it again, as if the old man, the Baal Shem with his gentle miracles, was sitting there, watching the girls learn. Right away then I decided. I knew I wanted to come and teach. I wanted to be part of this, whatever it was. I put aside the purpose for which our rebbe had sent me to San Francisco. Why should I found a Lubavitcher school, I asked myself, when the spirit of the Baal Shem is already here?"

Rae's face, lit up for a moment by the flare of a match, had the forlorn look of a little girl who has just been scolded for a misdeed of which she is, in fact, innocent.

"I am distressing you?" he asked, keeping himself carefully on his own side of the car.

"You're not distressing me," she lied, because she did not know how to tell him how much he moved her and for how many years, without ever being aware of it, she'd imagined that some day they would be far closer to one another, somewhere, somehow, without hurting Naamah. "Go on talking. Jacob, go on talking."

"About the Baal Shem Tov."

"About the Baal Shem . . ."

"So then . . ." He shifted uneasily in his seat. Vaguely, he looked around for his glasses, which Rae was holding in her hand. And now his arm, moving, it seemed, of its own volition, reached out for her. "Tell me, Rae. Tell me. What is this grief you will not let me see?"

She took his hand very carefully from her arm and held it up to her lips. She had done it perhaps before, in some extravagant mood that seemed to have required an extravagant gesture. But now, knowing he would take it as a typical Shadmi move, with no particular intimate meaning, she felt ashamed of herself as if, already in this, she were betraying both him and Naamah. And then, for a single instant, she held his hand against her breast before she moved away from him, opening the door to the car.

It was dark. The moon had not yet risen. There were a few stars, but their light was faint and far away, the feeble flicker of a dead planet, mocking them.

Jacob had pulled over next to the lake where, years before, he'd come for evening picnics with Naamah and her little son Michael. It was here he'd carried the boy on his shoulders as he and Naamah walked around the lake throwing crusts to the ducks and gulls and he had listened to her talk about the house on Scott Street, the old woman's leadership of their sect, her cousin Maya who was married to a wealthy man and Rae, whom he knew slightly—the tall, intense woman with red hair who was expected to carry on the tradition.

Rae had taken his arm. She was standing with her back to the car, looking up at the sky. She could not believe she had come home to renounce him, to give up all possibility of claiming him one day. And was it because, she now asked herself with a bitter certainty, already knowing it was: because she belonged to the old woman and the sect and could not of her own volition choose a mate? The man intended for her had already been marked out and she would take him, with or without love, knowing he was to be no more than a bedmate and companion, never her heart's central purpose or inclination.

And then she felt the loneliness again, that sense of being excluded from the common fate of humankind. They were walking fast, back and forth on the small grass border close to the lake. Jacob kept himself from wincing because he could feel how much Rae needed to hold on to him like that, her fingers tightened around his arm. Two ducks, asleep under the leaves of the shore plant, came out moving fast, down toward the water, their wings flapping. Rae glanced at them, seeing nothing. But Jacob automatically reached into his pocket for a few crusts of bread. He came to the lake every evening on his way home from the school, to stand there in solitary vigil, feeding the birds, to commemorate his love for his wife. Rae had put her head on his shoulder. She was taller than he was and had to bend her knees. It was an old, playful gesture and he had to smile, even now, knowing this time Rae needed him to be there, totally devoted.

"Jacob," she said and then stopped herself. She would never speak about loving him. Never. "Jacob," she went on toward some more possible destination: "Have you ever felt so much pity you could die of it? And at the same time, so much hatred it seems you could actually kill? One or the other, even one minute apart, that would be tolerable. But pity and hatred at the same time? It makes you wild, the struggle between them. And what can you do? You have to run away. You have to run far from anyone and anything that can make you feel this way. Here's my confession, Jacob. It's so simple. Isn't it, really? I hate my grandmother and I pity her with all my heart. She has the stuff fanatics are made of, she's a tyrant, an opinionated, sectarian old bigot. And still the greatness is there, undeniable.

"But when the school burned down and my mother was killed, she never recovered. She would stand at the table in the kitchen and call my mother's name. I'd listen to her, Jacob. Jacob, I couldn't tell if I were asleep or awake. I used to have a dream. My mother running down the street, burning. Her hair flaming, her clothes on fire, reaching out her arms to embrace me. Once I ran out of the kitchen in broad daylight. I jumped down the stairs into the garden and raced over to the altar because I thought the roof was coming down on us.

There were showers of sparks and that great cracking noise of beams falling. Would you believe it? I was coughing and choking. On smoke I'd never breathed. I was asleep at grandmother's house the night the school burned down. It was my parents who were trapped, burned alive in the fire. For weeks after that grandmother stood in the kitchen, stamping her foot to insist my mother answer when she was called. And then, because she heard nothing, because she did not have the power to summon the dead, her face would become so terrible. Worse than rage. I can see her to this day. That proud, terrible woman . . . broken. And by what? By the loss of her daughter or the loss of the school?

"After that, when it was built up again, it was never the same. When my parents were alive the board had no real power. But now I used to go with grandmother when she walked to the meetings. She still wouldn't let any of us drive. 'Every day is holy,' she used to insist. 'Why only the Sabbath?' She'd cover her head with the old shawl and take my hand in that grip of hers. But when she came into the meeting she wouldn't pay attention to the rules of order. After all, it had been her school. 'Yiddish and Hebrew in the curriculum,' she'd insist, 'only for girls.' Who cared what she said? My parents were dead, the board wanted to do it their own way. She had never let my mother take out insurance for the school. 'Against Chochma you will insure yourself?' Bubbe would say.

"The board built the new buildings from money they raised. The old woman was an encumbrance, an embarrassment. What did they care about her sect and its traditions? For them, even in the Shtetl, it was women's nonsense—tolerated, when it was noticed at all, because it seemed so silly. I remember the night they voted to drop Yiddish from the curriculum. Maya and Naamah and I were all there. Even Maya's mother, who knows why? Our grandmother stood up and beat her breast. Naamah and her mother went to stand next to her. But Maya laughed. She sat there, leaning back in her chair, laughing and shaking her head, and her own mother, who hated Grandmother, had to put her hand over Maya's mouth to keep her quiet. But Grandmother Shadmi kept repeating, beating her breast: 'Yiddish and Hebrew. Yiddish and Hebrew. Only for girls.'

"What did I do? Could I laugh? Laughter was too easy. I was dying of shame. I hated her, Jacob, she was so pathetic, standing there, shaking her finger at them. This great, powerful woman reduced to that when she went out now into their world. And of course they smiled at each other with that triumphing, embarrassed smirk. And then Sam Goodman went over to take her arm to lead her out. But I ran faster, I pushed him aside. With me she walked out, her head trembling. Her mouth was frozen in a funny grimace. After that she went up into the attic. She went up and shut herself in her room. All alone, Jacob. For years, alone in that room . . ."

Maybe for this one, Jacob thought, because he was suddenly frightened by her grief; maybe for this one it is better not to let go? They were standing at the edge of the lake. Rae pulled away from him and bent down. She picked up a stone and sent it gliding out over the water, her face closed, hard and bitter. Jacob saw a Rae from long before. A child seven years old, making up her mind that she would not cry after the fire. This was Rae watching her grandmother lose her hold on the world. Rae comforting Maya when Maya's mother did not write. Rae stuffing her mouth with grass to keep from crying that time her dog Zipka had died. This was Rae Shadmi, he told himself, who knew how to keep herself from breaking down.

Rae and Jacob stood there long after she became aware of his arms around her. They stood there while her longing for him came up through her legs, aching in her belly. And then, as they began to walk back toward the car, she knew what she was going to do. Slevka, little wrestler, her grandmother had always called her? Well then, she would wrestle—with the old woman, with the sect, with the birthdoom that had embraced her from her mother's womb. She would not run and she would not bow down. She was Rae Shadmi, who refused to be called Isarael. Rae Shadmi, who had spent ten years on the East Coast making a career for herself. Rae Shadmi, who might someday marry and would certainly write other books and who would, if she chose, travel to Europe on her own terms. She had come home to cast the truth of herself in the old woman's face.

Jacob, watching her, with that intense scrutiny he usually hid so carefully behind his tenderness, held out his hand to her. "You, who are always so ready to laugh," he said, "this time you shouldn't laugh at me. At times like this I seem to remember what it is I believe. It is so close I think if I will only reach out I can touch it. And then I don't dare."

Rae laughed. And it was that old, childlike laughter that was,

Jacob thought, her greatest charm. She took his hand in her own and lifted her arm, holding their hands out above them. And then Rae, who intended it as a challenge, threw back her head. She kept laughing and she said, getting it out fast: "But I dare, Jacob. I dare. I dare."

The Death of Sarah Rachel Shadmi

The Past: 1840–1974

6

Wh e n they were children the old woman told them the story of her life on regular occasions, each week, over the years. This is how it was done. She would wake them early on the Sabbath, take them downstairs in their pajamas, settle them on the bear rug in front of the fire, fill their laps with sesame cakes and poppy-seed cookies, and begin to talk. Although the story was never exactly the same they could, after a time, tell when changes were going to occur. The old lady would lift her chin, raise a finger toward the ceiling, shake it once or twice and speak very slowly, her voice growing deeper and more husky as she leaned forward toward them. They knew then that they were being given something new, and that they'd better listen.

For these were not ordinary storytelling sessions, in which you could drift off in your own thoughts, or play with the cookie crumbs in the long, white hair of the rug. They were supposed to be learning by heart the words the old lady spoke. She would frequently interrupt herself. "So," she would say, pouncing forward with her sharp look, to test them: "I was born, where?" And then one of them would sit up straight and shout out, "I was born in my father's village, in Chernik, in the Ukraine . . ." and go on reciting until the old lady sat back and resumed the story herself.

It happened, in this way, that all three of the girls could tell by heart the entire story of the old lady's life, as well as the family's in-volvement with the Flame Bearers, by the time Rae's mother had died and these sessions came to an end. For a long time after that their grandmother had kept to herself in the attic room, avoiding even her students, who came and went to light the candles and set out the offerings of incense and sweetmeats at the altar in the garden. The story was remembered. It had been heard and repeated too often to be lost, although Maya remembered some things differently than Rae, who had the best memory of all three of them, according to Naamah. But what did it matter? The old lady had changed the story a little every time herself. They preserved it for her, with her gestures and intonations, that slowing down and speeding up that were as much part of the story as the expression on her face, and all those interruptions that punctuated the telling over the years.

It was after Rae had gone away from home that these stories stopped changing. In the Home for the Jewish Aged, where their grandmother insisted upon living, away from the family, to leave herself free for the concentration, she had smeared her lips with wax and pressed them together. Then, she closed her eyes and rocked herself back and forth, her gnarled hands open on her knees, the palms facing the ceiling. She was trying to discover the fate of her beloved Isarael, using the old skill, as it had been taught for generations. Sitting near the window in her old black dress with its buttons of polished bone, she was following the thread of recollection that ran back into her own childhood and then yet further back into lives that had ended hundreds or thousands of years before she herself, as Sarah Rachel, had looked out from her mother's house at a little village in the Ukraine.

It was hard work, it exhausted her. Maybe it even shortened her life. There she sat, in her gray chair next to the window, looking for the pattern of births that had flowed into Isarael's life and would shape her destiny. But what she found, that made her put her fingers against her eyes and rock herself, moaning.

"The blindness," she muttered, "this one, what does she know? The power from hundreds, from thousands of years, given into the hands and she, what does she do? She runs to the world, *oy vey iz mir,* to the world she goes running . . ."

It was then she had called to Isarael in the old way, adding her voice to that larger call Isarael was resisting. She saw how easily Isarael could fall by the way, breaking the inheritance that had come down to them since the time of Naamah, Solomon's Ammonite wife, who had instructed Rehoboam, her son and Solomon's, in the ancient worship. She knew it was dangerous. She knew Isarael was not prepared for what she was receiving. She could be broken by the sudden eruption of powers that had been quiet since childhood, when she herself, their grandmother and guardian, had interrupted their training. She blamed herself. But what could she do? Naamah, she knew, would not be suited for this mission that would find the way back to Kiryat Sefer, the ancient city of the Flame Bearers. And Maya? Was there any need to think of Maya? If she served her purpose she would one day bring Isarael home, drawn back by the turmoil that was a Flame Bearer's lot, but even more by the love these two felt for one another.

And then they would see what could be made of that stern, un-yielding stuff Isarael was made of, her stubbornness, her insistence upon going her own way, that stiff-necked self-reliance that hid a sensitive and deeply feeling heart. All were needed. And that streak of wildness she shared with Maya, and the rooted dreaminess that was her own and the capacity to love and to renounce love for some even higher purpose. They needed everything Isarael had been taught to be, through countless lives and deaths and destinies.

The old lady sat hunched over on the narrow bed that had been brought into the small room at the top of the house in the old people's home. At dawn, and during the long dusk of the summer evenings, when the call would be carried across time and distance by the voices of children at play in the twilight, and by the movement of breath through the branches of tall trees and by the ripple of light over water and by the sharp, toothed messages of the leaves, she moved her lips, pressing her hands against her eyes, telling the story of her life to Isarael. In dreams and visions she sent it to her, in case she had forgotten it, telling it over and over again, the way she had when Isarael had been a child with unruly hair, her fist pressed into her cheek as she sat with her legs folded next to Maya, on the bear rug, leaning against her, elbows propped against her knees, her lips moving responsively, her eyes watchful as the old lady, beginning always with the story of her mother, Raisa Shadmi, who had been born in Kashevata, talked and talked . . .

c   h   a   p   t   e   r

7

Sarah Rachel's Story (1)

My *m o t h e r* was, who? My mother was Raisa, the daughter of Hadassah, the daughter of Ruth. At the age of fifteen she took in marriage the young man Pesach Flexner. Raisa came from the Shadmis of Kashevata. And well known it was that the Shadmi girls always chose their own mates.

I was born in my father's village, in Chernik, in the Ukraine, twelve years after the birth of my sister, Hannah Leah. But my birth the women of our village took note of. And why? Because by that time Hannah Leah had run away. A year later she came home again, with one eye blind, the hair pulled out on her head. And then she sat, rocking my cradle, and she told me such things I was not able to speak a word until I was three years old.

But that comes later. First I tell about my mother and my father. For it happened that long before Pesach Flexner went to visit in Kashevata, the women of his village already talked and gossiped about the Shadmi girls. They were known all over the Ukraine as members of the *Flam-Troger* sect. And these women, as we say, go all the way back to the beginning of days.

Now this, of course, about the Shadmis, would be enough for plenty of stories. But the Shadmis went even further. In our village it was said that one Shadmi, from every generation, became one of the *Hovrodnikim*. You know what it means? *Lovers of the people.* They are the seven sacred women to rise up in every generation.

Well, of course, the women of the village were curious about Raisa Shadmi when she arrived in their town. And of course they were disappointed. "This one, anyway, is no Hovrodnik," they said among themselves. They had been expecting, what? A woman larger than life. And Raisa Shadmi was a short, thin little person, with a stern, pale face, a small mouth held tight against the lips, and a broad forehead. She of course never called herself a Hovrodnik. What sacred woman would do that? But it was clear from the first glance that she gave herself airs. Refusing to shave the head, refusing to wear the *shaytl*, the wig of orthodoxy, even for a concession to her husband's family. But who ever heard of a Shadmi who made concessions?

Now believe me, the Flexner family was, in its own way, important in the village. They couldn't claim to be giving a sacred woman to the world, of course. But they were Hasids, father and son, followers of the Lubavitcher rebbe for many generations. And a Hasid, after all, is something everyone knows about. But the *Flam-Trogers*, who in that village were not well established? What could be said for them?

Now it's a fact, and this my children I told you already before. Every woman in the village heard of the *Flam-Trogers* since she was a child. That was so in every Jewish village. And no doubt, before the age of four or five years old, a girl growing up in Russia, in our time, had even met for herself some member of the sect. A peddler maybe, who came into the town and gathered some of the women together to remind them how to celebrate the holidays. Would it be possible for a girl to forget it? Because these peddlers frequently arrived dressed as a man, in a rough sheepskin coat. And maybe a girl only discovered the truth if she happened to wake up at night and go looking for the mama who was not in bed. Where was she? *Nu*, sitting up, next to the stove, with a cup of tea, whispering with this peddler who suddenly was a woman.

Now, Avram Flexner, the father of Pesach, my father, was the steward of a Ukrainian landowner. He lived well, with his whole family, in a house with its own synagogue. There were large rooms, beautiful silver, there was expensive furniture, carriages and horses, there were even servants. So naturally, the village was curious to see what would come of this marriage between these two families. But in fact nothing came of it. Old Man Flexner approved of his daughter-in-law. He liked what he heard about the Shadmi family and the sect. Who knows? He maybe was waiting for someone to stand up to him.

In Raisa Shadmi he was not disappointed. Right from the beginning she insisted on living alone with Pesach in their own house. She opened a little bakery, where she baked bread only for the Sabbath, loaves in unusual shapes. A hand, intertwining rings, birds, a nest, a fish, even a menorah. A year later, Hannah Leah was born, and by then Raisa had made them independent of Old Man Flexner. Pesach maybe was not so happy with all this. He had sisters, a younger brother, they lived, all of them, with their children, in his father's house. So, why not Pesach, the eldest son? But Raisa would have none of it.

Hannah Leah, my sister, was a wild girl. She learned how to walk at the age of seven months. And after that she was for Mama a living torment. By the time she was a year and a half old, who could keep her in the house? She would run out and take herself off to the ends of the village. She was forever going into the forest. And one day, when she was maybe three years old, she came hollering down the street so loud Raisa thought someone tried to murder her.

What was it? Hannah Leah had been going about in that way she had, looking at everything. She was, Mama used to say, a girl with eyes that see too good what is in the world. "*Nu,* where will you keep what you take in there?" Mama used to ask her. And that was, believe me, all her life the problem with Hannah Leah. She saw too much. And what she saw she could not forgive the world for making that way. Hannah Leah was impatient. Always impatient. But she had, believe me, a tender heart. You maybe won't remember this when you hear the story. But the tenderness was there, always, from the first years.

Well, what happened? My sister stopped to look into the little yard behind a peasant's house. A peasant was killing a chicken. You know how it is. She takes a few steps, the chicken runs away, the woman swoops down and puts it against the stump of a tree. Then she whacks off the chicken's head. That's how it's done. But my sister was watching this with her own way of looking. My sister had such eyes, the color of a small green stone under water. Flecked with gold. Now with their watching they got very dark. The peasant put the chicken down, a thing without a head. This, believe me, would be enough already for a sensitive one like Hannah Leah. But now, what happens? The chicken begins to run. Around and around in a circle it runs, the blood pouring out. And meanwhile the head, with the eyes open, is watching from the ground. Well, the woman laughs. She takes a look at Hannah Leah, she puts the hands on the hips and she begins to roar. My sister, who is at this time maybe three years old, throws herself at the woman, she pushes her down and spits at her. Then she goes through the village screaming.

You think this wasn't enough? What does she scream, at the top of her voice? It is this: "Where is God?" she shouts. "Where is God? Why is he hiding?"

After that Raisa knew the time was there when it was necessary to start the school. Always the Flame Bearers wait, they look for the signs, then they follow. There was of course no cheder for the girls to study in, so Raisa had Pesach build on a little shed to the side of the house. Then, she invited certain girls from the village to come and study with Hannah Leah.

The truth is, the other women were expecting this. It was the way the Shadmis did things. It was the way a Flame Bearer must do. Always we are looking among the girls and the women, for the ones who have in them the *heylige ikra*, as we say. It means the *sacred spark*. These are the girls who will be called to carry on.

Raisa taught them to read and write properly in Yiddish, for Yiddish is the cradle speech, and through it the mother gives to the children all the love that cannot be given any other way. Then she instructed them in Hebrew, for they should know the tradition of the other Jews, the Jews they lived among. She taught them Russian, to be able to go among the people who lived outside the Pale, if there would be need for it. And at the last she taught them Ugaritic, the sacred tongue of the Flame Bearers, for we speak as it was spoken long ago, in Canaan before the Hebiru came up out of the desert with their hordes.

So, Pesach and the rest of the men, what did they know about the sacred language of the Flame Bearers? The mysteries we keep to ourselves. They knew nothing about Kiryat Sefer, the ancient city, or the earthquake that took it out from history and hid it away far from the cities of men. These are the secrets. And how a Flame Bearer gets back there every twelve years, this, too, is a secret. We are old, my children. Not so old maybe as the green tree growing and the grass but we have come down, we, too, from the earlier time. From Canaan of old we have come, from the women taken by the Hebiru in violence, when they took in violence our land. From that time we kept it, the old worship. Through the years of struggle and the years of the conquest, under warriors and judges, under kings and the sons of kings, in the Temple we kept it and in the captivity, taken away to

Babylon, and in the coming back also to Canaan we kept alive the names of The Mother. But these things no one would tell. Not even the smallest girl would tell it who first got the story in her ears.

The girls came home, they could read from the Torah with their brothers in Hebrew. Pesach was proud, of course, he was like that, and he went home with Hannah Leah to the house of his father to show off. But for the others, what did it matter? "Learning is to a woman like a silk shirt to a sow." That's how they talked in the village in those days. But women, as everyone knows, are good at keeping a secret. When they heard a speech like that, would they argue? What would be the point?

The point is, you should remember. About Hannah Leah you should remember. And about Kiryat Sefer. And about my mother Raisa, who taught the girls. You should remember also about the *heylige ikra*, the little sparks burning also in you. And why? Because one day you are going to grow up. And then, at that time, when you are thinking maybe all this is only stories the Bubbe told you, one day will come a knock at the door. A woman will be standing there. And she will say, what? She will ask you, what? Maya, you are listening? You, Naamah, you have ears to hear? This will be the Hovrodnik. With the three questions. And then you will remember what the Bubbe told you and you will answer the questions. You will bow down the head. You will open the arms and hold them the way I showed you, the palms facing up. And she then will give you the key. Isarael, you are listening? She will give you the key worn around the neck of the great scribe, Rocha Castel. And she will tell you the way to Kiryat Sefer. For the in-gathering of the people in our ancient city. On the shores of Kinneret. In the land of The Mother, in Canaan of old.

8

It w a s at this point in the story that the old woman's voice would change. Her eyes, with their heavy lids, would seem to waken from their rapture and become again bright and piercing and demanding. At such moments Rae loved her best, catching at those times the urgency of the woman, this need that they receive from her the tradition to which, from birth, she had been dedicated. It was in her voice, in that husky, lingering, insistent way she brought out the promise in which they believed, looking forward to that day when the knock would sound and the door would open and the Hovrodnik would stand there with the message that called them into the sect, each one with her own mission and unique destiny.

"So, the questions, what were they?" she would demand, letting her gaze move heavily from one to the other, "who wants to tell?"

Usually, it was Maya who would answer first. "What is the name of the old land?" she would cry out, before Rae and Naamah could open their mouths. "What are the names of The Mother?" she would continue, as Naamah tried to get a word in, somehow. "Where is the first stone of the old path on the road to Kiryat Sefer?" she would conclude, glancing at them from the corner of her eye. And then, before the old woman could say another word, she would leap to her feet and lean forward and make her little hands into fists. "And the key? What is the key?" Maya would shout. "The key is for Ha Melamed Gadol, for the Great Teacher the next time she walks on this earth."

After that they waited. The old woman was not looking for facts or for simple verbal repetitions. Searching their faces, she was watching for that opening inward, through which some larger knowledge could speak.

For these sessions of hers were not what they appeared. Through them, it was true, they learned the history of the family, and were given always some further history of the sect. But this storytelling— with its repetitions, incantatory style of delivery, the rhetorical flour- ishes, the slight swaying forward and back in the old woman's body, the stylized gestures and self-answering questions—had as its central purpose the induction of a trance state in which the girls would relive the scenes she was describing.

In this, however, the old woman was always disappointed. The sensitivity she had as a girl, the capacity to enter into the old stories as if she were living them, none of her granddaughters seemed to possess. Even Isarael, who could remember every word spoken to her and would recite whole stories without a single error, would sit for hours, swaying and rocking, her face deeply absorbed but not yet rapt away.

The signs of the trance were familiar to the old woman—the suspension of breath, the slight rigidity of limb, the gaze fixed, un- blinking, the gradual brightening of the fine pinpoint of light at the center of the iris. Familiar also were the stages of induction, the sense of something distant coming closer, voices calling just beyond audibil- ity, the flickering of scenes not yet visible, the gradual closing down of one's awareness of the body and its immediate surroundings, as one began to drift in spirit, across boundaries and divisions most people imagined fixed and immutable, until finally the transposition was complete and one had entered another life, another time, another world.

She herself, in her youth, had been particularly adept at such crossings. She knew their difficulties and above all that danger one could enter so fully into another time it was almost impossible to cross back out again. Patiently, year after year, she sat with them, telling the stories, entering into her own past and the far more ancient past of the sect, but never in this crossing letting herself sever her connec- tion to the three girls entrusted to her guidance.

And then finally some progress was made. Maya, listening to her, had one day cupped her hand over her ears and looked up with a delighted, half-startled expression. "Do you hear?" she asked, turning to Isarael. "Bubbe, what is it? Something sighing? Far, far away," she whispered, with an expression of utter astonishment and awe. "It sounds like a soft popping, do you hear? Like a cork going out of a bottle. Like a drumbeat. Do you hear it?

And then Isarael had heard it too, the low calling of the grouse at daybreak hidden away across the swamp of a forest that would endure for as long as there was someone to tell the story, with its dense underbrush, lighted here and there by the filtered sunlight falling over the uprooted trees as the little girl named Sarah Rachel made her way, walking behind Mama, her high socks and long dress wet from the matted grass and she would close her eyes, following only the hoot and silence as the bird led them to itself to pay their tribute to the spring. And then Naamah's face had been covered with the clinging, fragrant damp, there were burs in Maya's hair and Isarael, her face flushed and awestruck and outraged, had reached up to pluck the leaves from an amber-colored aspen, and had held them in front of her, there on the white rug, staring at them, her hands shaking.

And then the tragedy had occurred. The school had burned down. Esther was dead. The beloved daughter, dead. And she, Sarah Rachel Shadmi from the Shadmis of Kashevata, she who always before now had been able to tell the future, this time had not foreseen it.

She retreated to the upstairs room, there to summon the guides, passing her hand through the fire, holding the burning coals in her bare palms and finding—nothing.

She covered herself with ash, mourning the loss of her daughter, calling her by name, demanding that she respond to her—nothing.

And then it had all begun to slip away, the world of her life in the house on Scott Street. The world of childhood lost to time and space, those forests of unforgettable awe. She was adrift in a trackless region, without the familiar signposts of progression that marked her passage between the worlds. It had happened to her before, when she was a small girl in her mother's house, as if she were buried somewhere under the earth. And it had happened later, when she had already gone to live in Baron Guzman's house in Petersburg. Her eyes were filled with sand. Her skin burned with the scraping of nettles and burs. Fingers came to pluck at her skin, to tear away her fingers, to uproot her limbs. And then the fire got her, eating away at the marrow of her bones, until at last she was indistinguishable from the howling of winds.

She would waken from this annihilation to the touch of a small, soft hand in hers. A girl's voice whispering against her skin. There was light, drifting and re-forming, the cloud shapes of sensory perception settling slowly. And from it Naamah's homely little face, inches from her own, would swim up, anguished and tender and watchful.

"Bubbe, Bubbe," the distant voice would be calling and the days would come again, each in its orderly progression and divisions, tea in the mouth at the first light, the spoon with its round globules of fat floating in a sea of golden liquid as the light hummed and buzzed against the window and then the merciful coming, in slow and measurable increments, of dusk.

She would be talking again, the words thick and ungainly in her mouth, and Naamah, the eldest, who must know and remember and guide the others, Naamah would be sitting next to the bed, where something lay mottled and gnarled, broken winged things that had fluttered down and lay gasping in their death agony as the girl stroked and kneaded them, fingers, palms, wrists, elbows, back to life.

"Tell me, yes? You will tell me, Bubbe? The Hovrodnikim, what are they? The *heylige ikra,* Kiryat Sefer. You remember, Bubbe? The story of Raisa?"

Then, she would reach out to the girl, with her own arms of flesh, to quiet the agony she heard in the girl's voice. "I told you already the story of Raisa, my mother?" The old woman, alone in the room with Naamah, spoke also to Maya and Isarael. And now for a time there would be no more echoes.

9

S a r a h   R a c h e l' s   S t o r y   (2)

S o ,   w h a t   can we say? Day to day, maybe, the women of Chernik didn't like Raisa, my mother. Maybe they had nothing to say to her if she came into the butcher and stood by herself, with her little bright eyes. But in their hearts they respected her. And every one of them was pleased if she stopped by their house to observe their daughter, sat down at the table with the child and wrote and drew with her on paper. The ones she selected for her school carried themselves different from that day. And their mothers, were they proud? Do you wonder?

The *Flam-Trogers* didn't invite just anyone to join their sect. From the little girls in Chernik studying with Raisa maybe one would become a member? Maybe none at all!

There were a lot of stories told about the *Flam-Trogers* and the Hovrodnikim. Some said the Hovrodnikim existed from the beginning of time. And of course everyone knew if there were not one at least of the seven sacred women to rise up in a generation the light from the sun would go out. And the moon with it. And all the stars.

You know what this means? It is part of the mystery. It tells the way the human being is stitched into the universe. This is our chant, to sing to the Hovrodnikim on our high holiday of compassion, Yom Chovdur.

> *Seven there are, there are seven.*
> *Seven in the exile where sorrow is.*
> *Seven in the heaven where Chochma lived.*

Seven in the fire where the sparks don't die.
Seven, there are, there are seven.

Of course, in the village, some women told stories about Flame Bearers that maybe were not true. When the peddlers came, or our singers, dressed up like men, with the true stories to instruct the women, they found always quarrels and disputes about what was right.

In our village it happened once, in the ritual bathhouse, a fight broke out. It was between Zipa, who sold kefir in the marketplace, and fat Devora, the beauty, married to the rabbi's son. What was the big dispute? Zipa claimed her family went back to Rocha Castel, the scribe from Soria. You know the story? How Rocha gathered together in secret the women to write down the teachings? It was the first time, after the destruction of Kiryat Sefer, they were written down. But many women, even in that time, thought the teachings should be given only from mouth to ear, as the saying is. From mother to daughter. And so, there was a division. My mother, of course, was a follower in the tradition of Rocha, a scribe. But I was intended for the other side, to keep the story living in the mouth.

These writings of Rocha Castel and her sect did not go among all the women who were Flame Bearers. They were kept by themselves, in the big chest we have still in the family. The key to it Rocha kept always around her neck. In our day the key is lost. It will be found, we say, only by Ha Melamed Gadol, the Great Teacher, the next time she walks on this earth. But then, when Rocha was living, the key was passed to the successor. And from her it went down to the successor who came after. And it was from this great-granddaughter of Rocha Castel our Zipa claimed she was derived.

Can you imagine? What could Zipa the kefir seller know about all this? Could she read the languages? I ask you! She was still an ignorant woman. And Devora even more so, no matter she was married to the rabbi's son.

Well, my mother is sent for. She gives a look to the two women and takes each of them by the chin. Now my mother knows the time is here to teach about Chochma and to tell the old stories about Kiryat Sefer. This is what we mean by reading the signs. Here, she thinks, even here in all this quarrel and ignorance the *heylige ikra* is burning. And now she takes Zipa, and she takes Devora into the school with the girls and begins to teach them how to celebrate the Sabbath in the old way, with the calling to Chochma, the Sabbath Bride, to come to be among her children from the first to the second dusk. She sits them down on the hard bench and she tells them the names of The Mother. Asherah of the Old Land. Lillitu of the winds. Anath of the sea. Elath of the sorrows. She talks to them about Chochma, who gave birth to all the other goddesses and to the gods and to the mortals.

Our village was next to a forest. It was a pine forest, with a dry air, very pure, always smelling from resin. In the summer people would go out there, to swim in the river, men and women separate of course. They would put up a hammock, at night maybe they would light a fire and cook a little meal. This was the Ukraine. There we had our own kind of Jewish life.

So, very slowly, over the years, my mother began to go out to the forest on the Sabbath eve, with her pupils and a few chosen women, Zipa and Devora among them. And this, if you want to know, is why my mother came to Chernik. Because the women there lost the tradition, they forgot to say the ancient names, they forgot the old stories. And she chose Pesach, why? She chose Pesach because, of course, Pesach was the kind of a man who wouldn't interfere.

Pesach didn't ask what the women would be doing when they went off into the forest. There they would make a fire with two sticks. But not with rubbing, the way another woman would do. Raisa would hold out the hands over the twigs. She would close the eyes, she would speak the blessing and from themselves the sticks would bring forth the flame, burning without consuming.

We say, in every woman who is a *Flam-Troger*, the sacred spark is burning so hot they could call the whole world into fire. But the Flame Bearer makes the sparks into compassion, to heal and not to destroy. And so also a Flame Bearer can light the Sabbath candles using only her hands. In our lamps is burning always the same oil, never burning itself out. So it has been since Canaan, and so it will be for so long the mothers tell and the daughters listen.

Raisa would make the fire, the women would chant and they would sing and they would dance with the girls. In the full moon and in the dark of the moon, leaping into the flames and taking up the burning coals in the hands. We say, on the eve of the Sabbath, Chochma, the wise one, rises from among the creatures where she lives with the birds and with the green trees and with the plants and with the green-growing things and with the flowers. She comes then to dwell with us, right inside, the second soul we get for the Sabbath, to rest with it and to rejoice. This is what my mother taught.

My children, you are listening? In the beginning there was no division between the earth and the heaven. The winged spirits and the four-legged spirits and those with gills and those with scales lived sometime here and sometime there, in the sea, on the land, in the sky. Chochma, the Bride, looked over them all, over the goddesses and gods and over the humans too, women and men. But then her own son, he who sat at her right hand, rose up against her to call himself Shaddai, the Almighty. And now he took captive the women and men she made to rejoice in her earth. And so Chochma, what can she do? She who we call Mother Compassionate, what can she do? She went out of heaven to live only with the earth, to console the women and men she made with sparks from her own fire. That is what we teach. The trees, the birds with their wings, the flowers in their glory, the salt sea waves, the grass of the fields, these are the Handmaidens. By night and by day they cry to us, calling us to rise up from our sorrow and from our forgetting to worship her again. Children, you hear them? This is what my mother taught. But this story of course is very old and everywhere there are Flame Bearers you will find it, among the women, in every land.

We say the Hovrodnikim see Chochma in everything. They live close to her each moment of their life. They understand the language of her creatures, they talk with the birds, they fly up over the trees with the blinking of an eye. And you my children, if you will listen good and understand what the Bubbe is saying, you, too, will make your nest in the neck of The Mother, there on the left side where lives the understanding. And then, when you come back, you will be maybe also Hovrodnikim and you will take on the burden of the generation, to struggle against Shaddai, who asks always the suffering of the innocents. You will be maybe a teacher. Or you will be one who knows how to heal in the ways of the earth, with grasses and with herbs and with spices and with flowers. We have also warrior Hovrodnikim, bound by a sacred pledge to lead the people only in protection, never in attack. Or you maybe will be a wandering Hovrodnik, who goes out among the people all over the earth to bring them back from the forgetting. Who knows? Who knows? From among you will come maybe even Ha Melamed Gadol, the Great Teacher we are waiting for. And then, then my children will come the Day of Days and our people will go back to Kiryat Sefer and all people will live each day in Canaan and the old land will become the land of all the earth and we will be Flame Bearers, women and men together, Goyim and Jews and The Mother will lie down with us, here on the earth.

Now you are wondering how you can recognize a Hovrodnik among all the women who are *Flam-Trogers?* This is something a woman learns from herself. From the torment and from the burning of her own *heylige ikra* if she tries to keep silent or remain away from her true work in the world. Such a one, if she does not answer the call, would burn herself up with her own fire, that is what we teach. The voices will come to her but she will not understand. She will run from the messengers and try to keep away from her destiny. And she will be broken like the tree is broken in the wind. And she will be cast down like the stars are cast, falling in their burning out of the sky. And the earth will tremble and the earth will shake and again for a time the roads to Kiryat Sefer will be lost. Children, you understand? When the knock comes to the door you go there and you open it up and you make welcome the messenger. And you find out if she is calling you to be the Great Teacher. The one who will go out to gather in the fallen sparks. To speak again the names of The Mother. To find again the way to Kiryat Sefer.

And now you will hear the story from my sister, from Hannah Leah. And you will think on all these things the Bubbe told you and you will ask yourself. Hannah Leah, you will say, was she a Hovrodnik? Or was she one of those who run away?

10

The story of Hannah Leah, which the old woman had told them many times when they were children, had made a deep impression on Maya. She remembered it, even during those years when it was only Naamah who went up to the old woman's room in the attic and sat with their grandmother, rubbing the old woman's hands and chest with dried raspberry leaves to bring her back out of her wanderings so that she could talk with her and tell the stories again, more or less as she had when they were children.

Many times Naamah tried to make them go with her, begging, cajoling, threatening. But to no avail. They were in rebellion, Rae and Maya, against the old woman. In her absence, they had begun to go out into the world, venturing beyond the neighborhood, where the other old ladies kept an eye on things. They had been to the neighborhood school. They had met children who knew nothing about the sect and did not care to know. And they themselves, what did they care? They lived, during those years, in a peculiar suspension of that larger purpose in which the old woman had kept them, practically from birth. They whispered and gossiped among themselves, keeping a curious eye on their aunts, as if they really had been aware of them before.

The old lady had taken them over so long ago, to teach them their role in the sect, the girls had practically never noticed their own mothers. Before the fire had destroyed the school, they lived for those occasions when they would come together in the old woman's house, where her presence filled every waking moment. Within a few hours of walking through her door their own mothers became for them as unimportant as they were also, it seemed, to the old woman. Esther, Rae's mother, had been given charge of the school. She was a humble woman, content with her work as the school's administrator, and this quality, of serene self-subordination, became even more pronounced as the old woman's powers began to decline. Elke, Naamah's mother, took charge bitterly of the old woman's daily affairs. But they too, on the Sabbath and holidays, seemed of no more significance than their sister Sonia, who had never managed to find a meaningful place for herself in the sect.

In the first year after the school had burned down Sonia was still with them. She had not yet married again and gone away. She was there all the time, always occupied with someone else's business. Soon, she gave up the cramped little upstairs apartment near the park, where she had lived with Maya. She moved right into the house on Scott Street, installing Maya in Rae's room and taking over the old sewing room next to the kitchen on the ground floor. From there, she kept watch over everyone's coming and going, commenting on everything they did, listening to their conversations on the telephone, the door to her room kept always slightly ajar, the room itself cluttered and anomalous in the ordered and impeccable house. If Rae were reading in the kitchen she would come over, watch from a respectful distance to catch her eye and then, when Rae could not resist her any longer and looked up questioningly, she would pounce. Soon, she was reading along with her niece, her arm around Rae's shoulders, following the text with her finger and sometimes even taking over the book completely, moving it gradually toward her until, finally, it was Rae who had to lean over Sonia's lap if she wanted to go on reading.

If Naamah was cooking, Sonia would be certain to come for a taste and then stand there, too close for comfort, until Naamah finally yielded, letting her stir and flavor and sample to her heart's content. Sonia was a busybody and a gossip, looking to stir up trouble and then stand back to watch the results. And all this was done, not from maliciousness, but from a restless need for activity nothing in her life was able to quench. Where Aunt Elke, her older sister, was hard-working, solemn, and industrious, Aunt Sonia seemed to be possessed of an innate frivolity, as if she were born to take things in the most superficial manner imaginable. How this daughter could have descended from the old woman, with her high visionary sense of moral purpose, no one had ever been able to say. For years, before she fell in love and went off to Europe, she had been the naughty girl of their household, more childish and rebellious than was Maya herself. She was small and quick, darting about the house with a dapper flutter, dressed in bright colors, singing softly to herself under her breath, smelling always of lemon or rose oil. The first time Rae had seen a hummingbird she called it Aunt Sonia and jumped up out of the oak tree trying to catch it in her hands.

Aunt Elke was a different matter altogether. Although she did everything possible to keep it hidden—wearing shapeless dresses, tying her hair back, covering her legs in thick stockings, stooping as she went about her work—her beauty remained evident, an alien presence, poking its way through her drab investiture.

She had one of those perfectly ordered and harmonious faces you see only in pictures. Arms with a long, sinuous curve to them, graceful shoulders, a long, proud neck, high full bosom, a tucked waist, slender hips and thighs. She was a beauty of the old school and she carried it all as if it did not belong to her, but had been borrowed and would one day be demanded back unless she kept it hidden.

Maya, who was good at drawing, used to creep down the hall and peer through the keyhole into Aunt Elke's room at night. She told Rae that their aunt used to get undressed and stand in front of the window, looking at her reflection in the dark glass. She would hold her hands beneath her breasts and turn herself from side to side, with a puzzled frown on her face, as if she were trying to figure out who was looking back at her. And then, humming to herself, she would comb out her hair and let it fall down all the way to her ankles, Maya said.

There was no knowing whether Rae believed her. But she liked the drawings Maya made of their aunt and she kept them for years and years, even after she had moved away to the East Coast, rolled up with a piece of tattered ribbon that had once been tied around Maya's braids.

But even in those days, when they were already grown up, Rae and Maya knew no more about their Aunt Elke than they had as children. They did not know whom their aunt had married or where she had lived when she went away from her mother's house or what had happened to her husband or why she had come back one day, with her few boxes of belongings and a little girl by the hand. It had all happened before they were born and it never occurred to them to ask Naamah. Their aunt remained a mystery and they liked it that way. A grim, drab, hard-working mystery and that much more fascinating therefore to their newly awakened curiosity.

And so, while Aunt Elke plodded among them, walking heavily up the stairs and down the stairs in that melancholy self-absorption that seemed only to enhance her embattled beauty, Aunt Sonia had fallen in love and run off. And still the old woman did not come down from her room. Aunt Sonia had gone and she did not write. Rae and Maya did not speak of her, not even late at night when they lay awake in Rae's room, sitting up back to back in the narrow bed trying to guess each other's thoughts. But their old game no longer held the meaning it had when they were children. It had become nothing more than a private language, their own cipher of bonding, the secret way they set themselves apart from the children at the school and even from Naamah, who in those years was beginning to be more and more like the silent woman who was her mother, drudge of the household, mother and daughter working it seemed day and night to keep it clean, preparing their meals, buying clothes for them, making sure they did their schoolwork.

By the time their grandmother had come downstairs again to take part in the life of the house, Rae and Maya had discovered boys and they would climb out of the back window at night to meet with them under the fig tree where the wood carving of Asherah used to stand during the twelve days of the spring festival.

Those were the years when Rae and Maya used to climb up into the oak tree and sit there as it grew dark, chewing the bark, in that easy camaraderie Rae had never forgotten. Just as Maya had never forgotten the stories of Hannah Leah the old woman had started to tell them again on Saturdays, in the kitchen, Naamah watching their faces to make certain they did not smirk or laugh or look bored.

"We say that a girl, when she is eleven or twelve or thirteen years old, when her blood begins, must find out what she is to do as a Flame Bearer. But of course it is possible to make a mistake. How else? A Flame Bearer is a woman. Even the Hovrodnik is also only a woman . . ."

And so they had grown back into the familiar stories, sitting there from first dawn on the Sabbath until late in the evening while the old woman talked. She was different now, her puckered face so deeply lined it seemed to Rae there was no room left for one more wrinkle. She was older, perhaps weary herself of this endless telling, to what purpose now she, too, must have wondered? Now that the school had been lost and the board had triumphed over her and her own pupils, the ancients of the sect, had begun to die off.

If Rae listened at all it was out of pity for her and because she did not dare to take from her the last hope and consolation, now that her own blood had come. She was disappointing the old woman, she imagined, just as her mother before her must also have done. Her grandmother had been waiting to find out if one of them might be a Hovrodnik or even the Great Teacher, Ha Melamed Gadol. She had tested and taught and waited for two generations as each, in turn, had let her down. And now there was only this endless telling and retelling of her old stories, to which Rae listened, when she could.

"Now my sister, when her time came, made such a choice my mother wanted to close her out from her house forever. But this cannot be. 'What the daughter is, the mother is also,' as we say. My mother knew this. Raisa knew. But, did they quarrel! From my first years I heard them. You see why I didn't want to talk? My first memory is the face of my sister leaning over my cradle. But such a face! Gray it was, ashen, like a burnt-out fire. But her one eye bright and burning, like a coal."

Maya kept an eye on her cousin as the old woman talked. And then, when the story of Hannah Leah seemed to run inside her again, as familiar as it was each time strangely new, she forgot Rae. She forgot to think about her mother, who wrote sometimes and once had even come to visit. She did not wonder where she was or when she would see her again. That vague yearning for closeness and communion that she felt always and never spoke of, even to Rae, fixed itself upon Hannah Leah and she would hear that muffled hooting far off across the forest. Pines and the resin of pines and the green-blue of the lake with its smell of mating. A lizard scurrying over the white rock. A hammock swaying, voices calling, coming closer, through the woods into the clearing where the small fire in its ring of black stones was already burning.

"My sister wore then, like the other women in our village, a *shaytl*, the orthodox wig. But this was to laugh at, or to make you cry. Because in this time Hannah Leah was still a Flame Bearer right down to the smallest toe. She wore this wig only to hide the fact that she had no hair on the head. Not a single hair. And why she had none I will tell you, but in its own time. My sister had taken the way of violence. And my mother insisted no *Flam-Troger* would do what she had done. And so they quarreled. Hannah Leah claimed she was Hov-rodnik, one of the sacred seven, who alone knew what is needed for the world . . ."

11

I *l o v e d* my sister, how else? To me, whatever she did with her life, she was a loving sister. And I loved my mother, too. She was a patient woman, very quiet, with her dark eyes. If she said a thing you would believe it. That was her tenderness, to give to the children the feeling she, the mama, knew what was right. Could I choose between them? Such suffering I saw in Hannah Leah until she ran off again. And this maybe is what makes a Hovrodnik in our time? Mama said the Hovrodnik must rise up from compassion and from love. And my sister, she was a *destroyer.*

Children, you understand? You are wondering why did I say this, that in our time a Hovrodnik is one who suffers? Now, to this question it is not so easy to give an answer. It has to do, this answer, with the way a Flame Bearer thinks about the world. Always, we are reading the signs, trying to figure out what Chochma needs from us. The Mother is there, who could doubt this? But she cannot interfere with what her children are doing. Maybe she looks and sees what is happening and then she weeps. She knows Shaddai, who calls himself Almighty, would be cast down out of the heavens if the hearts of women and men would open and see the world again in compassion. And so also the Flame Bearers are weeping and they are going out into the world with a terrible mission and a terrible burden. How else could it be? Could it be easy to open up the hearts of women and of men? And yet, one day it will happen. This is what we believe. And so we are working to bring it a little faster, this Day of Days, when will be no more division between heaven and earth and among the peoples of the earth.

But here I better tell you about the time when all this was taking place. We lived then, the Jews, in a world separate from other people. We had, as you know, our own pale of settlement and if we wanted to live outside, in Kiev maybe, or St. Petersburg or in Minsk, we needed a special permit or a higher education. But we knew, of course, what was going on in the world around us. It is our business to know.

In the year, called 1862, when Hannah Leah was born, it was already the time of the Czar Alexander the Second. He was called by the people the "Czar Liberator." And why? Because in the beginning he took away all the restrictions that kept the Jews separate from the Russian people. But this wasn't all. He made reforms also for the others, for the Russians too. In the courts, among the peasants. He did good works and there was such a spirit among the people in that time, how can I tell you? There was hope, and hope in Russia you didn't see so much. But then he changed and the people saw it was all only promises. He talked, he promised, nothing happened. What changed? Everything went on as before, the bribes, the abuses in the courts, the anti-Semitism. And so there ran now a big disappointment among not only the Jewish people. The Russian young people felt it also in themselves. And they began then to go out among the peasants, to help them during the famine and to teach them.

Now it happens that in this time, while Hannah Leah was growing up in our little village, there arose a group among the Flame Bearers and they were called *di Kalye-Makhers.* The Spoilers. These women were all young. They split themselves off from the older women, they went about dressed up like men. Sometimes one came into a village and presented herself there as a cantor. Maybe other women in the town, who also were secret members of the Spoilers, already were busy telling stories to prepare the way. So, the rabbi would go over to pay his respects. Did he want to be left out? The two would walk together, talking of this, talking of that. They would go into the synagogue, the rabbi very proud to have this famous cantor in his town. Then, when the moment would come for the cantor to chant the Mizmor Shir L'yon Ha Shabbat, suddenly strange words would come out of the mouth. The men of course would begin to tremble. Maybe a dybbuk was present? And now, where the cantor was, a woman suddenly appeared, standing there, in front of the congregation. And then, just as quickly, she vanished out the door. The other women whisked her away and the fear spread. The Shaddaim, the devils, it was said, were taking over among the women. And of course there was trouble and worry in that village for a long time.

This was what the Spoilers wanted. They were young, I told you this. And sometimes they went about and took the mezuzah from the doorpost and took away the usual inscription. You know of course what it is. *And if you will carefully obey my commandments.* But now they wrote their own words. *The fire never obeys. Be thou like fire, destroying that thou mayst renew.*

These pieces of parchment they put not only into the mezuzot, but into the tefillin as well. And when the men wrapped them on themselves, to pray, suddenly they would be struck dumb. The lips would move, the tongue would move, but not a word coming out from the mouth. Even, in some places, these Spoilers set a synagogue on fire and burned it to the ground. Or there were girls who would go, on Simchat Torah, dressed up like young men and they would dance with the men in the synagogue. There, they would press the sacred parchment of the scroll against their breast. And why? Because among the Jewish men always it was taught if the woman's body would touch the sacred scroll it would be no longer sacred. Or scribes of the sect would go into the synagogue at night and they would rewrite portions of the Torah. Or they would go forward if a stranger was called up to read Torah in an unfamiliar town. And they would cry out their own teachings. *Blessed is transgression. Blessed they who trample what has severed its roots from the living fire.*

Whey did they do these things? In those times the women sat apart in the synagogue, separated by a rail or upstairs in the gallery, behind a screen. And who doesn't know the morning prayer, recited by the Jewish men, praising God they were not born a woman?

These young girls, they didn't like this. Bad things existed already thousands of years, from the time the Hebiru came up out of the desert and took captive our land. But now they wanted to strike out against the Jewish men and these were the things they did. It wasn't enough for them we had our own sect, our own practices, our own ways of worshiping. It wasn't enough we did the work of The Mother, giving to the world the seven sacred women in every generation. Now they wanted to fight back against the men.

For Mama, these acts were not in keeping with our tradition. For Mama the fire was not to destroy, not even for the purpose to make new again. For her these Spoilers were too violent. She did not believe in them. She did not think they were Flame Bearers. They were, she insisted, from Shaddai, part of his confusion and part of his shadow during the Days of Shaddai. But when Hannah Leah heard about this group she could not keep her spirits inside her.

What would I today say about the Spoilers? They belonged to their time, who could deny it? But they had been touched by the *Tsayt-sam*, as Mama used to say. It means the *time's poison*. What they did among our own people, others outside also were doing. Soon the whole world would be in the Cycle of Destroying. That is what the Spoilers believed. The destroying was needed, they said, to clear the way for the coming of Ha Melamed Gadol, the Great Teacher.

We all in that time, all the Flame Bearers, believed it was soon the time for the Great Teacher to return. But what happens before the Teacher comes? Does the heart open and the knee bend and the head go back in awe to worship? The coming of the Teacher is felt by all the creatures. Then, the trees get more green. The birds sing louder. The creatures with the four legs come out from the forest and they are seen in the towns. Only the hearts from women and men do not know what is happening. Something they feel, pushing inside them. But this thing makes them afraid. They don't know this is Chochma, pushing from inside, trying to get back to them. It is this fear Shaddai wants. Because he knows, from this fear he will make his own power. Shaddai we say is the Lord of Fear. But The Mother rules only in love and with compassion.

That's how it is. And this becomes then our work, to teach the people what is coming and to prepare them for the Teacher, who comes to bring again the worship of Chochma. Our sect in this time went out to speak the names of The Mother. But the Spoilers taught that before the Teacher comes and before Chochma rules again in the human hearts, there must be violence, to tear down the old order and destroy the world of men.

Mama always argued against this. She used to say, "For violence, who needs us? There will be hands enough to lift up the rock. Let us be the ones to lay it down again."

Well, the Spoilers never came to our village. Hannah Leah looked out for them, but it did her no good. She wanted to run off and join them. But it was not yet the time of her blood. And so she waited.

Then, before she left finally and went out into her own life, something happened to her.

Since she was a little girl she used to go off by herself in the forest. This was unusual in our time. Most of the girls in the village would help the family, in the orchard maybe, or working in the kitchen garden. The family had perhaps a cow or a goat to take care of or they would go to the marketplace to help out the mama or run errands for the father if he would have a trade. Always there was something for the girl to do.

But Hannah Leah, this wild one, would have nothing to do with these things. She always would be by herself. She loved to climb up into the pine trees and swim in the river and leap off from a high rock. So of course, the peasant boys knew about her. But they left her alone because they were afraid of her. She had a funny little face, with small, glittering hazel eyes, a pug nose, a wide mouth, and such an expression as if she wanted to jump up and slap you in the face. She scared people, she had a certain look in the eyes, as if these eyes knew what everybody was thinking. "She'll die young," Mama said from the time she was a little girl. And now Mama, too, was afraid for her. She knew the time was coming when Hannah Leah would go off away from home. "This one," she used to say, "this one will become a scourge for the world." And this now is the story I want to tell you. One day Hannah Leah came home with bloody knuckles and broken lips, from a fight in the forest with a peasant boy who tried to rape her.

"Hach, you should have seen him," she shouted when Mama tried to dress the wounds. "This is nothing," she yelled, stamping the foot and pushing Raisa away. "I smashed him, I beat him with a rock, I knocked him silly." She lifted up her fist, hammering on the thigh. And then she tore herself away and ran to the window. She stuck out her head and shouted down the street. "Here I am. You. Pyotr Vasilev. Do you want to try again? Eh, you potato? Where are you hiding?"

That's the kind of girl she was. And Pyotr? What can you say about him, the only boy in the village who would dare this thing? He was a rough one, he came from rough people. "As the ground is, so also is the vegetable that comes from the ground," Mama used to say. "When a boy like Pyotr falls in love, what else does he know but rape?"

But now something happened to my sister. Can I explain it? All this was, of course, before I was born. The next day after the attack by Pyotr, Hannah Leah goes off by herself again. She walks into the peasant village, she starts asking for Pyotr Vasilev and comes finally to his house.

Now the peasants were not poorer than the Jews. Who could be poorer than a Jew in Russia? Only another Jew. But the peasants lived in a different way. In our village was wide streets, with small wooden houses, painted white. There was bright blue shutters, little wooden fences, gardens in front, a nice gate, maybe even a poplar tree. But in the peasant village nothing would be kept up like this. Maybe it was different somewhere else, but we thought their village was just a place filled up with mud, with pigs and every kind of animal going in and out from the houses. There no one knew how to read or to write. They were ignorant, they drank up the vodka and they had, of course, no ritual bath.

Now all this Hannah Leah knew since she was a little girl. But this time it made a certain impression on her. She found Pyotr Vasilev lying in a clump of rags, in a little dark hovel without a bed. He was in a fever, he could die even because of the beating she gave him. She stands at the door, she takes a look and a small little moan comes out from her lips. You see? This is what I am trying to tell you. Hannah Leah had a heart. This is what made her wild. It was the biting and scratching of the heart against the rough world that made her torment. And so now every day Hannah Leah goes over there and she brings to Pyotr the raper something to eat. Some milk from our goat, a loaf of bread Mama would bake for the Sabbath. She sits down on the floor next to the rags, she takes the head of Pyotr into her lap, she feeds him with a spoon and she rocks him. Hannah Leah, the violent one. So of course, Pyotr gets better. The day comes, the swelling goes away from the eyes, the eyes open again and what does he see? This funny little face from Hannah Leah looking down on him. After that, the two of them go off into the pine forest and Hannah Leah tells Mama she is teaching Pyotr to read and to write.

Mama, you think, would not let her daughter behave in this way? Going off by herself, into the forest, with a Russian boy? And such a boy no less who tried to rape her? But, could Mama stop Hannah Leah? She was then almost eleven years old. And a girl like this, headstrong in her violence and knowing always her own mind, you just won't find anymore in the world. She came up out of her time the way you, too, my children, come up out of your time.

Then, something else began to happen with my sister. She, who lived always apart from people, begins to feel something new. It was then the spring of 1874 and soon was coming the "mad summer," as later on it would be called. For in that summer, what happened? In that summer thousands of young women and men from the cities suddenly took off into the countryside to work with the people. This was "Chochma's Madness," the "Madness of Kovahl," when a person puts away the thoughts from their own small life, and goes out to serve among the people.

Now my sister, of course, knew nothing about this. Later, we found out that in Petersburg, where a Flame Bearer lived, there was a house where these young people would go, to receive money, peasant clothes, addresses in the provinces, forged papers, propaganda texts, to instruct the people about the unjust tax system, about their poverty, about the social injustice. Here you see the sort of work a Flame Bearer would do, reading the signs from her time. Many Jewish girls and boys also were involved in these things and many who didn't call themselves a Flame Bearer. But mostly it was Russian students, and they would go off in twos and in threes and sometimes they went off alone, barefoot, looking for work among the people.

Well, this was a time of famine for maybe half of all Russia. In that time the suffering of the people was worse even than usual. For three years one after the next there was bad harvest. So now these young people, they went to share the suffering of the peasants. When the Flame Bearers came, they insisted always on very practical work. They made hospitals. They brought food and they brought books and they offered education. But for the Russian students it was a crusade, they wanted to live the humble life of the people. The Flame Bearers don't care so much for the way a person lives. "Even a rich woman," we say, "can do the work of Chochma, why not?"

Now Hannah Leah, as I said, at first she knew nothing of this. But all spring, after the fight with Pyotr Vasilev, she was in such a state, who could describe it? It was, you could say, an exaltation. And what was it she felt, this violent one, who kept herself always apart, even from Mama? It was *narodolyubstvo*, as it was later called. *Love of the people.* But this love of hers was not like the love of the usual Hovrodnik, working among the people to teach, through this loving, the memory of The Mother. This love of Hannah Leah was now *only* for the Russian peasant. She wouldn't hear of anything else. Every day, she wanted to go down into their village and teach them to read and talk about how they were living. "There is coming," she said, "a new age. And for this, who needs Flame Bearers? Who needs even the Jews? We are the last," she would say, with a clenched fist, arguing with Mama. "After this, there will be only one people. And we, the Jews, will be dissolved into them."

All this was of course very upsetting for my mother. Always, from the time her daughters were little girls, she would be looking on our body, for the birthmark, the sign of the flame. Sometimes, of course, the mark would come later. But always, for the girl who should become a Hovrodnik, sooner or later, the mark appeared. The Shadmis have never broken the descent. Never, from the time of Naamah the Ammonite, wife to Solomon, mother of Rehoboam. Never we failed to find one at least in every generation to carry on. She is maybe only a humble worker. The way Esther, my daughter, the mother to Isarael, was a humble worker. Who is to say what is small in the world and what is large? You think only the Great Teacher matters? Or even, only the Hovrodnik matters? Even the grass matters, every blade. And the weed growing next to the grass. One single spark, we say, one smallest piece from the *heylige ikra*, this is enough to make new the whole world.

But now one day Hannah Leah comes home from the forest and goes into the little shed where Mama is teaching the girls. She slams the door and spreads out the arms. Shouting in that way she had: "For behold, it has happened."

Well, naturally, with all this shouting everybody turns to have a look. Hannah Leah stands there, looking back, with those eyes of hers. And then she tears open the blouse, pushes forward the little chest and sure enough. Right there, on the left breast, is the mark of the flame. But all around it the skin is raw. And now Hannah Leah insists a great pain came down on her when she was lying on the sand next to the river. And this pain, she tells them, marked the sign of the flame.

So, why not? It could be. Stranger things have happened. Mama gives a look and makes herself not cry out. She opens up the arms to Hannah Leah but my sister laughs. "Now, it has happened," she repeats and then she slams back out of the shed and goes off to the forest and nobody sees her again for weeks.

In this time my sister was struggling with *Kovahl.* You know what it means? It is the story we write, each woman for herself, from the story that is already written. It means the life the way Chochma intends we should live it. But what happens if a woman tries to write the story another way? And what happens if a woman runs from the story already written?

By then of course the "mad summer" began to happen. Even to us, in the Ukraine, the student crusaders were coming. Soon also came women from the Flame Bearers in Petersburg, and my mother found out this was a new movement, and the Flame Bearers, too, were a part of it.

This was not easy for Mama. Now she had to think Hannah Leah maybe didn't burn the mark onto the breast herself. Maybe Hannah Leah had seen ahead, the way a Flame Bearer can? Maybe even she was a Hovrodnik?

Mama went out to look for her daughter; she found her in the forest. These were hot nights and Hannah Leah, who all that spring ate only berries and nuts, was lying in her hammock. Mama brought a kid, a very small baby goat. She brought milk with her and now she cooked up the little animal very slowly in the milk. This is the initiation, very simple, between mother and daughter. The daughter tells how the Hovrodnik came for her. Maybe in a dream, maybe in a vision, maybe right there knocking at the door. The mother listens, she gives the blessing. The two of them eat together, tearing the kid, the sacred animal, with the fingers. The evening passes, the sky grows dark, they close their eyes, the sun is there again and the daughter is now a Flame Bearer. Most of the time the initiation takes place at the coming of the first blood. Eleven or twelve the daughter is then and most often she is thirteen. And for this reason also the Jewish men make their bar mitzvah when the boy is thirteen, to imitate these practices among the women, which we have since the ancient day. But of course, for a boy, what is so special about the age thirteen?

What happened between Mama and Hannah Leah I don't know, because this kind of talk, between a mother and daughter, when the daughter begins her blood, and finds her own destiny, no one is permitted to repeat. Hannah Leah, when she already was half mad because of her suffering, did not tell me a word. I know only Mama persuaded her she should come home for seven days, before she left. And then Hannah Leah, young as she was, went off to live in the

Flame Bearer house in St. Petersburg and work there with the new movement.

It was hard for Mama, I know this. Her daughter was, how old? Eleven years old, but already a woman. And this work she took on was very dangerous. These students could be arrested, they could be put into exile, or prison, and maybe they even would not receive a trial. You know what the prisons were under the czar? Can I tell you? Some people went in there for maybe a few months. They came out broken. Blind, maybe insane, their health ruined. It was a common thing. But Hannah Leah had chosen, what could Mama do?

Then, a few months later, the police managed to smash the movement. By the end of the summer they raided all the provinces and the centers. They arrested maybe sixteen hundred people. And many of them they kept in prison until the year called 1877, when some of them came on trial.

Hannah Leah escaped. And this you will hear again in the life of my sister. Always the escape. Until, at the end, she ran right into the arms of the Guide. But this was later. It was not in Russia. For now, my sister escaped. This is how it happened. She was in the back room in the Petersburg house, where the printing press was hidden. When she heard that certain kind of a knock at the door, right away she poured oil over the papers in the room and set the whole place on fire. On fire, I tell you. And then she ran out screaming and in the uproar she and some others got away.

And now begins the part of my sister's life I don't know so much about. Mama knew less even than I knew. What my sister told me when I was a little girl I remember. But, could she tell me everything?

So, she disappeared. She went, as the saying was, *underground.* But who knew anything about this girl with the mark of the fire on the breast? She was a child still, with a girl's figure, still undeveloped. And this is why she was so useful in that movement. In the earlier form it was maybe smashed. But something was started. And now it had to go a definite way. The czar broke his promises to the people. Where was the land reform? Where was the reform in the courts? After the year called 1874 he arrested the students who went out to the people in love. So, what could be hoped from him? The movement could not be stopped. But it changed its nature.

It began again a little more bitter and with a big disillusion. Mama of course saw all this before it happened. That is why she never liked what Hannah Leah chose or that the Flame Bearers should be part of it. Now more violence was coming and Hannah Leah wanted it. That, too, is what Mama knew.

You remember the question? You remember what I told you to keep in the mind? To ask in yourself if Hannah Leah remained a Flame Bearer in this work or instead became something different? We have been many things. Scholars and teachers and healers we have been. And women with visions. Builders of cities and women who work the soil. Prophets we have been, foretelling the going down and the coming up. So why not also a destroyer, clearing the way? But now you must listen. And not forget. The stories from men they write down in their books. In libraries they keep them. But our stories, the women's stories, what becomes of them? And what became of Kiryat Sefer, our City of the Book, and the libraries we had there and the houses of study? In the heart they live, where else? And in the memory.

So, you are sitting here. You are looking with big eyes at the Bubbe, listening with the ears. You are asking inside, was this the work of the Flame Bearers or was it instead part of the Great Error? Well, children, what was it? A new thing for the Flame Bearers, a necessary thing? Or was it only the shadow from the Days of Shaddai, part of the *Tsayt-sam*, the time's poison that ate up the love and compassion even of my sister, my Hannah Leah?

My sister disappeared. And then, a few months later she was in Moscow. It was now November or December and the Frichi had come there, from Switzerland. You know who they were, these young girls from well-off families? They were studying in Zurich. They worked there with the revolutionist Lavrov. They had there a debating society and a big pot of tea and a table in the kitchen where everyone could sit down for a sip and a holler, as we say. So of course, with all this, they became very radical. But then the czar called back all the women students who were in Zurich. And now these girls, with some Georgian men they met, arrive in Moscow and they begin a new organization, a conspiratorial society. It was still the same thing, Populism, going to the people. But now it was workers and intellectuals together. The Frichi went to live in the factory district. They distributed books and tracts to the workers and they spread propaganda. Soon, they were sending Hannah Leah over to the men's dormitory, where the men factory workers lived. They sent her with a message for a husband or a brother and that's how she got inside. But then, once she's inside, she begins to read to them, out of her books and journals, educating them. These were rough men. Did they care if a woman was a girl still, only a child? They took one look on Hannah Leah and they're already thinking that kind of thought which also was in Pyotr when he tried to rape her in the forest. But Hannah Leah, what does she do? She points a finger at them. "Look, you men," she says, "you think I don't know what you have in the head there? I know. And I didn't come here for that. For that you get someone in the streets. Me, I came in here to give you something better. So sit," she says and you know what? They sit. "And now you listen," she tells them. And what do you think? These big men, sitting there in the rough clothes, with the face unwashed and the dirty hands on the knees, they listen to Hannah Leah.

Well, all this is good. This is the kind of work a Flame Bearer should be doing. But then one day comes the factory manager without a knock at the door. He walks in. He takes a look to these revolution-ary books and pamphlets. He sees what he expects to see and then, of course, he seizes the books.

Again, Hannah Leah escapes. This is the second time. Who knows how? The men helped her. The Frichi got her off into hiding. And the organization meanwhile is growing

Hannah Leah goes now to live in a hotel with two others. One of them is Tsitsianov, a Georgian man. And the other is Nina Kuzmet, a rich woman from a well-off family. But all this was still new in the world. What did they know about making a revolution? Right there, in the open, all over the place, they have their books and their jour-nals. They have a chemical solution to put the passports in to change the name on them. There, on a table in the kitchen. That's where they do their correspondence, in code. They have money. They have even peasant clothes, for the disguise they need. So of course the police come there and they find these things. That's how it is. Each time more violent. Tsitsianov tries to pull out a gun. He points it at the policeman and they throw him down on the floor and they start to kick him. They grab hold on Nina Kuzmet. She gets free. She throws herself on top of Tsitsianov, under the kicks, to try to protect him. And meanwhile, Hannah Leah, what does she do? Does she run out the door and escape? Not she. Not my sister. This is what she is waiting for. Maybe all her life for this moment she is waiting. So now, she grabs Tsitsianov's revolver. It is lying there, under the table, where the policeman kicked it away. She jumps down under the table. Every-one looks and Hannah Leah fires.

Well, this you could say was violence to defend life. Maybe it was. Maybe it was. But this, I tell you, it did something to my sister. She was then almost twelve years old. A girl still, but for the second time she almost killed somebody.

And now from that moment, in the Moscow apartment, time was not on the side of Hannah Leah. After this, time was running away from her, trying to get away from her life. And she, too, was running. She went into the Crimea with Nina Kuzmet. They were hiding on the family's estate. But sooner or later they had to be ar-rested.

In Russia in this time a political prisoner should be kept apart from the others, even in a village detention hut. That's how it was done. But, if the political prisoners refused to identify themselves then they would go into a common cell. Hannah Leah refused. And that was almost the end of her. If she died then there would be no big sister for me when I was born. There would be only a story about a sister. This was a dangerous thing she did, going into the common cell. The new arrivals would be attacked by the others. These were brutal people in there, also the women. Day and night in that place you would hear the screams from fights and beatings. My sister never forgot it. She went away from our village, and from our mother's hosue, maybe ten months before. And now, for the rest of her life, when she tried to sleep, even after she came home, she would sit up in bed with the hands to the ears. Because these cries, they came with her.

From the first minute my sister went into that cell there was trouble. Right away someone yelled at her. "*Zhidovka*, Jew girl," they shouted. Who could say why? My sister certainly did not look Jewish. But now Hannah Leah gives a look at this woman who is coming over to her, the hands out, the nails ready. "You," says my sister, pointing a finger in that way she had, "that's the end of you." The woman looks surprised. She takes a step back. And now Hannah Leah picks up a pail and throws it at her.

After that, right away, my sister was put into solitary. It was a little space, so small you could hardly lie down in there. There was not even a bunk, it was completely dark. A few months in these holes and people got scurvy, they got typhoid, they got consumption. It would be all over for my sister too. But finally her friend Nina Kuzmet convinced them to let her out. She got her released to her own family. She says Hannah Leah is her younger sister. Those things happened too.

Hannah Leah maybe didn't like it but what could she do? Make a liar out of Nina? This is *Kovahl*. The story the way it must be written. Not the way we want it should be. My sister came out of there after six months. She was already blind in her one eye from the fight in the common cell. You know why she had no hair? When they put her in solitary she made a fire with her clothes and stuck her head in it. She did this. She made up a bundle out of her clothes and with the old blessing which Mama taught to her, holding out her hands, she called up the flame. And then she bent over and put her head into the fire.

Why? Why did she do this? It was because she tried to kill. I know, did she have to tell me? She should be dead, but the guard saved her.

And now maybe you think she would stay where she was and recover her health? The Kuzmet family would give her a home, she would have comfort, a big room for herself to sleep in, a window from upstairs to look over the fields. She told me there was a river flowing right there through the poplar trees. One night she looks out the window and she sees a wild swan flying by and she knows, this is the Hovrodnik, keeping an eye on her. She stayed only four months, my sister. Then, she disappeared. How else could it be? "In quiet," we say, "the heart is speaking."

All this time my mother and my father didn't hear a word from her. But rumors they heard. They knew what happened in Moscow, with the Frichi and the police and Tsitsianov and Nina and the man Hannah Leah almost killed. The women from the Flame Bearers, who now were not part of this new organization, tried to keep an eye on Hannah Leah. But she escaped even their eyes. That is why Mama believed Hannah Leah was not anymore a Flame Bearer. We lost her. No one could find her. Not in dreams. Not in transportations.

If you ask me, this, too, can happen. For a long time a Hovrodnik can be lost to the others, lost maybe even to herself, and still she could come back. But Mama said, even if somebody would be dead, we could reach them and give them guidance. But Hannah Leah, she said, was more than dead. She had trampled *Kovahl*. This is what happens.

My grandfather, the father of my father, went out to look for

Hannah Leah. He was, as you know, a wealthy man. He knew people. He had connections, even if he was a Jew. He went into the prisons, he went down under the earth, he looked in the cells, among the women. But Hannah Leah, she had vanished.

Then, in December in the year called 1876, when she almost was fifteen years old, they heard about her again. They thought she must be dead in some village detention hut, with a different name and no way to find her. But in January a woman came from Petersburg, saying there was a demonstration in front of the cathedral. The cathedral was called Our Lady of Kazan.

There were rumors a special service would be there, for those who died in prison. Many young people gathered. But the crowd did not break up, even after the service was over. Then, a boy in a peasant sheepskin coat brought out a red flag. It said *Zemlya I Volya. Land and Freedom.*

Another boy jumped up on a ledge and made a speech against the government. The police whistle sounded. And soon, from the Central Market, near the cathedral, came the market porters, the butcher boys, the various helpers and apprentices. They attacked the protesters. Right away, there was cracked heads and blood running and the sounds of shouting and the groans of pain. But now a girl, with a worker's cap on the head, with one eye blind and scars all over the forehead, picks up the red banner on which is written Land and Freedom. She shouts to the people, she begins to lead them in a procession. And this, said the woman who came to talk to Mama, this girl was Hannah Leah.

By the time the police came, my sister managed again to escape. The two boys were arrested. But she had disappeared. And this time Hannah Leah came home. She came, with her ashen face, the terrible scars, the head without hair on it. I was born in February, in the year called 1875. By the time I was one year old my sister was home again. And there she sat, with a matron's wig on the head, and the blind eye, rocking my cradle.

By the time I was two years old the trials began. In Moscow. Later, I found out Hannah Leah received messages in code, telling her to stay hiding. The organization had a man in the police headquarters, to let them know what the police were doing. So, she found out. For the police, the little girl in the Moscow apartment with Nina and

Tsitsianov was now identified. They thought she was a member of the Kuzmet family. Their reports said she was dead.

But the others, her comrades, were given terrible sentences, even the women. For the sake of the organization my sister stayed in hiding. But all this while her heart was driving her. Most of the others went off into hard labor in Siberia, and in Kara, to work in the mines. And Hannah Leah, what did she want? My sister, brooding over my cradle, she wanted to be in Kara with them.

12

"**S**h e wanted to be in Kara with them," a voice said. The old woman sat up in bed. She stared around her with a look of outrage, as if someone were playing a joke on her. And then she saw that Maya and Isarael were laughing at her. They were holding up the white rug over their head, lifting up the feet, clapping and dancing. "She wanted to be, she wanted to be, oh yes she wanted to be in Kara," sang Maya, whirling around in front of the tile stove.

"Stop, go slow," the old lady said, as the shifting scene tumbled into itself, making her feel dizzy. Was it now? Was it then? Was it the kitchen? the little garden? the street in Chernik? the attic room?

"Bubbe, Bubbe," said Isarael's voice, far away now and filled with an indefinable longing. "Bubbe, wait for me . . ." The old woman pushed her hands down on her lap, looking around her. Where were the children? The little room, with its sloped ceiling and narrow bed, reminded her of some place she had been before where she had not been happy. Was she in exile?

Then the blue curtain on the window began to move. She saw the fog outside, heard the cooing of a dove, the low moan of the foghorns on the bay, and she knew many things all at once. She was in San Francisco. In the Home for the Jewish Aged. The children were gone, grown up, away in their own lives now. And she knew that she never again would see Isarael.

"No," she said, putting her feet down on the floor and shaking her head. She was looking up at the ceiling, toward the corner of the room, where she had noticed a bird's nest the day before. "No," she repeated, in a firm tone, as if it were still possible to negotiate. "Not this. Too long already I waited. I won't have it."

There was no answer from the nest. And now, the silence made her angry. "It wasn't enough you took Esther away? Now you take me? Now, when finally Isarael comes home again?"

Then she realized that her granddaughter was already there. There she was, sitting in the old gray chair next to the window. She was bent over her knees in that way she had, leaning on her elbows, with the chin in her two hands, smiling.

The old lady recognized this smile. Sad it was, and stubborn. It reminded her of Hannah Leah. Dying, in the hovel. In Paris. Still insisting to go her own way, as if there was no regrets, no memory of the suffering.

Then, she was awake and she knew she had been wandering. She looked over at the gray chair next to the window to make sure. There was no Isarael . . .

The old lady did not know how to cry. "Tears, what for?" she used to say when she was a little girl. "If Chochma didn't want it should happen, would it happen? And, if she wanted, what need to cry?"

"Born old, this one," Raisa would say of her, shaking her head. "No good will come of it. A little one already not living like a human."

"H'unch," the old lady muttered, closing her eyes to keep out the light and taking up again the old disagreement with her mother. Why should she cry? She never had cried. Not when Hannah Leah went away and didn't come back again. Not when Raisa died. Not when she had to leave everything behind and come to the New World with her three children to bring the teaching of the sect. "Tears, what for?" she reminded herself when the news came about Esther, the one daughter capable of understanding burned so bad only bones were left and teeth to make the identification.

It was cold in the room. A cold light inching its way across the painted floor. She stood up, heaving herself from the bed with a terrible effort as if all alone in her one body she could overcome the earth-call of Chochma, pulling her back down to the dust. Never? Never with these eyes to see again Isarael?

"Isarael," she said, looking down at the grown girl who had wrapped her legs around Maya and was resting there on the white bear rug, gazing up at the Bubbe, her chin on Maya's shoulder. "Isarael, give to me the hand. So, the palm up. You see? This line, the small one that goes from the thumb out into the middle. In this line is the meeting place from your one life and the life of our people. What do you see there? Two forks in the road. It means, a growing apart. And later, a coming together."

She bent forward to take the girl's hand in her own. But Isarael, so tall now, jumping to her feet, grabbed the old lady's hand and brought it to her lips and kissed it. That was the time. That was it. After the fire. After the coming back down out of the room. Out of her whole body the tears ran, one drop from every pore. The arms wanting to open, to take the beloved granddaughter inside. She fought. How she fought to keep the eyes dry. To make the tears go back. To sit again, straight up in the chair, back straight, shoulders back.

"*Alte beheyme,*" she muttered, wrenching herself into the present. She hobbled over to the gray chair and dropped down heavily near the window. This was her life. To wake, to drag herself out of the past, to pull herself over to the chair, to sit there, fighting the sleep, keeping watch over the street, waiting.

"You foolish old cow," she moaned, pressing her hands down on her knees, "she loved you. You didn't know? Even then, already grown, the child loved you. And you? Too proud for this? You wanted her in the name of her mission? Too frightened to bind her through love?"

She sat back, closing her eyes to shut out Isarael's face. The hurt running over it. The eyes forked, spitting the poison, shutting off the love. She sat very still, thinking she was dead maybe. "Oy, Mother," she moaned, "how will she know? How will she know I love her?"

But she could not. She could not stay there, in the desolation, dying alone. The whirling came sick and furious, she grabbed the chair with her hands, clenching her teeth tight, fighting the dizziness. This time she did not fall into the past. She was sitting still in the gray chair, wearing the black dress with the bone buttons. It was not the wandering, it was the far-seeing, over distance. She heard Isarael getting out of the car. There she was, with Jacob. There, in the park? "Child," she called out, "child. What do you do there? Walking by the lake when the Bubbe is dying?"

She got to her feet. She was shaking all over. "Hurry, hurry," she urged, crouching down, trying to gather up her power, to drive it out into the universe. "This one wish," she said, throwing a fierce look at the nest, terrified by the hope she felt. "For now I saved it. Never before I asked nothing for myself. This one time. To put the hand on her head. To give her the blessing."

It was there, the anguish. Bigger than all the wisdom she had from the time she was a little girl looking out from her mother's house in Chernik at the streets running with blood no one else saw. She put her face in her hands. She understood. It was growing, taking a bit from here, a bit from there. One drop from the grief not cried for Hannah Leah. Another from the sorrow never mourned, Raisa dead. Rushing, swelling, pushing from inside. Big was this pain and hot. So it came. The tear, finally.

"Chochma," she said, speaking in a clear voice. She raised her index finger and pointed it at the ceiling, majestically. "Chochma," she repeated, narrowing her eyes. "Remember the promise. The Hovrodnik can choose the hour of dying. Chochma, remember."

And now finally she was with the children again. She was there, in the house on Scott Street. It was the Sabbath. They were listening. The old lady fixed her gaze on the three girls who sat on the white rug, looking up at her. "I loved my sister," she said, and this time she heard in the words a sound like the dropping down from far away of heavy tears.

"Did I know what was beauty, what was ugly? What could I know?" She looked down at her granddaughters, stern, frowning, measuring, prodding. Deep, deep she gazed, demanding from them more than they were able to give. The one tall and restless with the red curls and the smile stubborn. The one dark and beautiful in the wooing power of Jezebel with the dark hair. And the other, with the eyes that knew, in these things, there is weeping? For her was the story.

c h a p t e r

13

S a r a h   R a c h e l' s   S t o r y   (4)

Ye s, I loved my sister, of course I loved my sister. I loved even the
eye that was closed, with the white scars on it. But maybe also she
frightened me?

I grew up not wanting to talk. I listened, but I would not speak.
I was shy, I hid under the table when people came to visit at Mama's
house. Pesach, my father, would take me up to his shoulder, but I
kicked and grabbed his hair. I never wanted to go out from the house.
If Hannah Leah put me on the lap, when I was older, I looked out
from the window. I saw the street with the white houses and the blue
shutters and the little gates. I saw the poplar trees. But to me they
looked broken and burned. I saw it always that way. In the pine forest,
where I would go with Hannah Leah, only there I saw growing things
and green things that didn't scare me.

Mama didn't like all this. From the time I was a little girl she was
disappointed with this daughter that didn't talk. She taught me to
bake. It was to give me at least a way to make a living. More she didn't
expect from me. That's how it was. And she taught me. She told me
we came from the Rhineland, before we lived in Russia. From there
we brought Yiddish, we brought also our stories about Berchta, the
German goddess who cared for the vegetation. Berchta, you recognize
it? From this goddess we have the special challah bread for the Sabbath, the *berches*, baked with the nipple on top of the loaf.

Mama loved me. Of course she loved me. A mother loves the
child. But Mama was more than a mother. She was a teacher, she was
a scribe. She was a Shadmi, from Kashevata. She was looking, all her

life, for the ones to take into the sect. And for the daughter, who could become maybe the Hovrodnik. Hannah Leah disappointed her. And now there I was, born to take the place of Hannah Leah.

Mama let me sit next to her when she would be writing. I liked this. But I thought, Maybe it is to make up for Hannah Leah, who never let Mama touch her? Every night, after we ate the dinner, I sat next to Mama by the stove. There I was happy. But other times I saw things people didn't see. It was in my nature. Sometimes it was in my sleep, and I would wake up screaming, only no sound came out.

One night, I remember, Hannah Leah and Mama were in the kitchen. They were arguing. I woke up, from my bed I shared with Hannah Leah. Mama was sitting at the kitchen table, with the box. It was night, Mama of course was writing. Hannah Leah was sitting up on the oven, looking down at Mama. And then I saw an angel was there. She was very large and I thought she could not fit in the kitchen.

Each night Mama shut the door to my room. But each night it was open again. And this time when I looked out I saw that the angel sat down next to Mama. When Mama stopped writing the angel put a finger on Mama's hand.

I liked the angel. She had the wings folded up over the head, and a bright light in the face. For the first time in my life I wanted to talk, to tell the angel she was beautiful. But now I noticed she was looking at me. She stared and I became afraid. I wanted to pull up the covers. But I looked at the angel. For hours I looked and then the sweat came out of me and I wanted to cry. Finally, I couldn't look anymore. And then, the angel lifted up the hand and pointed. I felt a burning mark on the throat. "But what about Hannah Leah? What about my sister?" That is what I wanted to cry. But still, no words came. And then I hollered for Mama. For the first time in my life I talked and she came to hold me.

Later, when it was almost morning, I woke up again. Mama was rocking me. And now I felt her bend over me. I pulled at my night dress. "It burns, it burns," I said and then she saw the whole throat was one big mark of fire. I heard her muttering. "Strange child," she said to herself. "Who would imagine? This one, the Hovrodnik?"

After that, my sister stayed indoors most of the time. She didn't go off into the forest. She never went to visit in the peasant village.

Sometimes, with a kerchief on the head, late at night, wrapped up in a big peasant shawl, she would go out to meet my father when he came home from his father's house.

Ours was not a Hasidic town. But we had, here and there, a few families, and the Flexners among them, who followed the Lubavitcher rebbe. These men would meet at my grandfather's house on Mondays and Thursdays, to study and argue over the books. And Hannah Leah sometimes would go there and listen outside the window. Do I know why? In the daytime she never talked, not to Mama and not to Papa. She would sit whispering with me, and draw faces and animals in the ash from our fire. I thought my sister was, what? The word is *doomed.* I felt her sorrow eating away at her. At night when Mama was asleep, my sister would go to the fire and take up a coal in the hands and put it against the breast. But, did it help? The mark was fading. It was growing away. The more she burned herself, the more the mark from the fire got lost in the scars. And this, I thought, was because the angel put on me the sign of fire. I thought it meant now I was chosen instead of Hannah Leah.

She had gone in the way of violence so far as a Flame Bearer should go. Even further. Now, she should turn back. We do not think there is sin. We believe only in the Forgetting. Hannah Leah, with the scars and the blind eye, could make herself better again. She could begin, once more, out of love for the people. But this she wouldn't do. I thought it was because of me. Because I had come to take her place.

In code, and by voice too, messages came for her and she finally went off again, at night. I woke up the next morning and she was not there. Mama went about her day. It was Friday. She made the Sabbath bread, with my father helping. I was then a little bit more than three years old. That day in our house I thought there was ash over everything. I was rushing about, with a rag, trying to wipe away. But the more I scrubbed the more ash came there.

That day Mama went out, as usual, to teach the girls. This time she took me with her. It never happened before. Always before she left me with Hannah Leah. Now I knew something would happen. It would happen to my sister. I knew, Kovahl was eating her up.

I opened up the mouth to wail and again no sound came. Mama was stern—always apart from us, looking down waiting for us to join her in the higher place where she lived. That was her nature. But now she says something; very soft she says it, with a tender voice that was not like Mama. "So, you see?" she says. "Now is the time for you to be talking." After the night with the angel I didn't talk again. I didn't want the voice if it took away something from Hannah Leah. But Mama says: "You don't know why the angel brought you a voice? You didn't figure out yet what she wants from you? She wants you should tell the story of your sister."

Mama set me down on my feet on the big table in the shed. She put the arms around me and gave me a good deep look in the eyes. It was my turn. I knew this. It came early for me, that can happen. Because of the angel we didn't have to wait for the blood. Mama put her hands on my head, to give me her blessing. She told me I would have the gift of speech. She told me I could put even a burning coal in the mouth and it would not burn me. She told me I would live a long time, to be an old lady, I would have riches and sorrows and I would survive, the last of the many.

Later, when I grew up, I heard her tell all this again. She was dead by then. I heard it in the old way of hearing. And I remembered then what in all those years I forgot.

Well, after that day, Mama began to teach me languages. She saw, of course, after the angel came I was chosen to be a teller. She saw the future kept out an eye for me, as we say. And now, what do you know? For all those years I was silent I made up. When I was not yet five years old I could speak Yiddish, Russian, Hebrew, Ugaritic. Mama had grandfather find a girl to teach me French, and English too because she said I would live one day in Paris and after that I would live in the New World. From this time she took a very special care of me. But I felt, in her heart, she was still waiting. She was hoping maybe another would come, better than me, to take the place of Hannah Leah.

The French I learned was very good. But not the English. Later, when I came to New York, before I came to San Francisco, I opened up the mouth to speak and such a look came into the face of the people I talked to I shut the mouth again and didn't want to speak in English for a long time. Sonia, my daughter and already a butterfly, was holding on to my hand. You know how she is. Always ready to give a laugh at somebody. So now she throws back the head and she begins such a laugh, never, if I live to be a hundred years old, would I forget it. Esther, my youngest, who was a humble girl and very loyal, gives her a look. She takes Sonia by the shoulder and begins to shake her. That's how we came to the New World. Elke stands there, she says nothing. Elke, the beauty. But I saw a little smile in the corner of the mouth, bitter, mocking. That's how it is. In the child is already the woman. How else could it be?

Well, that comes later. My sister never came to the New World. When she went away from home she was living in Kiev and also in Odessa. Later we found this out. She went there to be part of Valerian Osinsky's group. And she did there very dangerous work. At night she would go out to put up the proclamations. These announced the "execution" of a certain spy or official. The proclamations were sealed with a dagger and an ax and with the words *Executive Committee of the Social Revolutionary Party* written in a circle. But all this was invented by Hannah Leah to scare the police. They were only a small group. A little later most of them were arrested and hanged.

Then, for a time, my sister came home again. She now was one of the living dead. I with my own eyes could see the life running out from her. She would take my hand and put it to the blind eye. She wanted me to heal her. By then I mended the broken wing of a bird. I made better a sick child who was dying. Even the peasants came that I should heal them. Pyotr Vasilev came, with his little son. He was, you remember, the boy who tried to rape Hannah Leah. Now he was a tall man, he worked in the forest, with rough men. But Pyotr remained always the friend of Hannah Leah.

My sister I could not heal. She didn't burn herself now with the coal at night. But she sat with the head bowed, pressing my hand to the blind eye. She wanted to see again because of her work. But, could I heal her for the purpose to do violence?

When she went off again I was five years old. That time she woke me up. She told me to bless her. She bend the head, but I could not reach out and touch her. I wanted. Believe me, with my whole heart I wanted. But I was not able.

"Heal me, little sister," she cried in a muffled voice. "Make me new again. Give back my destiny."

My hands froze in my lap. Hannah Leah left me. She gave a bitter laugh, she put her face next to my face and she was gone. It was the last time I saw her. The last time until more than twenty years.

This time she went off to join her friend Sofya Petrovya in Petersburg. She knew Sofya during the time she was living underground. Once, Sofya came to our house in the Ukraine, with a different name.

I met her and right away I didn't like her. But now she had a new organization. That's how it was. A group came up, it worked for a time, then it was destroyed by the police. So often it happened already from the time Hannah Leah first ran off to Moscow. Then, a new organization would come up, each time more violent. Now, they called themselves *Narodnaya Volya*. The people's will. And they were planning to kill the czar.

To you this seems only the talk of young people, who are impatient, who dream up some impossible task? But for them it was very serious. On August twenty-sixth, of the year 1879, they condemned the czar to death. Then, until March of the year 1881, they made eight attempts to kill the czar. Hannah Leah was part of this all. And all of this failed.

But then, on March first, something changed. And from this time the whole world was different. For us, for the Flame Bearers, it was surely the beginning of the Days of Shaddai. My sister believed the czar should be killed so the people would understand he was only a man. She wanted to show the people they could strike out. Even against a czar. And they could be successful. Then, she said, the people would believe in themselves.

This is the way my sister would talk. She told me in secret she was baptized in the Greek Orthodox faith. She wanted to be with the Russian people. To give her own blood for the new day that was coming. Well, the new day came. But it was not what she imagined. With violence it began, with violence it is going on. How else could it be?

My sister stitched herself into history. But for us, for the Flame Bearers, the time was beginning when we would be lost to the world. If there is violence, where will the *Flam-Trogers* be? They will not be in hiding. They will not be lifting up the hand to strike. So they, of course, will go down with the stricken.

This, my children, has happened before. It will happen again, before the Day of Days. There are times for casting down, for lamentation. So also we mourned when the Hebiru came up into our land. And again we mourned when Sargon of Asshur took captive the ten tribes of the North. In Babylon we lamented and on the way to Babylon we cried. For the fall of the Temple we mourned, where we had also Asherah's shrine. The Days of Shaddai cast the shadow many times. Many times the Great Teacher must come to be among us.

Narodnaya Volya knew that on Sundays the czar would ride out to take the parade from the Michael Cavalry Barracks. Usually, he rode in his sleigh through Malaya Sodovaya Street to get there. And this of course Narodnaya Volya also knew. So, now they put a mine under the street and they plan to kill the czar on his way back to the Winter Palace. But they had men also with hand bombs. These were volunteers and they expected to die, because the bombs must be thrown from very close up.

Sofya Petrovya and Hannah Leah were there also. They were keeping out an eye for the czar's party. He rode out that morning with six Cossacks. And now they saw him take a different way and go back by the Catherine Canal instead of his usual way.

All this my sister told me later. She was an old woman by then. Blind in both eyes. Living in a worker's hovel in Paris. Somehow, she learned I, too, was in Paris, with the baron's family, and she sent for me. When I came in and went over to her she reached out and took my two hands and put them on her eyes. "Heal me, heal me, little sister," she said.

Then she said, joking: "So, from me, at least is a good story?" But I could see. I knew at once. She never regretted. She thought she lived the way she should. It was her way to say she had still her own destiny.

I sat down on the bed. It was dark in there, a place to live under the ground. The bed was a door held up on boxes. Hannah Leah was wearing coats and sweaters, all one on top of the other. Next to her, on the bed, was books and notebooks and newspapers and pamphlets. "As we live, so also we die," Mama used to say. My sister could hardly talk. The voice came out in a choking whisper, very low. I bent over and she held on to my sleeve. "I ran back," she says, "I ran so fast. Who told him to take the other way?" And then she tells me what happened the day they waited for the czar. That was the year 1881. Remember. For us, for the Flame Bearers, it was a big division in the road.

My sister went back to tell the bomb thrower the czar changed his route. She went to show them where to stand. She placed them along the railing of the embankment, every few meters. Sofya, when the time came, would wave a white handkerchief to let them know the czar was coming.

It was, my sister said, in those minutes very quiet. Later, all her life, she remembered this quiet. "Like the sound of God taking in his breath," she said. The banks of the canal were covered up with snow. The ice was all over the canal. When she looked, she saw a blue light over the ice, burning with a cold flame. My sister was breathing very hard. She saw the cloud of her breath in the air. She looked at the dark branches of the bare trees and she thought she would not live to see them grow in green again. Well, she lived. But to me she said that never again the leaves came back on the trees. For her, after that day, the world was frozen.

It was two fifteen p.m. Only a few people were hanging about. But my sister could feel there were eyes watching. They looked down out of the branches and out of the sky. And then there was, she said, the roar from the white handkerchief. There were the Cossacks, and the sleigh from the czar, and the cloud from the horses breathing. Hannah Leah thought this was her own breath. She thought it was she who was running toward the sleigh. Rysakov, the volunteer, lifted up his arm. And then there was never again silence. When the smoke cleared they saw the czar was not hurt. The bomb hit the back of the sleigh. But, with their bomb, they had wounded a passer-by, an inno-cent one. "Thank God I'm not hurt." This is what the czar said. And Hannah Leah, she meanwhile was listening.

Then, she was rushing up to Grinevitsky, the other volunteer. He was standing still, with his hand to the chest, not moving. He was frozen there, also listening. She rushed at him, to get the bomb from his hand, to throw it herself. She lurched on him and he came back to life. His lips moved, he rushed forward. Again smoke. And this time there were bodies. There was blood in the snow. Timofy, another member of this group, rushed up to Hannah Leah. He had still the other bomb in the hand. He was holding Hannah Leah, dragging her away. Then, the third bomb was thrown. There was the boom and the cracking. Hannah Leah heard it, she the doomed one, mixed in with the cries from the beatings in the prison. She heard it always, for the rest of her life she heard it. She looked back. They were lifting the czar into a sleigh. She saw the blood pouring out from him, steaming in the snow. "Is he dead? Is he dead?" she kept muttering and Timofy put his arm over her mouth.

Then it was finished. Time, always running from my sister, now got away. My sister was eighteen years old. She had thrown Timofy's bomb. She it was who killed the czar. He was dead. The czar was dead by the time they arrived at the Winter Palace.

The others of course were arrested. On March twenty-sixth, in the year 1881, they came up to trial. They were given death sentences. Most of them were hanged. Two of her comrades, who were pregnant, had the execution postponed until the child would be born. And Hannah Leah, she once again escaped. But this time Hannah Leah could not keep on running. She came to visit Gesya Gelner and Anna Yakimova in the Peter Paul Fortress. From her own desire she came there. And now of course finally, the way she always wanted, Hannah Leah was caught.

You understand the fate of my sister? You believe she helped our cause? Ushering in the violence, going down into it, to serve in the coming of Chochma? Can I say what is error, what is truth? All my life, for my sister I mourned, believe me. But, what do we know? If she fell away from us. If she went the way of error, maybe this made her one of the sacred seven who do what must be done? You understand this?

For four years Hannah Leah and Anna Yakimova were kept in a cell below the ground. Dark it was, the walls running with water. When Anna gave birth to her baby, she insisted to keep it with her, in the cell. She stayed awake, to fight away the rats. My sister was put into a strait jacket and tied up to the bed for trying to help her. But what did it matter to Hannah Leah? Tied up or not tied up, she wanted to die.

For four years my sister was in the Peter Paul Fortress. Underground. Buried alive. There were no books. No letters. No extra food. There was only dysentery, scurvy, the insane prisoners also kept down there, below the earth. But Hannah Leah did not go insane. In those years, even after she was transferred to Kara, to the prison there, in exile, she was thinking about Mama. That is what she told me. And about the village we came from, and the mission of the Flame Bearers. She came to the conclusion her whole life was lived in a mistake. Later, she changed her mind maybe. But in those years she thought she chose wrong. It can happen. She had taken the *heylige ikra* that was her birthright and used it to the wrong end. For a Flame Bearer, this is dangerous. Their going wrong will never be in little things.

They will drag a part of the world down with them. It was this thought that burned my sister, she said. For her this thought was the coal she used to hold up to her breast.

Four years she was in Kara. In that awful wasteland there, with the mines and the starvation and the beatings and the hopelessness. It was there somehow Pyotr Vasilev found her, to share the exile with her. You know who he was? You remember this boy that tried to rape her? Somehow, he found out where Hannah Leah was. Who knows? Maybe he was a member of their group? From these years she told me little. "I was waiting to die," she said. "Every day I looked at my life, kicking at it like a dog. 'So,' I'd say, 'don't you have enough yet?' But I didn't die. I couldn't. That was the curse from the Flame Bearers. Always, we are born too strong."

Then in the year 1889 she was moved from Kara to Bargusi, on the east shore of Lake Baikal. She and Pyotr managed to escape from there, through the mountains, on the old tribal paths. They went abroad. But from this part of her life I know nothing. When I met her again it was the year 1905, in Paris. I came there in my own life, part of the Baron Guzman family. I came there in a time I, too, was lost and living in the Forgetting. And by then already the Flame Bearers began to disappear from the world.

It began six weeks after the czar was killed. First in Yelisavetgrad in South Russia. Then in many places, all over Russia. It was the first time we used the word *pogrom*. The Russian papers blamed the Jews for killing the czar. People came out from Petersburg to incite the peasants against the Jews. The word *pogrom*, you know what it means? *Nu*, the word maybe was new. But everything else was familiar.

We, as you know, have always women who can see ahead. Now, in the weeks before the pogrom, they went about to give warning. But, who listens to a sage? A few people maybe here and there. But the rest go on as they must, living from day to day. Should we blame them? From the cities, from the larger villages, all over Russia, the Flame Bearers moved into the countryside to be with the people.

Mama, in our village, was successful in warding off the attack. She went down to the peasant village, she found Pyotr Vasilev, she took him by the arm. This was before he ran off to find Hannah Leah in Kara. And then, for three days, after the events in Yelisavetgrad, she and Pyotr walked up and down the streets together, arm in arm.

That was it. All day and all night they walked there, saying not a word. The tall man with his peasant shirt and high boots. The little Jewish woman in the black dress with a scarf over the head. But it made an impression. They went through every muddy street in the peasant village, up and down they went, and it was enough. In our village, through all those weeks with the looting and the raping and the burning and the pillage by the peasants, nothing happened.

Here and there, in other places, the Flame Bearers also had a success. Maybe they warned people and the people listened and took measures to keep safe. Or they managed to keep the peasants from rioting. Sometimes they helped the children escape.

Later, we learned that from this pogrom maybe twenty thousand Jews were made homeless. One hundred thousand were ruined. There was raping, there was killing, it went on until the year 1882. More than eighty million dollars' worth of Jewish property was destroyed.

Narodnaya Volya, Hannah Leah's group, still had a few members of the executive committee that weren't arrested. And they now put out a leaflet saying it was a good thing. Yes. They said it was a revolutionary thing the peasants did in turning against the Jews. I ask you. Could it be? This is what they became. These "people lovers" Hannah Leah gave her life to. They joined all the others making a scapegoat from the Jews.

This is what happens. Over and over again it happens. And you know why? Some people say it is because the Hebrews fought against the worship of The Mother. They say, from that time, until this very day, the curse came down on them. But Mama, if she would hear this, she would get so angry. "Hach," she would snort, "and which of these father-worshipers didn't kill The Mother? Only the Hebiru were guilty? This nonsense is what you believe?"

But you know how it is. In a sect is every sort of person, believing every kind of thing. There was among us women who believed the Jews gave themselves to history, to be the sacrifice, the atonement for the great fight against The Mother. And this is why, they said, the Flame Bearers stayed always with the Jews, sharing the fate. They stayed with the Jews because of the suffering, and the wanderings and the exiles. And because also there is the promise, one day, we should bring them back to worship The Mother. In Kiryat Sefer. In Canaan of old.

I was six years old when the czar was killed. That day, I saw blood running down the streets of Chernik. After we moved back to Kash-evata I saw more blood and I again became silent. I did not want to speak. I was afraid if I opened my mouth Hannah Leah's voice would come out through it.

14

The old woman kept her eyes fixed on the ceiling. She was watching the blood move through her veins and she noticed it was growing thicker. Then she saw Jacob's old car driving along the ocean. It, too, moved slowly, as if the air through which it passed had become turgid and thick. Straining her eyes, she saw the flock of birds on the horizon, moving toward her; she saw the rocks covered with a white mist and the clouds, shaping. And she knew that she was dying. The death flock was coming. She would not be able to resist death any longer.

Then she saw the little sand-glass Hannah Leah made from bottles. The white sand from the river, which Hannah Leah put in there for telling time, was all in the bottom.

She tried again, to turn back the sand-glass, to lift it in the mind's eye. But her mind lurched, not able to hold the concentration. She saw instead the early morning. She was in Raisa's house. The bread was baking. It was time for Mama to come, wiping the hands over the big apron over the breast. Bending down, with the smell from yeast and salt and the rye flour, to sit down on the bed to listen to the morning prayers.

"Come, O Bride," said Sarah Rachel the child, getting confused. Was it already the Sabbath? "No, no," she insisted with a worried frown. It was the weekday, early morning.

She slipped down under the feather quilt. The heart beating so hard it would break soon right out of the chest. "*Oy vey iz mir, oy vey iz mir,"* she moaned, stuffing the pillow between her teeth. Where had they gone? The words to the blessing?

Already, she could see the look on Mama's face. The lines above the thin lips going in deeper. The quiver in the corner of the mouth. The eyes getting one bit darker, with the look in them, the disappointment.

She was so frightened she woke up, fully awake, in her black dress waiting for Isarael in the gray chair by the window. She looked outside. "Chochma," she muttered, "this late, already?"

She looked out at the purple domes, the cobbled streets, the square with the red tiles and the splashing fountain. "Kiryat Sefer?" she gasped, recognizing the ancient city. And there was the Teacher Beruriah, with her pupils, just like Raisa promised, going through the marketplace, asking the questions. "Where is the first stone of the old path on the road to Kiryat Sefer?" Beruriah said, taking the arm of the tall girl who was walking in front of the others.

The old woman closed her hands into two tight fists. The Hovrodnik did not have to go with Beruriah when she came. For those who served, Raisa said, more time would be given. An hour, maybe. Two hours, even. She tightened her shoulders and held on. First, to turn back the sand-glass, to lift it in her mind's eye, to make one grain of the white sand, only one, fall through again. Then, to resist the longing to be there, walking with the girls, in the teaching procession with Beruriah.

She saw the car turning out of the park, moving fast into the road along the ocean. "Isarael," she called, cupping her hands to her mouth. "Little one. Hurry. Kiryat Sefer is already here."

"First, the death flock," Raisa had told her when she was a girl. "When the time comes for you to be dying, the white cranes will come, remember. The birds with the dark underfeathers." Sarah Rachel remembered. "Then you will see the grains of sand. One grain for each breath you took during the lifetime. The cranes and the sand, these are for every woman. But for the Hovrodnik there will be also Kiryat Sefer. And maybe also Beruriah to be the Guide. Little one, you are listening? You have ears to hear? Then finally the seven Hovrodnikim. The old wise ones who have been with us since the beginning of time. You will see them, sitting down together at the fire to hear all over again, from the beginning, the life story. You understand? You then will know your small life is pouring over into the large life of Chochma. And you will let it happen, and you will not have fear."

Shuddering, the old woman pulled herself straight up in the chair, shaking in every limb. She stared at the room. Her hands clutched, finding nothing. Nothing. She stared at the emptiness and then she gasped, understanding at last a truth she had not wanted to have since Isarael went away from home.

"Elke, Elke keeps the secret," she cried out, relieved to be shouting. "Elke, the bitter one, keeps the secret from Isarael." She beat her fists on her breasts. "My fault, it was mine. Never enough I loved Elke. Always, I was waiting for the successor. Storing up the love, keeping it back."

The little wooden puzzle Papa had made for her from white pieces of bark from the birch trees rose up from the floor in front of the fire. She watched it, laughing; her whole life was there. She saw the little clearing in the pine forest where the fire in the ring of black stones was already burning. She saw the light coming from the tile oven onto Mama's back, bent over above the writing. There was the carriage from the Guzman family, the baron's wife with the handkerchief to the face looking out the window. And the angel, the wings folded up above the head. And the bowl of white milk with blue all around the edges. And Rebekah, the little sister . . .

But now she moaned, fighting the understanding that was wringing itself out of her, a pain that could not forget. It was not Sarah Rachel who was the last. It was not Sarah Rachel. It was Rebekah, waiting for the successor. And then, the last piece went right into place. "Rebekah alive?" she gasped, her mind clear now like the woodland pool without even one ripple in it. "*Veh iz mir,*" she groaned, taking it all in, all the implications: "Never I wanted to know there was still living Rebekah."

Cutting, sawing, snipping, tearing. Mama put the life thread to the lips. Biting. The thread snapped. And then her spirits went right out of her body and she was crouched, in the nest in the corner of the room, looking down at the old woman Sarah Rachel in the chair by the window. Dying alone. She saw the car screeching down the street in front of the home. The rattle-tat-tattle of Isarael's steps, mixing in with the rattle from Hannah Leah's little saber, mixing in with the chopping from Pyotr the Shabbas goy, running, tramping, hammering, booming. And then Rebekah was there (where? where?) waiting for Isarael, the arms open wide, Isarael stooping down, making herself small, to fit into the arms of her great-aunt.

Sarah Rachel sat in the nest, keeping an eye on everything. Slowly, aiming precisely, she picked up the eggs and began to toss them down into the room. The egg hit, splattering on the old woman's forehead. "Not for you, miserable wretch," she called, with a bitter cackle. "Unable in the life to love. Unable in the dying."

Sarah Rachel watched, crouching in the nest, as Isarael took Rebekah by the shoulders.

Sarah Rachel tossed another egg at the old woman down there in the room. Splat. Bull's eye. Right into the chest. "Hooch," she snorted, gleeful now. "You were the last, you thought? You didn't want to know about Rebekah?"

The pieces of bark rose up in a spiral, spinning so fast she got dizzy, trying to watch them. She saw the cranes coming, the death flock coming closer, the long pointed toes, three of them, lowering down on the long legs out from the dark underfeathers in the bird's belly. Slowly, slowly now, settling into the nest, the long metallic beak bending down over her. She opened her mouth, cheeping and crying, reaching for the worm.

Mama sighed, rocking her against the breast. Hannah Leah laughed, putting the finger, covered with jam, into her little sister's mouth. And Rebekah, such a beautiful old woman she was, drew Isarael to her, in that way she had, tucking her arm through the arm of Sarah Rachel's only love.

The tiny splinter of light that ran throbbing between herself in the nest and the old woman far, far away in the room below, beat itself out. Never, she would never go back there again, into that wretched shape, slumped in the chair, that made the error.

She saw the little girl, Sarah Rachel, sitting quietly next to the fire. "So this anyway," she murmured, "this is the way Raisa said it would be." She saw the Hovrodnikim sitting there, the little old one with one gold earring in the left ear picking up the coals, blowing on them, handing them to the others. Very fast they were talking, jumping from one thing to another, like the pictures in the puzzle. Hurrying, to get done with the story. Sarah Rachel listened. And now finally she took her breath between her lips, shaped it very carefully into a smoldering mass, and spit it out through her mouth.

The cranes wheeled, crying overhead their cry, with its pitched ache, longing. Overhead, overhead they went. And she moved out with them. The wind like a big hand coming to carry her, in the roaring spiral, under the belly as the wings went up and up and they reached out and they held.

15

Sarah Rachel's Story (5)

"**Th** i s is the story of Sarah Rachel Shadmi," said the wise old women who were sitting around the fire. "This is the story of Sarah Rachel Shadmi," they repeated in a dutiful tone, echoing one another. "This is the story. This is the story. This is the story . . ."

Sarah Rachel joined in. "Now begins the story of my own life," she said, talking to the Hovrodnikim as if they were Naamah, Maya, and Isarael.

"Her own life," said the crones, nodding their heads, their hands held flat down against their knees, their legs folded in front of them, backs straight.

"And this, I tell you," said Sarah Rachel, rather insistently, because she had noticed that one of them was yawning: "this was the big sorrow in my life."

"The big sorrow," the old women agreed.

"From two sisters," Sarah Rachel said, looking sternly at them: "there should be only one story. What do we mean by this? We mean, if the sisters get separate, both are grieving."

She waited for a moment but none of the Hovrodnikim seemed inclined to contradict her.

"I was six years old when the czar was killed," she went on, finding at last the words she had used one day in the winter. It was the first time she told this story to the girls. "That day, when the czar was killed I saw blood running down the streets of the village. Later, we moved back to Kashevata. Then I saw more blood and I became silent again. I did not want to speak. I was afraid if I opened my mouth,

Hannah Leah's voice, from the exile, in Kara, would come out through it."

For the last time the wise women sighed. "Shall we? Shall we wait?" They looked at one another, their heads tipped to the side, their eyebrows raised. They were wondering how much time there was, after all.

"We shall, we shall wait," the eldest among them said. And then they got up slowly, they crossed the clearing, entered the forest, and climbed back up into the spruce.

"Why we went back to Kashevata is of course also a story," the old woman went on. "It is the story of the way I went off from the family and began my own life. But this story you can only understand if you know the ground it was growing in. The seed from the grass grows here. And the seed from the grass grows there. But, is it the same seed if the ground is different?"

By now she was fully absorbed. "There were, after the pogroms, children homeless all over the Ukraine," she said, no longer paying attention to the old women who found her in fact quite dear, especially now that they could look down at her from the lower branches of the large tree at the edge of the forest where they were waiting patiently for the cranes to fly over.

These children the Flame Bearers brought together in Kashevata. There was, in that neighborhood there, on a big estate, a very wealthy Jewish philanthropist. His name was Baron Guzman. He it was who gave the money for the orphan-building.

For Mama this decision to go back to Kashevata was not so easy. The Flame Bearers came for her. They sat all night talking at the wooden table in the kitchen. They talked low, in the sacred tongue, but Pesach was such a man, even if he understood he wouldn't listen. I sat up in my bed. Of course, listening. I could see how the mama was suffering. She grew attached to her pupils in Chernik. It always happens. Papa of course never wanted to leave his family. This, too, she knew. She had a heart, Mama. A big heart, if she also was stern and silent. That night she comes over to sit on my bed. "So," she says. "With the big ears, always listening?"

"Don't go, Mama," I begged her. "Hannah Leah, how will she find us?"

"I should stay for Hannah Leah?" she asks, very sober. "I should let the orphans starve for the sake of Hannah Leah?"

Then, she waits. She's waiting to see how I will decide this question. In the kitchen the other women are waiting too, looking over at me. There are times like this. Always they come, when the choice is there, between the heart's wanting and the heart's knowing. I shook my head. One shake. That was all I could give to them. But that shake was enough. With it, I gave up Hannah Leah.

We moved to Kashevata in order for Mama to build up the home for the orphans. You understand? We knew already these were the Days of Shaddai. In this moment the Flame Bearer scatters her life all over the ground.

Now, in Kashevata, my mother's people were very poor. Her sisters were dead by then. She had a niece, with a grown-up daughter and also some cousins. They were not like Mama and her sisters. They were not interested in the Flame Bearers. For them, it was only stories. But they heard about me already by the time I got there. And they were curious. They wanted to hear me speak in all the languages. They wanted me to make the plants grow better in the garden. They had such faces, I cried when I saw them. I could not find the *heylige ikra* in their eyes.

So now, of course, they have a good time laughing at me. Instead of languages, instead of a girl who could heal the birds, there came a pale one who hid in the chimney when someone came over to visit.

Mama was busy with the orphanage. And of course Pesach helped her too. But he was not happy there. He wanted to be in Chernik, with his family. Sometimes, with his father, he went to Petersburg, looking in the prisons for Hannah Leah. And when he came home he was always a little bit thinner, with a white face and black shadows underneath the eyes. He would come to look for me, to put me up on his lap and tell me he found out nothing.

Could I tell him Hannah Leah was alive? Thinking her terrible thoughts? Blaming herself for the pogroms that happened to our people? Waiting to die and staying alive only for the punishment?

From the time Hannah Leah was arrested I shared her fate. From that time I did not speak. I never went out from the house. It was the early years of my life all over again. Mama thought, maybe in that early time I was getting ready for what came later.

Often, a woman came from the Flame Bearers in Vilna to sit with me. From Vilna come our healers. She put her hands on my throat, she looked in my eyes. In her, I saw the fire burning. I felt it inside her fingers. I wanted to go over there, to hold my hands to it. But I was keeping myself with Hannah Leah, inside her suffering. I wanted to take the suffering from Hannah Leah and make it come into myself. The woman asked me to talk, she told me to whisper, she said I should think only and she would listen. But I put out my hands to push her away.

Every night, from the time we came to Kashevata, Mama sat by my bed. The Flame Bearers have many kinds of healing. Mama tried all of them. She caught a hare with her bare hands, she took off the skin, she roasted it over a fire, she cut up the hare into little pieces and brought them to me. She had songs for me and stories. She brought in the grasses and the herbs. She caught a bird, it got tame, and she put it on the edge of my bed. At night, she covered my body with a soft light. I would wake and find myself burning in the fire. But I did not get better. The minute I closed my eyes I saw my sister. I saw her in the mines. But I did not know what the mines were. I saw her in the mountains. I saw also Pyotr Vasilev there. And I knew finally she got away.

One day, when I was thirteen years old, it was over. It was finally over. My sister was free. Her thoughts went on, but they were softer now. They did not scald me. I heard on top of them the sounds of the world. I woke up one morning. I heard the knocking at the door. It was, I thought, the Hovrodnik, coming for me. I saw an ant walking on the window. I heard the ant singing.

It was then the year 1888. When I went out from my room I found out there was now a little sister living in the house. Her name was Rebekah. She was, I tell you, the most beautiful child I ever saw. More even than Maya was beautiful. She had little black curls, brown eyes with a violet band around the pupil, a tiny red mouth, and pink little cheeks. She was maybe eighteen months old. But already she could walk and talk. When she saw me, right away, over she came with her plump little hand and put it on my leg.

Shall I tell you the truth? Right away, from that moment, I hated her. I knew she came to take my place. She came because Mama decided I could not be a Flame Bearer.

Rebekah was that kind of person, people loved her from the first minute they put their eyes on her. Always, all her life she was like this and I knew from the beginning she would eat up all the love from Mama and Papa. From the time she was a little girl she knew everybody in the village. Women would drop in to bring her an apple, or a piece of cake they made. "So, where is she, Rebekele?" they would say from the minute they came into the house. And then Rebekah, she would come flying, with the dark little curls. She would throw herself into their arms, for the hug and the kiss. "With this one," Mama used to say, "even a stone would fall in love." But me? Who would fall in love with me? The women would give a look at me, with such a surprise on the face, as if in those years when I did not go out from the house they didn't know a thing about me. But Rebekah, right away, as soon as she had the apple in the hand, to me she would come running. It was always like that. To give me the gift they brought for her.

My sister loved me. All the love other people gave to her she carried over to me. Who can say why? Between sisters, sometimes, it is like this. I had the feeling, maybe she loved me with Hannah Leah's love. Sometimes I thought, she looked, in spite of the beautiful face, like Hannah Leah. But I was never kind to her. I never did the things an older sister should do. All the things Hannah Leah did for me.

You know why? Shall I tell you? It was because she took away my place, as the younger. I thought it meant I had to go in the way of Hannah Leah, cast aside from the destiny, making the wrong choice, going to my destruction. At night, when Rebekah slept, I went over to her bed and there I stood, wishing that my power could be used to hurt her. Yes, I did this.

But, she did not die. She grew older, always prettier, singing always and chattering and laughing and dancing and clapping the hands. Could I love her? In me, like a poison worm, was only hatred. It was an illness, part of the *Tsayt-sam* left over from Hannah Leah. With the Flame Bearers there is this danger. We feel the best and we feel the worst. But I now, with the better part of me, was afraid. Sooner or later, I thought, Rebekah will catch this poison. Finally, for my own sake, and for the sake of my sister, I made up the mind. I decided to leave home.

But where? Where would I go? I was not Hannah Leah. I was afraid of the world. I thought I should go to a small city and teach the

Jewish children. And now I'm going to tell you the worst of all. In those years I hated not only Rebekah. I hated in those years even the Flame Bearers. I hated them, because now I thought I could not be a Flame Bearer anymore.

It was in this time the visions came again. With my own eyes I saw roots being pulled out of the earth. Everywhere, I saw the Flame Bearers dying. And I was glad. That is how much the *Tsayt-sam* lived in me then. If there was a pogrom, or an illness or a famine or a whole village ailing, the Flame Bearers would go there, to take the suffering out of the people into themselves. Before, they could heal the illness. But now the suffering was too much. No one could heal it. The shadow from Shaddai was everywhere. And the Flame Bearers, they, too, began to die from it.

These were hard years. They were bitter years for our people. After the killing of the czar the reforms all were taken away. The chief adviser to the new czar was called Podedonostsev. He had his own solution for the Jews. One-third of us should leave Russia, he said. One-third of us should convert. The remaining third should be left to die in hunger.

Now this, believe me, was happening. Thousands of Jews were expelled out of Moscow. They were deported from the villages, driven out from the universities. So of course, with all these persecutions, some Jews began to convert.

The Flame Bearers went to be with the people in trouble. To console, to preach the coming of the Great Teacher, to tell about the Return, out of the exile, of Chochma, Herself.

We had, I told you, many singers in our sect. And they now went among the villages, telling these stories. Some of them sang the Lamentations, right out of the holy book of the Jews. "He has sent a fire from on high down into my bones; he has laid a snare underneath my feet; he has brought me down; he has left me deserted, and ill all day long." Against Shaddai they sang these words, to show the way The Father deserts his people. But they knew the Flame Bearers would go down to be destroyed, along with the Jews, women and men together.

In this time Mama came to believe I would be still alive at the end of the long cycle of destroying. I would remain, she said, the last of the many. To pass on our tradition to the Great Teacher, in the New World. She believed this but it broke her heart. She didn't understand why I was chosen for this mission. She did not think I was worthy. I knew, in my heart, she preferred Rebekah. She didn't have to say this. I knew.

But this, of course, was my error. It was the *sam,* the *poison* making me see things in this way. Mama knew I was passing through the Seven Years of the Disbelieving. It did not come to every Flame Bearer. Not even to every Hovrodnik. But to some it came. And these forgot themselves. They forgot what they were born for. They felt cast aside. They no longer, in this time of their doubting, could believe in the healing of the world.

Oy veh, I tell you. It is a terrible blindness. It drove me finally out of our house. I walked about in our village. I was looking at things the way Hannah Leah, my sister, looked before me. I saw evil every-where. I saw always the suffering of the innocents. I thought we surely were living at the end of days. Wherever I looked I saw the hand of Shaddai, the Almighty, asking for suffering. I did not believe Chochma would come back. No, I did not believe it.

We say a true Flame Bearer has another eye, living inside the head, behind the two eyes that see the world. This other eye goes right down into the heart. She who sees with this inside eye sees always the meaning in things. But if the eye is closed off from the heart, what happens? The seeing remains but it becomes now evil. In this kind of seeing, without the heart, the world loses the sacred fire.

This happened now to me. I walked in a world of shadow and ash. I believed nothing. I had only the fear, soon I would cause Re-bekah to be dragged down with me.

I told you already we had in our neighborhood a wealthy man, he was a baron, although he also was a Jew. And his name was Baron David Guzman. His home was in Petersburg, but he had also a country estate. It was some kilometers away from Kashevata. I knew this al-ready of course. How else? Everybody in the village received some help from Baron David.

It also happened, from time to time, that the carriage of the baron's household came right into Kashevata. He brought his wife and his children, too, so they should learn about the suffering of their people. And in our town this was always a holiday. The people would gather around the carriage. They would reach out with the hand, run-ning alongside, next to the window. Finally, everything would have to stop. The horses, with their bells, would stand pawing on the earth.

Then, the baron and his wife would climb down to talk with the people.

This was, believe me, a brave thing. People rushed at them. They wanted to kiss the hands of the baron's wife. They wanted to touch the hem from her skirt. Women would reach up to touch Baron David by the shoulder. Everybody had a problem. Everybody wept. Everybody had a story to tell. The baron's wife would write it all down in a velvet book. Always help was given. To the wife with the sick husband, to the daughter whose mother died, to the girl who needed a dowry. Nothing was forgotten.

But now, what do you think? One day, when I went out to the marketplace, I saw this sight and it made me ashamed. I was ashamed from the begging and the weeping and the beating on the breast. There was one woman, Zipora, the wife of Baruch, who died without leaving behind even a hammer. And she now threw herself down in the dirt in front of the feet of the baron's son.

I saw this thing. I looked at it with my eye that was seeing only evil in the world. And now something happened. I ran over there. I took this woman by the arm. I drew her up to the feet. I did this, me the shy one. I shook her by the shoulder. "Aren't you ashamed?" I cried. "Aren't you ashamed to behave like this? Go better and ask my mother. Go to Raisa, she will tell you what to do."

Well, naturally, everybody looked on me as if I was insane. This of course was nothing new. But a violent burst like this they didn't expect from me. And now I went beyond myself. I saw the other children looking down from the carriage. I saw the wife looking at me. I went over. I lifted up a fist, I shook it at them. "You, too?" I yelled. "Who are you to come here and gape out of the window at the suffering of the Jews?"

I said these words? Even to myself it seemed Hannah Leah was talking through me. It was her hatred talking, for the mighty and the wealthy, no matter if they would be Jews.

And now, all of a sudden, I started shaking. The whole earth shaking under my feet. It was I thought the earthquake that took away Kiryat Sefer. I threw out my arms. A strange voice was coming out from my lips. I felt the voice burning. It was, for the first time in my life, the voice the angel brought. It was not the voice from Hannah Leah.

Later, this happened again many times in my life. And each time, with the angel voice, I saw into the future. This was the first time. It made me weep. I stood by the baron's carriage, I felt the earth shake, and soon I was wringing my hands. I was sobbing, for the coming of the sorrows. For the destruction of our people. Now, suddenly, I saw everything clear. I was fourteen years old. I knew this was the first step I was taking. It would lead me away. Away from the village, away from our people. I would be always just ahead of the violence. One step ahead of the three great cataclysms I foresaw.

So it happened. But for me, the way to my destiny, it never ran straight. Who can say why? There are lives like this. They are the twisted ones and sometimes they are almost broken. These lives you judge only from the later years. Or from the dying.

Well, after that day I went to live with Baron David and his family in their home in Petersburg. All this Mama saw before it happened. She saw even the way I would go out into the marketplace.

The baron's house in Petersburg was built by the grandfather of the family. He founded there also a bank with his own name. The Guzman Bank it was called. Then, he acquired a building that had ninety-two suites in it. It was in its own way almost a village. Inside were courtyards. In the vestibule was a statue of Moses. This statue was the first thing I saw. Right away I knew I had to be careful. I had gone over into the house of those who worship Shaddai.

Mama and Papa agreed the baron should take me to Petersburg. He was, from the first minute, interested in me. He wanted to educate me with his children, in his own home. There, they had a French governess and a Russian teacher. The chief rabbi of Petersburg came also to give the children lessons in Hebrew. But now the baron had a surprise. Who would expect this strange girl from Kashevata could speak already all the languages he wanted the children to learn? I was given also dancing lessons, I was given piano lessons, they taught me to draw. In that house, with its big library, with its many suites, there was also a place, on the ground floor, for Jews who were in hiding. Among them, every day I went down to look for Hannah Leah. These people stayed until the baron could get permits for them or help them go abroad. They lived always in the house, never going outside. I began to be the one to bring food to them.

And now I have something to tell you. Would you believe it? The entire Guzman family took a liking to me. Who can say why? They told me, even, I was a beautiful girl. Who ever thought such a thing?

Suddenly, I found myself in a place so different from Chernik or from Kashevata or any place where the Flame Bearers would live. You would think I should feel unhappy there? Or lost? You think I would be all the day pining for our village? You think, since I had this vision with the earth shaking, and I saw again what would happen in the world, I would be more than ever on fire to serve with the Flame Bearers? To become a Hovrodnik, if I was able?

But that is not what happened. In the beginning, in the first weeks and months, I was watching myself each minute. I was telling myself, this is only the first step. I am going out now into my destiny. But then a funny thing happened. Soon, I even forgot about going down to look for Hannah Leah. It was after maybe six months in that house. I saw myself one day in the mirror, when I was not expecting. I looked. Who was that looking back in a long dress with lace? All the women wore in that time hair down to the waist. But in the morning a servant came to comb it and put it up with pins. Another servant came to help with the corsets and the buttoning of the dress. And I maybe didn't have to look once at myself in all this time. In Mama's house we never looked in the mirror. "In the eyes of the people a Flame Bearer sees herself." That is what Mama always said.

I imagined I was very ugly. I thought nobody liked me because of an ugly face. But now I saw a girl with a round shape, a big bosom coming out of the dress, dark eyes, a pale skin, hair black like the crow.

The baron's wife, Matilda Guzman, was a beautiful woman. She treated me always like her own daughter. Now I saw her looking over my shoulder into the mirror. I saw, if she was beautiful, I, too, was beautiful. There was the same look to both of us.

So it began. It was *di Farfalene-tsayt*, The Time of Growing Away. And this, too, can happen to a Flame Bearer. For me, it was a forgetting. I knew what happened before, I remembered my sister, I got letters from Mama and Papa, telling me about Rebekah. In my dreams too, there was still sometimes a memory from the woods near Chernik, with the little fire burning between the black stones. But now it grew dim. It was there, but it faded. Little by little I didn't find it strange anymore I lived in a house with Moses in the vestibule.

The baron had students come to his house to learn from him. He was, although a baron, nevertheless a Jew. And he therefore could not teach at the university. But the professors sent over students to him, to study history, or Hebrew or Arabic or Turkish. All these languages I, too, learned, very fast, the way I did before in Chernik. There was a big lecture hall in the house and sometimes, when the baron wanted to show off with me, he called me up to the front and I talked with him in many languages.

Then, maybe a year later, a daughter was born in the house. Her name was Sophie and I, the minute I put my eyes on her, I was afraid it was the same thing all over again. Like Rebekah. She came to take the love away from me. But this time I didn't want it should happen. I ran to the baron and found him in the big library, with the bookcases sent over from Paris. There he had his ten thousands of books, with his other thousands of rare manuscripts. He had even three volumes with the pages singed and burned from an auto-da-fé in Spain. I found him at work. He was making a catalogue from his collection and there you would find him most days, in the morning. So I now went in there, without even a knock on the door. I went over to the baron, standing near the window. I felt the fire in my throat again, the voice the angel brought me. And I said, with a sob: "Make me, too, a daughter. I, too, want to be a daughter."

The baron was, I told you, a kind man. He often was by himself, with the books, in the study. He liked to teach and to discuss ideas. But he didn't like balls or concerts or parties. He was a man who reminded me always of Papa. And now he looked down, with his glasses and his small eyes, and then he lifted up the eyebrows. "A daughter?" he said. "Why not?"

After that, I loved Sophie, my little sister. I was with her all the time, I took care of her the way Hannah Leah took care of me. And then the years began passing. In the summers, for two or three months, we went to the estate, I with all the family. With the carriage I went also into Kashevata, to visit my parents. Mama and Papa were old now, Rebekah was growing up. I heard from Mama she went about by herself, a girl nine, ten years old, to talk in the villages, always with that look that made people love her. But one summer, when I went to visit, Rebekah was gone. She had moved to Zhitomir, to the house of a Flame Bearer who in that time was making a dictionary from the Flame Bearer dialect spoken in Russia. And in her house Rebekah met the *Hovevi Canaan*, the *Lovers of Canaan* who soon would leave Russia, to go back to the homeland. That was the way she chose.

But I, inside myself, when I heard this, I was laughing. Mama's village, Kashevata, with its hovels and its little stores and the inn with the bedbugs and the orphan home even, where Mama was raising the girls. What did it matter? So, maybe even Rebekah was the Hovrodnik from our generation. What did it matter?

Later, Rebekah told me, one time when she visited at Baron David's in Petersburg, she heard the land of Canaan calling to her, the desert and the dry land and the wasteland, asking her to come back to bring trees and to plant them. That was the time we quarreled. The first time. I laughed at my sister and it broke her heart. She was not used to people who did not love her. In all her life I was the only one. And this dream she had, this destiny as a Flame Bearer, she had until now told to no one, not even to Mama. But I laughed. She had taken up my hand, to hold it against her cheek while she was talking. She wanted my blessing. Why from me? I saw only, in her eyes she loved me, she respected me. And then the poison came back. The jealous feeling, the angry feeling because she stole Mama away. In her eyes I saw what I almost had forgotten. I saw the Flame Bearers were carrying on. I thought maybe I, too, had work in the world. Maybe I, too, could be a Hovrodnik? All this, my life in the baron's family, was maybe only a step, a preparation? I was then twenty-six years old. I had done, what? Nothing at all for our people. I had wasted my years. These thoughts it was that turned me against my sister.

Rebekah looked at me with her eyes full of love. She never was one to put a mask over, to hide what she was feeling. I saw the hurt come into her eyes and it ran right down into her heart. The tears came, but her face, with its big dark eyes and the violet rings around them, never changed. She gave a look on me and then she shook her head. She pressed my hand against her lips. "You don't see?" she said. "You don't understand? Between us is no problem. From the Shadmis one Hovrodnik in every generation. Isn't it so? So, why not you? And why not me also?"

I thought she was mocking me. I thought this, about Rebekah. She, with her fierce and her gentle spirit. She mocking? A terrible enemy she could be. Or the loyal friend. Later, she proved it. But to mock was not in her nature.

"Oh," I said, "Me, a Hovrodnik? Not me. And not Hannah Leah also. This we leave all to you."

I made then a little curtsy. I had a fine manner, I learned it from the governess. And Rebekah went running out of the room. She went down the stairs and through the vestibule and out the door. That was the last I saw her for thirty-two years. Never in all that time I heard from my sister. I tell you, I broke her heart. And I, in my own way, for thirty-two years, I never forgave her.

My sister went to Palestine. She went by herself, a girl of thirteen, on a Russian steamer. The money for this she earned by herself, teaching Hebrew to the Jewish students of Zhitomir. Of course, my father's family could help her with the passage, but Rebekah wanted always to accomplish by herself. She slept outside, on the wooden deck, using an old coat for a mattress. There, she met the other youths going to Palestine and she joined them, to sing Hebrew and even Zionist songs. But my sister was a Flame Bearer. She was never Zionist. What she did in Palestine was always for the love of the earth, and for teaching girls there. She was one of those who believed we would survive only on our Sacred Earth, where Chochma was waiting for us. There were many like her. Others had gone before, to dig up the ruins from Kiryat Sefer. Rebekah found them. She believed we would build up the ancient city, all over again, stone by stone we would restore it. She believed Chochma already went back to Canaan. And from there, she was calling the people, to save them. The Flame Bearers knew already what was coming for the Jews in Europe. Mama knew, and that is why she had me learn English, to make my way in the New World. Mama believed the way back to Kiryat Sefer is not from the digging up of old stone. In her part of the sect they were teaching the secret way to go back, crossing over outside of time, beneath the going up and the coming down of the ages. But many there were who followed my sister. Always, all her life, she kept the gift of love. Whoever set eyes on her, they fell in love. Not only with Rebekah the person. But with also the things she was believing.

I, in my own way, felt this too. It was this that made me bitter. When she left me at the baron's house I felt my better self pining after Rebekah, to go back to Canaan, to renew the earth. Many of the Jews felt this same call. It came out of the pogroms and the persecutions and from the knowing, even then, of the great holocaust that was coming. This happens to a people. Even in the most blind heart, there comes sometimes the foreknowing of disaster. It came after the turning of *Narodnaya Volya* against the Jews. It was part of losing the dream Jews could become, in Russia, like other people. From every class, from every circumstance, out of bitterness and hope and from old yearning after the Holy Land the Jewish people were turning to Palestine. And so, why not the Flame Bearers too? We say that in the heart of a Flame Bearer the pulse of the whole people is beating. My sister was such a one. It was her gift to take all this into the world. She was, in her time, one of the very great Flame Bearers, who could deny this? Later, when I learned about her life, I was ashamed for all the years of silence. But by then I had changed back. I remembered. It happened many years after Rebekah left me and ran out the door into her destiny. That day, I was alone with such a cold in my veins I thought maybe I could die from it. How could I know I was, even then, going in the way I must? To be saved. To be, when the smoke of the third great cataclysm cleared, the last Hovrodnik alive on this earth.

So, the years passed. I went to live in Paris, with Sophie and the other Guzmans, in their house there. But these years remind me always of the bubbles I used to make from the soap water Mama gave me, to blow between the fingers when I was a girl. There was the glitter and the color and nothing that could last. I did all those things a young woman, with money and a fine position, could do. I met writers. I met the poet Rilke. I went to the studio of Rodin. I traveled. I was in Vienna that time when the Boesendorfer Saal was taken down. We sat there, at the last performance, the whole audience, after the lights went out, for many hours, refusing to leave. I wept even, for the loss of this beloved place, where Chopin and Liszt and Rubinstein gave their concerts. That is how much I had grown away from our village and the Flame Bearers and my mother's house. But, all this was the bubble. Behind it, back in the village, was my life. Waiting. And soon it caught me.

This is what happened.

I was living then in Paris, but I traveled to Berlin and Dresden and to Vienna. I filled my days with the cafés and the concerts and the theatrical performances. I had the finest dressmakers in Europe. I spoke many languages. I heard from everyone I was a beautiful woman. I was wealthy, with the wealth of the Guzmans, one of their own children. But always, in all those years, I did not dream. Never a dream. Think of it. Not one, ever.

But now suddenly, one day, in the middle of a walk, I felt myself lifted up and carried away. That's how it happened. I was talking with my friends, we were strolling in the Bois de Boulogne, I saw a horse with a lovely chestnut color coming toward us. I smelled the smell from Sophie's perfume. Then all at once I was back in Kashevata. I was there, in my body, watching the orphanage burn.

It was then the year 1907. I was thirty-three years old. But in that moment I became a child again. My old powers came back. Across space, through time I saw. The orphanage indeed burned to the ground, killing the girls and killing also in the fire my mother and my father. The way I saw it, that's how it happened. Three days after the vision.

Later, they told me, my whole body flamed up. I was running with sweat, but my hands were cold and my limbs were shaking. That time, too, I spoke in the angel's voice, with a high, clear ringing, they said. I told them Mama was dying. I told them a great battle was coming in the world. And then, after this, would be another battle and the Jews would be eaten by fire. But all this I didn't hear myself saying. I remember only I was walking in the Bois, arm in arm with Sophie. Then I was in Kashevata, and the next thing I knew I was in a train, I was going back to Petersburg, and Sophie was with me.

I arrived too late. Sophie, a loyal daughter to her father, would not travel on the Sabbath. We reached the Russian border on a Friday evening and spent there the whole night in the waiting room. The following night we were in Petersburg, and the news was there too. But I knew already. I knew even when I sat down on the hard bench in the waiting room it was too late. On my face, on my breast, against my arms, I could feel the fire.

For Mama I mourned. How else? And for Papa, too, I grieved bitterly. But most I mourned for the lost, the wasted years of my life. I tore my dress, I sat by myself in the room. I took up a razor and cut off my hair.

Again I was late. Three years before I had Hannah Leah in my arms, in the worker's hovel in Paris, when she was dying. She couldn't be lifted even into our carriage. I sat with her, in that dank place, like a tomb under the ground. I put her head on my lap, I stroked the scars. I listened to the story about the way she killed the czar. And from that I took away more bitterness, more anger at the Flame Bearers, driving us to all this. Then, Hannah Leah asked me about Rebekah. I saw her make herself live, pulling the will together, the way a Flame Bearer can, to hold off the dying.

Her last words were for the little sister she never saw. "Give me to Rebekah," she said. It was the way, among us, the succession is handed down. And I, in my heart, laughed and tore at myself. She, too? I thought. She, too, without ever putting eyes on her, a lover of Rebekah?

Did I ask myself how Hannah Leah knew about Rebekah? How she knew even her name? I asked nothing. When the heart closes, what remains? Not even the smallest spark from the hunger to know. I heard only the yearning in my sister's voice, the deathless yearning after Rebekah. That sound hammered my heart. It hammered the little bit of remembering that remained there. From that day, until the orphan home burned down, I lived in my *brittle self,* as we say. With the high-pitched laughter, the feverish, glittering eyes, aching under the surface, bitten with emptiness.

Now, in Petersburg, all this I saw with a painful seeing. The baron and Matilda and Sophie and I set out for Kashevata. There, everything was the way I saw in my vision. The orphanage was in ruin, a great smoldering heap on the ground. Our little house, too, was no more. Nothing was left of us.

I, of course, went to look for the old box. How else? Maybe Mama buried it? To keep it safe? But I found nothing. It was all gone. All the writings that came down from the time of Rocha Castel, from Soria, as we call the land of Spain. In that time I did not cry. "What for?" I used to say when I was a small girl, "if Chochma wanted it that way, what need for tears?"

Later, I figured out, in that time I passed through the final step to become a Flame Bearer. It was, as we say, the *place of the rock.* The place where water is not and no light is there too. Silent it is in this place. Empty and barren. And after, if I survived, would be the new beginning. But I, how could I know this?

By the time we went back to Petersburg I was mute. I forgot how to talk. I couldn't say a word. I was for a long time not living in my flesh. I wandered, in my spirits, back to our home in Chernik. I lived it all over again. I wandered farther even than my own life. I lived in Hannah Leah, before I was born. I saw the chicken with the head cut off. I saw Pyotr in the forest, throwing himself down on Hannah Leah from a tree. I saw even my own birth, and the face of my sister, looking down with the blind eye into the cradle. I saw the city of the Flame Bearers, Kiryat Sefer on the shores of Kinneret. I saw the people coming back out of Babylon, following the Great Teacher Metzulah, who brought them back to Canaan after the exile of Nebuchadnezzar. I saw Rocha Castel with the key on the neck. I saw my great-great-grandmother Vera Shulkin Shadmi, who burned herself in the fire that time the peasants came to kill the Jews. And then, even further back I saw. I heard the turtle dove. Over my head was a nightingale. Around my cradle walked goats and sheep and the gazelles with their spiraled horns. There were blue thrushes in the air. The black-throated chat of the Galilee. I heard the singing of the pipit and the robin with the white throat and the dipper with the red belly. In my hands were the flowers from the desert. The crocus. The iris of Astarte. The asphodels that bloom for Elath of the sorrows, when she is weary. And then I saw, over all this came the vultures, with their huge eyes glittering yellow, to perch on the burned tree over my cradle, in the city of Kiryat Sefer, watching.

So it was. This seeing with the other eye, that goes down into the heart, happened now to me. It went on for months. And in all this time I did not live in my body. I traveled in the spirit, I went out to walk in the world of what was to come.

There, I smelled the burning from human flesh. I heard the shrieking from the ones fallen. I saw, once again it would happen, as before it had happened, when the Temple fell and down from the walls of the City ran the blood of the slain, crucified, hundreds of them on the walls of Jerusalem that time Titus came with his legions and Bar Kochba fought, defeated in the caves of Murrabat. And the burning of the people in Soria, in the land of Spain. And the massacres in Cracow, in Lvov, in Posen, the wandering out of Lithuania and the expulsion from Khazaria and the terror from the Crusades. I saw the torment of the Jewish people, over and over again, and the Flame Bearers always alongside to bring comfort, to remind them of Chochma. But this time it would be even worse than before, burning and torture, and the toiling of slaves.

Then, I saw Rebekah, with all her orphans, struck down and killed on the hills of Talpiot, above Jerusalem. Rebekah dead, the little sister dead. I saw the earth accept the seeds she buried there. I saw green trees grow out from them. But the voice of our people was heard no more in that land. We died out. Our singers dead. Our prophets dead and our healers and our scribes. And our great warriors too, who rose up to defend our people in this last cycle of the cycle of years before the Great Teacher came. All fallen, all in shadow and ash. And I saw the way I, always a lonely one, was cast out in a world alien, looking for my successor.

When I woke up out of this seeing I was sitting by myself in the library with the old box from Rocha Castel on my knees. Inside, Mama's papers and the other, older papers that came before hers. Did I know how the box came there? Who could I ask? I, with my voice the angel brought me, I would carry our box out into the world.

I sat there, with the hair growing back, and the bones growing out of my wrists from hunger, and I heard Mama speaking, with a clear, still voice, telling me what was to come.

The door opened. Baron David came in. He gave me such a look I thought I in my life never had seen before. And then he, who was always a shy man, kind and patient and with great angers also, but never one to make a big gesture, he opened his arms to me.

After that, day by day, I got better. At first, I could speak only in Yiddish, I ate only infant food, warmed milk and a piece of bread dipped in it. Then slowly, the languages came, Russian, Hebrew, Ugaritic, then the others. Little by little my flesh came back to live in my body. And my time of *the tender seeing* began.

From my window, on the second floor, I looked out into the courtyard. There it was already spring. I saw a light come out of the tree, like wings it came, fanning and beating the air. I saw angels dancing there, in every leaf. They were looking at me, laughing, pointing the fingers. Then, they had gone, and there stayed in the tree a blue light. It was of a beauty made only on this earth. It was the beauty of The Mother Herself, smiling. And then I, with my own eyes, I beheld Chochma. My throat aching with longing, I wanted to speak in our old tongue, to tell the whole world about her beauty.

So it was I got better. And soon, of course, with the weeks and the months passing, the time came for the celebration. It was for my recovering and for Baron David and Matilda too. It was then the year called 1908. A dance was held in our house. For them, it was the silver anniversary. For me, the third month of my recovering. I came, with Sophie and the baron's youngest son, down the stairs together. But then, when I walked into the ballroom I saw instead of the festivity, the baron lying sick in his bed. And he was dying.

It was again the same thing as in the Bois de Boulogne. The same as would happen many times in my life. I was carried upstairs, and this time I heard the warning. A vision came. It was Mama speaking. She told me again, I would live on, the last of the many. From my generation I would be the only one left, who passed into the secrets and still returned. Beyond the three great cataclysms I would live. And in that world where I was, the story of the Flame Bearers would be almost forgotten. To speak, in the words of that time, of this we loved would be almost impossible. That is what Mama said.

I felt a fiery finger against my lips, sealing them to the mission. And I understood. What was for us the world of ourself would be for the others, who came after, only a story. Words in the air. The lips moving. For them, Rocha's box and the angel, and the way the tall grasses speak, to instruct the Hovrodnik in healing, all this would be only smoke with no fire. And still I must go out there, to find the successor, to bring the story of the Old World into the New.

To hear of this was for me the most terrible thing, worse even than the life of Hannah Leah and the death of Mama and Papa. It was worse even than my lost years of the bubble. All this, I knew, happened already before. When Kiryat Sefer vanished, with our books and our scrolls and our beautiful images of Elath and Asherah and Lillitu of the winds. The Mothers broken, with their big bodies swollen in the belly and in the breasts for bearing of the generations. And before that too, the Mothers torn down in the cities of Canaan, where we lived, worshiping the corn mother, the little mother of the vine, and the beloved Chochma, with her arms open like the wings of the dove, calling always to her children.

So it was, as I lay in my bed, with eyes blind and my ears hearing only Mama's voice, I came to know that I would tell and tell and who would believe me? The old women would gather around me, waiting, waiting. Shadows of a shadow, ashes of the ash. Waiting, for the Great One who would come after, out of the new world, out of the forgetting. Hannah Leah was called maybe to raise up the hand against the injustice of the world, to bring an end to the old order. Rebekah was called to bring again the trees and the grasses to the dead land of Canaan. But to me was given the task, I should find the successor.

Two years later the baron died. He died in the same bed I saw, with the same book in the hands, that night I went down with Sophie and the baron's son David into the ballroom. It was December. We went through the snow, walking. Nearby was the River Neva. I heard, from far off, the sound of the Kaddish and the sound also of the waters on the earth.

But I already was away from there. An old woman I was, again in silence, by myself, dying alone, in the chair by the window. I was calling, in the old way, with dreams and visions and the voices that ride in the air. In my lace dress, I called, with hair black as the wings from the crow. And there came, with her hair of fire, and the hazel eyes that also were the eyes of Hannah Leah, tall as the birch that grows with the pines in our forest, my beloved Isarael. Little Slevka. The successor.

c h a p t e r

16

R *a e* was afraid she might be too late even before they drove out of the park and along the ocean, where a last ribbon of light was holding itself together on the horizon. Pressed against the window, her back to Jacob, she saw the clouds shape themselves, very deliberately, into that death flock her grandmother had told them about since they were children.

A couple was strolling near the stone embankment and a few late, solitary walkers. But the district had already been taken over by the dope dealers and prostitutes. A woman in a gray slit skirt and high heels watched them as they drove by, moving fast. At the corner they passed another woman, standing by herself, waiting to cross the street. She was tall and well built, with something arresting in her carriage, her hair tied up in small braids each coiled about with silver threads. Beyond, where the churning foam was still visible, beating against the rocks, a strange, fluorescent haze hung over the water.

Rae watched the clouds, wondering how much she was permitted to say to Jacob. And then, right over her heart, pinching and squeezing, she felt the emptiness, as if someone had just taken a childhood trinket she had lost track of all those years and held it up in front of her eyes for a single mocking instant. Just long enough to let her remember how precious it had once been. Before tossing it away, forever, into the ocean.

She remembered how she had come as a child to stand next to Maya and Naamah at the head of the table, to receive the old woman's blessing on the Sabbath. She remembered how she had loved her grandmother then and how her chest had filled with a painful pride, to notice how long their grandmother kept her there, so much longer than Maya or Naamah, her hands growing hot and heavy on the child's head, so that once or twice Rae had wanted to pull away in fear because she thought the old woman was trying to burn her.

Rae stretched out her legs and began to fiddle with the knob on the wing window, which had been stuck for as many years as she had known Jacob. But now, tugging violently at it, she succeeded finally in breaking it off. "I won't apologize," she muttered, rolling down the window and tossing it out. "At least this way the damned thing will open."

She felt a sudden weariness, as if she could put her head down on her knees and fall instantly asleep, the way a child might. Jacob reached over and took her hand. And then, rushing at her, there was a vivid, piercing sweetness. It brought back the memory of that night, in her childhood, when she had gone out into the garden to take the little cookies from the altar. The wind and the fig tree were part of it, and the wooden image, with its heavy breasts. The throbbing was there, too, of a day in spring at Stow Lake in the park, Maya laughing up at her through her child's eyes, so full of challenge and curiosity and a willingness to be loved, as she stretched out her arms from the hard earth, calling Rae back to it. The oak tree of late summer in the garden, she and Maya chewing the bark as they leaned against each other. And now, present with a truly horrifying actuality, her grand-mother's face. This was the death vision. Her grandmother, calling to her for all those years, had finally reached her.

Then, Rae was somewhere else. She was here too, in the car with Jacob, his large hand wrapped around her fist. And she was there, wherever it was, with her grandmother and she had reached out to take the tiny, blue-veined hands in her own. She practically had to kneel to bring her face level with the old woman's. And then, as she smiled at this tiny, withered tyrant, Rae saw her for the first time in her life. Saw without the enlargements of a child's seeing and without the bitter disparagement that comes to the adolescent girl, her heart broken by the loss of her earlier illusions. But she did not expect the old woman's tenderness. Her voice, rasping from the years of silence. "Isarael," she murmured and the fierce eyes filled with tears.

Rae bent forward so that the old woman could whisper in her ear. "*Mayn kind,*" she said, "*Ikh ken zen in dayn likhtigen ponem du bist take a khakhome.* My child, I can see in your bright face what a wise one you are."

Rae opened her arms but the old woman raised a crooked finger and shook it at her, playfully. "So many years, who needs them?" she said. "You kept me waiting, Isarael. Better you should have come home before."

Rae kept trying to look at her grandmother but a light seemed to be passing over her face and the harsh features faded away in it. It was the only word of reproach the old woman uttered.

Her grandmother was patting her on the arm. "Dear girl," she said, "you are looking at one who already is talking to death. And even better," she went on, with a crooked little smile, "even better. Death is telling a thing or two to me. Isarael. Death talks Yiddish."

"Is this forgiveness?" Rae asked. And the old woman, shaking her head at her, began to wheeze and laugh. "Wisdom. Not forgiveness. Wisdom that knows already, what is there to forgive?"

"Nothing to forgive? Nothing?" Rae cried out. And now, for the first time in all their years together, she saw the old woman hunch over, pressing her hands to her face, the tears falling between her fingers, dark as blood. "What good is it?" her grandmother moaned. "What good is it I know and I forgive? Where you are going you need now a better friend than my forgiveness."

And then there was that old, stabbing fear. The fear that had driven her away from home, running from the certain knowledge she belonged, from birth, to a destiny that must be chosen. To deny it was possible. Oh yes, it was. Just as possible as denying her need to breathe and eat and drink.

Jacob turned the corner sharply and Rae lurched against him, torn back out of the death vision in a rupture that made her feel sick to her stomach, her hands blue and icy, a disgusting taste of copper in her mouth. She leaned over him. "Hurry, can't you? Why is it taking so long? Do you know what's at stake here?"

But how could he know?

Rae felt as if she had fallen through the thin walls that enclose the present. From far away, she felt the wind blowing as she stood with the old lady. Where? At the door to the house on Scott Street. The old woman wrapping her shawl around her before she reached out to take Isarael's hand. And Rae, grown up, sitting in the car next to

Jacob, felt confusion. It seemed to her that her legs were very short and that her grandmother was towering over her, as they hurried along in the wind.

"*Nu meydele,*" the old woman was saying, "what is to fear? When the wind blows, that is Lillitu. Or maybe even, the breath from Chochma. So? You see? They come to visit you. To remind you, even when the Bubbe is not here, they still are keeping watch."

"No," Rae cried out. She had her hands on Jacob's shoulders and was shaking him, violently. "You can't. Not yet. Not yet . . ."

"Rae, I'm driving as fast as I can. What is happening with you?"

"Jacob, she's not going to wait for me."

He said nothing. He had learned during his years with the Shadmis when to be silent. But he was keeping an eye on her, glancing rapidly as he clutched the wheel with both hands.

Rae had drawn away from him. She was hunched up with her hands covering her face. Then she was looking up at him with unseeing eyes, wringing her hands. "Rae, tell me. What is it?" he insisted. He could never have imagined Rae so completely beside herself.

She was pleading with a child's voice, her arms wrapped around her waist. "Wait for me, Bubbe. Wait for me. I'm coming. I'm coming . . ."

Her voice had trailed off in a desolate wail and she was reaching out for him, throwing her arms around him. Then she was sobbing against his shoulder. Her grief burned through his thick sweater and he recognized it immediately. These were the tears she had held back for thirty years. "Jacob, make her wait. She can do it. Tell her to wait for me," she begged. "Don't let her go before she knows . . ."

"Oh, Rae," he murmured. "Rae . . ." Did she believe that, really? He managed to get one arm around her but she had pulled away and had raised her fists to her temples. Did she really believe the old woman could choose the time of her death?

"Jacob, Jacob," she said to him in a voice he would never forget. There was exasperation in it, an undeniable note of condescension, and above all a desperate yearning this time, finally, to be understood. "Jacob, have you lived with us all this time and not grasped it? Of course she can choose the time of her death. Don't you know who she is?"

She had slumped against the seat, her head back, her mouth

slack. Her hands had fallen open in her lap. "She, a Hovrodnik, and she never forgave me," Rae said. "She never forgave me." She was shaking her head, with such mournful bitterness he had to wonder if this could be Rae. And now they had turned the corner, they were skidding to a stop and Jacob realized he had just witnessed the collapse of everything Rae had taught herself to be since she was a small girl.

The Home for the Jewish Aged stood on a hill above the ocean at the corner of the street. It was a large building, painted white, with a wrought-iron fence, black shutters, a carefully tended flower box, and the general atmosphere of a prosperous, Mediterranean villa. From the upper stories there was a good view of the sea and the two windmills at the edge of the park. But Rae, leaning out of the car, knew that her grandmother would be completely indifferent to all that. She could see her, sitting at the open window, straight up in her chair, her eyes fixed on the street.

"Bubbe," Rae called, leaping out of the car. "Bubbe," she cried, waving her arms as she ran through the park on Scott Street. And then she was running up all the stairs she had raced up as a child, to throw herself in the old woman's arms, in those days before the fire had destroyed the school and killed her parents.

The matron came out of a room at the top of the stairs. Rae wanted to shove her aside and go on running. She stood still instead, looking desperately at the old woman, panting for breath. "Twenty minutes ago," the matron said, beating on her breast, her voice hushed in a reproachful whisper. She had recognized Rae at once. "Twenty minutes ago Mrs. Altdorf found her. Did I say twenty? Ten minutes ago. She went up to bring her the cup of soup. She sees her sitting there, by the window, like always, looking out."

"What's she saying?" Rae asked, looking around wildly.

"Oy," the matron went on, shaking her head, "like always, sitting there. Would you believe it? Ten minutes longer you'd think she could manage to live. Ten minutes, after the waiting all these years."

Jacob had come running up the stairs a few paces behind Rae. He put his arms around her but she turned to face him, burying her head against his chest.

"Oy," the matron muttered behind her, "you know what they say? As we live, so also we die."

"Shut her up, Jacob," Rae said to him in a voice so controlled and quiet he had to guess at her meaning. But then she was turning away from him. She looked back for a moment with an expression of forlorn confusion, as if she were still expecting him to take it all in hand and make it come out right. Then, he saw that she had thrown her arms around the little old woman who had served as matron at the home since Rae was a small girl. She was begging forgiveness, drop-ping down onto her knees. "*Bougemois,*" the matron shrieked, "vas is this? Rae Shadmi? Is this Rae Shadmi?"

Jacob went over and drew her to her feet. "Rae," he said in the voice he used to wake Brucha from a nightmare. "Rae, my friend," he repeated, gathering up all the authority and reassurance of which he was capable. She had reached out to touch the tears that were pouring down his face. "Am I crying?" she asked.

He walked with her toward the door of the old woman's room. She reached out to open it but it swung back as she approached and now he stopped, to let her enter alone. He went over then to lean against the railing. He understood, finally. Either way, it could destroy Rae. To find out like this, that the old woman was not able to choose the time of her death. Would that be worse, he wondered, than be-lieving she did not choose to wait for her granddaughter?

Rae walked toward the old woman. She walked so slowly that it must have taken her thousands of years. Her hair turned white before she reached the gray chair near the window. A scar, which no one had seen for a long time, appeared on her forehead. It looked something like a sickle moon and something like a small flame. And then, she was a very small girl again. She had bitten fingernails, her pants were torn at the knees, she had been crying and the old woman was taking her up into her lap.

Rae sat down in front of the gray chair and looked up into the old woman's face. She saw an ancient, withered creature, whose hair had been braided back into two long strands and pinned up on her head, as raven black as ever. She saw the grim, unsmiling, thin lips, the pointed chin, the skull-like cheekbones, and the black eyes that looked out so fiercely at the world. She put her head on her grand-mother's knees. Then, very deliberately, she took the old woman's hand and placed it down heavily on the head of this granddaughter who had come too late.

Rae sat there for a long time. It was twilight when she and Jacob arrived at the home. It was twilight of the next day's morning when Rae finally moved. She got to her feet and kissed the old woman's hand. Then stooping, with one of those reverent gestures that came upon her unexpectedly from time to time, she placed both her hands very gently on the old woman's head.

part three

From This Ash

The Present: Spring–Winter 1974

17

Th e week of mourning, in retrospect, seemed to have gone by very fast. But at the time Rae felt as if she were moving through thick syrup. Each day, before it was light, she would go out in Jacob's car, with the broken seat and the damaged window, to gather in the few old women among her grandmother's students who were still alive. There was Frau Altdorf, who had looked after the old woman during the last years and who lived still in the Home for the Jewish Aged. There was Zelda Zemanski and Miriam Katz. These two had remained close to the house on Scott Street, where they shared a shabby room in the basement of a once grand Victorian.

When Rae and Frau Altdorf arrived the two old women came upstairs in their best clothes, faded garments that must have endured for more than half a century. Rae watched them walk toward her down the long hall, with its high chipped ceilings, its damaged ornamental plaster, and the devastated magnificence of its staircase. With their bone combs, their hand-knit shawls, their high-button shoes, the long-sleeved dresses that buttoned at the wrist, the old women looked astonishingly alike, Rae thought, as if they had come from a single family and common root. She kept all expression from her face, but her heart seemed to be roaring and banging about in her chest, as they reached up, each in turn, to salute her with the traditional greeting. Taking her by the shoulders, bowing their heads. In acknowledgment of the successor.

"My dear old women," said Rae, "you're making a big mistake. You don't want me. I'm a coward, a fool, and an ignoramus."

She had always been inclined to talk to herself but she went at it now as if she were fighting for survival.

"I've forgotten everything the old woman taught me. I'm a convert to conventionality and I feel like taking to my heels and getting out of here."

Rae did not know that her hair had turned white. By the time she looked at herself in a mirror the scar had faded and was covered again by her red curls. A streak of white hair had remained. But it was hidden away at the back of her neck, where only a barber or a lover would ever see it. Rae had reverted to that mocking, superficial self she had pieced together with such strenuous effort during the years of her absence.

Frau Altdorf looked over at her with her eyebrows raised.

"Look at that, she thinks she can read my thoughts," Rae said as Frau Altdorf frowned, shook her head, and began to look distinctly worried. "But don't worry," she went on, silently addressing herself to the little old woman who had hobbled forward to take her arm, "I'll stick around for a bit to see whether you've got any interesting tricks up your sleeve, okay?"

"Uh-kaey," the old woman echoed with a quick, sly glance. And Rae, for some reason, burst out laughing.

Then the seven days of it ran together and began to seem the same day happening over and over. Each day the old women entered the car in the same order, deferring to Frau Altdorf, who had been so close to the old woman until her death. Each day they sat without speaking, holding themselves straight, their lips tight together, their eyes fixed ahead of them. To Rae, glancing at them through the rearview mirror, it seemed that they were no longer individuals. They were there as *Flam-Trogers,* members of the Flame Bearers, to observe the death of their teacher and acknowledge the woman she had selected as her heir.

Rae knew what they were up to. Their teacher Sarah Rachel had lived before and would live again; she would find them in other lives and lands, when they might in turn be her guide or instructor. They gathered now to commemorate the passing of a long life, well lived; with the exception of Frau Altdorf they had severed their daily connection to her years before and had, each in her own way, kept an eye on the restless, troubled world that surrounded them and on whose behalf they lit incense, spoke the blessings, and continued to set down the various stories of the sect that had come down to them since they were children.

"They know they've got me," Rae said and she didn't care if Frau Altdorf were listening in. "You think it makes a difference to them if I don't share their view of my role here? I can turn and twist and make an enormous pretzel of myself for all they care. They know perfectly well the snare will only grow tighter." She was helping them out of the car at Naamah's house and up the stairs into the small living room. They surrounded her as she walked into the room, they remained standing until she had seated herself, they sat down on the hard-backed chairs across from her. But they did not know, Rae was sure of that, how little understanding she had of those mysteries to which their lives were dedicated. They joined in the storytelling, adding an anecdote here, a detail there, none of which revealed anything to those outside the sect, but all of which was filled with an ambiguous significance Rae sensed but could not herself decipher. They expected her to find the way back to Kiryat Sefer. They were prepared to tell her what they knew about this journey outside time. For years, their grandmother had been waiting to teach her, keeping herself alive for that time when Rae would be ready to understand. For years, in the little upstairs room, she and her students had been setting down the instructions that were to serve as her guide in the event that she died before Rae was ready for the initiation.

"Bubbe," said a small voice in Rae, which was quickly silenced. "Bubbe . . ."

Naamah's living room, in which the family was assembled, was cluttered with the various projects that had kept her busy over the years. Sacred hangings, stained-glass lamps, hand-woven cloths for the Sabbath challah, the Havdalah candles she made herself, her clay figurines of the ancient fertility goddess, clay pots and masks and countless miniature paintings, enameled on brass in the old style of Russian icons—all these, for the first time took on their true significance and became the appropriate setting for this week of reminiscence and storytelling—the only form of death rite they observed.

Naamah, holding a surprisingly docile Brucha by the hand, led the informal procession that began the Havdalah ceremony.

"So, Michael?" Naamah said to her son, who had been loping about on his long legs in the kitchen. The old women had been watching him from their straight-back chairs near the window. He came into the room, walked up to Maya's daughter Ruth and took her hand. They were both self-conscious and ill at ease—Michael hitching up his shoulders and sticking out his chin because of his lesser importance as a male; Ruth because she had recently begun to menstruate and knew that she would soon begin lessons with Naamah and Frau Altdorf. Her cheeks covered with red blotches, she stumbled as she walked forward next to Michael, caught her breath and held tight to his arm.

By the second day Rubin Spaeght was there and seemed to have been there from the first moment. Tall and boyish, wearing a blue knit sailor cap, he came forward slowly with that lilting walk of his, way up on the balls of his feet, holding out his arm for Maya, who seemed to respond better to him than to any other person present. He had the same exuberantly curling light-brown hair, regular features, and pale blue eyes that had made him the prettiest little boy in their grandmother's school, when it had been rebuilt after the fire. But in those years he had been that pesky, obstreperous little Rubin who used to follow them home from school, kicking at pebbles and walking along with his hands in his pocket, while Maya would tease him and tousle his hair and try to leap in and give him a wet kiss on the cheek, before he bolted away.

Rubin had returned to San Francisco from Jerusalem, where he had been living during the last decade or so, to organize an alternative treatment center for people in acute states of mental crisis. It was for this reason Aunt Sonia had invited him to the Havdalah ceremony, going out of her way to renew an acquaintanceship with his mother, although the friendship had lapsed thirty years before. It held, apparently, in the minds of both women sufficient nostalgic claim to entertain them during those late hours of the afternoon when Rubin might be expected to drop in. Aunt Sonia, who had recently moved back to San Francisco herself, got involved in Rubin's affairs, joined the board of his little center, made substantial monetary contributions, and persuaded Rubin to take an interest in Maya—not trusting to his own fondness for "the girls" with whom he had gone to school.

Rae remembered him well. She had always cherished (with some humor and a great deal of affection) a memory of Rubin romping about in the schoolyard with some other boys. She and Maya and a few girls from their class had been strolling with a new teacher, who had arrived from Paris and had smitten them all with her tall good looks. They were shoving each other aside, trying to get hold of their teacher's hand and walk beside her. It was late in the afternoon, during the required break in Hebrew lessons. One of the boys had thrown a ball, which soared above the head of his companions. And Rubin, dashing over and leaping up at the last minute, had knocked the ball aside, before it hit the new teacher. That's what she recalled. The way he had run back and shoved the boy who threw the ball, "Watch what you're doing," he had said in a good, loud voice. "You almost hurt my beautiful teacher."

Maya and Rubin won favorable glances from the old women, as they came forward together and bent down to touch the floor in a low bow. The old women glanced at one another, muttered together in subdued voices, and then Frau Altdorf (breaking centuries of tradition) reached out and touched Rubin's head—offering their blessing to him, a man. "Good years," she wished him, "long life, time enough to remember."

Rubin smiled happily and glanced over at Rae, but Maya gripped his arm possessively. She drew him aside. "Good years," she whispered to him, "you understand. Long life you understand too. But, what are you supposed to remember?"

She spoke with a sweet little voice, as if she were offering instruction to a beloved child. And Rubin, who seemed to have remained a tender-hearted man, bent down toward her and let her teach him.

"What am I supposed to remember?" he said. "Well, I don't know, in fact. What *am* I supposed to remember?" He had spoken without the least trace of condescension and Rae, who was watching them closely, liked him for that. It couldn't have been easy, she thought, to approach Maya with exactly that combination of dignity and kindness. But then Rae decided not to be taken in. She narrowed her eyes, suspiciously.

Maya looked up at Rubin with a delighted smile. She lifted her finger and shook it gently. "The Mother," she said, lingering on the word so that he could not fail to take in its larger significance, "you are to remember The Mother."

"What's he doing here, actually?" Rae, who would have liked an answer to that one, had just picked up a whiff of Aunt Sonia's meddling. "Don't tell me she brought him along to take care of Maya?" It was a good guess; she knew nothing as yet about Rubin's treatment center. "So that's what it is, eh? Professional kindness? Let's see," Rae said to herself, shoving her hands into her pockets. "The old women give him their blessing . . . Oy, Rubin," she said, "you want you should live as long as that? Hach," she went on, savagely figuring it all out. "Someone's cooking up a wedding here, if I'm not mistaken." But there she was getting it wrong.

The old women did not seem to notice Maya's strangeness. But most of the time Maya sat by herself, muttering inaudibly. Occasionally, she would look up suddenly and stare at a fixed spot on the ceiling, shaking her head sadly. Once, Rae thought she heard her say, with a sigh of great anguish: "How ever did they get you into the nest, old woman?" Then, without taking her eyes from the spot she began to wring her hands.

Meanwhile, the three old women sat straight in their chairs, waiting with their monumental patience as each member of the family approached. Frau Altdorf, who seemed to be their elder, sat with her chin lifted slightly, her head tipped to the side, as if she were listening to instructions. Jacob went over, bowed down before them, his left hand touching the floor, and they blessed him too and took him by the hands, nodding their heads and glancing approvingly at one another. Then Zelda Zemanski actually rose from her chair and put her cheek next to his. "You get that?" Rae practically shouted. "The next thing you know they'll be taking him into the sect." But she managed, in that way, to miss the blessing.

During the first days Naamah delayed the storytelling while she waited for her mother. But each day she was surprised and disappointed and then perhaps even alarmed that Aunt Elke did not come. Something had happened between Aunt Elke and Maya on the day of the old woman's death. Naamah, who knew, kept promising to tell Rae, who kept promising to listen. And meanwhile, both of them were far too absorbed with the storytelling sessions to take time for themselves.

Apart from this, however, day for day the event went smoothly. Each day, Maya's mother joined them at noon. It was an acknowledgment that Aunt Sonia had been estranged from the old woman but was seeking now to maintain the bonds of kinship. She came dressed up in high heels, in a little hat with a black veil, redolent of French perfume and her anomalous life of giddy leisure, and immediately she began to intrude and interfere as if no time had elapsed since she had lived with them. There was even an extremely funny incident when

Aunt Sonia, fussing about as usual, tasting wine to make sure it was properly flavored, rubbing dried leaves between her fingers from the little spice box, sniffing and prodding the breads and arranging candles on a tray to distribute among the other guests, got into a loud quarrel with little Brucha.

The child, who that day was in an officious mood, flew after her great-aunt and contradicted every word she spoke in the older woman's very voice. "The yellow candles next to the red? Shall I believe my eyes? So, give me the tray, you heard me? Move sharp now, hand it over," Brucha said, rearranging the candles on the tray, pouring the wine into larger glasses, placing a cover with an embroidered tree over a bread shaped like a hand. Aunt Sonia, beside herself with irritation, finally plucked up the little girl by the waist, carried her, legs dangling, into the kitchen, sat her down at the table, poured her a big mug of spiced wine, clapped her hands, and chanted so that Brucha (who would always be obedient to tradition) had to drink it down without a breath. She succeeded in getting the little girl thoroughly drunk. Thereafter, Brucha wandered among the guests, who arrived each day in greater numbers, until the house was filled to overflowing, children sitting on the stairs, older people looking down from the landing. The dining room and kitchen, even the screened back porch, were packed with well-wishers and distant relations and with far too many curiosity seekers.

Among this multitude Brucha made her way, speaking a peculiar nonsense babble that sounded vaguely like a mixture of Hebrew and Ugaritic and was accompanied by strange little squeaks, odd facial expressions, and florid hand gestures. Maya, who had been keeping an eye on her, began to follow her about, also babbling and muttering to herself. And Rae, who was suddenly overcome by an uncontrollable desire to laugh out loud, saw that people looked at them as if they imagined this bizarre behavior might be part of the Flame Bearer ceremony.

Most of the time Rae went among them with an aloof, self-protecting politeness, which hid her sense of inner vacancy. The word had of course spread that she had been chosen as successor; people with only the most remote connection to the sect, or who knew about the old woman through hearsay and rumor, came forward to touch her shoulder or squeeze her hand in sympathy and respect or merely to have some physical connection with what they seemed to imagine was her new power. But she herself, struggling now with a sense of failure and inner collapse, moved among them through that thick syrup of her despondency, making bitter observations beneath her breath and biding her time until the week had passed and she would be able to sit down with Naamah and confess the full extent of her inadequacy. Stiffly, she accepted the tribute of the old women, whose eyes never left her face, and who seemed, when she herself was telling stories, to sit in a shared state of virtually suspended animation, scarcely breathing, their faculties strained apparently to the uttermost, so that they could register every slightest inflection and nuance of her voice.

As the week drew to a close, Rae began to feel that she would not be able to keep going much longer. "See there?" she muttered. "The time is coming, soon enough, when I won't be able to resist. They're getting to me, in that way they know how. Wearing me down with their old stories. Soon, you'll see, I'll be remembering things better forgotten, feeling things I finished with years ago. It's too late for you, little friend," she insisted to herself, "you're in the net and thrashing wildly." But she herself had grown intensely weary of her ironic sallies.

And there were times: sitting there, reciting the familiar words, when she lost track of the story. She forgot to fall silent and let someone else pick up the thread. She was aware of Naamah's scrutiny, Jacob's presence next to her, the eyes of Rubin Spaeght, curious and respectful, Brucha sitting sometimes on her lap, Maya's rather spiteful expression. But she felt that she was engaged somehow in restless combat with the old woman. She had a mental impression of bird flight, a quick, terrifying rush through her of winged creatures, as she spoke. Sometimes, looking across the room at the old women, she seemed to see seven of them sitting there, their forms flickering with firelight and shadow, the deep wrinkles cut even more harshly into their faces, on which there were expressions of severe, all-knowing joy. There were moments (and they were startling, deeply disturbing times) when she felt a hand pressed against her forehead, burning there with its claim. And then, when the week had passed, and the other guests had departed, and the family gathered at the door to bid farewell to the old women, something had happened that shook Rae to the very foundation of her being. This can't be happening, she had said to herself, I'm telling you, this can't be happening.

Nevertheless, it was.

She had been standing a little apart, while salutations were exchanged, the candles were snuffed out, the last cup of wine was shared among them, the spice box was closed, and the final blessing was spoken, softly. She had stepped forward to allow Frau Altdorf to take her by the shoulders.

"Still sticking around for the tricks?" the old woman had said. Rae smiled; she had remembered by then how often Frau Altdorf had played this mind-reading game with them when they were children. And it was, really, with a child's sense of the respect owed to an elder that she bent down to the old woman and bowed her head to receive the blessing. And then, when she stood up again, she had looked into the face of an old woman she had never seen before.

"This cannot be . . ." she had said because she knew it couldn't have happened like that. She had closed her eyes; she remembered this clearly. There was that odd sensation of choking she had felt years before, that time she had tried to tell Maya about the forbidden cookies in the attic room. A feeling of tremendous heat had rushed through her and her eyes had opened again, forcing themselves against her inclination to keep them shut forever.

The old woman was there. She was looking at Rae with . . . what? Distrust? Suspicion? It was an expression of very careful scrutiny! And of course, she reminded Rae of their grandmother. But that face, Rae would never forget. Later, she could just manage to recall the firm chin, the high cheekbones, the wide mouth. A beautiful old woman's face it was, certainly. But that was the least of it. At the time, it had made upon her an impression of peerless intelligence. Of deep inner struggle, successfully surmounted. And yes, there was a capacity for charm long since disciplined to some high, spiritual task. The woman was much younger than their grandmother. But she, too, had come from an old world, whose lessons were cut into her features with the same harsh strokes. She was wearing steel-rimmed spectacles, her hair was knotted into a thick white braid and pinned up on her head. Without doubt, she was a stranger. And yet she seemed to be waiting for acknowledgment.

Rae felt her knees beginning to shake. "You want to be recognized, is that it? But I tell you, old woman, I've never seen you before." Nevertheless, she felt something forcing her down in recognition to her knees. "No," she insisted, because she felt that actually she was longing to cry out "Yes, take me." Tall and well built, the woman leaned heavily on a gold-tipped cane and moved slowly, as if she were in great pain or were reaching out to Rae from across great obstacles. Fascinated, Rae watched the old woman's arm raise itself up with infinite effort and move toward her. And then, there it was: a pale, freckled hand on her arm, resting so lightly it seemed impossible this almost weightless flesh could conjure up so much feeling.

Rae fought back. She struggled as she would have if she'd been pulled out to sea or down into quicksand. Sweating and choking, her entire body beginning to tremble, she resisted, narrowing her eyes in that way she had, clenching her jaw, refusing to take in the wild freshness in which she seemed in spite of everything to have been plunged, as if someone had thrust open a casement and tossed her out into a stormy night. And then she felt that inrush of power that had come to her also in the months before the old woman's death. And again, as on that day which seemed to stand so far away it might have occurred to another person, in some other lifetime, the rage and refusal came over her—this outraged sense that she was being forced to become what some power larger than her own will wished her to be.

The door opened. Naamah and the others escorted the three old women to Jacob's car. Rae could see them walking slowly across the street, Frau Altdorf hobbling along on Jacob's arm at the rear of the procession. She watched them with a strained attention, trying to fight off all other sensation, because she knew that her forehead was burning in that way it did whenever she was caught up in one of these episodes. And she knew, too, that the stranger, saying something she simply could not understand, had pressed close against her and placed in her hand a small silver key.

18

In e x p l i c a b l e things do happen. Rae was no fool. She had moreover already passed through "occurrences" that only a year before she would have thought impossible for a person of her day and age. They were strange, but even in their strangeness belonged to that sphere of mental events which allows for all sorts of subjective expansions.

Years before she had read about a woman hired by the police force in Norfolk, Virginia, who could solve crimes and locate missing persons by listening to messages that came to her from "the beyond." The letters that had come to her from the West Coast during her years of absence informed her that several at least among her old friends consulted psychics, made appointments with faith healers, guzzled concoctions of bitter roots, and had small Oriental needles stuck with considerable efficacy into their meridians.

Dipped, as she called it, into this unwholesome brew her own visions would be right at home, she knew. But that key, which she held in her hand in all its palpable, objective existence, that key undid her.

Rae waited, upstairs in the guest room of Maya's house, and she held the key in her hand. She waited for some communication from Naamah or the old ladies that would tell her what she was to do next. She waited, fully aware of the contradiction, for the moment when she could make some formal renunciation of her role as successor. And gradually, as the days passed, and the savagery of her sardonic self-arguings failed to sustain her, she realized that she would wait in vain. It was up to her now. She must take the next step. Oh yes, they would leave her, quite alone, to her own devices, struggling with the unwelcome mystery that had been thrust upon her.

Jacob stopped by to pay her a visit. "Still hanging back here, Rae?" he said as he walked into the room. "You think the world is no larger than the twentieth century?" He had a way of making himself at home, taking off his shoes and sweater, running his hands through his hair.

She greeted him in a gruff voice, as if to reproach him for disturbing her solitude. But they both knew she was delighted to see him.

"This is the most dull and prosaic age in the history of the world," he announced, coming over to kiss her on the cheek. "And why? Because maybe we're still recovering from the Holocaust?" He liked to take up a conversation where they had left off last. He wanted to see if he could take her by surprise, confuse her a little, catch her napping. "Maybe," he went on, knowing perfectly well that he'd never succeed, "we have grown afraid to be excessive even in our imaginations? The nineteenth century sounds always from our point of view as if we made it up. Those Russian terrorists, if they would be alive today, would be for us only a bunch of young hotheads. They'll kill the czar? These babies, with the big dreams? Who could believe it? And yet, what happened? They killed the czar. Or take even more the young Zionists. They were, what? A bunch of ragged Jewish intellectuals from the ghetto. Without even a single decent suit of clothes among the whole lot. They sit sharing a cup of tea, smoking a cigarette, and staying up late in a tiny apartment in Zhitomir. *Nu?* This group is going to go and take back the Holy Land? Would you believe this if you heard it from a group of young people today? And what happened? Fifty, sixty years after they start their crazy dreaming they are winning a war for the independence of Palestine on holy soil. What does your grandmother want from you that is more unlikely or more absurd? Always there have been truths that live outside the history book, among the people. In my opinion, what we have here is a fragment of one of these great, hidden truths."

They stood for a time in silence looking out at the view. She heard a fog horn on the bay and tried not to hear it. "Truths, Jacob?" she said, finally, renouncing the desire to run from them again. "To me it all seems a remarkable concoction of self-inflation and fantasy woven about with fragments from an undoubtedly genuine folk tradition. I know the Flame Bearers existed for hundreds of years, telling their stories from mother to daughter. I can even imagine a female underground tradition of legends and tales, that date back to Canaanite times, in one form or another. I spent, after all, more than four years on a thesis to demonstrate the presence of Asherah worship in the Old Testament. I gave my grandmother's stories a solid, scholarly substantiation. But can you really believe there is a way to get back to a city that was destroyed hundreds of years ago? Do you ask me to believe the Shadmi family really has some special 'calling' to be legendary saints? My grandmother took literally what was in reality a great and beautiful fable, the compensation no doubt on the part of generations of women for their exclusion from intellectual and spiritual Jewish life. You men have the legend of the thirty-six Just Men? We have the tale of the seven Hovrodnikim. You have the struggle to win back Zion? We have the journey to Kiryat Sefer. But I, who have no need of this compensation? Why should I believe my grandmother knew a secret everyone else has forgotten?"

Jacob was sitting in front of the small woodburning stove, chipping away at the oak logs to make kindling for her while they talked. Whistling between his teeth, without looking at her, he tied the thin, surprisingly regular pieces of wood together with a bit of wire. "Why should you believe in the old lady?" She was stomping around the room behind him. "You make me impatient, Rae. You talk sometimes . . . what should I say? As if you came to all these questions for the first time yesterday."

"Today, yesterday, what does it matter?" She loved to imitate him but he never noticed and would only look up with a puzzled expression when she stood there grinning. That made her more seriously go on with it and now she said, with a fair amount of exasperation: "I'm no closer, am I? Not one bit closer really to an answer today than I was when I left for New York ten years ago."

"And how could you be closer with this life you have been living? You imagine the answer to questions of this kind will be found in reading, or for that matter, in writing a book? These answers that you need will be found only by living the question . . . at risk, Rae, at risk. This little mind you are carrying around at the top of your head, it cannot figure out mysteries. If it could, they would not be mysteries. To solve these puzzles your grandmother left to you, you must figure out first of all when to stop thinking. Yes, I'm telling you, Rae. Better you should go out and pick up a leaf off the ground or hold a snowflake in your hand than to stand here at the window trying to solve these questions as if they were chess problems. From the leaf and the snowflake you would learn at least something worth knowing."

"You want to know why I moved to New York, Jacob Paltiel? It was to get myself away from people like you. You think anyone there would sit up all night speculating about what exactly it takes to believe in the possibility of traveling to a city that vanished, how long ago now?"

"Beware, Rae," he said lightly, drawing up his knees against his chest and wrapping his arms around them. They were both sitting by that time on the floor, leaning against the canopied bed, plucking lint out of the rug and making small piles which inevitably in a rash or exuberant moment would be scattered back across the floor. "Beware you do not commit this old mistake of taking too literally . . ."

"Oh, if it were only a question of symbol and metaphor . . ."

"I am thinking," he went on, doggedly, "of the mistake some people make trying to keep themselves one remove from the hazard of living. You want to know how to travel to Kiryat Sefer? You don't figure that out sitting in the guest room here. You pick up the traveling bag, you stick a few clothes inside it, and off you go . . ."

"Easy for you to talk . . ."

"Yes, that is true. The talk is easy . . ."

"Tell me, Jacob, tell me what it is, Jacob." She was referring to a conversation that started up and then got broken off between them almost every time he came to visit. "What is it you don't ever quite say to me?" His eyes at such moments would take on an expression of startled yearning but he would manage each time to keep the conversation off himself. They would sit quietly and then she (as he had predicted) would begin to pick away at the inevitable questions.

She closed her eyes; it seemed to her that she was no longer the Rae Shadmi she had always been. It seemed to her that she was being hollowed out and violently uprooted from herself, so that something, or someone else could grow up in the place where she had been. How else can one describe it?

Night came, Jacob came tramping up the stairs, carrying a pot of tea, two cups, a plate of sugar cookies twisted in the shape of bows. He found her standing in the darkened room and he bustled about, without talking, to lay the fire, pull down the shades, light the kerosene lamps (there was electricity up there but Maya had never put in electric lights). Then he came to stand next to her, his arm around her shoulders. "So, talk," he said, "what is it this time you've worried to death during my absence?"

"We never had a chance." She said it in that way she had. Abruptly, in the middle of a thought, as if all day they had been talking together. "Did you ever ask yourself why Maya married Lev? Why precisely that bulky, ponderous, pedantic bore? He made a lot of money adding and subtracting long columns of financial figures for far wealthier men; he bought her an expensive house in Pacific Heights and bored us all to feverish distraction with his endless calculations of the odds for and against Israel's survival. The only unpredictable thing about him, if you want to know, was the way he died. But even that, who knows? Maybe he went off to war the way some men do because what was happening in his own family was even more appalling? We look at Maya today and we say, how could it happen? That wild, beautiful girl, reduced to this? But sometimes I wonder, Jacob. I stand here at the window, I look down into the street, and I have to wonder. Wasn't Maya always a little bit odd? A bit too temperamental, too quick to take offense and fly off into a tantrum? Or take Naamah's shyness. What does she have to be so shy about? Or my . . . call it my perpetual retreat from what I am feeling. Is it just that my parents died when I was a child? Or is it rather that if once I opened myself to what I feel . . . You were there, weren't you? You saw what happened to me the day the old woman died. You want me to step right out and snatch up the work she left unfinished? But what precisely is this work? A question of making the Old World fit somehow in our lives now? She brought the story of the Flame Bearers to America. Good, why not? I can see the value of an old story. But the rest of it . . . all these mysteries and secrets, who needs them, Jacob? Who asked her to drag all that baggage with her from the Old World?"

"Rae, to speak such nonsense! Your grandmother did not come here at the bidding of the Old World. The Old World has no need to graft itself onto the New. It is we, I assure you, who need what we left back there. Why do you make me tell you what already you know? If really you have forgotten, if to this degree you no longer know the head from the tail, go back to New York, find someone to marry, it won't be hard for you. Close yourself up in this normal life you stand here and pine for and forget all this. What's stopping you?"

"As to what's stopping me, Jacob." She had turned to look at him, angrily. "Did I say I wanted a normal life? I said I'd never been able to so much as want it. She made freaks of us, we fit neither in the Old World or in the New. And I, who have acquired at least a little protective coloration, so that I can pass for a perfectly ordinary assimilated Jew, I should give it all up now and figure out some way to . . . to . . . why are you hammering at me like this, Jacob? I'd be furious at you if I didn't think you were talking as much to yourself as to me. What's going on in there?" she said with a quick pounce forward, to tap her hand against his chest.

"And what, for that matter," he answered, because he was as much as she a master of evasion, "what happened to you since the old lady's death that you are not telling? You, Rae, crying out like this because you have a destiny? For this reason you are thumping on your breast and wailing? No, I won't believe it."

Hours that pass can move fast or slowly, depending upon one's mood. But events that take place out of time, in some other dimension that has its own style, continue to occur long after the immediate sensation of them has vanished. Squeezing the key violently in her fist, Rae leaned against the french door. Yes, that's what it came to finally, day after day. And then she lived again through that event which could not have happened and which had left behind this small silver key that had been worn around the neck of Rocha Castel hundreds of years before in Spain.

She could see the family in Naamah's living room, at the door. She saw exactly how the old ladies had been standing, Frau Altdorf a little apart from the others. Jacob, holding Naamah's hand, was carrying Brucha on his shoulders. Maya was keeping her distance from Ruth; she had placed herself behind Rubin Spaeght and was peering out at Rae with a wrathful expression. Michael, who had grown several inches during the last year, was shifting about nervously, as if he could not get used to his awkwardness. He was waiting for his mother to blow out the candle. But when Naamah hesitated, looking over at Rae with a sudden, quick turn of her head, Michael had bent forward and breathed on the candle, which flickered but did not go out. And then Rae had come forward a few steps to accept the farewell greeting from Frau Altdorf. This was the part she went over again and again. She had been standing only a few feet away from her. Frau Altdorf had already reached up and was holding out her hand. And then the stranger had been there, the old lady with her steel-rimmed spectacles and her gold-tipped cane. She had been there, with all the stubborn immediacy of actual encounter. It had been neither a vision or a transportation. It had happened, it had taken place. How could she doubt it? She was holding the key in her hand.

But that key. Once, when she woke from a restless sleep the key was burning her hand. She leaped out of bed in alarm, caught up in the old nightmares of her childhood—her mother running down the street, her hair flaming, reaching out with burning arms to embrace her. But most of the time the key lay dormant. It was a simple key, rather crudely made and no larger than her little finger. Sometimes, when she turned it over beneath her lamp, it was possible to decipher the initials F. T. scratched lightly into its surface.

At other times, she had noticed a rough line drawing of a female figure with large breasts, huge, rounded abdomen, and full thighs. But this, too, was not always apparent. She turned the key in her hand, she closed her fist over it, she put it on a chain and wore it sometimes around her neck. She wondered what would happen to it if she tried to throw it away and give it back to the void from which it had come. And meanwhile, she told no one about it. Not a word to Naamah, who stopped by occasionally after school to bring something to eat and a word of greeting. Nothing to Jacob, who came to visit her at night. It was a well-used key, badly tarnished. When she slept she held it in her fist, beneath the pillow, half hoping it would disappear by the time she woke. But in the morning, waking suddenly, fully awake before it was light, she grasped for the key, alarmed that it might have taken itself off again, before she had forced it to explain its existence.

"You make it all sound so easy," she said to Jacob on one of their long walks after midnight arm in arm through Maya's neighborhood. "Just suppose, purely for the sake of argument, it could happen that in a person of our time, strange, atavistic powers suddenly emerged. Think how I'd feel if I mumbled a few strange words, put out my hand to light a candle and it burst into flame. You don't think I'd be terrified and want to run away from what had just happened? A power I couldn't name or control and which therefore would necessarily be in control of me? This mind we have, with the ego riding so proud and triumphant, you think it will give in just like that, fall down on its knees and with open arms welcome these archaic forces?"

"This, Rae," he said, "is how you should talk. This is the issue, finally. You have been born to very great powers you do not understand. This is terrifying, I know that . . ."

It was a cold night; Rae had put on one of Lev's expensive fur-lined jackets but she was shivering anyway and kept tying her wool scarf closer around her neck. It had been raining, they were tramping about through puddles of water and oil slick, dark-hued purple rainbows floating beneath the lights. It was one of those San Francisco nights; you might as well be out at sea, she thought, feeling the tug of the mist and the foghorns and those steep hills like a storm wave mounting with that same sharp cleavage of vision. "And you?" she said to him; they had stopped at the corner; the narrow, grass-grown steps plunged down into the bay with its arched chain of amber lights stretched out over blackness, "what were you born to that you are running from?"

"What I was born to . . . ? You think you've guessed my big secret? But that is I assure you, Rae, a purely personal concern which one day, why not? I will discuss with you. But it is not the same problem as for you. You want to make this whole question of what you should and should not do as successor purely a personal matter. But for the whole culture I tell you it is a question of powers returning, not only in you or in the Shadmi family, but everywhere now in the world and to all kinds of people. If you look around you will see it is not only these friends of yours in Berkeley at whom always you are mocking, who discover old ways to put down plants into the ground or to reach from one mind into another. You Shadmis have hundreds, maybe thousands of years of handing down the knowledge of these so-called mysteries. That is why you are important. And for you, Rae, the question is most of all important, because it is you who are meant to find out the meeting place of the old and the new. If this feels to you, inside yourself, a disintegration, so how else could it be? What is happening in you is happening also in our whole age. We, too, we begin to disintegrate, we have taken these great accomplishments of science and reason as far as they can go. Now we must turn around again and dig up what science and reason have buried. How can you not know these things? You, who sat at the old lady's feet when you were a child still? We Lubavitchers, we have behind us in the figure of the Baal Shem Tov a tradition like yours, with rabbinical courts handing down successions from father to son, telling old stories, going out among the people, preaching and working miracles. The stories, some of them, and the teachings we brought to the New World, but the miracles we couldn't bring. This is why your grandmother is significant, Rae. She came here with not only the old stories of miracles, but with the miracles themselves. The Baal Shem, our founder, once climbed up on a mountain. You know this story? So deep in prayer he was walking along that he didn't notice he stepped off the mountain. But right away, what happened? Right away, another mountain moved itself over and came to stand next to the mountain where he was walking. So we say, this is a miracle of faith, a legendary tale, not to be taken literally. Yet, how are we so sure? How, I ask you? Have we gone up there, in this ecstasy of prayer, to walk off the edge of a mountain?"

She wanted to say: "Take me in your arms, Jacob; now finally, do it, do it." What she did say was this: "The old woman, Jacob . . ." Her voice was very rich and dark. "She should have made you her successor."

Yet, what he said was true (although she would never have admitted it to him); if she was being hollowed out and stripped down and torn apart, these acts of disintegration were not merely destructive. In the mornings, waking before dawn, she would sense an inherent order to her life, as if she were living through the last days of the person she had been and would shortly arise, significantly altered. These intimations were always connected to the little key. If she lost track of it for a moment, forgetting to put her hand into her pocket or to reach, repeatedly, for the chain around her neck, she would feel an acute alarm. She remembered, at those times, other occurrences she had slighted in the past, rushing into explanations that no longer served to keep the fundamental mystery of it all at bay. Once, for instance, when she had been working in the stacks, taking down old books of biblical scholarship and thumbing through them, a page had fluttered to the floor. Picking it up nonchalantly, she had realized that it could not have come from the book she'd been studying—a tortuously argued German tome of the early nineteenth century. It was a piece of ancient parchment, singed at the edges, the page itself blackened heavily, as if it had been snatched, in the last instant, from a fire. Even then, she had remembered the old lady's story of Baron

Guzman's library, with its rare collection of manuscripts, some of them rescued from an auto-da-fé in Spain. She had picked up the page, looked it over curiously, and placed it back in the book with a light shrug of her shoulders. That had been her typical stance in those days, when confronted with anything that challenged her sense of what was possible.

Another time, when she had been walking about through the bazaar in Algiers, a fruit seller, giving her change for a large bill, had presented her with a fistful of coins insisting with gestures and some incomprehensible words that she count them over. Well, why not? Rae studied the coins; she never had been much good with foreign currency and she really couldn't tell if the woman had cheated her or not. Nevertheless, she nodded back and winked vigorously to indicate her good will and the woman, turning finally to another customer, seemed relieved.

It was not until some time later, emptying her pockets in the little hotel room with its tiled floor, that Rae had noticed an ancient coin. Its edges were bent, its markings nearly effaced, and she had kept it carefully for a time in her pocket, taking it out occasionally to pore over its imprint. Then she had lost track of it. But it seemed to her now that it should have astonished her. It had been marked with Ugaritic words and with that blurred, heavy female figure that was scratched on the key and marked on the old lady's traveling bag and crudely drawn on the singed page from the library. If she had dared she might have wondered if she were holding in her hand a coin from Kiryat Sefer. But she had not dared.

Rae placed the key on her desk. Had it come to remind her that the rational order of things was simply inadequate to account for the world? Sometimes, when she touched the key it burned cold to her hand and brought back a time when she had listened with simple belief to the old lady's stories. If, in those days, a knock had sounded at the door and she had gone to open it and a woman had placed this key in her hand, she would have accepted it without question, knowing perfectly well that it had come to her from Rocha Castel.

There were times, particularly in the late afternoon, when it seemed to her that the key was humming and buzzing; if she put it to her ear there was a just perceptible sense of a song shouted across great distance; it was a haunting, siren call, as of children laughing and calling back and forth to one another in the twilight, and she would feel a mounting rapture of longing, as if she were about to reach out and grasp the edge of great secrets.

And then, one day, the enchantment broke, all of itself. Who can say why? She was walking down the stairs, softly, because it was early and Maya, she thought, was probably not awake; she heard the sound of a voice in the street, calling out to someone not to forget something he had almost forgotten; Rae stopped, taking a deep breath, with a feeling that she had not breathed in all those days since the Havdalah ceremony had come to an end. Time moved again and she moved in it, making coffee, poaching an egg, standing by the toaster, watching Maya come into the room and sit down heavily at the table, rubbing her eyes. She had expected relief, but she had found instead the sense that she had failed. The key the stranger had placed in her hand had given her an immense tug out of the circumscribed rational world in which she had always, since she was a young girl, wished to maintain herself. But it had not brought her out into that mythical sphere where Frau Altdorf and the other old women lived.

She sat down at the table next to Maya and pushed the plate of toast toward her. Maya pushed it back. "Shall I cut it into little fingers?" she asked, having just remembered the way Maya, as a little girl, liked to eat her breakfast. Her cousin smiled at her. It was an enchanting smile, heartbreaking in its acknowledgment that here, too, time had no power to keep childhood locked in that closed box in which the past should remain. "I want strawberry jam," Maya said, in the proud voice of a little girl who has just learned how to command the world through speech. "Please, may I?" she added, twisting Rae's heart. "And orange juice and a soft egg?"

Then, there came nausea; in the days that followed, during which she took care of Maya and the house, forcing herself to fix her attention on routine details, she was visited by a sense of dislocation so extreme she imagined at times a person would be able to die from it. The roots of life's meaning run deep, she knew. But the roots of her life's coherence had just been trampled. She was no longer the woman who could take pleasure in a conversation that lasted until morning. Jacob came by to visit her late at night. What did it matter? He said things that made sense, that moved and excited her while he talked and helped her to move out of the inertia and immobility. But when he fell silent again the nausea rose and she knew (or was it rather that she insisted?) . . . the words brought no comfort.

"Jacob, Jacob," she cried out to him one night in mock despair, "if I didn't know better I'd think you'd lost your head and not only your heart to the Shadmi family."

He smiled and wagged his finger at her but he got the impression, in that quick way of his, that their late night conversations were coming to an end. "You know me, Rae," he said, more than half wishing he'd finally managed to tell her what was on his mind, "in me, the heart lives in the head. And therefore, forgive me, unlike you, I'm able to see with that other eye of the Flame Bearers. What do I see with this extra eye? I'll tell you. I see a woman trying to pretend she has not changed. A woman running still from the truth of her life. And why? Because, maybe, she is too stubborn to admit that years ago, when she went away from home, she gave up everything that could mean the most to her?"

"I don't know what to make of it, Jacob," Rae said, with that wonderful capacity to leave unanswered the challenges he threw at her. "All of a sudden you and Michael and even our good old Rubin Spaeght are invited to know all the great mysteries. You don't have to tell me. I can tell. Naamah's let you into the secret. You know all about Kiryat Sefer. You know all about Rebekah and that work of hers, digging up the ruins of the old city. Maybe you even know how to get back to that sacred city of ours, which cannot be reached by crossing an actual ocean or stepping on to a literal plane? I can just imagine you and Rubin talking and gossiping. He's very busy with it all. He comes by, he talks to me for hours, trying to make sense of the family stories. He's a sweet man, would I deny it? When he puts on that little knit sailor cap and lets his curls fall over his ears I'm almost tempted to run off to sea with him myself. But really, Jacob. Don't you find it a bit silly? Rubin Spaeght, getting involved with these women's mysteries? You've been hanging around the Shadmis for a long time. You, Jacob Isaac Paltiel. And even you can't quite figure us out."

But it was no use, she could not keep it away. It would come over her even before Jacob left, taking her arm as they stood at the door looking out into the empty street where the world's good citizens were at their sleep. Say what she would, she no longer could believe in the words she spoke. She knew she would go back to her room, lie on her bed and wallow in a confusion that could no longer altogether keep at bay the knowledge that somehow, beyond the nausea and dislocation, something momentous was stirring and building and shaping.

19

R *a e* was sitting on Maya's bed. It was late, the curtains were drawn, the night was cold. A fire was burning in the white-brick fireplace and Maya was snuggled up against Rae, sucking her thumb. Rae was reading to her from an illustrated book of Russian fairy tales. It was a dog-eared volume, which had been handed down from Hillel to Ruth and had now arrived at its most unexpected destination— having become the bedtime companion of a mother whose thirteen-year-old child was now, in almost every sense of the word, far older than she was. Ruth had gone to live with Naamah and Jacob.

The phone rang. Rae picked it up, grimacing at Maya and rolling her eyes. Someone who had been told by someone else that Rae was back in the Bay Area. "I am?" Rae said, winking at Maya, who giggled with delight. "I suppose that's how it might seem to someone else. As for me," she went on, not even caring what her friend might make of it, "if here is here, and I exist at all, I suppose I'd have to admit I have come home again."

Then there were other calls from people with whom she had been active in the student struggle during the sixties. "Well, why not?" she asked Maya, who was already beginning to scowl with jealousy. But Rae, who had learned how to handle her, made a sweeping bow. "I shall go for a visit, if you will permit me."

Maya perceived no irony. "Don't go, Rae," she said, snuggling up to her as she stood next to the bed. "Stay here with me. If you don't, you know what will happen . . ."

During the last few days Maya had become very mysterious. Now, too, she winked at Rae and put a finger to her lips. But when Rae came over and sat down again for a long talk Maya fell silent, shook her head with a gesture of infinite sorrow, and sighed deeply. "They don't want me to let you know yet," she said in a resigned voice.

Maya had always been given to self-dramatization.

"Tell me a story," she said, throwing her arms around Rae's neck. She tugged at Rae and pulled her down against the pillow. But then she drew up her shoulders and put her hands over her ears to drown out Rae's voice.

During the next few weeks Rubin Spaeght dropped by regularly. He assured Rae no harm would be done to Maya by keeping her at home. His little treatment center was not yet ready to receive "guests." Money had been raised, a building had been purchased, renovations were under way. But Rubin was still training his staff, working nights and weekends with a zeal Rae admired in him and would not have expected.

"For you," he said, one night when she walked him out to his car, "it is a question of being there, just being there for Maya. Of course, if you're like everyone else you'll want to heal her." Rubin raised his eyebrows significantly. "But that's not in your hands. The best you can do is to do nothing. And that always proves, doesn't it, the hardest accomplishment?"

And for you, Rae didn't say, the hardest accomplishment—that surely would be to take yourself a bit less seriously?

Rubin had certain habits Rae for the life of her could not stand. The way, for instance, he held his hands when he spoke, palms pressed together in front of his lips as if he were a pious choirboy from a sentimental Victorian etching. Worse yet, he came right up to her and stood much too close and took her by the elbow whenever he had something important to say, as if to make certain he'd fastened upon her undivided attention. He did both these things while they were standing next to his car. He couldn't seem to meet her eyes. Several times he glanced back over his shoulder at the window of Maya's room. Finally, he put his hands in his pockets, jingled his coins, and couldn't manage to stop talking.

"You're making me nervous, Rubin." Rae always spoke to him in a tone of ironic banter, taking full advantage of their childhood friendship. "I get the impression you're either going to tell me something you think I don't want to hear or are feverishly debating whether or not to kiss me . . ."

"I'm in no conflict about that," Rubin joked back. "I've been wanting to kiss you for over twenty years now."

"Confession time, is it? That's what's making you so jumpy? It was the less beautiful cousin you were always secretly in love with when you used to follow us home from school?"

"The less beautiful . . . ?" He seemed genuinely puzzled. "That's what you think? I don't know. Maybe you are. But I certainly never thought so . . ."

Careful, Rae, she cautioned herself. Don't fall for it. And then she noticed again how he was standing too close to her, gripping her elbow.

"Seriously, Rae," he said, rocking forward on the balls of his feet. "I don't want you to think. I mean, the reason I stop in to visit Maya. It's not because . . ."

"Not because you're in love with her younger cousin?" Rae had started to laugh. "Don't worry, Rubin, I didn't think you were in love with me."

"I can't keep up with you, Rae," he said. "You're looking at me with such a fierce glare someone would think I had insulted you. But you don't even know what I wanted to say . . ."

"Tell me."

"I didn't want you to think I was coming to visit Maya because her mother had given money to my center. That's what I wanted you to know."

"How can you be so sure?" Rae's voice had lost its sardonic tone. "Which one of us is ever that self-knowing?"

"You've thought, all these weeks, that's why . . . ? You imagined that of me? And that's the reason you don't take me seriously? Do you realize, Rae, this is the first time you've spoken to me without . . ."

She put her hand on his arm. She was staring at him with an expression she herself would not have been able to decipher.

"Rubin," she said, "you were the most beautiful little boy." He looked at her closely but she was not joking now. "There was something about you. What is the word? You were a chivalrous child. You really were. But you can't come to us now and ask us to believe in you as our own private knight in shining armor. This is the real world, my friend. Terribly, terribly real . . ."

Nevertheless, she felt a distant hope. The faint possibility that he was there out of friendship and from some largeness of spirit that had drawn him to Maya's suffering because he believed in his own capacity to heal it. All this was in her eyes. The fear of being disappointed. The dread of being naïve. A terror of falling for someone you would be tempted to trust in such a fundamental way you might someday, in deepest trouble, risk turning to him.

"I refused the money. That's what I wanted you to know . . ."

"I don't want to believe in you, Rubin."

But the time came when she had no choice. One day Maya screamed, threw things, and grew wild without any provocation. Rae could not quiet her down. It took Rubin, whom Maya seemed to trust even more than she trusted Rae. And then there was the day Ruth tried to come home for a visit. Maya hollered as her daughter came running up the stairs: "Who's that?" she said, with a note of genuine outrage. "Doesn't she know she hasn't happened?"

Later, making notes for Rubin, Rae realized that Hillel had not happened, and that Lev also had not happened and that Aunt Sonia's remarriage had not happened. Maya confided in her one night when she came softly into Rae's room, that she could tell ahead the entire story of their life. And then she described what "would happen" except that she was not going to let anyone turn the page. It was, Rae realized, one of those "thought dislocations" Rubin had told them to look out for. But the truth was, Maya used to say precisely this kind of thing when they were girls together and Rae was spending a night at Maya's house, before they had both moved in with their grandmother. Then, too, she would insist that what would happen later in their life was like a story in a book, already written, but open to her influence. She would shake Rae by the shoulder in that way she had, insisting on this as if she really believed in it and didn't want Rae to smile. But Rae had kept smiling, because she didn't want to admit that Maya believed "that nonsense." And now, too, when Maya crept into bed with her as if she were still a girl of six or seven, closing her eyes and whispering, Rae in the darkness would smile to herself for an instant before she made herself notice what Maya was actually saying.

"You see, Rae? You see?" she would whisper, all curled up next to Rae in a long flannel nightgown with her doll Hadassah, "this is how you do it. You hold your breath, you count forward until you reach the year in which it would happen, and then if you don't like it you blow it out." She would make a peculiar puffing noise with a spray of spit and then she would clap her hands. "So, you see? Already gone. Now, all you have to do is write it over."

Rae said nothing when Maya talked like that; she would have believed happily that her silence was taken by Maya as an unspoken disagreement. But she knew that Maya took it instead as assent. And the doll was the other indication, Rae had told Rubin, that Maya had taken up "residence in the past." It was the doll she had been given for Purim, by one of their grandmother's old cronies a month or two before Aunt Sonia had left for Europe. It was made from a stuffed stocking, but it wore a beautiful dress of antique lace, tiny embroidered silk shoes, and a red satin cap. Maya had always kept it in a glass case, a "superb example of accomplished folk art," as she told Lev. But it was clear to Rae that the doll had always been precious to her, even in the years when she repudiated every other form of attachment to their grandmother.

Sometime during the last weeks Maya had taken Hadassah out of her case and wrapped her up in a scrap of blanket. She had taken a shoe box, filled it with scraps of cloth, covered it in tin foil, and made a cradle for Hadassah. Every morning as soon as it was light, she carried the doll and the cradle into Rae's room. Sometimes she sat with Hadassah by the window, whispering and chattering with her. When Rae kept her eyes closed, and tried to go back to sleep, Maya would walk on tiptoe, with her finger to her lips; she would sit down close to Rae on the edge of the bed, or curl up against her sucking her thumb and crooning softly to Hadassah.

And yet, in spite of Maya's steady withdrawal from the world the rest of them shared, none of them were seriously alarmed for her. Rubin gave them a long lecture on Maya's condition. They were gathered at the table in the kitchen, Maya was asleep upstairs. Ruth was there, looking pale and troubled, hanging on Rubin's every word. "It could be," he said, smiling too much and nodding his head at the end of every sentence, "that we are observing in her a regression that has as its hidden aim a healing intention. It's not so difficult to understand. She goes back into her childhood in order to come to terms with something that could not be resolved when she was a child. If we can fight down our own terror, if we can leave her to it, very possibly she'll come out of it again . . ."

"This is, of course, the view of mental illness that has inspired my new treatment center . . ." Rae echoed beneath her breath. But she knew there was no reason to be mocking this warm-hearted, impulsive man. He had already, in countless ways, proved himself a friend. Was it his fault he was far too pretty to be easily trusted, with eyes of an Easter-egg blue so sincere you immediately began to suspect him of who knows what duplicity?

He was a good man, she had no doubt of that. Jacob admired him, Naamah was grateful for his help. Ruth clung to his arm whenever he stopped in to visit. Michael invited him to sit in with his band. Rae told herself not to notice his little mannerisms. Cut it out, she warned herself, what he says makes sense and you know it. What difference does it make if he smiles too much?

She leaned forward and put her elbows on the table to have a good look at him. Rubin had reached the end of his sermon. He had taken off his jacket and rolled up his shirt sleeves; his face was flushed, he had stopped smiling. She liked him like that, his authority clearly evident, something very much like ambition in his eyes. He was assuring them that Maya was at the early stages of something that should be watched, "but without too exact or intrusive a vigilance." And then he ruined it all—tipped back his chair, put his hands behind his head, and looked over at Rae for approval.

Nevertheless, she was inclined to agree with him. There was a quality of self-indulgence in everything Maya did, a perceptible willfulness. That didn't keep them from questioning themselves, of course; it didn't mean they took her at all lightly. The situation seemed to call for a generous good will toward her, as Rubin suggested—a question of taking her "just seriously enough, without either undue worry on the one hand or exasperation on the other."

But for Rae there was no question of exasperation. To take care of Maya, snuggling with her in bed, preparing meals for her, listening to her babble at night, reading her a bedtime story, provided for Rae, who increasingly was in need of distraction, a welcome respite from the anticlimax with which she was living. If weeks before she had thought that she was on the edge of some momentous transformation, all that seemed now to have fled. If she had been confused before, and roaring with a sense that hidden deep within her despair there was a "certain growing something," now she could only look back with a violated credulity, against which even despair seemed a wholesome state.

The phone calls from Berkeley were a relief. So, too, was the opportunity for Rae to launch herself into the world. Kissing Maya good-bye, making sure someone was there to keep an eye on her, Rae drove across the bay to visit her old friends. She threw herself into her visits with a hectic exuberance, pretending to herself that she was, in this way perhaps, answering her "call." Who knows? she said to herself, with that lacerating irony. The way to Kiryat Sefer may have strange paths. Perhaps I'm to get there by slipping back into my past the way Maya is doing?

She talked to her friends about her grandmother's death. But what could she tell them about the silver key she was wearing around her neck? For a few days after the "enchantment" broke, the little key had been very busy. "Working overtime are you?" Rae would say to it, when she walked back into her room and found it humming and buzzing. She had given it a good shake at the end of its chain. "Watch yourself," she'd told it, "you're here on good behavior and don't you forget it." Since then it had lapsed into a state of dormancy, giving off shrill little hoots now and again, as desolate in their own way as a train whistle at night.

And what, for that matter, could she say about this last year of "signs and portents," during which she had been called back into the sect? Her friends knew her at a time when all that had been far away, in a childhood to which, on Sabbath evenings, she paid a reluctant and rebellious tribute. She had never spoken to them about her work in the school. She had never taken them home to meet the old woman. And now, because of this omission, her grandmother's death might seem to her friends a significant sentimental occurrence—but never an event of such ambiguous meaning she would never be able to measure its full significance.

And so, after a few weeks of dutiful nostalgia, she had stopped calling and returning their calls. On one of her last trips to the East Bay, she had driven over to the eucalyptus park in the Berkeley Hills, where she and a poet-boyfriend used to spend occasional afternoons ten years before, smoking banana peels in a little clearing above the lake, arguing about whether they were (as he insisted) high on passion, or whether the dappled brown skins were really as potent as Rae claimed.

It was early morning, the park not yet officially open. She hid her clothes under the bushes and made her way quietly into the lake, keeping an eye out for the helicopters that were frequently there, everyone assured her, to swoop down on naked trespassers and arrest them for indecent exposure. The water was cold and still, unrippled by the breeze overhead, up in the treetops. And it had been, in that sharp morning chill, a rare half-hour.

She was a strong swimmer, completely at home in the lake. A few yards ahead of her, in whichever direction she looked, a mist was rising from the water. She passed an old bridge, which arched over a still pond next to the lake and beneath which the water passed heavily, through dense reeds. She was swimming along the shore, close to the reeds, from which red-winged blackbirds would suddenly arise, dash out over the water, and again return, to perch quietly on the lower branches of a dead tree as she swam by. From the farther shore, which was heavily wooded, there came the sound of a dense warbling, the notes rising into a peculiar trill, which made her heart race.

She looked back at the shore from which she had come. The hills were just emerging from the mist, the branches and the tips of the highest trees nearly invisible. She felt the racing of her heart, the hammering of her blood in her temples, the sudden sharpening of her senses that had, during the last year, made her fear that she was breaking down. But this time there was no terror. The warbling, the mist, the cold water in which she was submerged, the old bridge and the quick shimmer of the black red wing, seemed to be speaking to her in a language she had once known fluently. Then, some high tension, which seemed to have been there for most of her life, suddenly resolved itself, as though a rubber band had finally snapped after years of being stretched to the breaking point. Something seemed to be falling, dropping soundlessly upon a place of great sensitivity, deep within her. She plunged down into the water and leaped back out of it, shaking her head. Then she swam back. She swam back along the shore of that pine forest of Chernik. She was there, the pine resin burned in her nostrils. The wild swans passed over her head, a feather fell in the water. And then she heard it, hidden away through mud and mist and shadow. The grouse beating out its message in the woods.

There was a wild joy. She wanted to shout with it, to hear its rapture strike back from the hills and rebound into the water, where all separation between her and the past had just come tumbling down. It was a moment only. She stepped out of the lake, dressed quickly, and walked away without looking back.

"I knew it, I always knew it. But I didn't want to know." That was it, then? The sharp rearrangement of inner attitude that would make it possible to take a next step? With a still and absolute clarity, she knew that for one moment she had moved out of her own life to enter the world of her grandmother's stories.

Rae was talking at the top of her voice, waving her arms, taking long strides through the pine needles, past the gashed peeling of the eucalyptus bark she saw with a vividness that took her breath away, the long strands lifting and rattling against the trunk of the tree.

"She wanted us to reach out and pluck a leaf from a tree. It's so obvious, how could I have hidden it from myself? From a tree I tell you that probably had been cut down by the Nazis when they invaded the Ukraine. And we did it, one time we actually did it, sitting there on her old bear rug.

"She wanted us to plunge into the pond in the forest, she expected us to sit in the kitchen with Hannah Leah and Raisa, eating challah, listening to their stories. It is, it is possible after all."

Rae in that moment was utterly without self-awareness. She wanted to shriek and prance and wave her arms but she lowered her voice because she had been trained since childhood to guard the secret. "It's so preposterous," she whispered, stopping to spread out her arms, "it's so incredibly ridiculous, who could take it all in? You tell the story, you induce the trance, you get into the events of the story and then, then you travel further back. That's the key to it. Right out of history, that's the key, into legendary time, moving at will from one story to another, what difference does it make if one event happened in the realistic sense of things and the other happened in the story-teller's imagination? It is possible, it can be done. That absurd, incredible old woman expected it from us. And, who knows? If she'd had time to teach us . . . If the school hadn't burned down, if she hadn't been driven half mad by the loss of my mother . . . She would, I tell you. I tell you. She would have pulled it off."

20

M *a y a* held the doll Hadassah on her lap. She was very worried about the little creature, who seemed to be suffering from some terrible pain. "Eat," she coaxed, "it's better when you eat." But Hadassah wouldn't open her mouth. Maya looked over at Brucha. "You never know," she sighed. "You wait, you worry, what can you do?" It was the voice of a little girl imitating her elders.

She was still sitting there, in the window seat of her bedroom on the second floor, when Rae came in. Brucha jumped to her feet and rushed over to Rae. She had taken to stopping in on Sundays with the little handwritten Ugaritic grammar Naamah had given her on the last day of the Havdalah ceremony. She came for Rae but she devoted herself to Maya, understanding without being told what Maya needed from her. She would sit with her on the living-room floor in front of the small, lacquered Oriental table, set out broken pieces of cookies and nuts, pour tea into tiny cups, serve the doll Hadassah, and chatter with Maya in a peculiar language they made up, a curious combination of pig Latin and ungrammatical Yiddish they called "snee-snaw."

Usually, when Brucha visited them, Rae would work with her in the kitchen, patiently going over the little grammar book. If Maya came in, Rae would wave her over and make room on the chair next to her. And then the three of them would sit there, as Rae asked them questions and corrected their responses. They were peaceful times, Rae thought, and they passed too quickly. In them, for moments, she would wonder whether it was perhaps her destiny to become, as her mother before her, a simple teacher. She would look over at them, at

Maya who seemed not a day older than the five-year-old girl who sat across from them; at Brucha with her sharp little eyes and her quick grasp of the ancient language. She would feel a rush of love and devotion, as if she had come home truly at last and was finding the way to make her place there. But then something would happen to shatter the illusion. Maya, jealous that Brucha was so much better at grammar than she, would manage to knock a cup off the table. Brucha would scamper for a cloth and Maya would begin to thunder. "Turn the page. Turn the page. I hate this story."

Maya's bedroom on the second floor had been made from three smaller rooms. Most of the work on it had already been finished before Rae had left San Francisco. The ceilings had been torn out and the rafters exposed. A huge stained-glass window had been cut into the roof and even now, in the late morning, the room was cast into a soft shimmering glow.

"Why's your hair wet?" the little girl asked as Rae knelt down to give her a hug. "Were you swimming?" she said, wrinkling up her nose. "You smell just like a fish." She laughed, grabbing Rae's hand and pressing it against her cheek.

"Siou, siou," Maya murmured to Hadassah, from her perch in the window seat, "what's to cry? Maya will make the blind eye better."

Was it love, Rae wondered, this piercing and anguish on behalf of another person, to whom one would gladly give one's life if that would make the difference? She glanced at Maya, who was huddled over Hadassah with a worried frown, rocking her against her breast and crooning to her with a shrill, unpleasant moan.

"Listen, sweetie. I want to talk to Maya." Rae had put her hands on the child's waist. "Mama will be here to pick you up in two minutes. Yes? You don't mind? I'll stop in to see you after dinner."

"What time after dinner?"

At the door she tore herself away from Rae, climbed up on the banister, slid down shrieking at the top of her voice, and went to stand by the front window.

Maya had always filled her rooms with too many objects. In the past there had been a sense of underlying order but now the room, with its silver jewelry hanging from the walls, its modern drawing board and antique easels, the Oriental rugs, the bits of faded tapestry and scraps of rusting iron, displayed haphazardly here and there, gave the sense of a struggle already being lost between a highly static, formal order and this surging abundance that threatened to become chaos.

Rae took it all in. Maya sitting in the window seat in her yellow bathrobe, her shoulders hunched up, her eyes blinking rapidly as she attempted to meet Rae's gaze—a tiny, haunted creature cast adrift in a rising sea that might at any moment swallow her.

"She's lost, she's utterly lost . . ." Rae walked over to the small window on the other side of the room and the words, fragmenting in that way they had, came with her. Lost . . . utterly lost, utterly, utterly . . . She was filled with fury again, with all her old rage and resistance. How could they? How could they let her break through into the secret heart of the tradition when this, *this* is what they were doing to Maya?

Maya's room overlooked a small brick patio. There was a rock pool where water lilies used to grow, but the little garden, cluttered now and overgrown with native plants, looked dreary and desolate. It depressed Rae, who had come driving home fast with a totally unreasonable hope and confidence. She saw now; there could be no doubt of it any longer, something was guiding her, taking her along step by step. And maybe, if that indeed was happening with her, the same thing in some other way also might be happening for Maya?

Maya had come to stand next to her. She had recently figured out how you could rub a hole in the story. That's what she called it. You said the words over and over again. Then, through the words, you could see everything clearly. You held it steady in front of your eyes and pretty soon you were there. It was as easy as that. You had slipped through into the story and could talk to Hannah Leah yourself if you wanted to.

Now, she saw Hannah Leah winking at her. Hannah Leah was lifting up stones from the earth oven and carefully setting the green leaves aside, so that she could raise the kid onto a wooden spit. There, it was almost dark. That didn't bother Maya because she knew time was different when you were in a story. Hannah Leah was walking from tree to tree, lighting the little oil lamps that had been hung out for the celebration. She would step up to them, wave her hand with a peremptory gesture, and the lamps would kindle.

"Hach," Maya said to herself, "so that's how she does it." She could feel a funny kind of itching in her palms, as if something were crawling about underneath the skin. She wanted to scratch at it to make it go away but she knew she'd better just put up with it. That maybe is where the flame came from? Then, she started to laugh. That's how it was these days. She stayed there in her room with little Brucha and pretty soon, what do you know? She figured out things Rae also wanted to know and just couldn't!

Maya put her hand over her mouth. "Better not tell her, whatever you do!" Ever since Rae came home from New York Maya talked to herself. "You'll be sorry. She'll gobble it up and take it for herself. And then where will you be, my little duckling?"

But Maya wanted to tell Rae. She had always told Rae everything. And what good was it anyway if Rae didn't know that Maya knew? She nudged her cousin and glanced up at her with one of those significant expressions. You see, she seemed to be saying, this is the sort of thing that happens in my life now. But then she frowned. "Look at them," Maya said, pointing to the seven old women she was sure Rae could not see. "Those filthy old yids. Who told them to come and interrupt her?"

Rae, who was rarely shocked by anything she heard, turned to look at her. But before she could say a word Maya took her by the arm and whispered in a lower voice, cupping her hand over her mouth so that the old women wouldn't hear her. "You can't see them, can you?" she said. "The seven Hovrodnikim? Or Hannah Leah?"

She broke off, afraid she would say too much, and now she looked around her apprehensively, holding her head absolutely still while her eyes darted sharply up, down, to the right, to the left and then back, with their fixed stare, looking straight ahead of her.

Rae closed her eyes and shook her head. She counted backward from a thousand, very slowly. But it was no use. When she opened her eyes nothing had changed. Hannah Leah and the old women were in the garden. They were there, a few feet from the rock pool. Hannah Leah was striding about in a large circle. Rae could not hear what she was saying. But it was clear that an argument was taking place. The seven old ones looked tired and sad. Rae had the distinct impression she would only have to lean forward, open the window, walk out onto the chipping cast-iron spiral staircase, make her way down into the garden, and she would have stepped out into a place where her own grandmother was still a child. Or perhaps, not even born yet?

Then, Rae felt a great yearning. It was far stronger than the desire to throw herself on her knees before the old woman with white braids pinned up on her head. She thought it might drag her down into the past where the seven old ladies were waiting. She could feel the fresh, cool air. Hannah Leah a small girl still, running naked in the woods hooting and shouting. There she was, climbing up into the aspen and now she turned back to wrinkle up her little ugly snub-nosed face, the dappled light of the great tree falling on her.

It seemed to Rae that she was practically there without taking a step further. Small star-blue flowers were growing at her feet. There was that dense crushed smell of forest earth and, really, it was only her love for Maya that kept her back, pulling her in the other direction, as if Maya and the seven old ones were playing at tug of war with her.

"Rae," Maya said. She had drawn very close to whisper in Rae's ear: "You have . . . everything. Please, Rae? Leave me Hannah Leah?"

"Maya, believe me." Rae was in that instant so fully in the present she could hear Maya's heart beating. "I would never, ever take her from you."

Maya began to cackle. That was the only word for it. "You? You don't love me. You never did. You just wanted me to give up my claim. Always, every day of our lives you were trying to get me not to be the successor. You can't fool me. I know what you came home for. You need me, Rae. They won't talk to you. They never showed you how to get back into the story."

"Save her. Why can't you save her?" Rae wanted to call down to them, there in the cobbled street where they were walking in a sedate procession in the long, slanting light of a late afternoon. She wanted to run down past the picket fence and the carefully tended cottage gardens and take them by the shoulders. But she choked on the words the way she had as a young girl, fishing out the burned dough from the Sabbath fire.

Maya was no longer laughing. She had been rubbing her eyes, holding them open between her fingers, staring down violently into the garden. Now, with a haughty scowl, she said: "Rae, you'd better not take Naamah's side. She wants Aunt Elke to be your teacher. Don't do it, Rae," she urged, her voice so stripped suddenly to its naked urgency Rae felt as if she were groping about underwater for something that shimmered, slipped away, appeared again, was squarely there in her hands. And she had to be so careful then not to squeeze down too hard, crushing it, in an effort to hold on. To hold on? To hold Maya. To keep her, here on this side. Talking.

"Aunt Elke's started to turn yellow," Maya rushed on, her voice thin and shrill now. "You know why? Because inside her is your mother and father. I threw water on her when she tried to come for the feast of unleavened bread." She had taken Rae's arm, tugging at it convulsively. "I drove her away before you got back. I wanted to save you. You see? I wanted to save you. Elke will burn you down too. She smells terrible, Rae. Even Ruth hates her."

But then she realized that she had slipped up. Ruth hadn't happened yet. None of it had happened. She made an urgent, rubbing gesture, both hands stretched out in front of her face. "Blot it out, blot it out," she commanded and her eyes flashed with a really terrible power. She ripped a page into smaller and smaller scraps, muttering beneath her breath, "whispt, whispt," in a stunning mimicry of a tearing page. "We don't want that story, do we, Rae?" she asked confidingly. And then she wrinkled up her eyes and shook her head with the irresistible appeal of a lost, beseeching child.

Rae wanted to pick her up in her arms, carry her over to the bed, and rock her to sleep. She wanted to get on a plane and return to New York. She wanted to reach out and shake Maya until she came to her senses. She even wanted to drop down onto her knees at Maya's feet and beg her to be . . . what? To be well again! To be again her Maya.

Maya hunched over and began to rock herself, sobbing softly, her arms wrapped around her waist.

Why Maya? Why not me? Rae glared around her. But there was no one to answer her question. The garden was desolate, the pine woods behind the house in Chernik had vanished. For an instant she thought she might ball up her hands into fists and pound them against her temples. The way the old woman had done when the school had burned down and Esther, the favorite daughter, had been killed in the fire. Progress for me, entrapment for Maya? That is what she would have asked them if they had still been there, those seven old ones who held, she knew, the threads of their lives. For me, a way forward? For her . . . madness?

She said: "Why did Aunt Elke start the fire?"

Maya was staring at her. And now there appeared on her face a

look so grateful Rae saw that other Maya of extravagant beauty, so
briefly present in her damaged features. She remembered Maya standing with her hands on her hips that day the old man who sold oranges
came down the street, his rumpled pants and patched jacket telling
what there was to know about his life. He was shuffling along sucking
in breath and crying out: "Oranges. Oranges. Does anybody want to
buy my oranges?" No, it probably wasn't like that, not really; but that
is what she remembered. Maya running into the house and dashing
after him with a fistful of crumpled bills. The old man had set down
the two pails carefully on the pavement next to him; he had bent over,
rummaging through the fruit, to find his best orange. Rae remembered
the way Maya had looked then, the radiance of her, reaching out to
accept the fruit, her hair tied back anyhow because of the summer
heat. And Rae, trying absurdly to reach that other woman, said:
"Aunt Elke was jealous, was that it? She thought Bubbe loved Esther,
she loved my mother, better?"

The words shattered the fragile bond. Maya frowned at her and
pursed her lips accusingly. "Don't patronize me," she said. "Don't you
dare. Not in my own house. If you believed it, you wouldn't have come
back here. And especially not today," she added, dropping her voice
to a whisper and glancing nervously out the window.

Outside, in the little patio, Hannah Leah was talking to Raisa.
She was pacing about, her hands behind her back. But then she
turned abruptly and leaned forward with a menacing gesture toward
her mother. "It's bad," Maya said to Rae, leaning close to her as if she
had decided to let her into an important secret. "Raisa doesn't want
her anymore. She wants Sarah Rachel instead. But it's a mistake. It's
a mistake, Rae, you see? Hannah Leah's trying to convince her. If she
chooses Sarah Rachel you know what will happen?" She shook her
head violently back and forth, pressing her hands against her cheeks.
"You know, don't you? Aunt Elke will have to take it in hand. She'll
burn down everything."

Rae felt that she had just crossed over into a region where she
would be forever helpless. The usual comforts (love heals, devotion
matters, sincere effort will be rewarded) couldn't thrive in this high,
austere place where the facts of existence loomed up sheer and naked.
She felt cold and out of breath, as if she had climbed too fast and
couldn't adjust to the sudden change in altitude.

Maya had retreated a step or two, groping behind her for support. She refused to open her eyes, even when Rae reached out to touch her hand. "Wait, just you wait," she said, as if she were threatening her cousin with a terrible secret. But she remained silent and Rae saw her open her eyes and peek out at her quickly, with an utterly childish look that might have been comic if it were not so urgent.

"Well, what is it, Maya?" she said at last, exasperated by her own anguish. "I can't stand here all day waiting."

"I've seen some terrible things," Maya said, and Rae had the impression she was hearing something that had been gone over again and again although it was perhaps never really intended to be spoken.

"I've seen why Hillel died," Maya had whispered it, and Rae just managed to keep herself from drawing back violently. "I've understood about Lev. They all die young, you know. All the men. Jacob wasn't the first husband, so he's been spared. But look what happened to your father." Spittle had gathered in the corners of Maya's mouth. She wiped it away impatiently. "That fire was meant to kill him, not only your mother. That's the way *they* work. They drive Aunt Elke to do it. She sets fire to the school to burn down your mother. But they want her to do it so she can destroy the man. You see? You see?" she rushed on. "That's how it is. It goes all the way back," she insisted, with a stabbing gesture of her hand. "Right back to the earliest time. I've seen them coming with their scythes and knives. They walk in a long procession, in their dark robes, over the fields. And then they cut him, Rae, they cut down the Lord of the Grain, they hack him to pieces and bury him in the earth. Your mother knew this. She figured it out. Always it happens. All the men. You know why? Because they need the sacrifice. But your mother stayed loyal. She wouldn't run out and leave her husband. Rae, you've got to believe me. I've seen it . . ."

She had taken hold of Rae's shirt and was tugging at her. "Don't you see, Isarael," she cried out in a mocking voice, "we're cursed. Don't you see?" But then her face changed, her contempt visibly crumbling. "Listen to me," she said, with an urgency so great Rae felt herself pulled down into it. "That's why Aunt Elke went away to live with a husband. She knew better than to bring back a husband into this family. And my mother too. She figured it out. That's why she divorces every few years. Better to spare them. But she was too late to save my father. And I was too late," she gasped out, suddenly sobbing. "I didn't understand. I never should have let Lev go to the war. And then when Hillel got sick . . . when Hillel got sick, Rae . . . when my boy fell ill . . ."

She began to pace, her fingers pressed over her eyes, cutting a precise path past the oak easel and the bed, back and forth, through these thoughts that were, Rae saw, a dreadful snarl of guilt and loss and envy and sorrow, the whole terrible burden of it finding now, finally, this release.

And Rae, in the grip of a dread that was not all on Maya's behalf, kept herself still. She had seen her own possibilities pacing about there in Maya. It was from this she had always been running away.

"Don't let them get me," Maya was moaning, pressing her face into Rae's shoulder. "I can't fix Hannah Leah. I can't heal the blind eye." And then she dropped down to the floor on her knees.

"Help me," she whispered, throwing her arms over her head. "I'm lost, Rae. I'm lost, utterly . . ."

Rae reached down to draw her up. It seemed to her that she was trying to pull Maya back from the edge. She felt her feet slipping; the ground crumbled out from beneath them and she was, she knew, letting herself down into Maya's madness. She took Maya's hand in hers, noticing for the first time in years the silver ring with its obsidian stone. The ring Maya had worn since she was a child. A gift from their grandmother. Rae had an impulse to tear the ring from Maya's finger. She wanted to swallow it down. Yes; and with it the fate this ring had settled on Maya.

It was a mad idea, she knew it, but she could not drive it away. It clung to her, gathering up the shadows she had not faced before. From the time they were children the old woman had neglected Maya. As if their grandmother had known all along. Known? That Maya was intended for nothing more than madness?

Unspoken, it seemed to stand there in the room with them. Maya sacrificed . . . so that she herself, the little wrestler . . . would be set free from the curse.

"Maya, listen to me." Rae was talking fast. "There's a line you can't cross. Neither of us can cross it, believe me. It separates what we fear from what we believe. There *are* patterns in families. Traits, qualities, tendencies, even the tragedies. The same kind of illness and ambition and talents and visions. But a *curse*, Maya? That, too, is only an attempt at explanation. It involves more than we need commit ourselves to—even we, who have inherited grandmother's stories. Maya, are you listening to me? Don't turn away. There are, I assure you, much better explanations for Hannah Leah, for what happened to my mother and father. Even, Maya . . ." and Rae hesitated before she risked it: "Even for what is happening to you."

Maya had always loved Rae's clarity; she loved her cousin's conviction you could make sense of everything. And this time, too, Maya, pressing very close against her cousin, could see the difference between a family pattern and that shadowy other thing she'd been imagining. For an instant the wonderful difference hung there so clearly, like a handle you could reach out and grasp. But then, as she tried, forcing herself to see it Rae's way, the words shattered. The deception exposed itself.

"You're just trying to get me to give in," she wailed. "You want me to give up the inheritance. You want me to step back and let you be the successor. But Hannah Leah's come for me. For me, I tell you. She's chosen me."

"Maya," Rae cried out, "we've been set against each other all our lives. There have been too many secrets, too much mystery. They make a certain atmosphere, especially for children. And especially for the kind of sensitive children we were. But that's still different from what you imagine. Many things are possible. More than I ever believed. We are a family dedicated to some legendary mission that stands outside time and yet somehow within history. We're not like any family I've ever known. But does that mean we're cursed and condemned? Maya, are you listening to me? You're dearer to me than anything on earth. And this much I promise you. I'll figure it out. I'll make sense of it, somehow."

She was going too fast. She was battering at Maya. She could feel the words bouncing back at her from Maya's silence. Maya was shaking her head; it was an infinitely weary, despairing gesture. And now, for the first time, it no longer seemed theatrical.

But then, unexpectedly, Maya said: "I counted on you, Rae. All these years I was waiting for you to come home. I thought, surely Rae will have the answers?" It was that aching simplicity of hers. It made you believe, surely this lost woman could be saved, somehow?

Rae was trying to talk but there was a choking sensation in her throat. She reached for the chain around her neck and took the key in her hand. It was still and cold to her touch. "Withdrawn" she might almost have said. As if it did not choose to participate in what was now to happen.

"You know what this is?" she asked. But there was no need to ask. It was clear that from the first moment, Maya had known.

This time Rae did just the right thing. It seemed far too melodramatic, even as she was doing it, but not at all false. She put her hand to her heart. It was that typical gesture of Maya's. "Maya," she whispered, "I swear to you. We are free, each one of us, to choose our lives. Here," she said, breaking the chain with a single, hard tug. "Take it. I give it to you."

Maya put her hand to her mouth to hide her joy. She leaned way back on her heels, thrusting her body forward and rocking herself with delight. She said, eagerly, with a trusting whisper: "You're not afraid? You're not afraid what they will do?"

Rae, letting go of all control, shouted back at her: "Terrified," she cried, with an absurd glee, "of course, who wouldn't be? But now suddenly it seems . . . Maya, why is it so strange? It seems suddenly the most wonderful possibility that you and I could make our way back to Kiryat Sefer."

And that was all, it was all over. They were alone in Maya's room, Rae's hand close over her cousin's hand, enclosing the key.

"We'll do it our way," Rae said, "we'll make the claim we want to make. I'm not going anywhere unless you come with me."

21

"**Y**o u think there's no one else here to take care of things?" Jacob said. He had come over on his day off to take Rae's place with Maya so that Rae could get out of the house.

Maya hollered at him, "Tear out the page, strike the sentence." She banged about upstairs, protesting the fact that Rae was going out.

"Go, Rae," Jacob said, "take a walk, go to the lake, have a coffee in North Beach. I have an ounce or two of sense in my head also. Trust me," he insisted, taking her by the shoulders and giving her a light push out the door.

"I'll stop in to visit Brucha," she said when he shut the door in her face and opened the little grille to wave at her.

"Brucha? Now you go over all the time to take care of Brucha? You know what you're doing, Rae?" he said, keeping his voice low, but glaring at her with a serious expression. "Shall I tell you?"

He had opened the door, closed it carefully behind him, and was standing on the top step, shading his eyes against the afternoon sun.

"Do you know what you're becoming, Jacob? Shall I tell you?" she teased back, relieved and exasperated at the same time because she knew that sooner or later, before she raced down the steps and jumped into his car, she'd hear from him exactly what she'd been trying not to tell herself. "You know that little man who sits in the woodpile and pesters everyone? *Alter tate onshikenish? * That's who you are, Jacob Isaac Paltiel. *Old Father Nuisance.* The only male mythic figure that ever made his way into the Flame Bearer stories."

"You won't stop me like this, Rae. I'm going to say it and you're going to hear. If you think you're becoming Aunt Sonia, maybe you're

right. And you know why? For the same reason she became Aunt
Sonia. So that you don't have to take care of the real business that is
before you. Leave Brucha. Leave Maya. Leave them please to me.
What happened to you, there in the lake—this is a breakthrough. Go
already, find out what Naamah wants from you. This way we'll all get
a little bit of rest around here."

Rae drove over to the park. It was not so easy to get to Naamah,
even if she wanted to. Whenever Brucha saw her coming down the
driveway, she would begin to hammer on the kitchen window, terrified
that her aunt would ignore her. She would run and throw herself into
Rae's arms. But then she would tug at Rae's hair, or open her mouth
in an angry snarl, pretending to be Teppele the dog. And therefore,
because there were times when Rae actively longed for the child, she
would stop in before dinner, take Ruth and Brucha, and go over to the
park. Always, to the park. Always here, where years before she and
Maya used to walk and sit, so wrapped up in each other. And where
today she roamed and wandered with a growing sense of restless impatience, waiting for Naamah and Brucha to get home from the
school.

It was a wild, wind-swept day in the early fall. Rae had parked
her car a few blocks from Naamah's house but she had been striding
rapidly, with her free, swinging gait, astonished by this sudden soaring
of her spirits. She noticed shadows, the sharp upward turn of a bird's
flight, the high massing of clouds in a sky so tender it could have been
draped, she thought, as a canopy for a newborn child to assure it of
the world's essential goodness. And yet, for Brucha her anguish had a
sharp, tearing tenderness and she imagined it would have been like
this that she'd grieve over some premonition of unhappiness for her
own child.

There was, to be sure, attention paid, even now that Naamah
had become so preoccupied with her work on their grandmother's papers. An au pair girl from Holland looked after Brucha. Ruth was
devoted to her. Michael took her out to the rehearsals of the band.
Jacob would sit next to her when she had her bath, keeping afloat the
little wooden toys that had already done strenuous service for several
generations of Shadmi children. They were made from birch, hollowed out inside, covered in wax and carefully preserved by each suc-
ceeding mother of the clan's youngest child. But it had become clear
to Rae that the vital connection between these people, which made

them a family in more than name, had been withdrawn. Naamah had taken it away with her, into her self-absorption and her growing obsession with their grandmother's papers. And now the little girl, in spite of everyone's efforts, had grown surly and angry. She would throw pieces of soap at the little wooden figures, push them down under the water and try to drown them.

Rae and Ruth frequently took her to the little playground where Maya and Rae had spent so many afternoons in those mythical days just after Maya and Lev had come back to San Francisco. It had been remodeled since the time when Ruth, with her stocky little legs, would clamber up onto the highest horse, shouting to her older brother, who hung back and hesitated and finally, after great encouragement, sat down on one of the low swans, grabbed the pole and held it tight, his sad, pensive face growing white with anguish and determination.

The old merry-go-round had been spruced up and painted since then. The dilapidated little animal farm had been refurbished. Brucha would run off with her red hair flying behind her, to find some older girl whom she could boss. But she'd be back soon enough, Ruth said with a knowing smile; and probably with some irate mother dragging her by the hand.

Ruth would wrap her arm through Rae's and lean her head against her aunt's shoulder. She was a short, stocky girl who had grown into an awkward and homely adolescent. She had small, intelligent eyes, a large nose, an expression of worried preoccupation, and a surprisingly fine, well-formed mouth, which would have been her best feature if it had not been marred by the way she held it in a tight grimace, chewing nervously on her lower lip. She had survived the deaths of her father and brother and was trying, to the best of her ability, to figure out what was happening to her mother. She worried about Michael, whose band was breaking up at the end of the year. She helped in the house and studied, with no particular facility, the lessons Naamah and Frau Altdorf had assigned her. Her one great joy in life seemed those hours of the afternoon when she could tuck herself up next to Rae and sit with her legs folded beneath her, chattering and gossiping about the family.

"Naamah says you'll make up your mind in your own good time. But I don't know. If it were up to me, I mean, if I were in your place, I might want to have a life of my own. Not everyone has to become a

Flame Bearer, do they? I mean, not every Shadmi? Sometimes I think it would be better if I were a boy. Michael is confused about where he wants to study. But at least he doesn't have to keep asking himself whether he's supposed to be a saint or a scribe or a teller of stories or a healer . . ." She looked up apprehensively at Rae to make sure it was all right to go on like that. She was keeping her voice low to protect Brucha, whose sharp little ears seemed to take in everything, even when the child was halfway across the playground kicking up a rumpus. "Maybe that's the problem with my mother. Maybe she doesn't belong either. There's you and Aunt Naamah. You have your assigned place. Everybody expects something from you. But what about Maya? And sometimes I wonder. Maybe it's this stuff that's messing up Brucha. She was always a little imp. But now . . ."

There was no denying it. Brucha had become an obstreperous child. She had begun to get into quarrels with the other children. Once she even punched out at a much bigger boy who sent her flying back into the sand with a shove. Rae and Ruth had rushed over but Brucha ignored them. Then, with tears in her eyes and her lips clenched, she picked up a fistful of sand and threw it with all her might at the tall boy, who suddenly lost his nerve and began to howl when the wild little girl flew at him, her hands scratching.

Ruth doted on the child and clucked and worried over her and Rae could never bring herself to scold her. And so, from month to month, perceptibly, now that Naamah's careful supervision had been withdrawn, the little girl grew spoiled and willful. Soon there was no point in Ruth and Rae trying to talk. No sooner had they really broken through their reserve than the child, sensing their bond, ran over and scrambled up on the bench between them.

There were times, sitting with the children, when Rae felt she had discovered the meaning of her life. She would close her eyes and lean back on the bench, stretching out her arms to enclose the two of them—Brucha perched on her lap, her thumb in her mouth, her head resting against Rae's breast. Ruth leaning against her shoulder. Briefly, they would grow together and become (or so it seemed to Rae) a single, still awareness. The playground, with its uproar of pushing and climbing and digging and shouting, had moved off and left them to the ache of intimacy that was enclosing them. It was a day like that when Rae finally decided she would never return to New York.

But today, wandering about in the park alone, as she waited for

Naamah to get home, she felt all that was expected of her. Maybe, she told herself, stopping to take a drink from the little fountain that Brucha like to fill with dirt and leaves, Jacob was right? She was back-sliding again, running away from it all, doing nothing more during these weeks than charm and enchant the children so that she could distract herself from the real task that stood before her?

A breakthrough Jacob had said? And if it had been? What then was supposed to come after?

She looked down at her hands, at the knuckles turning blue in the cold. She was a woman named Rae Shadmi, born in San Francisco in a particular house on Scott Street in the actual year 1941 and rooted, therefore, to this age and time. And yet somehow expected to step out of the tyranny that made one day follow another and kept a day that had already passed from again returning . . . no, it could not be grasped like that, not by the rational mind. Jacob was right. The idea was one thing. But actually to pull it off, to enter one day through the bronze gates of Kiryat Sefer, to stroll past the fountain where Be-ruriah would be sitting with her girls—that was another.

It was too early in the day for the tourists to be out, and Rae was alone in the arboretum except for one of the regulars, the old "squirrel lady," as they used to call her, who came daily to the bench near the duck pond. She was still dressed in her shabby green skirt and the old tennis shoes—was it possible? Ten years later? They were splattered with a coating of thick plastic bandages to cover the holes. She had on the same shabby sweater, wrapped rather than buttoned around her and tied with a long scrap of knitted scarf.

The old woman sat with her face turned away from Rae, tapping a peanut on the back of the bench, the squirrels racing against their shadows toward her across the wet grass. Rae had seen her often years before and then once on Thanksgiving, when she'd come out before dinner with Hillel and Ruth. The park had been filled with squirrel feeders that day, and the old lady had stood by herself near the gate, rather forlorn and desolate, Rae thought, watching the fickle squirrels scamper after the nuts brought there by the holiday children. Hillel, in his blue knit cap, without saying a word had gone over to the ragged old woman to stand next to her, silently. And now here she was, in full possession of her territory, a decade later, the squirrels crawling over her lap as Rae walked past stricken by the idea that this could be Maya—was it possible? Was it possible, she raged (it always came back

to that)—suddenly dashed down out of her high spirits, by the sense
of what Maya had been ten years before, in her wild, unpredictable
beauty. Running out after them to bring them the bag of crusts they'd
forgotten. Across the little bridge, to hug the children and draw her
arm through Rae's, the dinner left to itself, outrageously abandoned,
as they trooped across the grass to feed the ducks and geese, the great
swan, launched from the opposite shore, gliding toward them, out
from under the willow.

Rae glanced at her watch. There was still almost an hour before
Naamah and the children would be home from school but now the
time seemed to weigh heavily on her. It was as if the lights had gone
out in the single room in which she was standing, while all around
her everything else seemed to go on blazing for some perpetual celebration that had just excluded her.

She was walking slowly on the curving path that led to the
wooden pergola. Now, even a moment later, she looked back on her
joy as a transgression, a deliberate forgetting of Maya, and of that
urgency that was making her for the first time eager to talk to Naamah, because she knew perfectly well (although she was reluctant
even now to admit it) that Maya was approaching a crisis. There had
been a turn, some crossing made virtually behind her back, so that
one day suddenly she was aware just how cold and withdrawn Maya
had become, how she had stopped eating again, how overnight something monumental seemed to have taken place.

One morning when Rae got up Hadassah had been lying on the
stairs. Then, when she picked up the doll to give her to Maya she'd
had a sense that Maya was simply "no longer there." She didn't recognize or acknowledge the doll; she stared at Rae with an icy silence,
and then seemed to withdraw even more, with a sudden quick turn of
her head, listening for something inaudible to her cousin.

Rae sat down on the bench in the pergola, leaning forward with
her elbows on her knees. And what was it, in fact, she was expecting
from Naamah?

Again, Rae glanced at her watch. Not more than fifteen minutes
had passed since she had seen the old squirrel lady. But now her waiting took on fretful urgency as she walked across the street and went
into the Japanese Tea Garden.

She knew, from before, the way to enter from the back gate. It
was large and heavy but never locked. She pulled it back and slipped

into the garden. She loved it at this hour, after the tourists had left for the day. She felt that the pools and the fat carp and the bowed bridge and the red lacquered temples all belonged to her and to the Shadmi family.

She stopped before the statue of Amida Buddha. Someone had put birdseed and crumbs into the Buddha's tarnishing bronze lap. Sparrows and small wrens and overfed pigeons and a few intrusive gulls were going about busily on the folds of the metal robe, and then she remembered, standing there with her hands in her pockets, the words she once had been taught so she could call the birds.

It was one of those moments, she recognized them now, when something was about to happen. Her forehead burned, the air around her began to shake and shimmer with an excruciating lightness. From far away she heard the buzz and murmur of inaudible voices and she knew that she was going to do it. Quickly, she glanced behind her. "*Ziptsit, tsepsit, malkitsie, zipitsie,*" she whispered, feeling in the next moment exceedingly foolish.

The birds went on with their industrious feeding, scattering crumbs and feathers, their heads bobbing, their claws making sharp, scratching sounds on the Buddha's metal legs. "Ah well," she muttered, shrugging her shoulders, relieved and at the same time absurdly disappointed. "What the hell did I expect?"

She walked on down the path to the tea garden, listening to the rattle of dishes and knowing, with her keen sense of smell, that the hostess had poured herself a cup of green tea. At the same moment, from down on the avenues, she heard the chime from some neighborhood church she had never been able to find. She was breathing quickly, giving in now to the tightening in her chest and to that sense of eager yearning, as if she were about to pierce the veiled substantiality of the world.

A white-breasted bird with a dark belly, a short brown tail, and a pale line above its eye, flew by overhead and perched on a branch of the cherry tree above her. She felt an incredible tugging inside her. It was a longing to lift her arm, to hold it out at shoulder height the way their grandmother could do it. And then she realized where she was. It had been here, at this very spot, late in the afternoon, at this same hour, the old woman had first taught her about the birds.

"Bubbe, Bubbe . . . ," said the small voice inside her. But this time Rae could not silence it. "I came too late," she whispered. She covered her mouth with her hand. "I'll never see her again." She kept repeating the word. "Never, never, never, never."

Rae bent over her knees. She had opened a wound so darkly hidden she had never guessed before that pain could run so deep. "Old woman," she said. "Old woman, why did you let the fire get them?" The years that separated her from childhood had ceased entirely to exist. "Bubbe," she sobbed, raising her eyes, "you could have saved them."

Time was in shreds. The bird, tipping its head, stared back at her with its unblinking eye. The words were repeated; they were softer this time, even more reproachful. And then Rae felt the way someone was lifting her arm. "What's the matter? You don't believe in the Bubbe? You don't think the old woman can call the birds?"

Rae got to her feet with an uncertain smile. "*Ziptsit, tsepsit, malkitsie, zipitsie,*" she whispered, the old woman's fingers gripping her wrist. Rae wanted to tell her how much she loved her. Yes, she thought, the time has come. She turned her head, expecting to look into her grandmother's eyes. Her own face in that moment furrowed with a child's unyielding concentration. But now, from far off across the garden, a bird rose into the air and flew toward her. She kept her arm raised. A yellow-billed magpie, with its sweeping tail, alighted on the tree above her. She fluttered her hand. Faster, faster. The bird rose from the tree, its wings beating with a quick, incredible affinity before it settled, gripping her fingers with its claws. It was followed by a horned lark, with a black collar around its yellow throat. She saw the little girl Sarah Rachel walking through the wet grass, following Raisa. She heard the far-off popping sound of the grouse. A purple martin flew toward her, its shimmering, violet head and neck shading off into black wing feathers.

Then she remembered what the old woman had taught her about the birds. How the flycatcher makes its nest out of snake skins. How the wings of the purple martin look triangular in flight. How you could tell the difference between a horned lark and a water pipit. And Kiryat Sefer? She held the birds steady on her arm and posed for herself that supreme test. A memory of flight passed through her veins. The sudden quick soar, wing-spread over water, shrill, sharp cries in her throat. She closed her eyes and for a single instant felt herself rise from the ground and plunge upward. And then, when she couldn't stand it any longer she released them. With a light flick of her hand she let them go and threw herself on her knees to place her hands flat down on the earth.

The birds circled three times overhead, bound together in that brief instant by her concentration. They circled in silence, weaving a taut band of light above her head. She was trying to hold them but her mind was stretched to its breaking point. The charm broke; they flew off, shattered, separate. She was thrust back into herself, cramped and stifled in the earthbound heaviness of human flesh. A journey outside time to a city outside history? No, not yet; she could not go that far. There was something in her that could take nothing on faith. She would have to live through it all, step by step, if that was required.

She made a mark on the earth, an intricate entwining symbol, two letters curled about one another, indecipherable. But if that time should come, when it seemed even remotely credible that a woman could set out to discover a vanished world, she would take the ultimate risk, and hazard everything.

She got to her feet walking fast. She heard the old woman's footsteps fade away behind her. Down on the avenues a church bell that perhaps did not exist was observing the hour. In the tea garden dishes were being washed and the hostess in her silk robes was gazing at golden carp in the small pond, sipping tea that had not grown cold.

N *a a m a h ' s* little shed at the back of the garden. It should have been a dank, shabby affair, given its long history of leaking roof and rusting tools. But one step inside and you could not remain in the twentieth century.

"Am I disturbing you, Naamah?" On the few occasions Rae had managed to make her way past Brucha's vigilance she had always felt the same resistance. It was warm in there, the small room heated by a little stove that burned kindling and twisted paper. It smelled of myrrh and eucalyptus bark and the old books Naamah had inherited. But all that pleased Rae, who had often wished their grandmother had intended the books for her.

Rae stood with her hand on the door, hesitating. The room was filled with bunches of drying herbs and aromatic flowers. Naamah had covered the rotting walls with old tapestries their grandmother had left behind when she moved to the Home for the Jewish Aged. But that way of drawing you into itself arose above all, Rae suspected, from the old pine table at which Naamah worked. Or more precisely: it was the work itself that did it. Her endless poring over the old papers that had been entrusted to her. The ink she made. The quill feather pens with which she wrote. The candles in which she held her pen before dipping it in ink and ash. The never quite dying echo of that interminable chanting and blessing with which, painstakingly, from day to day, the work proceeded.

Rae, who had never really seen her at it, could imagine it all. And therefore, she crossed her arms over her chest to give herself courage. One more step and she would have entered the inner sanctum of the Flame Bearer tradition—to the degree, at least, that it could be established in the New World.

"Rae, what a question. How could you disturb me?" Naamah reached toward Rae with both arms. "Come," she said, smiling at her cousin. "What are you afraid of? You think you'll get swallowed up and never get out again?"

Rae looked around for a place to sit. The cluttered room was filled with their grandmother's furniture. The heavy chest of Spanish oak with its ornate brass fittings stood in a corner. But every surface was covered with books and notes and drying plants.

"As a matter of fact," Rae responded lightly, stepping into the room with an immense stride. "I do feel as if I had just been ordered to take a giant step and am in danger of forgetting to yell out before I move, 'Mother may I?'"

"This game I remember. Always Maya won. But you know, even then I suspected, somehow she cheated? Rae, how well you look," she went on, as she gathered up her papers, stacked them carefully together, and wiped the quill pen with a piece of fine silk that she kept, neatly folded, next to the ink pot. "What has happened? I haven't seen you like this since . . . since when? Since you were a little girl, maybe?"

Naamah made room on the chair in which she was sitting. Rae sat down, holding herself very straight. But then she leaned over and put her head for a moment on Naamah's shoulder. "Good," Naamah said, patting Rae's hand, "yes, it is good to have you here."

Years before, when Naamah had been involved in a project with a potter's wheel and huge pails of clay, she had used the little shed for a workshop. A few large, unglazed pots and figurines stood on a rough shelf nailed above the window. Naamah, aware that Rae was looking curiously at them, nudged her gently. Rae sensed it immediately—Naamah was feeling shy and now she would start talking and keep at it to hide her discomfort.

"You are wondering what happened to the rest of these pots?" Naamah said. "The rest I shattered. Yes, I did it. And why? Because always when you begin with something new a sacrifice is needed."

Naamah was speaking rapidly, with a note of insistence that reminded Rae of their grandmother. But Naamah had not always been like that. In the past, she would close herself off within silence. Or if she got nervous enough she would be driven, out of sheer desperation, into storytelling. It was completely out of character for her, Rae thought. But she did it splendidly. It transformed her looks, heightened the color in her cheeks, exaggerated her gestures and made her pale, sweet eyes flash with an unexpected zeal. This happened now, too, and it delighted Rae. Her lips parted, she caught her breath, drawing up her shoulders with suspense, and there, in the little room, before a minute had passed, were a storyteller and her listener.

"Did I tell you something that happened?" Naamah asked. "Well, what does it matter? How will it hurt to tell again?"

Rae, catching the familiar words, answered obediently. "You're right," she said, smiling slowly, "how will it hurt?"

"I had been making small figurines," Naamah went on. "Little fat shapes with a hole in top. They were clumsy, believe me. Very crude. So there I was getting dressed for a party at Rosa Reichman's house. You remember? Already before you left her husband came in as president of the board. Jacob and I were going there, it's part of our work and we try always, as you know, to fit in and be respectable. But, what happens? Just before we are leaving the house suddenly I get the idea I cannot go out without the little figurine around the neck. A thing of beauty it certainly isn't. Yet, it is also not a hideous thing. Well, to make a long story a little bit less long. I put on the little figure and I go in there to Rosa's house. It's noisy of course, everybody talking and eating and waving the hands. I go over to a group of the teachers; soon I, too, am talking and waving the hands. And then I notice, across the room, a woman is looking at me. *Nu*, it happens. I look back, she looks again, the eyes meet and soon, sure enough, she is coming across the room, she comes right up to me, she stops two inches away, she leans forward to look and then she says, picking up this rough little lump of clay I'm wearing, 'You must tell me. Where did you get this?'

"Now, who is this woman? Soon enough I find out. She is an Israeli, a famous archaeologist. Rosal Ynpee no less. And she, it turns out, has just been working on a dig in the Galilee, close up to Lake Kinneret. This is what she tells me. But this dig of hers had nothing to do with Kiryat Sefer. It was just an ordinary dig, for an ordinary buried city. But now, you know what she says? When she finds out I made the little figurine myself, she shakes the head and lets out such a moan, everybody in the room begins to look. Why? Because this little shape I made out of my own hands, in this little shack at the

back of the garden, is exactly like the images of the 'female diety'—
that's what she called it—they have been digging up in the last year
near Lake Kinneret."

There was a tiny point of hectic red in Naamah's cheeks when
she had finished speaking. "You are wondering why did I tell you this
story? Because, Rae, I want you should understand that what is happening to you in all these months is just the way it should be. Sit.
Don't get up. What are you afraid of? You think it's so strange I know
what has been happening?"

There was no room to pace in Naamah's little shed. Rae, looking
around rather urgently now, felt as if she were plotting her escape.
The little stove was drawing badly; a thin stream of densely scented
smoke leaked from the poorly fitted door.

"I'll open the window," Rae said, but she did not get up. Naamah
had put a hand on her arm and Rae remained sitting.

Then, there was a silence in which Rae grew even more uncomfortable. She had come to Naamah with a sense of her own power,
ready to offer herself to Naamah and to the old ladies in exchange
. . . for what? She wanted Naamah or Frau Altdorf to help her get on
with it. To bring her along even faster. She had come to tell Naamah
she would go out on whatever wild goose chase they had in mind for
her. But only if they would use all their skill and mysterious knowledge
to help her be in time. To save Maya . . .

"I've been studying this word *Shaddai*," Naamah said, because
she really was quite incapable of ordinary conversation. She picked up
a piece of paper and separated it carefully from the rest. "Why, for
instance, do the Flame Bearers use the word *Shaddai*? And not *Yah-
weh*? I've been looking it up in the Old Testament. I found it there
maybe twelve or thirteen times. I found it in Genesis, in Job, in Isa-
iah, in Ruth also. And I've been reading what the scholars have to
say." Naamah picked up a heavy book from the floor next to her and
placed it in Rae's lap. "You know the work by Friedrich Deletsch? And
William Albright? You came across them when you wrote your thesis?
Of course, we do not expect scholars to agree. They are limited by the
texts they study. They cannot go, as we can, back to the source. One
thinks Shaddai is a warrior god. Another says god of the mountain.
Another insists Shaddai is god of the plain. For myself, I hear the
word destruction, *Ke-shod*, in his name. The one who destroyed the
worshipers of the Goddess. It's important, Rae. Our work must be to

establish, also in a scholarly manner, that Grandmother Shadmi and the other old women in the Flame Bearers, have preserved an authentic legend, going all the way back to Canaanite time. You, in your thesis, do not succeed with this because you don't believe in it yourself, really. Even your scholarship seems ironic, a certain kind of sport, making a joke of scholarly methods. It is, in its own way, very effective; even, I suppose, it makes possible that certain people, who never would pay attention to our ideas, might want to read them. But it is not enough. In the use of this one word *Shaddai,* there is hidden a whole philosophy, a world view, a theogony. There is history here, even a secret doctrine. My feeling is, the time has come to make all this known. It can't be kept secret anymore. Not from men. The world needs it. Or here," she went on, in a breathless voice, her cheeks flushed and her eyes flashing with an unpleasant light. "You see these words? Three of them written in Hebrew. One in Ugaritic. These papers, some of them, come down all the way from Rocha Castel. But take this word, *mshngt ilm.* It is the Ugaritic expression for 'the wet nurse of the gods.' And now here, the Hebrew word *reharmim,* mercy. And here, *reharmim* combined with *rehem,* womb. And here, combined with *Ima,* the word for Mother. Now, here they are again, all written together, one on top of the other. This, I think, is a chant or lullaby or even a word game for teaching children. You remember '*ziptsit, tsepsit, malkitsie, zipitsie,*' the words you got from somewhere when you were a child for calling the birds? It's something like that. You can arrange them in all sorts of patterns. But basically, you have the same meanings. Mercy. Womb. Mother. Wet nurse of the gods. I've written them down in different variations. You see?" she asked, pointing to a little entwined circle of words at the center of a page:

Womb of Mercy, Mother of the Womb, Mother of Mercy, Mercy of the Mother, Mercy of the Womb.

"You see what an important idea is expressed? The Mother as the originator and wet nurse of the gods. A universe, fundamentally compassionate. You see why this is important? Soon, we shall be living again in the Days of Shaddai. It will be time for the Teacher to come among us. The world is going very close to its own destruction. All the signs are there. The building up of these stockpiles of bombs. The dying of the waters. The poison they are putting into the earth. Already the birds cannot make shells strong enough to hatch their young. But here we have these wonderful old stories that remind us the universe is hatched out of compassion, from the fundamental ground of mercy. Rae, you want to make mockery again? You think I am foolish sitting here with my old papers? But how do you know what matters in the world? You are so certain marching about in a picket line with a sign, and writing a petition and walking in Washington is more effective than telling an old story? Rae, I am asking you. Why are you so sure?"

Rae put her arms around her cousin. "My dear Naamah, my dear Naamah," she murmured, "I am not your enemy, I assure you."

"Yes, yes, forgive me," Naamah answered, suddenly pale. "I forget myself. Yes, I see, I go beyond myself. But, Rae, understand please. All this is only because I don't know how to do the work Grandmother Shadmi left to me. What, after all, is my real work? To bring you some comfort. To help you a little bit in this time of change. You, if you had the right teacher, if you did not have to do all this alone . . ."

"And just what is it I'm doing, Naamah?" She had spoken with anger. But then, shrugging her shoulders, as if she were finally weary of her own evasions, she said more simply: "What exactly has been happening to me?"

"You are receiving instruction. In the only way which now is possible. What can I say? We have been cut off from Kiryat Sefer. Something has gone wrong with the transmission. Some mistake was made, some wrong turning in the path. There are things the old lady didn't tell us. Those years, when I went up to her in the attic and sat by her bed, were for us lost years. We missed something and we were cut off from something. It was right for the old lady to come to the New World. But it was wrong for her to think she was the last of the many, the last great Hovrodnik alive on this earth. The Hovrodnik is the most humble of women. She knows only she must act and speak as she does and that she serves The Mother. This is true also of Ha Melamed Gadol, The Great Teacher. Perhaps, even, one recognizes them best from the way they are wrestling not to become what they are meant to be. Our grandmother did her work and some of it she did well. The school; the telling of the stories; the writing down of the legend with the other old women; what she taught Frau Altdorf, who now is helping me—all this was good work, we can be proud for her. But you know what I think? I think Rebekah is alive and waiting for you. She it is who will be your teacher."

Naamah stood up and moved to the other side of the table. She put her hands down on the rough pine surface and leaned forward toward Rae, a troubled expression on her face. "I think my mother knows about all this. That is the reason Maya hates her and threw water on her and drove her out of the house. You know what Maya said to her? Did she tell you? '*Du Kalye-makher*', she said to her, 'a Spoiler you are, worse even than Hannah Leah.' You know what Maya is trying to do? Have you figured it out? She is trying in her own way to heal Hannah Leah, to make her better, to heal the blind eye our own grandmother could not heal. And this means, what? It means our poor little Maya is trying all by herself to lift us, to lift up the whole family out from the shadows that live so close to us. Of course my mother did not burn down the school. But she did something she should not have done. She is keeping a secret you need to have, Rae. What my mother could tell you would give you the way to go on. To find Rebekah. To make your way into the destiny that is yours alone. You feel the power for this growing maybe even today in you? Good, I believe it. But the healing for my mother and also for Maya can come only when you find your way back to Kiryat Sefer, where the tradition lives. You think I don't know why you came to me today? You want to make a bargain? We should make an exchange? I will teach you how to heal Maya and you will take on this burden of successor you don't really want?"

Rae had the feeling that now, finally, Naamah was saying things she needed to hear. It seemed to her that for weeks, for months, perhaps for years, she had been hammering against some unyielding obstruction and then, whenever it seemed her knocking was about to be answered, she had taken to her heels and run away.

She stood up, she sat down again, she looked at Naamah with gratitude and relief. Why, she asked herself, why hadn't they spoken sooner? She leaned across the table and placed her hands over Naamah's. And then they both laughed at the same moment, remembering their old delight—Rae's hands, from the time she was a very little girl, already so much larger than her cousin's.

Rae shook her head; "I refuse to laugh," she whispered, catching sight of the impossibility, the secret catch that made it all unthinkable. "Naamah," she said, pointing up at the ceiling with a stabbing gesture: "Are *they* still mocking me?" And then her voice changed, and she did not bother to hide its ominous undertone: "You know I can't leave Maya. Whatever else I am expected to do, I can't do that."

"Yes, yes," Naamah nodded, "I know we must come to that." She put her hands behind her back and rocked herself slightly, looking up at the ceiling as if it were indeed from there she might receive guidance. She had narrowed her eyes and was biting on her lower lip, looking tentative and unsure of herself. The old Naamah suddenly, not this new, awesome person she had become. "What is happening with Maya . . . this is, you know, not insanity. For us, for the Flame Bearers," she added, as if uncertain whether to include Rae in this, "the problem is not that Maya looks from the window and sees Hannah Leah walking in the garden. The problem is not that she hears the voices or sees the vision of the sacrifice of the male. We know that in our ancient past this is what happened. We were once a simple, perhaps even a barbarous people. We sacrificed the male to make fertile the soil. It is good Maya is finding out these things. Do you give yourself grief over this? You, in all your study, didn't discover it? In all peoples was once this practice of human sacrifice. The gods, all of them, have been worshiped in strange ways. But what Maya makes of these things, that is the problem. She, too, is called, how else? It comes to each one of us. But how she responds to the call, that is the trouble with Maya."

"And with me?"

"You don't understand what has been happening to you, is this what you mean? Rae, I am telling you. You have been called and you have responded. And yes, at the same time you are running away. That happens. And it happens especially when the transmission is broken and a teacher is missing and there is no one to guide you through the initiation. The Hovrodnik does not come to knock at the door. She does not ask us the Names of The Mother. She does not try to find out if we know the Name of the Old Land and where is the First Stone of the Old Path on the Road to Kiryat Sefer. These ways to be called into the sect, for us they are not working. So then the initiation comes up out of itself, crude and terrifying, you think I don't know? But you, unlike Maya, don't make such a confusion of it all. Why Maya? Why not you? What can I tell you? You remember *Kovahl?* The story one writes for oneself, which at the same time is a story already written? So it is with Maya. With her whole life she is trying to write the story. But she is writing the wrong story."

Naamah's hands were shaking. She waved them at Rae to keep her from interrupting. But then she clapped her hands together several times, shaking her head. "Forgive me," she said. "Forgive me, I must finish. This perhaps is more important than anything else. We envy each other, how else could it be? We wrestle with each other for a place in the sect. We cannot blame ourselves for this. But you, Rae, you must understand *Kovahl* and what it means. For each of us there is a part to play. For each a place in the sect and in the family. Your part, I admit, is very dramatic. To escape somehow from time, to move back through history, to find your way to a vanished city. Yes, and maybe, who knows? Maybe to become, for our time, Ha Melamed Gadol? But, Rae, understand please. The Flame Bearers do not believe Ha Melamed Gadol is a woman more significant than other women. This is a mistake. Bubbe passed it on to us. Others have made it too. Perhaps it comes down from generation to generation in the Shadmi family. We have lived for such a long time away from our own land, among men who think in a different way. Always worrying who is on top, who is better, who is bigger. But in this error we see the degeneration of the Flame Bearer tradition. In the Old Wisdom each one of us is necessary to accomplish the task required for every generation. If this is true; if each one is necessary, how is it possible to say one is more necessary than another? What we do, each one of us, is mixed in with what the other does. All of it tangled together, all required."

"Is this sophistry, Naamah? Or are you trying to tell me that what is most dramatic cannot be confused with what is most significant?"

"Rae, listen. Maya cannot change the story that for her was written, not in this life only, but in all the lives she lived before. What she is not now, she may be one day. Also to her will come the opportunity to be . . . whatever she wishes. She wants to be the successor? She wants to be Ha Melamed Gadol? So good, why not? Someday, certainly, if she wants this enough she will attain it. But then she may discover it was just as good to be, who knows what? A scribe, a teacher, a humble woman like your own mother? Can you understand this, Rae? All equally important? Because without each one doing what she must nothing could be accomplished?"

Naamah fell silent. She folded her arms on her breast, took a deep breath, and glared up at Rae from the full depth of her concentration. "*Oy, veh, veh,*" she said, "perhaps in my whole life together I didn't talk this much?" And then, she rushed on: "You think I didn't give myself grief over this same problem since I was a little girl? Always

I knew it was you. You were the one the old lady waited for. The great hope. You ask me why? With words you don't have to ask me. I see in the eyes this is what troubles you. I knew already from the time you came home, this is the question you want to thrust at me. I know even the guilt you feel. From this you are running away. But you cannot make this struggle less by taking Maya with you. She cannot go; not because I don't want it, or Grandmother Shadmi didn't want it. In herself, in Maya herself, is the impossibility. She cannot go because her destiny is somewhere else. And this precisely is what the old woman didn't teach us. The destiny fits, like a good suit . . . The destiny fits, because we are born to grow into it . . ."

Rae got to her feet. She pushed the little table away from her, made a fist and placed it down very deliberately on a stack of Naamah's papers. "You ask me to believe in a fixed, implacable destiny? You ask that of a woman born in this day and age? As if," she went on, her voice growing belligerent, "we owed no loyalty to our own time and to the centuries of struggle to free the human will? I won't have it, Naamah. It's too much to ask. It's a surrender, a submission, a wanton throwing out, I tell you, of our struggle to create ourselves."

They were glaring at each other across the table, Rae flushed and excited, Naamah ill at ease but aware that the old lady had prepared her for precisely this argument. "You want to help Maya?" she asked, struggling with her voice. "You think even you might heal her? You have the idea you will stay here and take care of her and shut yourself up in the house with her until she is better? It won't happen like this, Rae, I tell you. Maya will be better only when she accepts her own chapter in this story written and written again, old and at the same time new, in every generation. And how will she do this? Only if you do what you must and find the way back to Kiryat Sefer. You think it is so strange that a person can step outside of time? You give yourself grief over this key that has been put into your hands? Of course I know about the key. Why do you look at me like this? I sit here, in the garage, I do my work, I find things out. That is my part of the story. You wrinkle up your nose? You think all this is nothing but hocus-pocus? But somewhere in your own knowing you know better than this. To me was given the work with the papers in the old box. You know what I do here? I write over again, from the beginning, mark for mark and page for page, what has been written since the earliest time. If I make a mistake, if I write one single dot or comma in the wrong way, I tear it all up and start over again, from the beginning. And why? Because I have nothing better to do with my life than make a clean copy of these old scraps that have come down to us? I do it, Rae, because, for the scribe, what is new will only come from what has already been written. One day, if all goes well with my work, I will take up a new page. I will think that I am copying something here on the table before me, but instead I will be taking down a dictation from a woman who lived maybe hundreds of years before our time and who died, maybe, before her own work was completed. Someone, Rocha Castel herself perhaps, who knew more stories than ever she had the time to write. Beruriah even, who never let her students write a single word. Think, Rae, all over the world, in drab little rooms like this one, there are women writing down stories that were told and remembered and told again, from mouth to ear as the saying is. Once, in Kiryat Sefer, we, too, had books, telling the history of the world as the Flame Bearers lived it. But even then, when Beruriah walked with her students, talking and reasoning with them, there were stories no one wrote, things that could be told only. And these things, and all the things that were written and destroyed when Kiryat Sefer was swallowed up in the earth, these may come again to the one who sits and writes from the beginning, never changing a mark or a dot from the few fragments that have come down to us.

"And now, Rae, I will tell you one more thing and then I will be silent and let you talk. You want to know what is the problem with Maya? She is trying to do what you should be doing. She is trying to get back to Hannah Leah and to Rebekah to find the missing pieces. And they, who knows? Perhaps because you do not answer when they call, they are trying to reach you through Maya. Who was it who put the key in your hand? Who was this old lady with the steel-rimmed spectacles? Rae, that was Rebekah."

"That was Rebekah," Rae repeated. "That was Rebekah." She had known it already. And still she did not believe it.

Naamah moved cautiously. "Rae," she said, her voice in that instant all tenderness and control: "Have you asked yourself? What happens to the person who gets into her hands what she cannot manage? In Maya the envy and the outrage is bigger than everything else. If she succeeds in what has been set for her, that will be her accomplishment. To find out how a human being descends into this turmoil and comes out from it whole. Then, yes, I assure you, Rae. She will find what is meant for her in this life and it will give her meaning. It will be big enough for her, I promise you this. As big as anything you, too, will someday accomplish. Perhaps Brucha will in her time need what Maya has learned. Perhaps this knowledge will make it possible for Brucha to play her part in the way she must play it. Perhaps some little girl not yet born will be saved because Maya has made this descent and has come back from it, knowing. So imagine, for one moment only imagine I am right. What would be left for you to do? Supposing even what you want most of all to do is to heal Maya? You would take from Maya's shoulders this task that is not meant for her. Then, it will be you who answer when Hannah Leah calls. It will be you who set out to find Rebekah. You who will let yourself slip through the crack and make your way outside of time. And then Maya, and my mother, and even I, Rae, can take our position in whatever place is right for us. So, I'm done now. This is what I have to say. Only one thing more I will tell you. So far as is in me to help you, I will give you that help. There is something I, too, haven't risked. I will risk it for you. I will do what for generations the women in the tradition of scribes have done when there was nowhere else to turn. I will burn the papers that have been given to me. Yes, I will set them on fire. I will make them into ash. This you don't know about, there was no reason for you to know. It is the way of the scribe. I learned it from Frau Altdorf, who learned it from our great-grandmother Raisa, when she was a little girl. I mix this ash with ink, I recite the blessing, I begin to write. From this writing, that mixes in itself the burned shadow of what has passed, comes new understanding. We risk everything, we who set ourselves out on this path of the *Flam-Troger*. How do I know I have the power to succeed? Perhaps I will burn up and not be able to replace the writing that has come down to us. This is the risk I must take. And you, what is your risk? It is the risk of loving so much you let yourself abandon us and go off into your own life. Perhaps you will lose yourself, perhaps you will not find the way to Kiryat Sefer and you will leave us as we are. Maya in this childhood she cannot outgrow because she cannot accept the destiny that is meant for her. My mother in her isolation. And me? You think I don't see the danger? I could be left here, with my handful of ash, not knowing even what truths and what secrets to hand down to my daughter. And why? Because something there is, something that cannot come through to us even in my work. That is the missing piece you must find."

Tears were streaming down Rae's face. "Poor lonely old creature," she said, not aware that she was crying. "To think of her, dying alone and so completely self-deluded. The last of the many? The last great Hovrodnik alive on this earth? That's what she thought? And all this while Rebekah was living . . ." Naamah said nothing. But she did not think that Rae would always feel like that. So far as she was concerned, their grandmother had done enough.

"I gave the key to Maya," Rae said, glancing down at her sleeve. "I promised her I would never leave without her." She was looking curiously at the faint damp spots staining the dark silk. "Why am I crying?" she asked, and Naamah, reaching across the table to take her hand, spoke so softly Rae could barely hear her: "Because already you know. It means nothing, a promise that cannot be kept."

J *a c o b* was standing at the kitchen window. He kept his eye on Marjan, the au pair girl, who was trying to bundle Brucha out of the car. But Brucha, catching sight of Rae, who was dashing across the street, drew away from Marjan. Shrieking with excitement, she began to scamper up the garage steps into the kitchen as Rae came thundering up behind her.

In the next instant Jacob had opened the kitchen door.

"What has happened?" he asked in a muffled voice. Marjan had come into the kitchen behind Rae. Rae was reading Jacob's face, trying to guess exactly what had happened in the last half-hour that had made them rush over, she and Naamah together.

"She's okay?" Rae whispered.

"Yes, fine, nothing's wrong," Jacob answered, with a frown. "I was looking out for you because . . ." He shook his head. "Who knows why? Suddenly, I felt you should be here. But she's fine," he repeated. And it was clear that nothing had happened—not yet.

Naamah had come in through the front door. They could hear her, in the hallway, talking to Maude, the young woman Rubin had sent over to help with Maya.

"Where is she?" Rae asked. "Has she gone to sleep yet? It's late for her. Have you been up to see her?"

"She will tolerate only Maude," Jacob said. "Rubin was right to send her. She won't have me or anyone else from the family. Nothing's changed . . . at least in this way, not. But she sent down a message." He reached into his jacket and took out a piece of paper. "It was rolled up, like this. She wrote on it I think with a burned match."

Rae took the scrap of paper and unrolled it with a sudden sense of immense fatigue. Maybe it had all been a false alarm? Maybe Maya was only acting? She looked down at the scrap of paper and saw a crude, childish drawing of a little house with a wooden fence, a garden in front of it. There was an X marked over one of the windows, with an arrow pointing to it. A nonsense word in a vaguely Russian alphabet was written into the X.

Rae shook her head. She wished Rubin was there. "It's hard to know . . ." She broke off and looked up at the ceiling. "You're sure? Maude's been up to see her? Did you call Rubin? It's extraordinary," she said as Naamah came into the room, looking almost as puzzled as Rae. "Half an hour ago, in Naamah's little room, I was suddenly convinced something terrible had happened . . ."

Naamah unrolled the little piece of paper. She took her lower lip between her teeth. But then her expression changed. "You'll forgive me?" she asked. "You don't understand?" Her voice had a very slight edge of impatience. "Maya is saying it is she who has gone to live in Raisa Shadmi's house, in the house of the Flame Bearers, you see? She is telling us she has become the successor, Rae. She and not you."

"You're so certain that's what it means? You have no doubt whatever?"

"Rae! Certain?" Naamah looked at her with surprise. "But what question is there? Am I certain what you mean when you speak in English?" Rae could feel that quickening inside herself, that sense that Naamah was now "off and running." Her voice had risen, it was becoming urgent and breathless and it affected Brucha even more strongly than it did her aunt. The child had been roaming about, looking into the large storage jars that Maude kept filled with herbal teas and beans and grains. But now suddenly Brucha jumped back with a little shriek as a huge jar of lentils crashed down onto the floor.

Marjan had taken a step toward her, clucking apologetically. She never was much use, Rae thought, watching the hopeless, incompetent look cross the girl's features. But Naamah had turned to look at her daughter with her hands on her hips. She was still, Rae realized, with some surprise, a patient, gentle mother.

The child came over and pressed herself against Naamah's legs. She was looking up at Rae, with her head to one side, her lower lip caught between her teeth. But her little eyes kept darting toward the ceiling. And suddenly Rae, looking closely at Brucha, felt her panic rising.

"They've come for her," Brucha said finally, but she looked very puzzled. "Hannah Leah and the seven old ladies have come for Maya."

Naamah touched Rae on the shoulder. "Listen," she said.

Rae had heard it before. A hushed and dreadful quiet in the house. It had awakened her on several nights, giving her the impression a door had been left open that she had never known existed. Then it had made her get out of bed and creep down the hall, to stand listening outside Maya's room. Now it was making her move with a catlike stealth.

Brucha tried to go after her as she left the kitchen, but Jacob, pouncing, grabbed her up in his arms. Rae put her finger to her lips, winking at Brucha. Fool, she said to herself, you think she'll believe it's a game? She heard the old clock winding itself up for a good long wheeze. It was almost seven o'clock. Shivering slightly, she walked faster. To get upstairs before the hour struck.

She was taking the stairs three at a time, sickened by the smell of burning flesh. She had a sense of extreme mental clarity. What does it take, she was asking herself, what exactly does it take to make this kind of idiot I am into a believer? And meanwhile, it seemed to her that something was pulling her up the stairs so fast she was practically flying.

Maya was not in her room. Rae, moving on pure instinct, ran down the hall and up the little spiral staircase to the guest room. She could hear Jacob and Naamah coming up the stairs behind her. Brucha was hollering at Maude, but the words were drowned in the loud pounding footsteps that echoed back at Rae as she ran. From far away there was the sound of a telephone ringing. Rubin, she thought with relief, and then she was at the door to the guest room, slowing herself down, stopping to catch her breath, to smooth down her hair, to compose herself.

"Maya? Are you there?"

She tried the knob. The room was not locked. She was wondering how to act, she was asking herself a million questions. She felt as if some slow, deliberate element in herself continued to ponder and measure and calculate, while she had already entered the room, with its heat and stench and sickening tension. And then she was at the

window, struggling with Maya, before her mind had shaped the com-
mands: Enter. Save her.

Maya had been standing outside the window at the very edge of
the little balcony with its treacherous, low railing. Her arms were
spread out in front of her, as if she had been caught in the split instant
after stepping out on a tightrope. She was wavering slightly, lifting
and dropping her arms, her head twisted at a peculiar angle, her back
arched painfully upward.

Rae leaped up onto the balcony and took Maya in her arms. Maya
was biting at her, trying to get her foot around Rae's leg to trip her.
She was tearing herself away, her head thrashing from side to side, as
Rae held on to her, pressing the naked, emaciated body against her
own. It had all happened in a few minutes. But for the rest of her life
it seemed to Rae that she and Maya were struggling on a splinter of
time where their lives moved very fast. For them an entire lifetime
seemed to come and go and stand ready to begin again. Outside their
frantic, timeless clutching, everything else moved with an excruciating slowness, while something in her was screaming for Rubin to
hurry.

Rae knew that the woodburning stove had been stoked up too
high. There was a blast of bitter cold. A smell of roasting meat. A
high-pitched, audible shrill of tension. Meanwhile, she had the leisure
to observe the spires of the Golden Gate Bridge rise up behind Maya's
shoulder, stunning in the clear brilliance of the fall day that stood
there, all over the place, shrieking reproachfully.

Maya leaped out of her arms. There was a cry of warning, a call
of outrage and terror. But is was Rae's own and instantly stifled as she
took it in that Maya had sprung down into the room and was throwing
herself against the door. Rae heard the latchkey turn. She heard the
rush of air as Maya tossed it furiously away behind her. And now Maya
whirled about with a face so lofty and sublime it struck Rae to the
heart. Madness, she feebly protested, was not supposed to be like
this—so suddenly and unpredictably controlled and lethal.

They stood there, Rae hunching forward with her arms spread to
keep Maya from racing back to the window. They stood silently,
caught between the reassuring limitations of the physical world and
that other terrifying dimension that had broken through there. And
Rae wondered if this were playacting after all. It seemed so urgent and
frantic, but at the same time crafty and intended.

Rae, whose attention was nailed to Maya with a tenacity that left nothing over for other impressions, now sensed a new danger. The doors of the woodburning stove had been left open. Maya was very slowly raising her left hand, the finger pointing upward. There was a shower of sparks into the room behind Maya. And Rae realized, with a sickening intake of breath, that Maya was commanding the fire.

Maya's face, still and frozen as before, had taken on a new expression. She seemed transported, lifted out beyond the reach of frenzies and torments. And now she said to Rae in a hushed, stilted voice, raising her other arm above her head, majestically. "You from flesh. I from this ash."

In some other chamber of herself, where everything was still occurring in an exaggerated slow motion, Rae listened to the words over and over again, marveling at their grandeur. Then, before she could stop her, Maya had leaped over to the stove, scooped out an armful of blazing wood, and pressed it reverently against her chest.

Rae was holding the hands of a woman with red hair. "Isarael," the woman was saying, and she knew this was her mother. She looked up at her, at the heavy breasts and thick arms. They were standing outdoors. There were other women, dressed in robes. It was a full-moon night, something was shimmering, there around her mother's neck. The little girl looked up, catching her breath. She reached out, trying to touch the silver key. And then one of the other women put a hand on her mother's shoulder to draw her aside. "It's time now, Rocha," she said. "Let's begin."

It was true, then? She had lived before? Her life was as insubstantial as an onion skin, which even now was being peeled back to some palpable core of recollection. It was true? The way the old lady had always told them? What Maya was doing, dancing with fire, had been done before and would be done again.

Rae heard someone pounding at the door, hammering at it, to break it in. It sounded to her like a far-off drumbeat or the rattle of a saber or like Pyotr the goy chopping wood or the rattle of death in her grandmother's throat or like Hannah Leah climbing a staircase. Beyond it, coming from a corner of the room, she heard the sound of sobbing. It was not Maya, whom she'd already picked up and thrown on the bed. Maya was as still and silent as the doll Hadassah, who was propped there on Rae's pillow, her lace dress torn to shreds, her doll face blackened with ash, the hair torn out of her head.

Rae realized that she had been moving in a quiet sort of urgent rapture, without having known that such motion was possible—so precise and intelligent her body seemed. She was wrapping Maya in the blanket, she was crooning to her, bent over kneeling on the bed, as if all had been nothing more than a moment of wildness before bedtime.

She heard herself saying, as she put her lips to Maya's cheeks: "Shah, shah, little one. Don't worry." But Maya seemed to feel no pain. She lay there with her huge, reproachful child's eyes, whispering to her cousin: "They told me I could walk on air. Hannah Leah told me. She said I could fly. Do you think it's true, Rae? She told me I could fly right over the world to Kiryat Sefer. She said the old ladies, all seven of them, would be there." The loftiness and grandeur were gone now. In their place was once again the voice of a lost child, who seemed to be wondering why Rae could not manage to protect her.

"No. You can't fly," Rae answered. "Don't you listen to Hannah Leah. You listen to me from now on."

Maya's eyes had begun to close. "I thought you were going away," she whispered. "I thought Rebekah had come to take you. Hannah Leah told me she'd stay with me always. She said she always wanted a little girl."

Maya yawned. She looked very tired, as if it were past her bedtime and Rae were keeping her up late.

"She has a terrible scar, you know? It goes from here all the way to here," Maya confided in Rae. "But I think, you know what? I think you like me better than Hannah Leah does."

Rae knew that Naamah had entered the room. She knew that Jacob had managed to drag Brucha away. And she felt in those instants before Naamah reached them that this time alone here with Maya would have more weight and substance, more ambiguous and problematic meaning than anything she would ever experience again in her life. It gave her a peculiar feeling of reluctance to be torn away and returned to that ordinary world from which any moment now they would all rush in, with their uncomprehending, urgent compassion.

Maya had reached out to put her arms around her cousin's neck and Rae understood, in the empathetic cringing of her own flesh, just how terribly Maya had burned herself.

Rae wanted to look away and close her eyes, but she took Maya's hands in her own and looked down. The entire underside of Maya's arms had been charred black. The skin on her chest was puckered and swollen. The velvet ribbon had left a charred ring around her neck. Just over her left breast the key had branded her with a raw and blistering tattoo. But the key itself had vanished. And Rae knew that Maya, alone there in the room, before she tried to walk out onto the air, had been dancing, with Hannah Leah. Their arms full of fire.

part four

The Sense of an Ending

The Future: 1974–

24

I*t w a s* there, that sense of an ending, even before they drove out along the coast, Rae and Ruth and Brucha in the old VW Rae had given away to a friend when she was leaving San Francisco. They were taking the curves slowly. Rae had put the top down, although it was still a premature, uncertain spring, a day before Purim. Brucha was bundled up in a red blanket, sitting on Ruth's lap. But she began shouting and trying to get to her feet when they passed Rubin's car and Maya glanced over at them with a little weary smile and lifted her hand in salutation.

"Did you see that?" Ruth asked, the excitement making her young again for the first time since Maya had gone into the hospital, almost three months before. "I don't suppose this means we've suddenly come back into existence?"

Later, they had passed Jacob and Naamah. Jacob was driving. But they could see, as they came up fast behind him, that he was paying no attention to the road. Naamah had her face averted and Rae imagined she was crying. A few miles later, as they had agreed, Jacob pulled over and Naamah got into Rae's car. Brucha, seeing her father drive off alone, set up her usual racket and they had to stop again, so that she could be put into the front seat with him. Naamah's eyes were swollen and red. But she slipped into the back seat with a quick motion of her hand, letting them know she didn't want to answer questions.

They had lost sight of Rubin's white Porsche. Jacob's wheezing Chevrolet groaned along behind them. But Rae was speeding up because she did not like driving in the mist. It made her feel that she had already set out on a journey that had no foreseeable end, no point of departure, and no guarantees, therefore, of homecoming or returning.

But when had it begun—this sense of an ending that told her now in so many ways she would not be with them long? She had been dreaming about departure. Trains pulling out of the station as she went running down the track, trying in vain to catch up with them. A bus hurrying down the hill toward her and passing her by, as she waved her arms and called out frantically. And had it been there already that late afternoon, when she and Jacob had been out walking in Potrero Hill? Michael was going all over the city interviewing musicians to replace the members of his band who were leaving for college. She and Jacob, once or twice, had gone with him. But why? What were they doing strolling about in this neighborhood she had so rarely visited?

"I'm ready," she had said, laughing, forcing her spirits high as they strode along together. "I've shed all my resistances. So, where's the legendary 'guidance'? Where's the 'assignment'?"

"Mock all you like, you unbeliever," he'd answered, with a light tap at her forehead, relieved that now finally, after months of despair about Maya, they were back again in their old mode. "But us you don't fool anymore. The head, what does it matter? The head doesn't have to believe. But the heart . . . that's a different matter. I take one look on you and I know. Here is a person in whom the heart finally is open. You even don't look the same. To me you look all scrubbed up, like someone that just got out dripping and steaming from a hot tub. It's all gone, all the bitterness. You'll forgive me? All the compulsive charm is gone too. What's left is my friend Rae, as I knew she could be. True and simple and the heart living in the eyes."

"And this," she asked, imitating him, "is a woman you could have fallen in love with?" She felt safe, knowing perfectly well he would take it for nothing more than banter. But she didn't want him to see her eyes.

"You're asking me?" he answered, taking her arm. "But didn't you know? You've always been . . . Rae, what is it?" She had pulled away from him, bending down to pick up a broken piece of blue glass that was shimmering at their feet. She couldn't bear to have him say it in jest. And then she turned back to him, as if she had brought herself at last to stop pretending.

"Do you know how long it's going to be, Jacob, before we walk like this again?" But she had thought of it as nothing more than an evasion.

On another day they had been sitting for hours together in the Trieste, playing the same three arias over and over again. The numbers for them had not changed during all those years she'd been away. L2, L3, and L4. She knew them by heart and would jump up with another quarter the minute "Celeste Aida" had ended. But that day one of the customers had come over to the jukebox to protest her repetitions and the owner had gone striding after him to take her side. "You been here, how long?" he'd said to the tall man who had appealed to him against Rae. "You don't like it here, you know how to find the door?" And then he'd walked back to the table with his arm around her. "Hey, Jacob Paltiel, you don't come here all these years, just like your cousin."

Later, Michael showed up at their table for a few minutes. He stood leaning against the jukebox studying them, their heads bent together, the two of them sharing the same cigarette, both fully absorbed by this intense, verbal rapport that was so foreign to him. Finally, with an awkward, self-conscious grin, having made up his mind apparently that they were never going to notice him, he had come to stand behind Jacob, his hands on his stepfather's shoulders. Jacob had reached back to acknowledge his presence. And then the moment was gone, leaving her aching for its passage. Michael, leaning forward to kiss Jacob on the head, told them in a happy voice that he'd just arranged with the owner of this Italian coffee shop in North Beach to bring his band in on alternate Tuesdays to perform Yiddish music. They had toasted him with tall glasses of iced espresso and he went off with the merest suggestion of a swagger to phone his lead singer, who had been angry at him since Michael had come in one night to a rehearsal with his arm around the au pair girl, Marjan.

Jacob leaned forward to take Rae's hand. "You got him this job?" he began. But she lifted a finger at him.

"Don't thank me for interfering," she said. "I know you don't approve. It all comes from my worrying. No matter how hard I try, I can't leave things in the hands of . . . you want me to start talking about fate? Or do you imagine the Flame Bearers have made their way to the scissors and thread and are sitting there ready to cut the cord of my destiny? And anyway," she rushed on, because she could not yet admit to herself that their days together were numbered and that she would be haunted for years by the longing to be with him here in North Beach as they were now, together. And then she reached out, half standing, to take his face between her hands and kiss him on the lips. "My Jacob," she said in a husky voice.

Jacob was right. Her heart had been opened. And it was this, she decided, that had given to all the events of the last weeks a sense that they were being imprinted. It was like fixing the memory so deep it could never be dislodged, no matter how much she went on changing. She was being marked with this place, and with the love she felt for them all. So that later, when years had gone by and she had been away for a time even longer than all the years she had already lived, she would know how to bring herself back to them?

The mist was growing heavier, fading out the edges of trees and houses, making things loom up suddenly from a nightmare landscape. She had leaned forward against the wheel, and was wiping the window with her hand. During all the years of their childhood, Grandmother Shadmi had not taken them across the bridge, either to Berkeley or to Marin County. She had never approved of cars. She had not brought them up this wild, wind-swept coast, with its weatherbeaten farms, bare trees, grazing horses, and herds of black cows. "It's not Jewish," Maya had said one day in another lifetime so many years ago when she and Rae were poring over a map, "past Petaluma and the chicken farms, I'm telling you, it's just not Jewish." And therefore it made no sense that this unfamiliar landscape, with its sloping hills and rocky headlands, so densely covered with thistle and gorse, struck home to her with the same aching familiarity and sense of loss. But when in fact was she going to leave, she asked herself more urgently now, as Naamah smoothed out Ruth's braids and combed the girl's hair down over her shoulders. And where was she going? And how would she get there? And when exactly had she figured out that she was leaving?

25

T *h e r e* was that day Naamah had been standing next to Rae's bed, leaning over her, when Rae woke up.

"Rae," she whispered. "She knows."

"Give me a chance, Naamah," Rae muttered. "Do you realize what you're interrupting here? How do you know I wasn't just about to dream the way back to Kiryat Sefer?"

She kept her eyes on her cousin's face but she knew perfectly well that Naamah would take her time before she told her. Naamah had always been fond of a little suspense. It was a trait you would not easily associate with her but there it was, contradicting one's desire to tuck up human beings into orderly and predictable packages. She had already guessed that Naamah was talking about her mother. And she might have figured out what Aunt Elke knew but she didn't find the knowledge exactly welcome. And anyway, she knew that Naamah wouldn't tell her until they were on the headland for their picnic, tramping through the high grass still wet from last night's rain.

Naamah had parked on the downhill side of the street in front of Maya's house, where Rae had been living with Maude and Rubin and a few other members of the Pine Street Annex while the old Victorian intended as the center was undergoing final renovation. Rae stopped to gaze curiously at the houses on the block. She had not noticed them during all those weeks of worry about Maya. She looked so young, Naamah thought, and terribly tired. She was drawn and pale and there was a look in her eyes as if she'd been gazing long and hard at shadows. And then they were in the car, Rae was rummaging through the picnic basket, breaking off pieces of egg bread and stuffing them ravenously in her mouth, while Naamah watched her with a smile, relieved to see her eating after so many weeks of near starvation.

Rae had called the hospital to check on Maya before they left. Maya's burns had looked far worse than they were, apparently. Or perhaps Maya had just healed fast? Naamah and Frau Altdorf had been to see her daily. That might have been part of it. The skin on Maya's arms and chest was lightly scarred but already the raw mark of the key was fading. She had spent two days in the intensive care unit of Moffat Hospital and then had been transferred to the closed psychiatric ward at Langley Porter while they waited for Rubin to get his treatment center opened. Meanwhile, she sat wrapped up in a blanket and ignored them, her face lit with the immaculate, cool lustre of the transhuman. The little key had not been found.

When they reached the headland, Rae leaped out of the car and began pulling out blankets and jackets and piling them up on the ground. And then they were moving fast, with an exuberance Rae could not suppress. Naamah, who kept reminding her that she was "a slow person," had to pant and struggle to keep up with her although Rae was carrying everything, blankets piled on top of jackets piled on the picnic basket. Finally, Naamah had to stop and catch her breath and she was sorry, it was good to see Rae like that and she thought Rae had probably already figured out what she was going to tell her.

Rae, who had been laughing at her cousin, set the basket down on the ground and began to walk in a circle around her, throwing out her arms. "There's a wild spirit lives out on this cliff," she shouted. "Grandmother Shadmi was right. Remember? Once, on Rosh Hashanah, Maya ran off and got an armful of wildflowers and scattered them at the rest of us. Do you remember? She kept insisting she had seen tiny little women in long skirts going about with coals in their hands, bending down and breathing on them and then burying them in the earth. Bubbe kissed her and cried out: 'Ale vayber hobn yerushe fun zeyer muter Khave.' What an expression. 'All women are heirs to mother Eve.' Does it seem possible? There was a time, it actually existed, when all our mothers were here with us? And you know what else?" she yelled, crinkling up her eyes at her cousin. "I dreamed last night about your mother."

"Yes, Rae, good," Naamah had said to her, taking her by the arm. "You know, then?"

"How not? Of course I know. Haven't I, after all, discovered all the old 'channels of transmission'? All I have to do is close my eyes and presto-chango—the hidden world stands revealed."

"Always the joking. I'll never keep up with you. It's just like Brucha. The same wild spirit."

"Are you going to tell me?"

"My mother is inviting us to come for Purim. She's been going into Mendocino to work with a women's collective, a little group of actors. They're preparing a Purim play to perform for the public. Maybe we could take Maya? It's not for months yet. By then, who knows? Perhaps she'll be ready? It will be good for her to see my mother as she is, a bitter woman, but not certainly what Maya imagines. And you could talk to her, Rae . . . you could talk to my mother, about Rebekah."

Then, for a long time, they were silent, walking shoulder to shoulder through the wet grass. And Rae, who seemed to be ignoring Naamah's hint about Rebekah, said finally: "There's no point pretending Maya's going to be well next week or even next year. If Rubin manages to get the center going she'll be there for a long time. It might even be the best thing in the world for her. We, at any rate," she said in a softer voice, "certainly have not come up with anything better."

"You have to leave many things unfinished," Naamah said. She had turned to put both her hands on Rae's shoulders. That was the time. They had both realized Rae was going to leave. And then, during the next weeks they had gone out many times to walk on the headland because that is where the Shadmis always used to go for their family "conferences." In those weeks Aunt Elke began to write regularly to Naamah. And Maya, one day when Rubin came to visit her, had looked up and acknowledged him with a quick wink.

"And so, the plot thickens," Ruth had said and they all began to wait eagerly for Aunt Elke's next "disclosure." But Rae, because she refused to make up her mind about Aunt Elke, insisted upon understanding why her aunt would have kept her "knowledge" of Rebekah secret for so long.

"You know how my mother is," Naamah said to her. "She hates our grandmother. And why? Because she gave up her life to work in her house and take care of her? It's more than this. The stories from the Flame Bearers she hates too. And in these years, living alone by herself on the farm, she became more than ever bitter. I used to call her up when I was working on the papers. I thought maybe she'll know something and could help me. At first, she slammed down the phone. She didn't want a thing to do with them. Later, she wrote me letters, warning me to keep away from it all. 'It's *sam*,' she would say, 'pure poison. Look what it did to my mother, and now you want it should do the same thing to you?' But I always had the feeling she knows something we have to find out. When my work on the papers was going well I thought maybe we don't need her anymore. But now, when I can't go on all these months, I've been asking her again. What else can I do, Rae? Where else can I turn? The old papers I have already destroyed. I burned them up, I made them into ash. But nothing helps. Nothing. Not even this extreme measure. You understand, Rae. I'm not reproaching you. The key is lost. Rocha's key that has taken hundreds of years to get back to us. We can't stand here beating the breast and lamenting. I assure you, Rae, you have tormented your-self enough. Now is the time to ask, what can we learn from this?"

"The night Maya burned herself . . ." Rae folded her arms over her chest. "That night, I was standing with a group of women. We were outdoors. It was a full moon. I looked up and saw the key around the neck of Rocha Castel. Naamah, Rocha was my mother . . ."

"Rae, forgive yourself. What you did, giving the key to Maya, came out of what is best in you as a woman. But it did not come from what is best in you as a Flame Bearer. Sometimes there is no struggle between these two. But sometimes indeed there is struggle. For you maybe there was no other way to learn what I told you already that day in my workroom. You cannot give away your destiny to another person. Bubbe knew you were descended from Rocha Castel. She knew from the moment of your birth, I tell you. For her own reasons, as a grandmother, she loved you best. But it was not because of love she intended you to be the successor. That choice was never left to her. For her, and for the other women in the sect, was only the one question. Did they have the power to recognize the right one when she came along?"

"The right one . . ." Rae repeated the words very slowly. "I am the daughter longed for over hundreds of years. Don't they understand how impossible that is? Even if I felt large enough to carry this burden, didn't they realize how much guilt and self-reproach it would involve? I'm stuck, Naamah. Here is the question beyond which I cannot move. It's only become worse since Maya burned herself. Infinitely worse since the little key vanished. You say Ha Melamed Gadol is no more important than a woman sitting somewhere in a small back room weaving a prayer shawl. For me to take that in I have to see myself as somehow large enough to accomplish the impossible. And at the same time, a woman like everyone else. Naamah, if I could manage that, the grandeur along with the humility . . ."

"'The Flame Bearer is only as large as she is small.' You remember this saying? It means no one is ever worthy to do what she is called to do. No one is ever significant enough. The mission is always larger than the one who goes out on the mission. The Flame Bearer is made up out of the same clay that makes up every woman. She is a Flame Bearer only because she knows, in the clay lives the spirit of The Mother. If Chochma waited for one woman who was more worthy than another, how would The Mother do her work in this world?

"I look at you, here beside me. You, with your slanting eyes and your high cheekbones and your red curls. What are you that makes you the chosen one? Why did the destiny of the Great Teacher settle on you? I cannot answer these questions. But I can say this. It had to settle on someone. Someone had to be able to do this thing. And so, why someone else rather than Rae Shadmi? Isn't that the question for you to ask?"

Rae had begun to smile. Then she laughed and put her arms around Naamah's waist and leaned her chin on her cousin's shoulder. "'Why me? Why me?' All these years. That's what I've been asking. And now you, with a shrug of your shoulders, you look me right in the eye and you say: 'Why not?'"

But Naamah would not let herself be diverted. She reached up to stroke Rae's hair but then she drew away from her and said: "We are waiting for something, all of us are waiting. You are finding out how to call the birds. But could you be certain, if you were in trouble and far away from us, you would know how to 'find a hole in time,' as Rocha Castel used to say? It is only the first taste. After this will come years of learning until you one day will know how to move at will in and out of the old stories. Then you will be able to summon Rebekah when you need her, you won't have to wait for a swim in the lake or for our grandmother's power to pass into you. But how? How will you go after it without Rocha's key? That is what you are waiting to find out. Maya, too, in her own way is waiting and now something happened. My mother's going to leave the farm. She offers it to us, for the school or who knows . . ." Naamah broke off and looked away from her. "You see?" she asked, with sorrow in her voice, and Rae thought she was about to tell her something about Jacob. But Naamah, holding her palms pressed together, sighed and said nothing further.

They had made a picnic in the little grove of withered pine trees perched dangerously near the edge of the headland below the Palace of the Legion of Honor. "Rebekah came to the United States from Jerusalem, during the thirties." Naamah had reached out for a piece of bread but her hands were shaking. She took the linen napkin and smoothed it out on her knees. "She and our grandmother had a meeting then, and that is when my mother met her. Rebekah was here to raise money for her school. That is what my mother says. But I say: Rebekah was here to find out if one of our mothers had been trained to do what you now will be doing. She was then a woman in her fifties. She and our grandmother were meeting for the first time in more than forty years."

The wind had died down but Naamah was still shivering. She expected Rae to begin joking that there was always another version to the story. No matter how much her cousin changed, this trait always was there, this hiding what she was thinking and feeling. And then, because she wanted Rae to say something, she had held out a glass, nervously, for Rae to fill. But her cousin seemed oblivious. She had crouched down on her haunches as she drained her glass. And then suddenly, springing to her feet, she swung out her arm and smashed the glass down onto the rocks below them. "To the willing suspension of disbelief," she shouted. "And to the Flame Bearers," she whispered, grabbing Naamah's glass and smashing it with a quick stamp of her foot. "And to Kiryat Sefer," she added, kneeling down to put her hands on Naamah's shoulders and rock her in a strong embrace. "And to you above all, my cousin. But how can you sit there with such equanimity? Naamah, have you any idea what you are doing? Shoving me off the edge of the world like this?"

"We became friends, didn't we?" Naamah murmured in spite of the joking. "We became more even than cousins. We became friends . . ." And then they were both hugging each other and Naamah could see that Rae had understood that it would really happen. The time was coming, it was not far off, she would set out alone in search of Kiryat Sefer.

Certainly, Rae had known by then that these months she had spent at home, gradually taking apart the life she had built up so carefully while she was away from them, were a preparation. And then slowly, through her urgent sense of reaching out to hold on to them all, she began to understand they were saying good-bye to her.

The day Ruth came dashing into the waiting room at the hospital trying to imitate Rae's ironic stance. She was holding a little notebook in her hand and now she tossed it down on the table next to Rae. "I've got it all worked out," she whispered in a voice of mock hilarity. "These are the questions we have to answer before we're ready to take the Final Step and pack you off to a mythical city."

She watched Rae open the notebook and leaf through the pages. She was trying not to say anything while Rae was reading but she was tense and overwrought and finally she couldn't sit still any longer. "I asked Aunt Naamah to read it too. She says there's no great mystery why her mother kept the knowledge hidden. That's how her mother is, she says. Do you think so, Aunt Rae?" she went on, lapsing into urgency and wrinkling up her homely face.

"Could be," Rae said. "We're all so very dramatic. Why not Aunt Elke?"

"But why would she make such a big secret out of knowing Rebekah?" Ruth was talking in a reckless voice. It reminded Rae of Maya's old impetuous enthusiasms. "And why is she telling it now? And anyway, can we believe her? I hardly know her," she rushed on, condensing her pages of question and surmise into a few rapid-fire outbursts. "But I don't like her. And I wouldn't trust her without proof. But what proof is there?"

"Oh," said Rae, hiding her smile, "if we waited for proof . . ."

"You know what I'm going to do? What time is it? I'm going to show my notebook to Maya."

Then she ran out of the waiting room and up the stairs with all the foolhardy daring of a woman who will never learn to protect herself against devastation. She returned with a strained smile. She sat down on the sofa next to Rae and leaned against her aunt, who drew her close and propped her chin on the girl's head.

"It went well," Ruth said, "at least in the beginning. I didn't even knock. I went in there, I sat down on the bed, and I told her about Aunt Elke and Rebekah. She actually looked at me, would you believe it? My mother looked, with her own two eyes, at me. Because I'm telling you, Aunt Rae. I don't think I could take it anymore if she kept on insisting I've stuck myself in to the wrong place in the story. But then she noticed the notebook and she got scared. I guess that's what happened. She suddenly jumped out of bed and ran over to the door and listened. Then she went to look out the window. And then she came back, grabbed the notebook from my hand, ripped out some pages and swallowed them . . ."

Ruth's face seemed to be trying to cry and trying to smile at the same time. A spasm of indecision passed over it and then she threw herself into Rae's arms. "You're going away, aren't you? You're leaving us, aren't you?"

"You think I wouldn't rather stay?" She said it almost with anger.

"Shall I tell you what I think?" Ruth had just figured out there would be plenty of time to cry and not much time for conversation. "I think Maya will be better after you go. Not all better. But just enough. I think she'll want Rubin to fall in love with her. I think she'll try to make him do it. You know what Aunt Naamah says? She says Maya could be Rubin's 'test case.' She says Maya would never be so withdrawn she wouldn't be aware of that. We can't judge Maya," she stormed on, her voice growing more and more frantic. "That's what Aunt Naamah says. We can't judge Maya. We have to understand, in her own way she's doing what she can. If you go, if you really try to find out about Kiryat Sefer, if there's really a way to get there, you see what I mean? Maya won't have to try so hard. And then, she can just come back to live with us. The way she used to."

Rae said nothing. She did not move. She was telling herself the healing of this girl was not in her hands. She could not interfere here any more than she could with Maya, or with Naamah and Jacob.

Ruth pulled away from her. "I can't bear it," she shouted. "It's not fair. How long this time? Will I ever see you again? You could get lost out there, you know. You could die even. And all because of those dreadful Flame Bearers." But then she clapped both her hands over her mouth, one on top of the other. "I don't really mean it," she said in a muffled voice. "I want you to go and find them and figure out what it all means. I believe in them. I really do. But I just can't understand why it has to be so painful."

"You think I'm not afraid?"

"You're not afraid of anything, I don't believe you," Ruth said, trying out a new familiarity with her aunt. "You're just stuck in your ways," she galloped on, knowing that it would be impossible to offend this woman. "It's just like Uncle Jacob says. You have a great big heart. That's what he told me about you. But you try to let the little head tell the big heart what to do."

"Oh?" said Rae, "ridiculous, is it?"

Ruth shouted. "Yes, ridiculous," she yelled, with a quick childish glee, pounding Rae on the shoulder.

But Rae had hesitated to accept Aunt Elke's invitation. She was involved in her own 'researches' and didn't like to believe she wasn't getting anywhere fast. She had realized by then what the little key had been for and how bad a mistake she had made giving it to Maya. Now, she was left to her own devices, picking up a hint here and there from what their grandmother had told them as children. She found, with practice, that it was easiest during the late afternoon and early twilight. Then, time seemed to grow thin, odd little cracks and transparencies appeared in its surface. Her concentration, freeing itself from other preoccupations, would fix itself on the distant voices of children ("when you did yesterday," "she found it under the desk," "over here not over there silly," "you did, you did so, you did it"). And sometimes she was not in the room any longer, curled up in the window seat with her head pressed against her arms.

Once, she saw a marketplace. It was early morning; she remembered, with a great tug of nostalgia, walking there with her older sister, carrying their jars of oil and honey and wine. She saw everything with a remarkable clarity (that was a rare day): the bronze statues of the goddess, the marble columns, the dancing figure with its rounded breasts at the base of the pediment, the itinerant peddlers who had traveled on muleback from the mountain villages. She heard the voices of hawkers crying their wares. Amber from the north, baked figs with anise, black sheepskins, cured olives, tamed birds. She did everything she was supposed to do; repeating the stories their grandmother had told them about Kiryat Sefer, closing her eyes, rocking and swaying the way the old lady used to, reciting everything she had heard about Beruriah, their great teacher, who had walked through the marketplace with her girls. But she couldn't enter. Not once, never again since the day she had stood looking up at Rocha Castel and had seen for the first time the little key that would have helped her, hundreds of years later, get back into the old tales.

There were times when Rae could not believe she was making

this attempt to slip past time. But she became aware, after a few weeks of effort, that she was receiving support from an unexpected quarter. It happened not once or twice, but on numerous occasions that Rae, finding herself right at the edge of really colossal possibilities, would encounter Maya there with her. Maya. Urging her on, adding the pull of her own longing to the nostalgia that tugged at Rae, until she felt at times that all she needed to do was let herself go and she would be swept out beyond the circumscribed rational world and be carried back finally to the woods and the women gathered there and the white sand beach of her grandmother's stories.

Maya, in her long nightgowns, with the doll Hadassah tucked up in her arms, snuggling in bed with Rae and babbling about the way to write and rewrite their story, must have been trying even then, from some forlorn, desperate part of herself, to enlist Rae's aid and to pass the burden over to her.

Without doubt, Maya knew what Rae was doing. If Rae went to visit her at the hospital after one of these memory sessions, Maya's face would be covered in perspiration, her hands would be hot and dry and Rae understood that it was hard work keeping herself in that state of lofty withdrawal. It required all Maya's concentration, she could not afford to let go a single strand of her attention.

Then, gradually, as Rae kept at her work, Maya began to "return" to them. At first it was only to Rubin; for him she dragged herself back and let him hold both her hands in his while she told him stories, talking until she was spent and her voice came out in a whispered rasp and she would tip back her head and drop right off to sleep in the chair, her mouth open, her hands spread out, twitching slightly, on her knees.

Rae, too, felt she was changing. She joked with Naamah it was true and did what she could to keep afloat her habitual ironic sallies. But the irony itself had been transformed and she knew it. In the past, it had been there to serve her bitterness and to hide the fact that as a young child she had felt betrayed by their grandmother, in whom she had once believed, fervently. Now, the irony was there to hide that lurching of her heart Jacob had correctly divined. She didn't want to love them this much if she would have to leave them. And if she had to leave them, she didn't want Aunt Elke to be the one to tell her where she would have to go.

They had begun to celebrate the Sabbath again. Naamah, who

had let everything drop during this last year while she was at work on her papers, brought them together, "as in the old days"—so they could acknowledge the sense of farewell that was pervading the atmosphere. But it was Ruth and her notebook who dominated their discussions. "Well then," Ruth announced, as they sat late over dinner on Friday night. She got up to pace around the table, shaking her head and flashing impatient glances at them. "What does it prove that Aunt Elke has Rebekah's letters? Does that tell us why she kept them secret in the first place? You know what I think? If we go up there, if we do what she wants and come for Purim, those letters won't be there anyway. You watch. They'll somehow, mysteriously, have disappeared."

And so it had gone on, hour after hour, until finally even Michael got involved. He had been watching them with his heavy eyes. Keeping score, Rae imagined, measuring and weighing one opinion against another while he, in silence, came to some judgment of his own. Did she admire him? The rest of them were all so outspoken. Blurting out whatever came to mind. Interrupting each other. Talking at the same time. Yelling, in order to be heard above the growing din. And meanwhile Jacob was going back and forth between the table and the pantry, bringing out new supplies of food. Naamah was pouring fresh pots of tea. And Rae, who knew that she would never again in her life find anything like this, ignored the discussion and let herself drown in the sense of loving them. It was far more than a kinship bond. It was, as she had said the day before to Rubin, the kind of elective affinity Goethe had described. As if they'd chosen each other for their shared intensity, their endless enthusiasm for solving puzzles and working out the mysteries of human motivation. She loved Rubin, too, in that moment and wished he were a cousin or even a brother so that she would not have to regret the passion she had tried to feel for him and couldn't. No, even now she couldn't.

Michael said, clearing his throat and speaking in a soft voice: "Grandmother Elke was always slighted." And then he stopped, waiting for their response. He looked over anxiously at Jacob, his large Adam's apple bobbing nervously. He was the strangest boy, Rae thought, looking at him for the first time with real affection. He stood rocking back and forth on his flat feet, waving those long arms of his, which seemed to grow before your very eyes. His sleeves, which always fit at the beginning of the evening, looked too short by the end of the meal. He had gigantic hands, with long, flat, sensitive fingers that floated at the end of his palms as if they had made claim to all his expressiveness. Jacob nodded, encouraging him. "Well, she was," he added, belligerently. "You remember how Great Grandmother Shadmi used to talk to her? As if Elke was just a slave?" Then, because they still didn't get it, he shrugged his shoulders and was about to withdraw.

A difficult boy, Naamah thought to herself, wishing he did not have to be given so much encouragement. But it was Ruth who blurted out: "What are you driving at? So, she was a slave? So? So?"

And now, because Ruth had given him the opportunity to get angry at her, he began to speak in a supercilious, condescending tone: "So? So? You can't figure it out for yourself? The secret made her important. Don't you see? It made her a part of the whole story. She knew what nobody else knew. You get it? It gave her a destiny."

Jacob had been watching him with a proud smile. And now it was clear to Naamah that the two of them had worked it out together. And that Rae, who had been leaning back in her chair, letting her eyes move from one to another, as if none of this concerned her—in fact had been impressed.

Brucha came back from her wanderings on the back porch, where she had been making life miserable for Teppele. She was dragging the little dog along with her, precariously tucked up under her arm. She came over to the table and grabbed a lump of sugar and held it between her teeth. But her eyes were riveted on Rae.

"She won't tell me what she knows," Naamah answered, looking apologetically at them; she had long since accepted the burden of her mother's peculiarities. "Now she insists it's for Rae's ears. I try not to be hurt by her," she added, catching the look in Jacob's eyes. His mother-in-law, he often said, was the one person in the whole family he distrusted. "To me," she went on, giving him a sad smile of acknowledgment, "all this is her way of saying she, too, like our grandmother, is choosing Rae. I have to forgive her. She felt, all her life, so insignificant. Michael is right. Our grandmother always preferred Aunt Esther. She gave over to her the care of the school. And of course, there was always Aunt Sonia catching everyone's attention, even if she was the pariah. But my mother? She hardly got away from home. She married my father in Europe and right away he was drafted. A few months later she got pregnant and he wrote to ask for a divorce. So, what could she do? She came back home. And after that her whole life was cooking and cleaning and caring for Grandmother's house. Was this a life? Until she went off to live by herself on the farm she had nothing for herself. But this now, the letters with Rebekah, her knowledge all these years about Kiryat Sefer, it was her way to be important. She'll tell only Rae, she says? Of course, only Rae. Now, she, too, has chosen. She, too . . . has a successor . . ."

c h a p t e r

26

Th e y stopped for lunch in Marshall, at a rough little seaside res-
taurant, with wooden tables outdoors on the deck. There was a chill
in the air, but the mist was getting thinner and Rae felt the buoyance
of the weather, an unmistakable sense of early spring. They sat longer
than they'd intended, eating french bread with barbecued oysters and
drinking beer. The filtered sunlight, the flash of white on the bellies
of the sea gulls, the rocking of the brown hills across the water, the
ripple of light against the stripped wood of the deck, gave her the sense
that she had been cut loose from her moorings and was already out on
that trackless wandering Naamah had predicted for her.

Rae was sitting next to Ruth, her arm around the girl. Maya, to
everyone's surprise, had sat down next to her daughter on the other
side. The owner, a tall woman with dyed red hair, a husky voice, and
a rasping cough, had taken Brucha over to the smoking barbecue pits
to pour sauce on the oysters. And Rae, taking it all in with that new
passionate nostalgia, believed for the first time really that Naamah was
right. Already, before she had left them, she could feel the loneliness
of the habitual wanderer who day after day finds herself homeless at
nightfall.

Maya, after pushing the oysters around in their shell and licking
the thick sauce from her fingers, went over to the barbecue. She stood
with her hands folded behind her and swayed back and forth on her
toes as she breathed in the pungent smoke. They all watched her. She
was a sad, remote, and tired woman, but just then she did not look
disturbed. The scars on her arms and chest were covered by a thick
turtleneck sweater, and today, in the easygoing atmosphere of the

place, her wide eyes and expressive gestures made her seem appealing, with a wistful, waiflike charm.

Rubin, who was the last to admit what this trip really meant, poured out the pitcher of beer, divided up the oysters as they arrived, and kept an eye on her. He was telling stories about his life in Israel, smiling too much and laughing eagerly at his own jokes. When Maya seemed to be growing restless he stood up and went over to the barbecue to stand next to her.

What a lonely man he is, Naamah thought. She had already decided that she would talk to him about Rae. But how to find the right occasion? Rae would tell him in her own good time, she knew. But she wanted the telling to come from herself also. Part of her pledge to keep him, after Rae was gone, a member of the family. She folded her paper napkin, pressed it against the table, and stood up heavily. But of course, as soon as she approached the barbecue, Brucha threw the basting brush into the pan and scampered away to pester Michael, Maya taking off after her with a delighted squeal.

Michael had been sitting alone at the table next to them, his head bent forward as he strummed his guitar. There was a deep and pervasive loneliness about him too, Naamah thought, looking across the deck at him and wondering whether he had inherited this withdrawn silence from his father. But the truth was, she could hardly remember what her first husband was like. And now, to think that she might be drifting away from Jacob too . . .

So why not Rubin and Maya? she suddenly thought, eager to push her thoughts off in some other direction. She had caught Jacob's eye. And once again that feeling of unfamiliar pain came up inside her. She should blame herself, she wondered? But why blame? It was he who had decided all those years to work at Grandmother Shadmi's school. Was it her fault, or the fault of Michael and Brucha he did not write more or become, finally, a philosopher? She smiled over at him, wondring if he had just had the same thought about Maya and Rubin. And then she took both of her hands and pressed them up against her cheeks, swaying her head back and forth.

Foolish woman, she was saying to herself, such thinking still, at your age? But to Rubin she said: "She's going to leave, you know this, don't you?"

Rubin's pale eyes darkened painfully. "She's going back to the East Coast? After all?"

"Back? Rae? Never."

It seemed to imply much more than he was able to grasp but the largeness of it brought him comfort. He raised his eyebrows, ran his hand nervously through his hair, looked quickly at Rae then back at Naamah, and finally just stood there, holding her eyes. It was, she reflected, at times like this you felt the substance of the man, this quality of intense, clear vision that was so much more compelling than his goodness.

Rubin folded his arms on his chest. "You were right to tell me," he said in a voice that made her wonder if she had been. "It was, I guess, obvious all along."

When they drove off again, Rae was riding with him. She was sitting on the far side of the seat, withdrawn and distant while he fiddled with the dial on his radio, glancing at her apprehensively. There was a light overcast, although the mist had been lifting as they ate lunch. A brisk wind was blowing and shadows were moving fast across the hills. But then the light broke through the clouds and Rae felt herself aching for those dusty small roads of a country she did not recognize. That sense of herself walking there alone, the old lady's leather bag in her hand, toward nightfall. Mountain villages with crumbling walls, donkeys grazing in the rubble, a young girl running past, hawking oranges. Vividly, she saw herself strolling out onto a pier to shade her eyes wearily against the horizon. Years and years of it; the unexpected homecoming in strange houses where the table was spread, the candles lighted, the Sabbath meal served as it had been in her grandmother's house during their childhood. And herself grown old finally in this quest for a city in which she still did not really (not one hundred percent, not wholeheartedly) believe.

Then she was trying to say something of this to Rubin, because she had known for months that he was in love with her and that in her sorrow about Maya she had let him believe her leaning against him was reciprocation. He had been there the way no one before him had been, with his bear hugs and tender gestures. That way he had of taking her hand and tucking it into his pocket when they walked together. Even with Jacob there was that feeling of reserve, of being on guard, of holding back and keeping hidden. At strange hours Rubin knocked at the door to her room and walked in, often uninvited, sensing the moments she needed him most. Rubin listened from a reserve of silence that was, she realized, his greatest gift. The secret of his capacity to heal, the quality for which in another life she might have come to love him. In his arms, tucked up against his father's old suede jacket, she had let herself feel terror for Maya and sorrow for the loss of everything she herself had been. And even then she'd known she was deceiving him. Lying next to him in the guest room where Maya had danced with Hannah Leah, she placed the blue knit cap on his curls with a nostalgic tenderness. It was too late to run away to sea with him.

"I have been thinking about Kiryat Sefer," she said in a quiet voice, without turning toward him. But he had caught the note of departure in it.

"From my point of view," he said, when she did not go on talking, "the question of course remains. Why can't you do whatever it is you want to do and stay right here in California? If Kiryat Sefer is a mythical city, and yet somehow your family needs and expects you to get back to it, surely the jumping off place might just as well be San Francisco?" He interrupted himself because she had sucked in her breath. "I must take these things metaphorically, it's part of my work," he added, feeling that nevertheless he had missed the point. "Maya talks about Kiryat Sefer and I hear in this her yearning for healing and wholeness. But for you to set out actually looking for a city that disappeared hundreds of years ago . . . Rae, are we having this conversation? I'm in love with you," he burst out finally and the car swerved over to the other side of the road. "With every word I hear you saying that you're going away. But why? Do I constrict you? I try to give you all the freedom you need. Do I ever ask you for an accounting? You come and go as you like. You stay with me, you stay over at Naamah's house, you have your own room at Maya's. You are free to go and come as you like with Jacob. Have I ever objected? I don't even feel any kind of inner objection. I take you, I really do take you as you are."

Rae kept silent; she was weighing the possibility of his understanding her but she did not think the chances were good. And then, still without turning toward him, she said: "It doesn't seem to be a question of choice. I haven't decided anything. What could I decide? I have no more reason to leave here than I have to stay. No, I'm sorry, Rubin. There are times when I feel that I'm trying very hard to be in love with you. I have to tell you the truth, don't I? But something has turned me in another direction. You remember the game? That's what I feel like. Pin the tail on the donkey. During the last year I seem to have been blindfolded and spun around and given a little shove forward. No one has asked me to believe in anything. I'm just supposed to set off with my arms in front of my face, groping. And the strange thing is, that's precisely what I'm going to do."

It was the first time she had said directly that she was going. And now, as they both at the same time took it in, she had turned to face him, her eyes making it evident how much it cost her to speak to him like that. He had reached over to click off the radio, spilling the ash from his cigarette. But then he realized that the silence was even more difficult.

"I wish I didn't feel so helpless," he said, trying to make his voice matter-of-fact. "I think it would be easier for me if you told me you were going back to some other man. Or that you were going to become a nun and enter a convent. I feel the same thing sometimes struggling to maintain contact with my patients. But with you, where it matters more to me than anywhere else, I can't even name my opponent. You're not in love with anyone else? I believe you. You're not planning to become a nun? You're certainly not going through a breakdown. But with every word you speak I see you growing more and more distant from me. You're very nice about it. I don't deny that. Anyone can see how hard you're trying to be considerate. But somehow that only makes it worse."

"Your opponent?" Rae took up the word. "Don't you see?" She was leaning over very close to him. "It's the sense that you regard as an enemy everything that has become most essential to me. You're afraid for me, is that it? You don't want me to go off on a wild goose chase? You don't want me to take this risk? But that only makes me feel that I could never share with you what most concerns me. As if I'd always be divided against myself, needing to get rid of half of what I am in order to make a bond with you. I've spent my whole life with this sense of inner division. I've always been running away from something. I won't do it anymore. Finally," she said, her exasperation out of hand by then, "finally I'm not trying to figure out what it is. All I'm asking myself now is how to follow it."

"I know what will happen to me," he said. "For a long time I'll pretend you're going to come back to me because without you my life is going to be far too small. And then, when I realize you're really lost, I'll forget that anything larger was ever possible. I'll fall in love again. I'll probably even get married. I'll pretend it's the same thing I had with you. I'd be all right I think if I could only remember that it wasn't. But I'll forget . . ."

He kept silent then, managing somehow not to question her or smile too much or run his hand through his hair or flick the ash from his cigarette. And finally, she said, with that sharp veering off he was almost used to from the Shadmis, something about the German poet Rilke, whom he had never read. And then, when he could take in her words, she seemed to be in the middle of it and he couldn't for the life of him figure out where she was going.

"You know that coffee shop Jacob and I like so much? It used to have a poster of Trieste on the wall. The first time I went to Europe I wanted to visit there. To see Duino Castle, where Rilke used to stay. But on the train I found out it had been destroyed during the war. Did I tell you this story? Rilke spent a winter there, he was staying alone. One night he was paying some bills. But suddenly he got up and went out onto the balcony. It was a stormy night and he heard a voice shouting out to him. Shouting to him, mind you, with the first words of what became *Duino Elegies*."

She had fallen silent and was looking at him with the expectant gaze that always made him feel so hopelessly inadequate. He knew too, from the familiar sinking in his chest, that he was out of his depth again. He felt small and irrelevant and he kept himself, in the last minute, from blurting out: "You don't say? That's very interesting." And now, finally, she went on, trying he knew to hide her impatience. "It reminded me of Naamah. Rilke regarded himself as receiving 'dictations.' So far as I know, no one ever has given much thought to figuring out from where, or from whom, or even why these 'dictations' came to him. We accept his words; we welcome them; we call them poetry. We regard ourselves as immeasurably enriched by them. And so I wonder whether the same isn't true for what Naamah 'receives.' You know what she's been doing these last months? She destroyed all of our grandmother's papers and since then she's been waiting for something to happen. For 'dictations,' you see? For her, as a Flame Bearer, they are imagined to come from Rocha Castel, the first of our scribes after Kiryat Sefer was destroyed. Or from Beruriah, one of our great teachers from before the earthquake. And now, in the last few days she's begun to hear a voice and to do some kind of automatic writing. You could scoff, of course. But I wonder. Why are we willing to accept Rilke's experience and yet feel so inclined to be scornful of

Naamah's? Perhaps the dictations that are 'coming through' should be accepted in their own terms even if one can't say a single meaningful word about where it's coming from? Or how? Or why?"

"It sounds to me," he said, knowing that she had for the first time directly let him into her preoccupation, "as if there really could be any number of explanations and none of them guaranteed to be the truth." He had no idea what he was going to say next, only that he was determined to please her. "I think . . . what does it matter? Someone who stayed at home waiting for the right explanation would probably never . . . set off?"

She leaned over toward Rubin and put her head on his shoulder, fairly drowning in her desire to believe that now, even for an instant, there was somehow safety in the world. And he, in the relief he felt, could hardly catch a word of what she was saying.

"So, what do we have? If we leave aside the whole question of explanation? A gift of inspiration, that's what it comes to. Like poetry. Like a dream. Something that remains fundamentally mysterious, no matter how much we probe. And our task then is to accept and value what we've been given?"

She was talking fast, with that intensity of hers that made her strangely dreamy and somehow at the same time vividly present. "You see what I'm driving at? It's not really a question of believing in anything at all. For the life of me I still can't honestly say I believe it is possible for a woman of our time to find Kiryat Sefer. And I'm certainly not able to take on faith what Naamah's been writing down lately. . . . You heard us talk about it? Naamah's 'ghostly guide'? She is telling her that the Flame Bearers have been meeting all along, in some kind of Druidic college, every twelve years or so. Our grandmother may have lost touch with them, but they don't seem to have lost touch with one another."

No, he wanted to say to her, no, he didn't see what she was driving at. It made no sense to him, these old stories of theirs that mattered more to them even than they mattered to each other. But what was the point? He was an interlude, he knew that.

"Naamah thinks there are all kinds of orders and chapters. She says they are spread out all over the world, keeping an eye on what is happening, sending out its members where they will be most needed. It all works through various sorts of intuitions and inspirations which we have ceased to understand. That's what Naamah says. Sometimes a woman receives it through a dream, sometimes through her own vague yearning to change her life and set off in a new direction. Sometimes it comes from a book that she suddenly gets in her hands. Every decade or so the call goes out and the women feel it. For most of us it remains only a restlessness, a sense of dislocation and turbulence. For us, as Shadmis, it should be different. But our grandmother failed somewhere, she didn't instruct us properly. And so the call to the ingathering doesn't make sense even to us. Me it terrifies, Maya it disturbs, Naamah it draws out of the family into that little room of hers behind the house. That's Naamah's sense of it. As for me, I can only say it's easier to think of setting out in search of the sect than leaping blindly out of time and tumbling somehow into Kiryat Sefer. I think, frankly, for me the whole question of belief has been outclassed. I have to trust some faculty other than my ability to speculate rationally about what's required of me here. Maybe in fact, all that's needed is an ability to be swept off my feet by it all? In a manner of speaking— to fall in love?"

He did not, even for a moment, fail to understand her. He was, for the time being, way out there with her in that high-stepping of thought he had always admired so much in her. And he said, without any longer trying to hold himself back: "What is it you want of me, Rae? To say that I want you to go? But how can I, after all? When I love you?"

And she, sitting even closer to him, her arms wrapped around his neck as if she were trying, in spite of everything, to lash herself to him, drew back: "I know it's preposterous. You think I don't know? But this is what I'm asking. I want you, who love me, to see that I have to do what I'm about to do. I want you—not to admire, not to approve—I want you to understand."

She had folded her arms over her chest and was looking at him with an implacable gaze. "Yes, I want that," she repeated.

And he said, simply: "Understand? But I do understand. It seems so obvious."

And then they were laughing, because some crisis that had been growing between them for weeks was now behind them. He was reassuring himself that if she were ever to love him and come back to him it was because he could give her this. He was thinking that if he was large enough to let her go he might be large enough to keep her. And then he had seen the real truth of his dilemma. He felt, in that moment, in his acceptance of his loss, worthy of . . . what? Of her? He shook his head. It was not that. It was simply, he thought, as he pulled over to the side of the road to bury his face against her, that he was large enough to let her go—now that he had clearly understood he had no choice whatever.

27

T h e y had left the coast behind them, with its wings and shrieks and occasional wind-beaten houses. They were driving through the woods, the chapparal stripped back scarlet here and there among the redwoods. Rae had gone back to the VW with Ruth and Brucha, who was trying to scramble to her feet, pounding Ruth's lap, waving wildly. Some imperceptible crossing seemed to have taken place and time began to kick and plunge, a maniacal horse trying to get rid of its rider. She was no longer wondering if Naamah were right or asking herself if she were willing to leave. She was already on her way, the preparation was complete, only the last step remained to be taken.

It was summer here, the sky swept clear of its cloud rack, and Rae drove more slowly now. She was disturbed by this speeding up of time that seemed to be tearing her away from them faster than she was willing to let them go. She had just realized for the first time really what it would mean to set out by herself, a woman alone, into the world. It would have been difficult even if she had known where she was going. But to set out wandering from city to city, hitching rides, going by foot, letting herself be guided by dreams and intuitions that could lead her, somehow, to members of the sect. It was like the burning of their grandmother's papers, Naamah said. An extreme measure. Something you resorted to when there was no other way. If Aunt Elke couldn't tell her how to find Rebekah, if their great-aunt's letters had no directions for her, she would have to do it that way.

Then Aunt Elke was there, standing by the gate. A stout woman, wearing jeans and heavy boots and a flannel shirt, there was no trace left of that earlier beauty she had tried so hard to keep hidden. She came striding over and reached in, to pull a kicking Brucha out of the car. Her face was heavy and deeply furrowed, her eyes sardonic, her mouth grim. She had combed her hair into a braid and tied the end of it with a piece of rope. She set Brucha down on the ground and kept a hand on her shoulder. She did not smile, or make any pretense of pleasure that they were there. She shook hands with Ruth. But it was clear that her interest was fastened upon Rae.

She reached up and pushed Rae's hair back from her forehead. "You didn't always have it," she said, narrowing her eyes as she peered at the raised birthmark that grew just under the hairline. "But then when you were three or four years old, what happened? One day all of a sudden the forehead began to sting and burn and there it was. The Flame Bearer birthmark. When the old lady caught sight of it, oy, I tell you, it was all over for you."

The farmhouse was a good way back from the road and they had to walk it. Brucha immediately started to fret and complain, kicking at the dirt and making little fists at them. But Rae snatched her up and set her smartly on her shoulder. Aunt Elke had turned to watch Jacob drive up, the old car heaving a rumble of relief as the engine was turned off. She looked for a longer time as Maya and Michael came down the path, arm in arm. "Calves for the slaughter," she muttered, shading her eyes with her hand. For Naamah she had a stiff, reluctant embrace.

And then it seemed to Rae, even before they got to the farm, that they'd been away from San Francisco for a long time. She felt disordered in her perceptions and had trouble adjusting to her surroundings. They were as confusing as those insinuating forecasts from her own future, the little villages, the dusty roads, the long loneliness of empty streets at dusk which set her heart racing.

Fragmented impressions began to swim up and pass away—the gray octagonal barn, which was the finest building on the place and had been built by Aunt Elke with the help of a women's collective down the road. The goat pen, where Brucha immediately set up an outrageous chatter, grabbing a baby goat in her arms and hugging him tightly around the neck. The little house, not much more than a two-room shanty, where Aunt Elke lived. It was neat inside, with a tiny kitchen built into one corner. There was a second room with a loft bed, a thick rug, a woodburning stove, and a fine walnut bookcase.

The barn was a two-story affair, divided into oddly shaped, unfinished rooms. A gallery looked down on a bare wooden floor. There was a central skylight, soaring up over the interior space, a smell of pine and sap, a thick rope swinging in the breeze outside the door. The barn had never been used and seemed to be waiting for its tenants. But it became clear to Rae, as they trooped in a ragged group around the farm, that Aunt Elke was drawing it out, building up the suspense, leading them on a merry goose chase. Her pride was the large garden that filled most of the remaining space between the barn and the house. It was carefully planted, flowers surrounded by vegetables, fragrant herbs and pungent plants hidden among them. Here they had stopped, as Aunt Elke named her plants with a laconic emphasis. She did not conceal her satisfaction that she had gotten them up there to witness her life.

Maya, who had been dragging along behind the others, holding tight to Rubin's arm, was staring at Aunt Elke. She watched Elke bend down to touch a plant and pull out a weed or pluck a sprig of fragrant leaf to hand to Naamah. Then, when the others moved on, Maya stayed behind with her aunt. Rae saw Maya's lips twitching and realized that Maya was reciting the names of the plants the way they had as children, standing on tiptoe to watch Aunt Elke transplant them. She used to do it by moonlight in the months when the moon had been full two times. They thought it strange the old lady entrusted that task to Elke. Everyone knew it was a sacred business. But Aunt Elke had to her credit certain odd graftings that had impressed Frau Altdorf when she came to harvest the herbs for drying next to the tile stove in the old lady's room. Rae wondered if Maya remembered the way she herself years before also by moonlight had taught Ruth to garden and it tore at her to see Maya like that, so close to what she had been, her face dreamy and gentle yet still so infinitely remote from them.

Maya glanced at Rae; she stood looking at her for a long time, hunched forward slightly, her palms pressed flat against her thighs. Then Maya came over to stand very close to Rae, pressing against her.

"I'll be better soon, I really will be," Maya assured her. She wrapped her hands around Rae's arm. "Please," she whispered, "Rae, don't be angry."

"Angry? But why would I be?" She couldn't for the life of her figure out what Maya was driving at.

Maya put her fingers against Rae's lips to keep her from interrupting. She stood up on tiptoe, tipped back her head, and said in a voice so soft it was hard to apprehend: "I know how to go through into the story better than you, Rae. But don't you worry. This time I'll show you." Maya was taking great pains to keep her voice low but certain words kept breaking away from her. "She'll never *tell* you," she whispered. "She *doesn't* want you to *know.*"

"Aunt Elke? Doesn't want me to know?" Rae considered it. "What does it matter, actually? I sometimes think . . . maybe we'd all be better off if we left the whole thing alone?"

Maya liked the way Rae was talking to her, as if the years had not come up to make trouble between them. "We've lost the knack of it," Rae said, and Maya, looking very sober and responsible, repeated: "We've lost the knack."

"I don't know." Rae was looking at the ground, shaking her head slowly. "Perhaps what we're supposed to have learned in all this is how to separate ourselves from it? Without slighting it or forgetting it? You know what I'm saying, don't you?" She had put her arm around Maya to draw her very close and Maya made up her mind then and there that she wasn't ever going to leave Rae again.

Rae said: "We need to give it a place in our lives, this great tradition of female knowledge we've inherited. We have to find some way to honor it, to pass it on, but without trying to live it in the old way. I'll never go back to New York. The years I spent there . . . They've vanished so completely . . . sometimes I think I could get back more easily to Kiryat Sefer than I could to the life I had been living all those years."

Maya had drawn back to look at Rae while she talked. Her eyes were fixed on Rae's lips, her own lips moving responsively as if she were calmly going over the words to extract their fullest implication. But then, without warning, she darted back and huddled up in Rae's arms.

"Not now, Rae. Not now. I'm getting better. Rae, don't leave me."

Rae looked up over Maya's head, helplessly. And were you, if you had witnessed, if they had let you see . . . bound forever, that's what Rae was asking herself, to someone who had stripped herself down before you?

Yes, she thought, probably you were.

She had wrapped herself around Maya, feeling the time had come to make a choice. To let it all go finally and find her life's meaning here with them as they were even now in all their trouble, together. But her eyes had been met; this time her despondency had been taken in. She knew that even before she saw Aunt Elke watching her from across the garden, her arms crossed over her chest, her eyes narrowing in that Shadmi way, measuring them.

"Maya, you know . . ." She had lowered her head to put her lips next to Maya's ear and in that moment she knew it herself for the first time, really: ". . . it's no longer in my hands."

An hour later Aunt Elke left for town with the four women, members of the cast, who had walked over from the sprawling farm collective that was her closest neighbor. She had given Naamah a careful set of directions on the back of the playbill. Michael went along with her to see about providing some additional last-minute music. Before he left he came over and stood very close to Rae, putting his arm around her shoulders. Is he saying good-bye to me? Rae wondered.

Maya was standing a few feet away from her, nodding her head up and down and dragging her left foot back and forth through the dirt. She, too, had decided. If Rae was going to leave her, she wasn't going to hang around here holding on to Rae. But still, somehow, she didn't like to stand too far away from her. They watched the truck pull out of the farm, raising a cloud of choking yellow dust. Rae looked around her, wondering whether for Jacob this place could provide the refuge he needed. All those years they'd accepted his sacrifice so unthinkingly, knowing always that the job was beneath him, telling themselves he'd find time, sooner or later, to do his own work. And now, before Naamah was ready to let him go, he had decided. He was leaving San Francisco. He was leaving the school. He was moving up to the farm.

Brucha was banging about between the goats, pushing them by the haunches, tugging the old billy by the beard. "Now, you come along here," she said in a grown-up voice to Maya, who glanced back to Rae to make sure she wasn't going anywhere. The little girl rubbed a spot on the bridge of her nose, she took an invisible braid between her fingers and gave it a tug. "Hoie," she sighed, putting her hands on her hips and hoisting up her trousers. "These goats need feeding."

Rae and Naamah were strolling arm in arm, back and forth between the house and the barn. Rubin, watching them, pulled nervously at his eyebrows. He could feel how completely their hopes had collapsed and he didn't know whether to let himself feel joy at the possibility that Rae might not be going anywhere. He plucked a blade of grass and put it in his mouth and then, walking fast to catch up with Brucha and Maya, he found himself whistling.

Rae put her head on Naamah's shoulder. "I told you, didn't I? She brought us up here to make fools of us. I don't think she knows a thing. And if she did? Do you see the way she looks at us? She hates the lot of us."

Ruth and Jacob had gone into the barn, and now they waved down from the upper story. "You should see the view," Ruth called out, trying to distract them. There was a dry wind, blowing up in the dust.

"We've done what we could, haven't we?" Rae muttered. "We've let Maya go insane, we've allowed you to burn up the papers, we've ruined your marriage, disturbed your child, torn me out of my life, roped poor Rubin into it all, broken Ruth's heart, and ignored Michael. Isn't it enough? What do they want from us now?"

Naamah was holding her hands in front of her face. She was walking by herself, back and forth in a small circle, bent over, biting her lower lip. "If only I were better at these dictations. It comes in such a rush I can't get it all down. But this I know. Next year, 9867 by the Flame Bearer calendar, there will be the in-gathering of the sects and you must be there. You think I don't know the danger, Rae? You could become like Maya, wandering after shadows. You could get lost. Out there, where you are going, you have to know how to summon help.

"And you, you are the sort of woman who gives away a key that hasn't been seen for hundreds of years in the world. We could, if we let you go off without guidance, lose you forever. And what if you do not find them by next year? For twelve more years you will have to wait, out there, alone, beyond our help. I don't like to think what these years could be like. It is now the pull is the strongest; later, it will all grow faint again. Now, before the in-gathering the locked doors open and voices that have been silent cry out. That is why your powers are growing. But these things you should have been practicing all your life. You should know by now how to travel in the old stories, how to summon Rebekah, how to listen to what the birds are telling you. That is our way and we have forgotten. This is why we need my mother. She has Rebekah's letters. Of this I am sure."

"Yes, she has them. She has them all right. Otherwise she

wouldn't have bothered to bring us here, to torment us by withholding them."

"Rae, don't you see? It shouldn't be like this. If things were right, if the transmission had not gone wrong, Rebekah would be able to maintain the contact with you herself."

"Naamah, it's a dead end. Admit it, we've just hit bottom." Rae turned and looked over her shoulder with a comical wag of her head. "Welcome despair," she said, bowing deeply.

Naamah ignored her; she had figured out by then the best way to handle her cousin. "Rebekah must have known something would go wrong when she came here during the thirties. Why else would she write, of all people, to my mother? Yes, smile, it's good. You think you were born with this charm for no reason? Go to my mother, do what you must, talk to her and get the letters."

The play was held in a large public hall at the end of town. The audience trooped in late, the men wearing country clothes, the women more extravagantly decked out in long dresses and heavy jewelry. No one had come in Purim costumes. Children ran up and down the aisles, a few dogs came in, Brucha kept dashing backstage, egging on the other kids and peeping out from behind the heavy green curtain.

It passed quickly—and that was saying a lot for it, Rae thought. She had always hated amateur productions. It was performed in modern dress, and had managed to update the drama so that Queen Esther talked about contemporary Jewish issues. Haman, a tall woman dressed in a checked gangster suit from the forties, personified all the forces of the modern world that live by violence. But the audience, mostly young and probably not Jewish, seemed to love it. They shouted and clapped and called out comments. Michael played an old piano at the back of the hall—it was out of tune, but he banged away bravely. There was even a moment when their Queen Esther came striding to stage center and held them all in a suspended silence, momentarily persuaded that here indeed was a woman who would now manage to save her people.

When the play was finished several girls went over to stand next to Michael, who shut the piano and leaned against it. Brucha, with a great burst of magnanimity, had gotten herself up onto Maya's lap. Rubin sat with his arms around Ruth and Rae. They all tried not to notice how relieved they felt when Maya let Brucha sit on there,

swinging her legs and clapping her hands long after the cast had re-
tired. Aunt Elke looked out from the faded curtain. She peered over
at the little family group. Half smiling? Or attempting to smile? Or
was it simply what it seemed to be—a knowing, malignant smirk?

28

The sun did odd things on this northern coast. Rae, who was out walking with Aunt Elke, observed it closely. It seemed to fall suddenly, springing on some small detail it wanted you to notice—the yellow triangular hinges on a darkly weathered outbuilding next to a white cottage with a red tar-paper roof. Or it selected a wooden picket fence and made her aware of the way shadow fell over it. She thought maybe she would come back one day, when it was all over. There were houses for sale, white cottages on the lower, less elegant, seaward side of town.

Aunt Elke, who had been living some eight or nine miles inland, knew the town well. People greeted her by name and with them she seemed to warm up and become responsive. But with Rae she had strolled along indifferently at first, wearing her heavy lumber jacket, a thick scarf on her neck. She admired Rae's tolerance for the sharp winds. She noticed her admiration for the picturesque, graying, anomalous New England town perched here in the California wilderness. After a while, she took Rae's arm, confidingly.

"You know what would happen if somebody came to visit the house? Right away, of course, she'd introduce them to the daughters. 'And this is Esther, the youngest,' she'd say. 'A girl to make you proud, always with the head in the book. And here is Sonia, with a heart made out of fire. And this is Elke, my eldest. From her we haven't decided yet what will be made. And that maybe is a destiny too? Someone maybe is needed to do what the ones with a destiny won't do?'"

"I never found her humor easy to take either."

"This was her humor? What humor did Mama ever have? Always, she was looking for her successor. To Esther she gave the school. But did this mean she found her successor? Don't you believe it. But me? Would she think of me? 'This one,' she'd say, giving me a push forward, 'a Shadmi without fire in the blood. Ima, tell me,' she'd call out, beating on her breast, 'tell me, Mother, what should we do with her?'

"Before you came, it was Naamah. Mama would go into the room after the child fell asleep and she'd begin to look. All over the body she looked for the birthmark. Even on me she'd give a look. She'd tell me, 'Roll up the sleeves. For you,' she'd say, 'the hands would show it. And maybe the arms. This is your nature.'"

It seemed to Rae that any moment now she was going to sneeze or cough or say the wrong thing. But she didn't have to worry. Aunt Elke had been silent for too long. On and on she went. It was the kind of verbal battering that made you close yourself off—and that, Rae knew, was dangerous. Just when you should have been listening, you'd have fallen asleep on your feet and would miss the few words that really mattered. The house on Scott Street, which should have been left to Elke. Sonia, who had been married five times and wasn't anything to look at. Esther, who always, from the time she was little, was Mama's favorite. Why else would she give her the school? Esther? With brains in her heels and a head like gravy? And finally Aunt Elke said, as they strolled out onto the sweep of grassland at the edge of the town: "You want I should tell you about Rebekah?"

There were two large dogs romping together through the high grass. A few people were strolling about on the headland, gazing out to sea through binoculars and field glasses at the gray whales visible off shore, leaping and sporting there like dolphins. It had grown dark, already in the late afternoon; now and again the light broke through the heavy overcast and fell, with its sharp luminosity, over the small clusters of white flowers. Rae had the feeling she'd better not show too much enthusiasm for the idea of Rebekah. She bent over, plucked a sharp blade of blue-green grass and held it betwen her teeth. But then, practically in the same moment, it made her furious. Aunt Elke knew perfectly well why they had come to visit.

"Oy, Rebekah," Aunt Elke said, casting a sly look at Rae. "Mama's big torment. And why? Because Mama never wanted to believe

Rebekah was the daughter from Hannah Leah. You understand this? You see why it was? If Rebekah was from another generation she too, and not only Mama, could be the Hovrodnik." Aunt Elke laughed, two short hoots with a heavy rasp. "They believed these things. The two of them. 'One Shadmi from every generation.' Yes? You remember? But Mama didn't want this. She wanted to be the last great one alive on this earth. But we heard from other women, from their little town. Rebekah, they told us, was smuggled back from Siberia, to the home in Kashevata. Raisa raised her like her own daughter. You know why? Because maybe, if somebody would know, they would try to kill this daughter of the czar's assassin. *Nu*, Mama thought I didn't hear all this. I was there to clean up, to take care. Never a person. And you girls, too. For you I was always only a rag with hands. Why shouldn't I be bitter? But now, I'm not. It's over. It's the past. I've given it up. I'm ready to leave. You want to go to Europe? You want to find Rebekah? I'll go with you."

She had glanced at Rae's face. "You don't know? Of course, she's alive there. I have even the address. Where she was and where she was going. Oy, Mother, believe me," she spat out, "to think it would be me? Me? To tell the successor?" She had put her hands to her head, the palms pressed flat against her temples. "You want to know why they quarreled, Rebekah and Mama? They quarreled because Mama insisted the tradition had to be kept secret, away from the men. She didn't want the men to know about the sect or about Kiryat Sefer. Rebekah and the others had a big mission to bring the old worship into the modern world. They thought it was time to tell the hidden tradition. But Mama, she didn't want this. 'These are the mysteries,' she would say and bang on the table with her fist. This quarrel they had already in Russia. And this quarrel they had again when Rebekah came to visit in the United States. But then the Second War in Europe came and we didn't hear any more from Rebekah. Mama had the idea she went behind German lines to save the Jewish children and bring them into Palestine. She thought Rebekah was captured. She thought Rebekah was tortured and killed. Don't ask me where she got her ideas from. Maybe it was from the voices? From the voices! This is how she could give herself airs. If Rebekah was dead Mama was the last great Shadmi in the Old World line. The last Hovrodnik raised with the old knowledge. The last to pass on the Tradition. Phtew!"

She spat again, kicking out at a hillock of grass. And Rae had to fight down a nearly overpowering desire to clap her hand over Aunt Elke's mouth.

"So, now what happens? You see the problem the old lady made for herself? She was, you remember, in the oral succession. Not supposed to write down the stories. She, who didn't want the tradition changed, who didn't want that the telling from mother to daughter should be broken, what happens to her now? What if she doesn't find someone to hand on to? What if Isarael isn't ready yet to understand? So she starts to work with the old ladies, with Zelda Zemanski and Frau Altdorf and the others, to write down the stories. Why? You are asking me? She wrote down the stories to give them to Naamah, to keep them for you. And you, what do you do? You go away from home. You don't visit, you don't write to her. It was you, Isarael the Beloved, you broke her heart."

"Yes, I did. That's true," Rae said, knowing she had just been released from the last unthinkable thought. "I broke her heart."

"Hunh," Aunt Elke muttered, without looking at her. "You think it matters you admit it now? You don't fool me, Isarael Shadmi, with your ways. I know you since a little girl. I tell you, you broke her heart. It was then, after you went away, I began to hear from Rebekah. Maybe she knew the old lady couldn't hold you? Maybe she knew you were getting lost to the sect? But now suddenly, Mama wasn't the 'last Flame Bearer,' anymore. She wasn't the 'great survivor.' There was another, who thought different things. And Mama, who believed always she would choose the successor, what would she have left? No more Isarael. No more 'last of the many.' And meanwhile, what if she died? What if Naamah wasn't a good scribe? What if the wrong person read what was written? What if there came to her a big punishment because she wrote it down?"

"You want me to laugh at her, is that it?"

Aunt Elke, who had been walking slower and slower, was suddenly moving fast again, waving her arms and shaking her head. There was a cold wind blowing up fast from the ocean; it seemed to carry the scorn Rae heard in her aunt's voice. The clusters of white flowers leaned away from it, pressing themselves against the hard-packed earth. The two dogs, circling back from their long romp, came over sniffing, their heads down, tails wagging. Aunt Elke was far ahead of her now and that was good. Rae was afraid her outburst might already have cost her Rebekah's letters.

"You don't know how lonely she was in that old-age home?" Aunt Elke turned, giving an impatient wave with her hand. "You came here to listen? So, listen. I'll tell you how lonely she was. She had cut herself off. Years before she quarreled also with the others in the sect. In Paris already she quarreled with them. They were always arguing inside the sect. One thought this, one thought that. These were so-phisticated women. What did they need with her old nonsense about Kiryat Sefer? They kept together and she cut herself off. When she left Europe she put them behind her. She was, maybe, the first from the Flame Bearers to go to the New World. And for what reason? To make a school here? She came here because she believed the Ameri-can Indians were the lost tribe of Dan. Hoie, I tell you. Mama and her voices. She told you about the in-gathering on the shores of Kin-neret? But did she tell you how to get there? You think you will get on a boat and arrive in Haifa and take the bus to Safed? You, with your head of fire, were you listening when she talked? Canaan of *old*, she said. The in-gathering on the shores of Kinneret in Canaan of *old*. But you, you think you know what are the names of the Old Land?"

For a moment, Aunt Elke stopped talking. She sucked in her breath, cast a quick, startled look at Rae, and seemed genuinely sur-prised at the Hovrodnik question she had just asked her. But then, snorting ironically and shaking her head, she lunged back into her harangue.

"You are waiting for the Hovrodnik to come and tell you how to get back there? But she won't come. The Hovrodnik won't come. And why? Because the old lady didn't teach you how to call her. Why did she come looking for the lost tribe of Dan? She came because she, too, didn't know how to call the Hovrodnik. She came so the Miwok Indians would teach her again.

"You listen to me. The Shadmis were looking always for the lost tribes. Rebekah, too, was looking. If you're a Flame Bearer you have to find a task. The world doesn't have enough suffering and sorrow? They have to go digging up in the past, looking for lost tribes, finding old papers, digging around for libraries from vanished cities. That was another reason for their quarrel. Rebekah thought she could find the lost tribe with papers dug up from the library in Kiryat Sefer. But

Mama, she insists to follow the voices. Why do you think we came to California? Why to San Francisco? You think she had anything in common with those German Jews who were here? Those Yekkes? She hated them. Why do you think they gave her always so much trouble over the school? A German Jew is an assimilated Jew, wherever they are. And if they become a Zionist, then they'll have also an assimilated Zionism, assimilated all the way back to the biblical language. It's their way not to be a Jew, not to speak Yiddish. The same thing, all over again."

Aunt Elke's voice had dropped to a low hum. She had reached out to take Rae's hand in hers. And now she kept plucking it toward her, with a convulsive shudder. A fine bead of sweat had broken out on her aunt's upper lip and Rae wanted to run from her. She wanted to shake off her hand and take to her heels. She wanted to put miles and years and silence between them. Aunt Elke was testing her. Looking to see where her loyalty lay. With her, in her bitterness? With the old lady and the tradition? And she, meanwhile, would have to listen. For days and days, a captive audience, she would walk and listen, in silence, not interrupting, submissive to the older woman. And even then, who was to say the letters would be given?

Aunt Elke was laughing again. But now the laughter had the rough edge of a sob in it. "My mother told us, already when we were children. We would go to America. We would find the Indians there. Hoie, I actually believed they talked in Yiddish. She believed they told their own Flame Bearers stories. She believed they had female deities. She thought they knew Ugaritic. Earth worship. Nature spirits. Who knows what she thought? In Paris, in the beginning, everyone made a big thing out of her. But she went too far with her visions and her voices and her old worship. She was a beautiful woman, with the same red hair like yours. Later it changed. Yes, I'm telling you. After we came to America it turned black. Baron David left her a great pot of money. She never wanted to marry. She had three children. Each from a different man. You think Esther or Sonia knows who their father is? If Sonia would ask her she'd wave her hand. 'What do you need him for?' she'd say. 'I'm not enough for both the father and the mother?' But she never loved anyone until she put her eyes on you. When you were fourteen, fifteen years old maybe, suddenly you started looking like her. You and Maya, you treated me always just like the old lady did. A fixture, part of the furniture. But who brought you up? Who made the lunch for you? Or dinner, or the snack in the afternoon? The old woman? You think so? That's what you remember? The mother you had after Esther died was me. You think you know the names of the Mother?" she asked suddenly, dropping her voice to a whisper, and this time Rae actively wondered if she had just heard a mocking echo of the Hovrodnik question the old woman had taught them to expect. "And you, what's to become of you now? You'll go off, you'll go away? You'll find the Flame Bearers maybe? You'll find a project for yourself? That's what they do. They figure out what's needed, all over the world. And they send someone out. Maybe they'll send you to Ethiopia," she said, and then that rasp of laughter came again. "Maybe you'll lead back a lost tribe of sheep to the promised land. Eh, teacher? Not that anyone seems so very eager to have them . . ."

And now she grabbed Rae by the arm and shook her violently. "You came here to find out the big secret? What's the big secret? A few years ago I could have told you. I myself, I could have said where you should go to find these Flame Bearers. Rebekah worked with them. All her life. They had the dig, near the Lebanese border, they had their kibbutz near there until a few years ago. They were very friendly with the Arabs in the neighborhood. They had a program for educating the Yemenite children who came in and the children from Egypt and from Morocco. All the Oriental Jews. But Rebekah's great dream was to find the Flame Bearers' library. Some bits of pottery with writing, and also some scrolls they dug up from a site near the kibbutz. But what could come of it? You think anyone is so interested to find out about the goddess worship? So of course right away they ran into opposition. And how could they prove definitely there was a library buried there? The dig would have to go under the orchards from another kibbutz. So what could come of it? Nothing. And again more of their nothing."

"That's it, that's enough," Rae said. "I can't listen to another word." She had raised her arms, the palms open, the fingers spread wide. She was not proud of this gesture. It came out of exasperation and expressed an unintended threat to shut up her aunt. The older woman cringed away. "What did I say?" she asked in a frightened voice.

Rae pitched her voice low. "You think I don't know how lonely my grandmother was? You stand there and ask me? I've carried her loneliness with me my whole life. Yes, right here," she went on, hammering her left fist, just once, against her heart, "here, where my own life should have been. Who am I, Aunt Elke? I am giving up everything I ever wanted to be. And why? You think because I want to follow in my grandmother's footsteps? I have never wanted it, I tell you."

Rae stopped talking and looked at her aunt. Elke had hunched up her shoulders and was gazing at the sky. "Tonight will be rain," she said. "Better I should get back now. You saw my little plants? Always there's work, taking them in, taking them out from the greenhouse. Am I my mother? Could I make a whole forest with my bare hands?"

"You think it was such a gift to me that Grandmother Shadmi made me her successor?" She had put out a hand to stop Aunt Elke from walking away and now she gripped her by the shoulder. But it was no good. There were people you could not reach even when you threw down in front of them the hardest truth you had. "You know that Maya resented me for it, always. No closeness we ever had could overcome her bitterness. Naamah, I admit, did not. Who knows why? Unless she knew all along she got the better portion. She had her work, a sense of purpose, our grandmother's love. But I? I have all my life been a creature half in and half out of her stories, a half-human, divided in every breath between my longing to set myself down here in this age and time and by that impossible tug backward into a past she refused to relinquish. You promise us Rebekah's letters and you hold them back? And why? So that you will have the one true version of the story? Aunt Elke, I tell you, it won't be like that. For us, the more we learn, the more the ambiguity grows. People are dead. They are buried all over the world. Facts are dispersed, hidden, disguised. We're caught between lies, embellishments, forgotten truths, great imaginative capacities, and, here and there, without our knowing exactly where they are, sharp splinters of reality that make it impossible to dismiss the whole thing and give it up in despair. After all these months I'd be a fool to think the way I did when I stepped onto that plane in New York. But I tell you, even now, I'm not a person who can sit down and believe any one piece of it. It has no place in the rational categories by which we make sense of the world. To accept it, I have to be willing to place myself outside my capacity to explain things. I have to be able to take some kind of fundamental risk. Trusting, what? That I can walk the thin line Maya has stumbled over? That I can venture out in this frightful legendary bog and come back telling my own story? I don't need Rebekah's letters. The old woman gave us enough. Yes, she cut herself off from the sect. Yes, she quarreled with Rebekah. Yes, I admit it, she puffed herself up with a false grandeur. But week after week she sat us down and told the stories. Put the letters in my hand, make it easier for me, and you will be part of this peculiar enterprise of ours. But even without you I'll find them. I'll find Rebekah, I'll find the sect."

Aunt Elke shook her head. "You won't find them. You'll get lost," she insisted. "It happened to me. I set out, I, too, before Naamah was born. I went back to Europe to look for them. No," she whispered, taking Rae by the elbow and pulling her close, "it can't be done. You know what it's like wandering out there? You have to strip yourself down. You have to give everything up. Sometimes the guidance doesn't come and this means maybe you haven't been chosen. But also it can mean maybe you haven't been given the right instruction. You, clever one, you know where is the first stone on the old path to Kiryat Sefer?"

Rae interrupted her, darting forward suddenly. "You're asking me, aren't you? You're actually asking me the Hovrodnik questions . . ."

But Aunt Elke went on talking as if there had been no interruption. "You think they're just sitting there, with a little office on a street corner in Paris? The women who call themselves Flame Bearers, these are not the ones who know even the smallest thing. You think you will go to the kibbutz and you will say, 'Hey, ladies, give me the train schedule for the in-gathering?' It's not like that. For the in-gathering it's different. You have to find them some other way. I know, I tried it. I went out by myself. I arrived in Safed and I gave everything away. The little suitcase with a few belongings. The identification papers. Even the money I carried, I gave it away. There I was, in the one suit of clothes. The old lady didn't tell you? That was her pride. She thought she'll figure out by then how to do it in the old way, with the visions and the voices. But these days that's not how it goes. These days nobody finds the in-gathering without the wandering. Years and years it could take. And how will you eat? And where will you sleep? But if you stay out there long enough, and if you dream good enough, and if you know how to talk to the birds and eat the bitter herbs, so sooner or later the guides will find you? They didn't find me. You maybe will be more lucky? Here it is," she said, with a sad little shake of her head, pulling the packet of letters out of her pocket and pushing them into Rae's hand. "But it won't help. Even Rebekah's letters won't help."

Rae watched her walking away, her thinning braid with its hank of rope flopping against her shoulders.

"I'm sorry," Rae said, not knowing for what exactly.

She had spoken too softly for Aunt Elke to have heard. But her aunt turned back and cupped her hands to her lips. "Always, I tried to protect you. 'What does she need it for?' I asked myself. I tried, didn't I, to keep the letters away from you? 'Better she has her own life,' I told myself. But you, you couldn't keep away from it, could you?"

29

Th *e* lamp, smoking darkly, rocked back and forth in the strong wind that had come blowing in from the coast. It seemed to Rae, who was curled up with Brucha, that the swaying shadows flung out over the rough boards of the loft gave to the barn the quality of a ship rocked indolently far out at sea, on quiet waters.

Brucha was falling asleep. She was lying on the floor of the barn and her voice had become husky. "How old will I be when you come back here?" Rae leaned over and whispered some nonsense at her. But she was relieved when the child dropped off to sleep again. Jacob, Rubin, and the others had driven into town for a movie. Maya was asleep in the small loft next to theirs, where they had thrown down the sleeping bags and blankets. Naamah, huddled beneath the kerosene lamp, was going over the letters.

Brucha woke up. She looked around her, saw that her mother was still working, and opened her mouth to protest. But then she sat straight up in her sleeping bag and said to Rae: "Will you forget me?"

"Forget you?"

Brucha looked right up at Rae without a smile. "No," she said, "you could never forget me."

That makes five of them, Rae thought. Jacob, Ruth, Rubin, and Michael had done it already. Now here was Brucha. Saying good-bye to her.

The letters were written in Hebrew, in a beautiful calligraphic script. Most of them were complete. But here and there Aunt Elke had removed isolated pages. There were passages in Yiddish and in Ugaritic and some of these reminded Rae of the old lady. But on the whole the letters were disappointing to her. They seemed to have been written by an educated but superficial person. They told her that her aunt had been living in Israel and had decided to leave for Ethiopia. It was hard to believe this was Rebekah. The guide, the link back, the living witness, the survivor.

There were descriptions of her travels, random scenes, reports of conversation. Rae was not surprised to recognize, from the Ethiopian passages, a landscape that matched the vivid imagery she had received during the last months. The mud-wattle huts, the starving children, the fierce mountain scenery of an underdeveloped country. But it all had a peculiar flatness, as if her aunt were writing from a sense of duty but intended to keep hidden the motive that drove her from Israel to Ethiopia and back to Israel and then to Ethiopia, from which the last letters had been written. Almost ten years before.

Rae sat up and put her elbows on her knees. From the moment she and Ruth had gotten out of the car to greet Aunt Elke there had been this same quick sense of deflation. It seemed too sad, too small an ending. A kibbutz? A collective settlement in the Galilee near the Lebanese border? An archaeological dig for the library of a vanished city?

Rae had never really allowed herself to believe in the sect and its mission the way Naamah did. She had let herself experience some remarkable things. But she was hardly the type to become a true believer. Down on her knees that day in the park drawing the interlocked initials of the Flame Bearers on the ground, she had been a woman in the grip of powerful feeling. But on her feet again, brushing the dust off her clothes, she had gone back to being a skeptic. The "progress" she had made over the months, her movement into the old stories, amounted (she had told herself) to little more than a determination to set reason aside as irrelevant to what she was experiencing. Slowly, with great effort, she had given up categories and the judgments that went along with them in order to leave herself free to feel. And she had, in this perfectly reasonable stance, overlooked the fact that her hopes and expectations were mounting daily. The last few hours of disappointment had let her in on the big secret. Pacing about on the farm, waiting for Naamah to get back from her walk with Brucha and Jacob, Rae had read through Rebekah's letters with despair. And that finally is the way she found out how much she had hoped for from them.

It was cold in the barn. Naamah was taking her time, having spread out her usual paraphernalia, and now she was swaying and chanting, lighting her candles, gesturing and invoking. Rae loved her too much to be able to laugh at her but she wanted to laugh. It seemed better than crying or cursing or giving way to the bitterness that had eaten up Aunt Elke's life and was once again nibbling at her own. She got to her feet and began to wander about with her hands in her pockets, stooping to keep herself from slamming into the rafters.

She peered over the half-timber railing that separated them from the unfinished loft in which Maya was sleeping. Her cousin was curled up on the pile of sleeping bags, sucking her thumb. Here, too, the progress they might have expected was proving illusory. Maya, when Rubin said good-night to her, had thrown her arms around his neck and sobbed, begging and pleading with him not to leave her. Nothing could quiet her until Rae lay down beside her and wrapped her up in her arms. But her restlessness had bothered Maya, who whimpered in her sleep and cried out, babbling about poisoned letters. She had grabbed Rae's hand and held it to her chest and Rae could scarcely ease her fingers out of Maya's grip.

Rae took off her jacket and spread it out on the rough floor next to Naamah. It was better than wandering about on tiptoe, trying to hold back her impatience, but it didn't help much. She had cast away the life she had led for the last ten years. But what came next? Years of hopeless wandering? More of that vain probing at the boundaries of time?

Naamah was sitting in front of a small window that looked down over the garden. The moon was full, the wind had died down somewhat, the shadows rocked themselves close to the base of the wall, an owl hooted from somewhere in the woods, and Rae, with a gesture of angry resignation, bent over the pages spread out on the floor. Then she remembered the time Naamah had taught her to read again after she had forgotten. After her parents had been killed. Then, too, they would sit on the floor and Rae would look at what Naamah was writing, interrupting her with a nudge of her elbow to ask questions in a timid voice.

"She doesn't say a word about the Flame Bearers, does she?" Rae had folded her legs under her and was leaning toward Naamah, but the sound of her own voice surprised her.

Naamah put her fingers to her lips. "Wait, wait," she whispered,

"I'm not ready yet." She had been dipping her pen in the mixture of ink and ash. Her hand, moving over the pages of Rebekah's letters, made the shape of letters and words but she wasn't writing. Rae closed her eyes and rested her head against Naamah's shoulder. She could scarcely remember that other Rae who had arrived in San Francisco less than a year ago. But the day itself was vivid. She remembered climbing up over the gate and jumping down into their grandmother's garden. The altar was there and the forbidden cookies. The wind had come up, the spray from the fountain touched her hand, and the statue, with its hollow eyes, looked over at her.

"This is what I think." Naamah was keeping her voice low but Rae could tell she was back in the mode of Naamah-the-Scribe. She opened her eyes, pushing her cousin lightly with her shoulder. And then she remembered, for the first time since she was a child, what the carved wooden figure had said. *Ziptsit, tsepsit, malkitsie, zipitsie.* It was the statue who had taught her how to call the birds.

But Naamah didn't want to be interrupted. She waved her hand at Rae. "Wait," she said, "it will keep for later? This is what you have to hear . . ." Then she took Rae's hand and pressed it against her own cheek. "Forgive me, I'm excited. You are saying, what? *Ziptsit, tsepsit, malkitsie, zipitsie?* The carved statue taught you? But of course, Rae, didn't you know? I figured it out already weeks ago."

Rae shook her head, laughing at Naamah. "It didn't occur to you to tell me?"

"I have an idea Rebekah was called to work among the Falashas, the Black Jews, in Ethiopia," Naamah said, because she just couldn't wait any longer. "You have been reading about them? So, you know how they live. Any day they can be raided by bandits. Even to this day they can be sold into slavery. They are hated by the Moslem right. And by the Marxist left. They are starving and dying of illness. And the government of Israel, meanwhile, is slow to bring them into the country. I think Rebekah, in writing about these things, was trying to call you into this work. The letters were written over ten years ago, just after you went away. She must have known by then that the old lady lost you. The Flame Bearers are a hive. What happens to one of the members will be felt by the others. And you, Rae, have been important to us for a long time. We have been following you through many lives. These letters, which sound like a travelogue, are really a call to you, an urgent message. But of course Rebekah had to determine whether you were initiated by Grandmother into the teachings. And how else, but by writing you these letters that you would have to understand in some deeper way?"

Naamah pushed the letters over toward Rae. "Take this word," she said, "*Charash*. It means 'smith.' A 'blacksmith.' Or maybe even 'craftsman.' It's a familiar word. Rebekah uses it about the Falashas. They are indeed well known for their ironworking skill. There are even people who believe they were the first tribe in Africa to have developed it. But you know that the word *charash* can also mean 'magic'?"

Naamah paused and wiped her lips. Rae, who had been half listening to her, sat up smartly and opened her eyes very wide, as if she had been asked a question and was supposed to shout out the story. But Naamah glanced over at her with a frown, impatient at being interrupted.

"Or take this word. *Nappeh*. A 'user of the bellows.' It also is given a feminine ending and it also is in the plural. Now, in this place, here it is together with *charash*. So, you could think, maybe she's talking about a tribe of women craftsmen? Women blacksmiths? Women artisans? It's possible. But I think she means 'women who work magic.' This is her way of saying the Flame Bearers. *Nappeh*, a user of the bellows, *charash*, a smith who works magic—it is the Falasha name for our tradition among themselves. You know, Rae," Naamah interrupted herself, "perhaps this is not a disguise at all. Perhaps Rebekah assumed you simply would understand how to read her meanings. Most of the writing I worked on before I burned the papers was like this too. It's a style, a Flame Bearer way of communicating at many levels all at the same time. I'll show you what I mean." Again, nervously, she pushed the letters over toward Rae and then leaned over and began to thumb through them.

"Well, for instance this whole question about the tribe of Dan. The old lady didn't tell us this part of the Flame Bearer tradition because over this she quarreled with Rebekah. That much at least we understand from my mother. And in this the old lady was wrong. The Miwok Indians, so far as we know, did not have the Flame Bearer tradition. But look here. In this place Rebekah mentions the decision of the Sephardis' chief rabbi, in 1972, that the Falashas were descendants from the lost tribe of Dan. But this letter was written, when? In 1964, before the decision happened. That, to begin with, makes us take note.

"Then, we ask, what is the tribe of Dan? Part of the ten tribes of the Northern Kingdom that revolted away from Judah and the centralized worship in Solomon's temple? That is the general knowledge. But we know the tribe of Dan insisted on having their own places of worship. They were 'idolators,' the Bible says. And that, as you showed also in your thesis, means goddess worshipers.

"Next, the tribes of the Northern Kingdom were captured by the Assyrians in 722 B.C.E. This, too, is general knowledge. They disappeared after their captivity. Jewish legend in the Midrash always said eventually they got away and went to live beyond the River Sambatyon. But where is the Sambatyon? Perhaps in Ethiopia?"

Rae was smiling. She had drawn up her knees and wrapped her arms around them, her forehead pressed against her legs. It was more and more like that time so many years ago when she had first come to live in the old lady's house after the fire and Naamah had taken her under her wing, writing down the old stories in a little notebook for Rae when she got sick, so she could read them to herself while Naamah was at school. It was with these notebooks Naamah had taught her to read again. And even then the stories had been written in Hebrew and Russian and English and Yiddish.

"You see what this implies about Rebekah's work? She went to Ethiopia to work with the Falashas. She was an old woman by then and we can imagine this work wasn't easy for her. This is why she would have called you, to come and join her in this task. Later, I think, Rebekah found proof the Falashas were the remnant of the same people who were taken away by the Assyrians, the goddess-worshiping tribe of Dan. And therefore, the Flame Bearers would be still active among them. This is what happens. When the people as a whole forget, the women remember. They keep the secret, now that it has become a secret. They tell it as stories, from mother to daughter. It is the same all over the world. Certainly, as we see from Rebekah's letters, in the Falasha tribe the women go apart during their menstrual time. They go to huts by themselves to work on their handicrafts and to tell stories. There are women in the Falasha villages who interpret dreams. She refers to them also as *charash*, 'the magic workers.' The Falashas are a tribal people, living in the remote northwestern mountains of Ethiopia. And under these conditions you would expect the 'magic workers' to be very influential.

Naamah began to cough. She took a folded handkerchief from

her sleeve and pressed it to her mouth, glancing over at Brucha. Rae, who had reached out to put her arm around her cousin, looked down at her curiously. She felt strangely remote from Naamah's urgency.

"Look here," Naamah whispered, clearing her throat. "Here, she talks about wanting to have workers to go to the tribes, and prepare them for going into Israel. But she doesn't write only the word *avodnik,* 'worker.' She puts it in the feminine ending. She adds to it this prefix, which means ancient. Here, she brings it together with the word, 'to learn.' She says the dream interpreters have seen a particular woman. You could think maybe she's describing the tribal beliefs of the Falashas. But in this place, the word *avodnik* is also associated with the word *stranger* or *sojourner.* I would translate it this way: 'The stranger, who has been sent from ancient times to learn from us. The sojourner, who will work for the Law of Return.'"

"The sojourner," Rae repeated, looking down at the pages. She was having trouble paying attention.

"This is important, Rae. It means, I think, all over the world something essential was forgotten. Maybe, in this sense, Rebekah, too, needed to be instructed by them, in the same way our grand-mother wanted to learn from the Miwok Indians. Maybe it wasn't only that our grandmother didn't pass on to us all the tradition she had. You see, Rae, how important this is? There may be a trouble within the Flame Bearer succession everywhere. It may have been going on since the time Hannah Leah and the Flame Bearers turned to vio-lence, the way the old lady always implied. If our grandmother did not find what she was looking for from the Miwok Indians, still, the basic idea might be correct. Perhaps that now is our task, to go out again among the Miwok and find who is left and who is still telling the old stories. Maybe the Falashas, because they are still a tribal people, have kept the tradition pure and know what we have forgotten about the in-gathering and Kiryat Sefer and the way to be called and the way to be guided?"

"The Falashas," Rae said. Naamah's words seemed to be making curious spirals, they were tugging at her, but she could not concentrate on them. "They have kept the tradition, you think?"

"This is a leap, I know. But it seems possible to me. And now, Rae, be patient. I'm going to make even a bigger leap. This word 'stranger' we are talking about? I think the 'stranger' makes a reference to you. I know, you're not convinced. How could you be? But have a look. Here, all together in one place, the word 'worker,' the word 'stranger,' the word for 'sacred learning' and now the phrase which is after all the meaning of the name Isarael . . . the one who prevails against God. You see what it could mean? God, the patriarch, the God of Israel, does not want to bring the Falashas back to their original homeland. But The Mother does. It is a pun, you see? It means all this, and it means Isarael Shadmi, too."

Rae was scarcely listening to what her cousin was saying. It all seemed to be taking place a long time before and to have that dreamy conviction the tales and speculations had when they were children together, when Naamah, four years older, was almost a grownup already and had from somewhere acquired the capacity to console. Aunt Elke had claimed to be her mother. But her mother had been Naamah.

This love she was showing with her explanations and her worry over detail brought with it a kind of conviction. It was a confidence that no attempt at persuasion would have been able to call up. She was impressed by what Naamah was saying because she believed—not in the accuracy of her scholarship, not necessarily in the interpretations she made. She believed in Naamah. It was as simple now as it had been during her childhood. As straightforward and simple as that.

And then, with her eyes closed, and Naamah's breath against her cheek, she saw the dark faces of famished children. She saw the mudwattle huts and the old woman in steel-rimmed spectacles and she wondered what it would have been like if she'd received the call ten years earlier when she was leaving for New York. She opened her eyes. Naamah was talking again, huddled over the papers, wrinkling up her forehead, biting her lower lip. It was cold in the barn, and Rae, who never admitted to feeling cold, took Naamah's hand and placed it over her shoulder. She had slipped down onto the floor and was resting in Naamah's lap. And then Maya was there too and the bear rug and the fire.

Rae took a moment to get used to the idea. It wasn't unpleasant. But it did make her feel that she'd been dropped down too fast from an enormous height. She noticed the old woman was sitting in her chair across from them. There she was, with her wrinkled old face, her eyes dark and glistening like two cooked prunes. Rae knew what would happen next. The old lady would lift her chin, raise a finger toward the ceiling, shake it once or twice, and speak very slowly, her voice growing deeper and more husky as she leaned forward toward them.

Naamah was bending over her. "Rae," she murmured, "is it possible? You look eight, nine years old. Does this mean you listened . . . you remember what Bubbe used to say? With the child's ears still growing?"

"Scrolls?" Rae sat up and looked over at her cousin. "That's what you're saying? You actually think she found scrolls? Like the Dead Sea Scrolls or the Gnostic Gospels? Dug up from a cave in the mountains in Ethiopia," she went on wistfully, as if she were longing to believe in it and were, at the same time, repeating it to get it right. "Dug up from a cave and sold illegally in Cairo. But is it possible? She has evidence the Falashas are really from the tribe of Dan? Written evidence they were once goddess worshipers?"

"Look for yourself. Here, in this spot. Either she's describing ancient Falasha crafts here, in this passage, or she's talking about scrolls buried in an urn and unearthed recently. And here, if she's not talking about antique shops in Cairo, she's talking about the illegal sale of these scrolls. And if she goes to Belgium to meet a man who sells antiquities, maybe it's not because she's a wealthy woman interested in purchasing something for her private collection. You see what I mean? It isn't easy to be sure. Frau Altdorf and the others wrote in such a flowery, embellished style. Much more in keeping with Yiddish tradition from the Shtetl. But Rebekah is using another mode, where everything seems flat and literal and insignificant. Until you get the idea that every word and phrase has also another meaning. It all sounds, from one point of view, like the behavior of a wealthy old woman collector. But if we read symbolically the way for generations the scholars of the Flame Bearer texts have been reading our writings then, suddenly, there is a new possibility of understanding.

"See, here. She says she must be in Israel by April 1975. That is less than two months from now. But it is more than ten years since she wrote the letter. How could she have known then what will happen two months from now in Jerusalem? Only if she were using the old skills and knew how to read the future in the old way, very precisely. We know because we have been reading the newspapers. There will be a meeting of the members from the Israeli Knesset with members from the various religious organizations and the various ministries. To decide what? To decide if the Falashas are indeed Jews and entitled to citizenship under the Laws of Return. Rebekah knew all this ten years before it will happen."

"Ten years ago I left for New York," Rae said.

Naamah touched Rae's cheek with her fingertips. There were tears in Naamah's eyes, but she wiped them away impatiently. "For us Rae," she whispered, "for you and me, no time is left. You think I don't want to put my arms around you, you think I don't want to let myself go and weep in your arms? We have no time Rae, not even for saying goodbye. You see, don't you, how important this is?"

Naamah picked up a page and held it up to Rae. "Here, you see?" she said, forcing herself. "Rebekah implies she must go first to Belgium, to meet the dealer in antiquities, as if she knows already this little trip is going to take her more than ten years. From Belgium there come no more letters. Not a word in more than ten years. Is she dead? Has something happened to her? That she came with the key tells us nothing. Living or dead she can be your guide. The point is, Rae, how do you keep open the communication with her?"

Rae had stood up and was staring out into the garden. For the first time, without effort, she was able to hold herself in both worlds at the same time. There she was, on the bear rug in front of the fire. Maya was sitting next to her, reaching up to stuff almond cookies into Rae's mouth. Rae had to laugh. She was twisting away from Maya, trying to keep her lips closed tight. Maya was tickling her, trying to make her laugh so that she could slip the cookie into her mouth.

Rae put her hand on Naamah's shoulder to steady herself. Maya was two years older, she liked to wrestle Rae, arms pinned to the floor. Rae put her arms around Maya's waist. Something was being torn. She said, Maya, what if we never see one another ever again, Maya?

She was trying to hold on to Maya. To Brucha with her bright little eyes. To Rubin, whom she had tried so hard to love. To Michael and Ruth and to Jacob. Jacob.

"Naamah," she called out, but it was too late, the present was shredding all around her. She saw how it would be possible to slip into the stories. Repeating the familiar words, entering through them into that little shed behind the house in Chernik. Hannah Leah had just come in to show Raisa the mark of the flame on her breast. The little girls were looking up at her. One of them had leaped to her feet. She was holding both her hands over her mouth but her eyes were wide and Rae knew the child would never forget it. One day she would have to sit down and tell the story.

In the small back room in Kashevata, Sarah Rachel, recovering from her long illness, was listening to an ant sing. Her hair was combed back in little braids, pinned up in loops over her ears. Wisps of hair were fraying out all over her head. She was missing Hannah Leah and Rae felt Sarah Rachel's anguish, knowing she'd never be able to make the blind eye better.

"Bubbe," Rae said. The child looked over at her with her hooded eyes. Rae saw how much she wanted to be loved, this little one who did not dare to reach out and put her arms around Rae's neck. She saw the little girl fiddle with the bedcover, her small, freckled hands keeping themselves busy. "Bubbe, hold on to me, don't let me go," Rae pleaded. But it was no use. It was too late. Her grandmother had become a child.

"Forgive me," Rae whispered, for the first time understanding the real kinship between them. The old woman Sarah Rachel had loved the little girl Isarael because she had seen her own loneliness in the child.

Rae sat down at the edge of the bed and gathered the child Sarah Rachel in her arms. "What is there to forgive?" the child said in her grown-up little voice. She was sitting straight up in Rae's arms, holding her back straight, her neck stiff. Then she leaned forward, very slowly. Thousands of years might have passed while she was moving forward. Rae felt that the child was flowing into her. The loneliness they shared dissolving between them. The long, aching hereditary sorrow.

The child's head dropped down onto Rae's shoulder and now, with a muffled sob, she gave herself over to Rae to be loved.

In the mud-wattle hut the woman with steel-rimmed spectacles was sitting on a wooden bench. Rebekah! She was an old woman and it made Rae glad to see her there. A little girl with short-cropped curly hair was sitting next to her, wrapped in a white scarf, spinning raw wool with a stick and spindle.

Rae could smell the thatch on the roof. Through the open door (there were no windows in the hut) she could see the patches of chick-

pea next to the mountain path. Rebekah was sitting on a bench covered with monkey skins. A chicken was pecking about near the jars of
grain. And now a fine, amber-colored dust rose up from the grain jars
while the girl lifted her head and looked straight at Rae, who had just
sat down on the floor, at Rebekah's feet.

a c k n o w l e d g m e n t s

I am grateful to my friends and to my daughter for the generous help they have given me with this manuscript.

Niki Chernin, Susan Griffin, Naomi Newman, Roz Parenti, and Michael Rogin were its first readers. Michael also read every subsequent draft with tireless devotion. Elisabeth Scharlatt is once again vividly present on every page. Angelyn Spignesi and Tracy Gary made important suggestions, which I have adopted. Elizabeth Abel and Anna Hawkin inspired me at a crucial time. Diane Cleaver believed it would all work out. Rachel Knoblock laughed and cried with me and helped me with the Yiddish. Renate Stendhal paid attention to every word and worked with me very closely on the manuscript, substantially changing its vision.